ADJACENT MONSTERS

ALSO BY LUKE TARZIAN

The Shadow Twins Series
Vultures

Adjacent Monsters
The World Maker Parable

The World Breaker Requiem

The World Reaper Odyssey

Anthologies
Dark Ends

Whimsy Hell

A Cup of Tea at the Mouth of Hell (Or, an Account of Catastrophe by Stoudemire McCloud, Demon)

ADJACENT MONSTERS

A DUOLOGY OF NIGHTMARES

LUKE TARZIAN

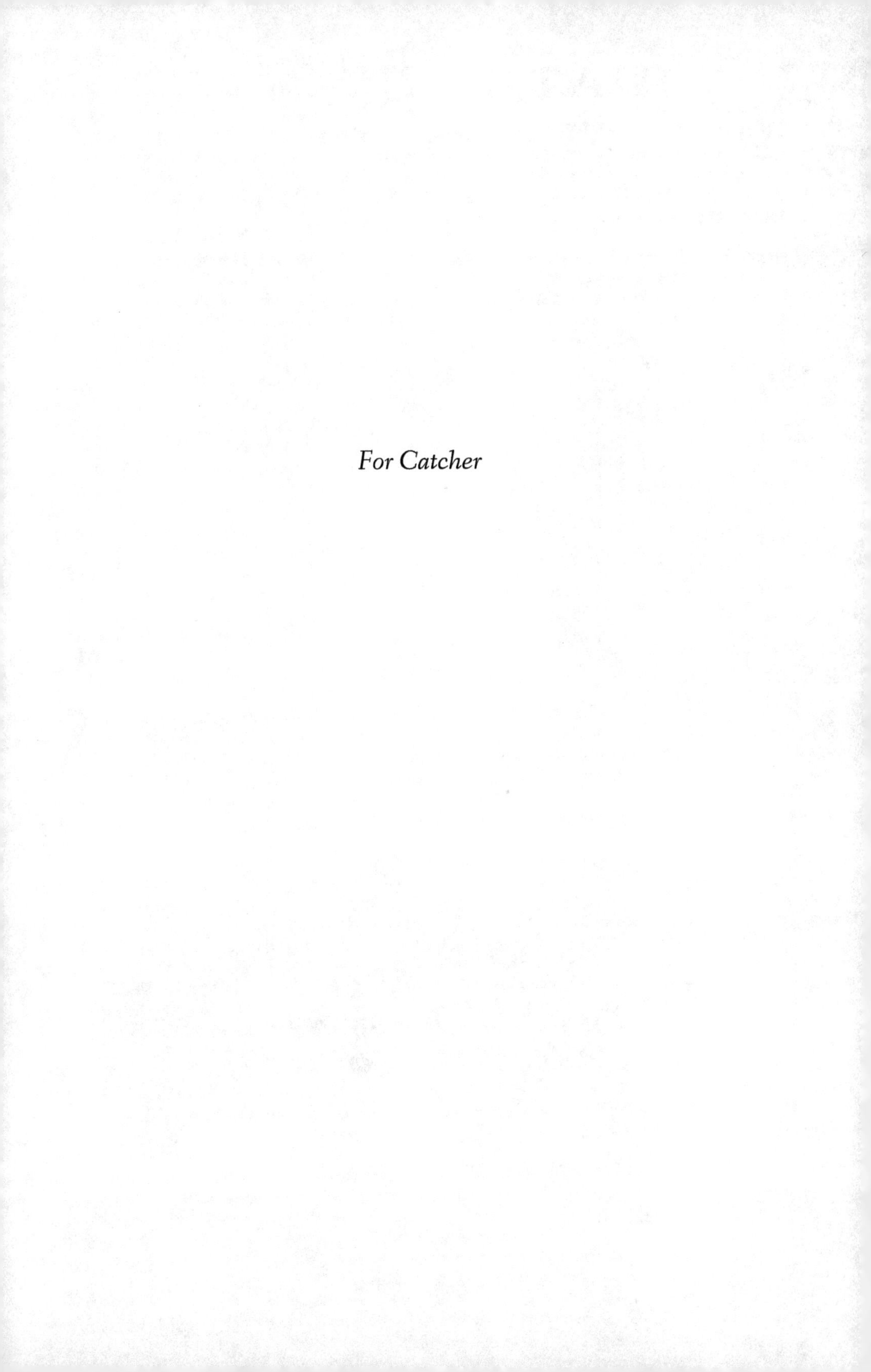

For Catcher

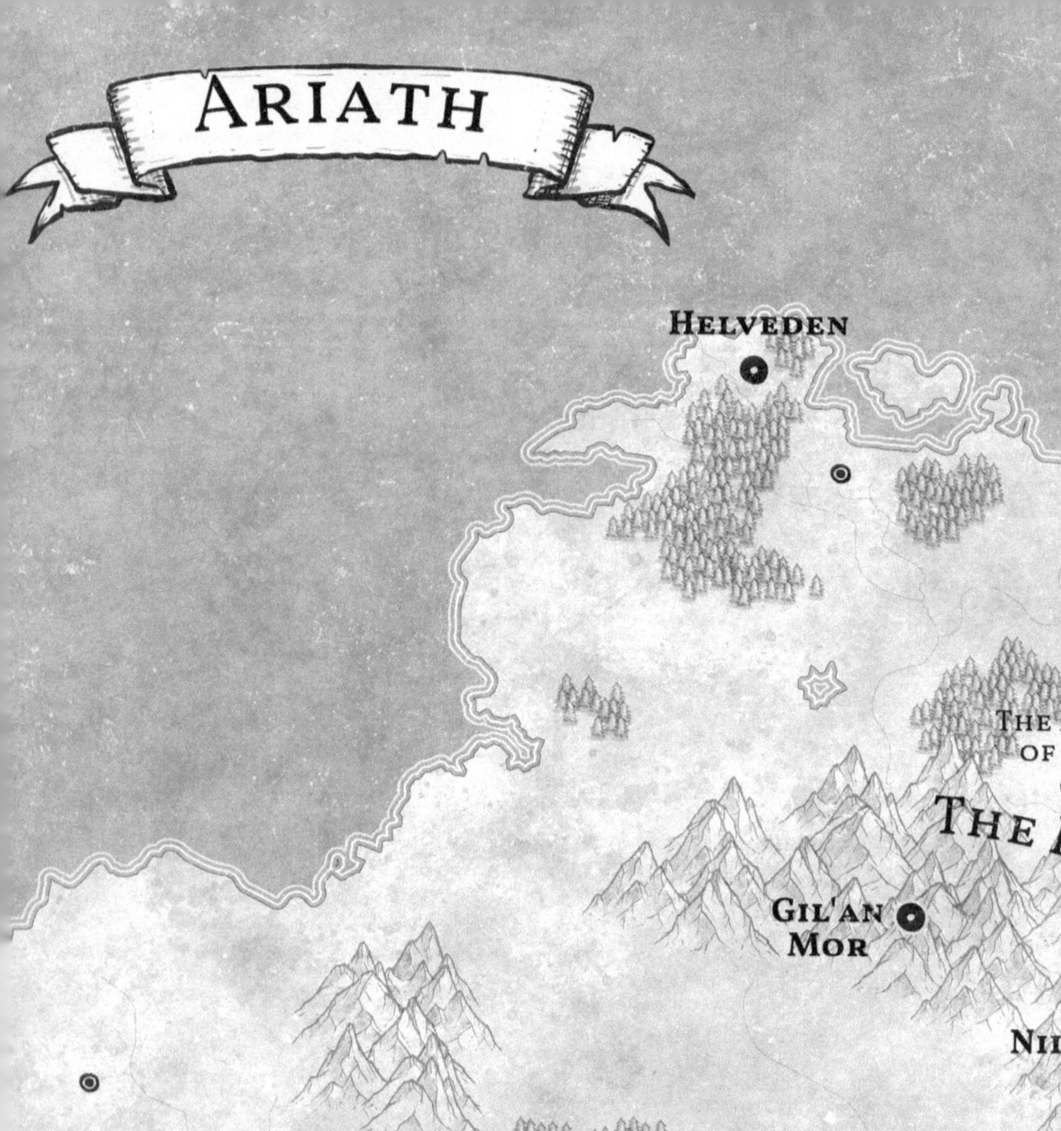

ARIATH
HELVEDEN
THE RU
of Ul
THE PE
GIL'AN
MOR
NIL-I
BANEROWOS
YL
OLD JÉMOON

THE SONJA OCEAN
E DREN
RACH
NA'SCHUUL

THE WORLD MAKER PARABLE

BEING THE FIRST NIGHTMARE

"Midway upon the journey of our life, I found myself within a forest dark, for the straightforward pathway had been lost."
— Dante Alighieri, *The Inferno*

PENDULUM DANCE

Hang-Dead Forest north of Banerowos was aptly named. Rhona had lost count of the corpses half a mile back. She towed her prisoner on a length of cord. Thus far she had ignored Djen's every word, half because she was tired of listening to the woman spit hatred, and half because Rhona wasn't entirely sure how to respond. Leading the woman you loved to the tree from which she was sentenced to hang had that effect.

"I do as the Raven wills," Rhona said.

Djen spat. "Fuck Alerion. Fuck *you* and your reflexive bullshit."

They ducked beneath a trio of low-hanging corpses. The dark bones were long picked dry. Only tatters of clothing remained.

"It's the truth," said Rhona. "Alerion's will is our command. Those who ignore him are a threat to the continued unification of home."

"You really *are* full of shit," Djen hissed. "Alerion's words are so ingrained into your skull they may as well be his hand shoved up your ass and moving your mouth." She heaved a sigh. "Never in all my years would I have thought you'd be the one to dance on strings. I suppose I never really knew you at all, Rhona."

Rhona halted. She had tried these last hours, these last days, to ignore the bitterness Djen spat her way. Some of it was rightly earned—Rhona didn't deny that. She just wished Djen could understand *why* she had done what she had done.

"I suppose if I had," Djen continued, "I would have foreseen you betraying me to Alerion."

"How could I *not*?" Rhona asked. "You *unleashed* the Vulture from her cage."

"I *had* to, you idiot," Djen snarled. "You and Alerion all but doomed us when you imprisoned Luminíl. What I did was for the future of our home. For the survival of this country and its people. If you would open your eyes—if you would *all* open your eyes—you would see how absolutely wrong you were to have kept such power in chains."

Rhona yanked the cord and they continued on the way. She focused on the forest; she had always found peace here among the dead. For that, some called her mad, but what did she care? She inhaled deeply. The trees smelled of death and fear, if fear could be said to smell like anything at all. To Rhona, fear smelled like a foul breath clouding in the night, and that too was a very particular scent. In Hang-Dead Forest a foul breath was defined as an odor of iron and rain—magic. Mirkúr.

They marched on through gnarled and twisted trees. Guilt nipped at Rhona's heels like a hungry dog and her heart stung. It wasn't supposed to have come to this. She loved Djen for all her flaws, for the gravity of her sin—could she really string her up to rot amongst the dead? Could she really watch Djen join the countless corpses in their pendulum dance?

"*You'll have to whether you like it or not,*" her conscience said. It called itself Fiel. "*Country over person—it is the Raven's way. Alerion's will is our command.*" It sighed. "*How could we have ever loved such a thing as Djen Shy'eth?*"

Rhona frowned. *Ever the formal voice of woe,* she thought. Fiel—the vocal trauma to her silent grief. Loving Djen had come easily to Rhona. In fact, it had been the easiest thing she had ever done, which made it all the more nauseating how quickly she had turned Djen over to Alerion. Had Rhona always been so fickle?

"*No,*" Fiel said. "*You are doing what you know is right. Country over person. If minds like those of Djen Shy'eth and Sonja Lúm-talé can be so easily swayed by the darkness of the Vulture Luminíl then what reason do you have to believe a word they say? The Vulture is the personification of entropy—Luminíl had to be contained.*"

They came to a small clearing in the depths of the forest. At the center was a tree unique from all the others: white of bark and black of leaves. For that Rhona called it the Lost Tree; it seemed so out of place in a wooded world of death and fog.

Yet by branches have so many lives been claimed, she thought. From the branches of the Lost Tree she would hang her beloved Djen; to its roots Rhona would give her own blood in reverence. Blood paid was a debt owed and it was best to curry favor where you could, especially in times like this where uncertainty was king.

"If you would stop taking sips from the wine Alerion serves," Djen said, "you would know how absolutely wrong he was, how wrong you are. You would understand the severity of what you did to Luminíl." She sighed as they stopped at the base of the Lost Tree. "You will..."

Rhona turned to look at Djen. It was the first time she had

done so since leaving Banerowos. For a moment she allowed herself to get lost in Djen's full-moon eyes, to imagine the taste of her lips and the gentle warmth of her breath.

"Keep your tongue," said Djen. "You have that look, but your words mean nothing."

Rhona flinched and it pulled her from her dream. She dropped Djen to her knees and drew a dagger from her cloak. "I wish things could be different."

Djen smirked. "No you don't—but you will. Get on with it."

"*Alf elo nor,*" Rhona chanted. "*Nor elo alf!*"

She punched the blade into Djen.

Then she did the same to herself.

———

"ONCE MORE YOU RETURN."

Rhona opened her eyes to the ethereal voice she had heard so many times before. Before her towered a lithe figure of smoke and wings. It called itself Equilibrium. It offered a hand and pulled her to her feet.

"It has been a while since last we spoke," said Equilibrium.

"It has," Rhona said. She gazed into the vast whiteness that encompassed them, feeling peace where others had undoubtedly felt dread. The Silent Place was many things to many different souls. She heaved a sigh.

"You have questions," Equilibrium said. "As you always do." The spirit brushed a hand against her cheek and she felt a modicum of weightlessness. "What brings you to the Silent Place this night?"

Rhona did her best to breathe evenly, composing her thoughts as best she could. She wanted everything to be presented as clearly as it could be. With her left index finger she traced the air, leaving gossamer symbols in her wake. Equilibrium reached out with its right index finger and traced them in reverse.

"So much conflict," the spirit murmured. "So much heartache."

The whiteness of the Silent Place dissolved in rivulets. In its place a meadow manifested. A sea of silver grass beneath a moon like none that Rhona had ever seen. Several yards away stood a tree. *The* tree. The Lost Tree. Equilibrium led her at an even pace, its great wings trailing into the ether.

"This is new," Rhona remarked. The Silent Place had never before been more than a brilliant void of nothingness. "Have my memories done something?"

"You are the first to whom the truest nature of the Silent Place has manifested," Equilibrium said. "This is a realm of memory and thought, a means for introspection, for retrospection, however they may be achieved. It is a haven for the dreaming dead."

Rhona brushed the trunk of the Lost Tree. She felt a tingle in her chest—but of what?

"Was I wrong?" she asked. "Has my life these many years been nothing but a lie?"

"You present your question broadly but you focus solely on the woman Djen Shy'eth," Equilibrium said. "What do *you* think, Rhona? What does your mind tell you that your heart does not, that it refuses to?"

"Only that I am conflicted," Rhona said. She felt stupid for her answer, for the ignorance and simplicity of her words. "I loved Djen, but I love Jémoon—I love my home. *Our* home. What Djen did threatened the livelihood of all I hold dear..."

"But?" Equilibrium asked.

"But...but..." Rhona wrinkled her nose. "*I* pushed her to recklessness. *I pushed her to unleash the Vulture Luminíl—but why? Why would she do something like that? And what did I do to push her away?"* She looked up at Equilibrium. The spirit gazed back from the darkness of its cowl. "I'm confused by it all."

"Condemning loved ones to their ends has that effect on everyone who swings the sword," said Equilibrium. "The guilt and retrospection manifest far quicker in some than in others. In you, long before Djen's end. The heart often acts on impulse; it is fueled by desire strong enough to suppress logic either temporarily or permanently. What did you desire most, Rhona? What did your heart scream for?"

She opened her mouth to speak but the meadow had already begun to fade. Like the whiteness before it, the meadow dripped away in rivulets until the Silent Place was an endless void as black as the abyss.

Then, she saw a light.

———

THE GRAY of Hang-Dead Forest was soothing to Rhona's eyes. The smell of rain and death upon the breeze eased her mind as she strung Djen's corpse to the lowest branch of the Lost Tree. As Rhona worked the memory of her time in the Silent Place returned and she found herself asking repeatedly the question Equilibrium had posed:

"What did my heart scream for?"

"A great many things," Fiel remarked. *"A great many things, amongst them Djen Shy'eth."*

Something more than Djen, Rhona thought. *Something strong enough to push her away.*

"Power has the tendency to do that," said Fiel.

Rhona frowned, turning away from the tree. *What are you saying?*

"*What, for the longest time, you sought yet at the same time denied you did,*" Fiel said. "*Control. Authority.*"

That's madness, Rhona thought.

"*Is it?*"

Rhona was silent. Her body ached, her mind howled with the pain of uncertainty. She turned to Djen and brushed her cold cheek. She looked her in the eyes and in them saw a thousand possibilities evanesce. The future was forever fickle. Did that mean Rhona was as well?

She pressed her lips to Djen's one final time.

Then she walked away, waiting for the words that Djen would never say.

OPEN WATER

Then

"I LOVE YOU," Djen said, and Rhona nearly toppled over the balustrade.

Rhona steadied herself and looked Djen in her brilliant, stark white eyes. Had she heard her properly? Had Djen said what Rhona had been dying to say? She took a deep breath then exhaled as smoothly as she could so as not to betray her nerves.

"And I love you," Rhona said. Whispered, really. She was trembling. The moonlight shone upon them, upon the distant lake, unobstructed for the first night in weeks; it made Rhona feel warm. She focused on that warmth as she once more tried to compose herself lest Djen think her words were false.

Djen took Rhona's hands in hers. Her trembling subsided almost as quickly as it had come and for that she was grateful. For Djen, she was immensely grateful. They stood in the silent night, the winter chaos of Banerowos's streets little more than a dull buzz below.

"I've dreamt of this for so long," Rhona said, caressing Djen's knuckles with her thumbs. "Of standing here with you, everything else little more than an afterthought." Her cheeks were hot. "Djen..."

Djen smiled. "Me too."

She pulled Rhona toward her. Their faces were just inches apart. Rhona could feel the warmth of Djen's breath and it smelled like mint. Her hair smelled of vanilla and... Rhona shuddered at the pure intoxication of her scent. She wrapped her arms around the woman's waist and pressed her lips to Djen's. A spark rippled through her body—this felt right. This *was* right.

"I've been wanting to do that for...I don't know how long," Rhona murmured when they finally pulled apart. "Years. Decades, even."

"Me too," Djen whispered. She turned, resting her elbows against the balustrade. "I've never seen the lake so bright before, at least not that I can remember."

"I saw it once," Rhona said, mimicking Djen's posture. "Long ago when Banerowos was little more than a skeleton of its current self. You were speaking to Alerion about something. I don't recall what, but it must have been important to you. You jabbed him in the chest with your finger and whatever he had been so eager about vanished from his face."

"Mmm. I remember that," Djen mused softly. "Don't remember what we were arguing about but I most certainly won."

"And Alerion's been calmer ever since," said Rhona. "Silly winged man."

"Careful now," Djen said. "Gods aren't fond of such talk."

Rhona rolled her eyes. "Luckily Alerion seems to have developed an aptitude for discerning sarcasm and fun."

"You have a point. Humility is an appealing characteristic for a god to possess."

"I spoke with the Vulture today," Rhona said. The abruptness of her statement drew a gasp from Djen. "Calm, now. You'd think I told you I murdered someone. I met her in the Raven's Wood for meditation."

Djen offered a slight frown.

"What?"

"Just...be careful around her," Djen said. "She can be volatile."

"As can the Phoenix," said Rhona, "but only if provoked."

"I suppose," Djen said. "Thankfully we've Alerion to keep them both in check."

"Exactly," Rhona said, leaning into Djen. "Besides, they helped to form what we call home. Without that winged trio of creation Banerowos would be little more than a dream. *Jémoon* would be little more than a dream. A fantasy."

Djen sighed. "I suppose you have a point. It's just...such power makes me wary. I'm not the only one. The three of them could destroy us with the snap of a finger. We're little more than playthings for gods if you really think about it, Rhona."

"I *have* thought about it," Rhona said. "Sometimes the notion makes me feel smaller than a speck of dust. But mostly...it makes me feel safe, if that makes any sense. It makes me feel important such primordial beings would see us as their equals in a way. They walk amongst us willingly. That counts for something."

"It does," agreed Djen.

Again, they stood in silence.

"It's enchanting," Djen said.

"Hmm?"

"Each ripple on the surface of the lake," Djen said. "A thousand possibilities manifest and evanesce repeatedly."

Rhona had never thought about it like that. "How many ripples do you think were involved in our creation? In that of Jémoon and Banerowos?"

"Impossible to say," Djen said. "To comprehend, really."

"Probably best not to lest we drive ourselves insane," Rhona said.

"Probably."

Djen draped an arm around Rhona's shoulders. They stood and they stared.

———

LUMINÍL WAS beautiful in the same way death inevitable. She was entropy where the Phoenix Mirkvahíl was creation. She was destruction for the greater good, for the evolution of their world, and her power was such that Rhona couldn't help but feel small in her presence despite being half a head taller.

Luminíl stood at the base of a great tree in the center of the Raven's Wood. Where the others bore leaves of red and green, this one's leaves were black and its trunk was whiter than virgin snow.

"I have been waiting for you, Rhona," Luminíl said. Her voice was a gentle breeze.

Rhona approached at a measured pace. She felt little reason to be afraid, anxious—but there was *still* reason. She stopped several feet shy of where the Vulture stood and bowed her head.

"You need not be so formal," Luminíl said. "Long have we known each other, after all."

"Of course," Rhona said. "What's on your mind?"

Luminíl turned to her. It was all Rhona could do to stifle a gasp. Dark veins webbed outward from her once-white, now-red eyes. Rhona had never seen Luminíl so...so...

"Something is wrong with me," the Vulture said. "I am ill and have been for some time."

"How?" Rhona asked. "What's happening to you?"

"I do not know," Luminíl said. It was the first time Rhona had ever heard fear in her voice. "It started in my dreams and has since manifested itself physically."

Luminíl had never mentioned her dreams to Rhona.

"Have you told Mirkvahíl or Alerion?" Rhona asked.

"I fear their reactions."

Rhona frowned. "But why? You are each one third of creation. And Mirkvahíl is your beloved. What harm could they do?"

Luminíl extended a hand. "I could show you. I could show you everything, Rhona."

A flurry of emotions swam through Rhona, curiosity and fear the strongest of them all. She had been invited to peek into the mind of a goddess—how many people could claim that? But how would she react to Luminíl's dreams? What would the Vulture's dreams do to Rhona? What would *Luminíl* do to Rhona?

"Well?" Luminíl took a step toward her.

Rhona extended a trembling hand. "This won't hurt, will it?"

"I cannot say for certain," Luminíl said. "I will keep you as safe as I am able."

The Vulture's words inspired little confidence, but she was Rhona's friend and you were supposed to help friends in need, were you not? She took Luminíl's hand.

"What now?"

"Be still," Luminíl said. The Raven's Wood swirled and dripped away in rivulets. "Be still."

. . .

Now

RHONA HADN'T THOUGHT about that night in the Raven's Wood in years. Probably for as long as the Raven's Wood had been Hang-Dead Forest. It had changed her, molded her. For better or for worse, she wasn't sure. On one hand she hated what she'd seen in Luminíl's dreams, hated what her exposure to them had done. It had cost Rhona her friendship with Luminíl. It had cost her Djen. But it had saved Banerowos, had saved the whole of Jémoon, and wasn't that the most important thing?

"Is that what you truly believe?" Fiel asked.

What do you mean?

"You tell yourself what you saw in the Vulture's dreams was the catalyst for everything," Fiel said. *"Is that really true, or it something you tell yourself to mask a horrible reality?"*

What would I be denying? Rhona asked.

"That you were always wary of the Vulture," Fiel said. *"That she tricked you into revealing your true nature—your desire for control, for authority over those who scare you most. Like Luminíl herself. Like Djen Shy'eth and Sonja Lúm-talé."*

That's ridiculous, Rhona spat. *In those dreams I saw the end of everything. What I did saved Jémoon. I saved Luminíl, whether she and her acolytes care to admit so or not. If not for Alerion, Mirkvahíl, and myself this world would be dead.*

Fiel chuckled. *"You say that, yet here we are having this conversation. Here you are, thinking to yourself you ought to have a conversation with Alerion, or Varésh Lúm-talé perhaps."*

Rhona growled. She continued through Hang-Dead Forest;

Banerowos was still a way off, probably an hour or so. There was a grain of truth to what Fiel said. Life was like open water, each wave, each ripple ripe with possibility.

What do you suppose I should do? Rhona asked Fiel.

"Whatever your gut suggests," Fiel said. *"One's gut instinct is more often than not correct, especially relative to the heart and mind. Do whatever you must to see the truth in all this madness."*

Madness. There was a lot of that going around these days thanks in no small part to Djen and Sonja. How had they been so weak of will? How could they have let Luminíl influence their actions? Alerion might have insight, as might Varésh. But there was someone Rhona felt would be more reliable.

She was going to request an audience with the Phoenix Mirkvahíl.

FLIGHTLESS BIRD

Varésh Lúm-talé was a failure. He had always been the least skilled Architect; the other Celestials thought it an affront he had risen to such prominence. The title of Architect and the responsibilities that came with such a rank were reserved for the most respected of the Celestials and Varésh knew he was on the opposite end of the spectrum. It didn't help matters he had been appointed to his current position by Ouran, the Celestial Emperor. It helped even less Varésh was the favored son of Ouran. He had yet to figure out why.

"Yet here you are, having wrought this world," his conscience said. *"Here you are, the false king of Harthe."* A Celestial word meaning Harmony. Another lie, the grandest of them all, Varésh had come to learn.

"What say you, O Crown of Harmony?" his conscience sneered.

Varésh walked in silence as the voice berated him. Before him sat a vast expanse of grass, a sea of gold, soft and gentle like the feathers of the Phoenix Mirkvahíl whom Varésh sought. He sought a great many things, redemption most of all, and Mirkvahíl was the grandest requisite.

"You assume the Phoenix lives," his conscience remarked as he waded through the tall reeds. The clouds shifted white to gray to gold and back. *"You assume you can so easily negate your idiocy and that, dear boy, is your arrogance shining brighter than the sun."*

"Do you have a better idea?" Varésh asked aloud. "This entire journey all you've done is whine. All you've done is chide and ridicule and hiss."

His conscience snorted. *"After everything you have done, Varésh Lúm-talé, after everything you have subjected me to, I think I have earned that right at least. Would you care to disagree? No—do not answer. My query was rhetorical."*

Varésh kept on at a measured pace. He had been at this for weeks, following the telltale signs of Mirkvahíl's rebirth. Life where once there had been death. Brilliance where once the light was silent. But most of all, the dreams. The images and whispers born of illum prying memories from the depths of the abyss.

"How naive I was and am and always will be 'til the end of time." One needn't cross the Temporal Sea to see that Varésh would forevermore be prone to idiocy. It was evident in his actions and his words.

"The irony," his conscience mused. *"As if Mirkvahíl could help you rectify your wrongs. As if this plan of yours will sidestep the ruin yet to come. Why do you think your father bequeathed this planet unto you? Have you ever sat and thought? Have you ever walked the tomb of memory in search of clarity?"*

Varésh had not—until recently, at least. Introspection had

always made him wary for the simple fact he had always been afraid to learn the hidden truths about himself and otherwise. It had taken holocaust to finally acknowledge what he had been, was, and always would be.

"*Failure,*" his conscience prodded. "*It rings in your ears. It buzzes like a thousand flies above a corpse. It is your legacy, Varésh Lúm-talé, and what a miserable thing it is. What a miserable thing she is.*"

Varésh shivered. She. The Vulture Luminíl. Entropy unbounded. Chaos freed by arrogance and lust and lies.

"*How many lives? How many, do you think?*" The question rang in Varésh's ears, high-pitched and unrelenting. "*Thousands? Hundreds of thousands? Millions, even? What would your beloved Sonja think could she see what you have done, could she see the monster you have made?*"

His conscience manifested at his side, hawk-faced with eyes of light and shadow and a mane of midnight hair. "*What would Sonja think could she see what you've become, could she see what you have done?*"

Varésh trembled at the question, shook with misery and rage. "You keep her name from this."

"*Just as you kept her life?*" his conscience sneered. "*Your Sonja deserved more than you were, Varésh Lúm-talé. She deserved more than you ever will be. She saw from the start what you needed a catastrophe to see. They all saw and for that they are dead.*"

Varésh tensed his jaw. "Mirkvahíl will help me make this right."

"*He said naively,*" mocked his conscience. "*You place your faith in the idea of Mirkvahíl as blindly as your people bow to your father's every whim—and look where that has led!*"

Varésh stared across the vastness of this place. He could feel it in the pit of his stomach, his absolute fear, the desperation of his endeavor.

"If you were strong you would strike your father down," his conscience said. *"You would sever ties, free your people from his madness and his lust for universal conquest. You would have them be true Architects, true World Builders, not the lies Ouran has made them.*

"But you are not strong. You are desperate and you are ignorant, and so you go about this task of yours. You seek to rectify a wrong you cannot undo and it will haunt you 'til the end of days whenever that may be."

The manifestation vanished. Varésh was alone with the grass and the clouds, with the wind and his thoughts. *It* will *work,* he urged himself. *It* has *to.* If not the personification of preservation and renewal, what could quell the destructive nature of the Vulture Luminíl?

"How could I have ever let it come to this?" lamented Varésh. A great ruin of ice and stone flashed across his mind. A dark world. A dead world. It filled him with more shame and guilt and disgust. He hated himself, and he hated that he hated himself. But that was part of the experience, he supposed. The experience of introspection in the wake of failure. The experience *of* failure.

And maybe that was why his undertaking had a chance to succeed. Success bloomed from the seeds sown by failure, or so he had taken to telling himself. His idiocy was a parable from which greater things could come if he made sure not to make the same mistakes again. If he was going to be an Architect, a World Builder in the truest form of the term, that meant giving a shit.

He walked.

Raindrops fell.

———

Varésh had seen much of Harthe in these last years. As planets went it was an infinitesimal thing, large yet scarcely populated. In his youth he had fantasized about the day he might be made an Architect, be made to shape and mold worlds, to nurture them from infancy to maturation. The notion of parenthood had always appealed to Varésh—what could be grander than fatherhood in the context of rearing an entire world?

"Do you truly believe you can set things right?" he asked of himself as the wandered through the rain. "How does a parent come back from *that*, from ignorance? From annihilation born of arrogance?"

"*And a false sense of unity,*" his conscience said.

"Of course..."

Varésh stopped. He was soaked to the bone but he did not care. He stood and stared, trained his ears to a faint but anguished melody behind the liquid misery and clouds. He had heard it so many times these last years, increasingly these last few weeks.

"Mirkvahíl," he whispered. The louder her song grew, the nearer Varésh knew he was.

"*Or perhaps you are imagining it,*" his conscience said, "*as you imagined so many things before. A man who fancies himself a god is the biggest lie of all, and all he does comes from a false heart.*"

Varésh choked back tears. He *had* fancied himself a god in his yesteryears—things were the way they were because of that. But he had changed. Celestials, he had *changed*! Why else would Mirkvahíl have called to him? Why would the Phoenix call to a man not pure of heart?

"What makes you think your heart is pure? What makes you think your motivation comes from a place of remorse? Truths are lies we tell ourselves," his conscience hissed. *"Lies we tell ourselves to mask the monsters that we really are. The truth, Varésh Lúm-talé, is not so easily discerned from madness. In fact, they are more often than not one and the same."*

His shadow twin manifested and caressed his cheek with a wispy hand. *"Which one of us is real, Varésh?"*

Varésh trembled at its touch. Its words chilled his blood.

"What makes you think me your conscience, hmm? From where, pray tell, did that little notion arise? His shadow twin grinned as its shape waned. Think on it as you walk, but remember this: I am not suck in here with you...

"You are trapped in here with me."

Varésh retched at its lingering touch. Retched as he never had before. He crumpled to the grass and curled himself into a ball, hugging his knees to his chest. It could have been the sickness, it could have been something else, but he was certain there were spirits in his midst, silhouettes of yesteryears gliding through the grass. They were silent, faceless, yet they filled him with fear, sorrow, with agony and shame.

"Stand up."

Varésh regarded the rainswept meadow with blurry eyes. Before him stood a silhouette composed of brilliant light.

"My dearest Varésh...stand up."

The world swam back into focus and he wasn't sure whether or not he was hallucinating.

"Sonja?"

Her laugh was unmistakable. Varésh knew the moment a smile

manifested on the silhouette that it was her, his beloved Sonja come to talk some sense into him—he hoped. For all he knew it was a trick of his shadow twin, a ruse to unnerve him, to further unravel his sanity and push him to the brink of utter madness.

Her touch was warm, gentle. Her smile and her eyes were as sweet as he remembered, as he had seen in dreams. Varésh reached for her but to his touch she was a ghost. How cruel a punishment that was.

"You need to stand," she said again, and helped him to his feet. *"This meadow is not the end of your journey. That, my Varésh, is a long time from now."*

He averted her gaze, shame rumbling in his gut. "I sometimes think I don't deserve to live. Not after all I've done..." He inhaled deeply, looked her in the eyes. "Not after what I did to you."

Sonja winced. Her expression soured slightly. *"I hate you for my death, Varésh. But I believe in your heart—even the worst of us, the most misguided can achieve redemption."*

Varésh swallowed the lump in his throat. Fresh tears fell from his eyes. He felt lighter for her words, yet still weighted down by his sins.

"The way forward is arduous," Sonja said. *"Far more than you can see. The game is long."*

"The game was always long," Varésh said.

"There are many pieces yet to be revealed," Sonja said. *"It is a game of shadows. I have seen the end."*

There was a tremor in her voice. Varésh frowned. "And?"

"It is not for me to tell," said Sonja. *"That is the way of things. That is fate."*

There was a long silence between them as the rain fell.

"I miss you terribly," Varésh said.

Sonja offered only a sad smile. Her form faded to mist, then she was gone.

———

It was dark when Varésh finally stopped for the day. Clouds scraped the sky but they were thin and the rain had stopped. The moon shone pale and the light was soothing. It made Varésh think of home, of childhood and all the nights he had spent gazing at the stars. Simpler times. Gentler times.

He leaned against the wall of the tower ruin he had taken refuge in. Its name had long escaped him and this realization was profound. He had always feared being forgotten. The notion made him feel empty inside, made him feel like little more than a ghost. If things and people were fated for namelessness, how important had they been to begin with?

"*You,*" his shadow twin hissed, "*have grown so sadly introspective in these last years.*"

Varésh ignored the jab. *My philosophical brooding is nothing new,* he thought. *Just...rediscovered. I was like this in my youth back home on Indris.* Celestials, he missed that planet so! Missed home so much it hurt—but he could not go back. *What do you care?*

"*I don't,*" his shadow twin said. "*I was merely remarking.*"

Varésh frowned and crossed his arms to his chest. *Why are you so convinced I haven't changed? You're absolutely hellbent on believing my intentions false, on convincing me my intentions are false—why?*

"*Because I know you, Varésh Lúm-talé,*" his shadow twin said. "*More than you know yourself.*"

Again you imply autonomy, Varésh thought, *and I am*

reasonably sure I *am real. If you are not my conscience then who
or what are you?*

"*Your lie,*" his shadow twin said. "*The lie you will always
carry with you. Worry not, Varésh Lúm-talé, clarity will manifest
soon enough.*"

The world was silent. Varésh closed his eyes.

"'Your lie,'" he whispered pensively. Lies were the founda-
tion upon which he had built his life—which one was this?

MANIFESTED FALSITIES

Then

Varésh Lúm-talé was a god. At least, he fancied himself a god. Considering the power he wielded and the place from which he'd come, he was at least on par with Alerion, Mirkvahíl, and Luminíl. So, actually, yes—Varésh Lúm-talé was, in fact, a god. And with great power came great emotional instability.

He wiped the snot from his nose and took another sip of whiskey. How in the high holy fuck had it come to this? Luminíl, corrupted and running amok, sowing chaos with every step, with every flap of those great, monstrous wings. Mirkvahíl, struggling to combat her dark lover. And Alerion?

"Fuck Alerion," Varésh slurred. "Fuck *everything. Especially* fuck Luminíl."

If not for the Vulture then Sonja would still be alive.

Condemning her to death had been the hardest thing he'd ever done, but what other option had there been? If not even Alerion or Mirkvahíl had been able to free her of Luminíl's corrupted will, then what chance did Varésh expect to have? He raised his glass to the memory of his wife then hurled it across the room. It hit the wall and shattered, glass and whiskey flying all directions.

A knock on the door. It opened before Varésh had a chance to tell whomever it was to piss off into the night. He calmed slightly at the sight of Rhona, perhaps the only other person in this city to whom he could relate. Only a week ago she had hung her beloved Djen Shy'eth, another of Luminíl's acolytes. Another soul lost to the corruptive nature of mirkúr.

"A drink?" Varésh asked as Rhona took a seat across from him.

"Please."

Varésh poured her one. She took it from him and downed it in a single gulp. It seemed that kind of thing was going around. He offered a sympathetic frown. "Know how you feel. At least I think I do. I hope I do."

Rhona leaned back in her chair. "And how do you think I feel?"

Varésh opened his mouth. "I—"

Now

"THAT'S NOT HOW IT HAPPENED," said his shadow twin, pulling Varésh from his rage.

Of course it is, Varésh snapped. *Why would it not be?*

"Why does a jealous lover manifest falsities?" his shadow twin asked as it took form. It extended a wispy finger to Varésh's temple and pressed, drawing a wince. *"Relax and let me kill this lie of yours. Let me show you what I saw through borrowed eyes while I was still able."*

Then

VARÉSH DWELLED at the north-most tip of Banerowos in a home without a door. As he had mentioned to Rhona years ago, he was horribly claustrophobic.

Rhona found him in the parlor with a drink as she so often did. It made him small in the best of ways; it dismissed the general air of prestige that came with being slightly less than a god. She took a seat opposite Varésh and accepted a drink.

"You seem conflicted," Varésh said.

Rhona smiled ruefully. "Djen is a puzzle. She makes me question the morality of her death."

Varésh sipped his drink. "Love is strange in that respect. Profoundly powerful." He looked Rhona in the eyes. "Go on, now. Ask me what you wish—I can sense the question ravaging your mind."

"Sonja."

Varésh set his glass to the side. "She would have destroyed Jémoon."

"But she was your wife," Rhona said. "You loved her deeply."

"As you surely did Djen," Varésh said. He had a faraway look in his eyes. "I have found, in all my countless years, the right thing and the hardest thing are often times the same."

"Of course." Djen flashed across her mind. "How did you cope?"

Varésh offered a melancholy smile. He poured another drink and swirled it in his glass.

Rhona's heart sunk—actions spoke far louder than words. "I wish I could ease your pain."

Varésh reached for her hand. "And I yours." He sighed. "Reconciliation eludes me."

"In your heart of hearts, do you believe your actions right?" Rhona asked.

"Yes," Varésh said. "And no. Judgment is requisite for order, but must every criminal be hanged? Must we frown so heavily upon idealism if it makes Jémoon a better place? I cannot help wondering if perhaps there might be a flaw in the design."

"How could unity be flawed?"

Varésh stood and started from the house. Rhona followed and they came to rest at the edge of a garden overlooking Banerowos. The city was a jewel beneath the moon, its dark streets and architecture capturing celestial light. It was beautiful enough to make one momentarily forget the Vulture had been freed.

"What do you see?" Varésh asked.

"The city as she stands." Rhona tilted her head. "Should I be keen to something more?"

Varésh gave another melancholy smile. "The people. In them, what do you *really* see?"

Rhona hesitated. Was there a specific answer he was looking for?

"I see fear," said Varésh. "I see frustration. I see anger and I feel it too. I feel their emotional distress where once I did not. They crave harmony; a people united can do great things. But more than that, they desire autonomy. I hear their whispers in

the night—they think the tenets too rigid. They think punishment too extreme."

Many people had been hanged for speaking out in favor of
Luminíl. Many more had been hanged for less.

"If the tenets are given slack...what then?" Rhona asked.
"What do you foresee?"

"Truthfully?" Varésh shrugged. "Emotion is fickle; discontent has a long memory."

Rhona tensed her jaw. Their conversation had led somewhere she had not expected; she was more conflicted than she
had been upon her arrival. If Varésh of all people doubted the
tenets of Jémoon, what was she to think?

"Perhaps Djen was right," Fiel said. *"Too much wine dulls the
mind. Are you ever going to think for yourself? Or are you too
afraid to have an opinion all your own? Deep in the confines of
your mind, what do you truly believe? How do you truly feel?
How have you* always *felt? What have you* always *thought?"*

Rhona swallowed. She had no immediate response. Her
body tingled.

"There it is," Fiel said. *"The coldness of uncertainty creeping
up your spine. Centuries of stout conviction ripped apart by the
moral quandary of your almost-god. How does it feel to have
lived so subservient a life?"*

"I should go," Rhona said.

Varésh nodded. He was silent as she left.

Now

"Are you absolutely sure that's how it really went?" Varésh asked.

"*Quite,*" his shadow twin replied. "*Unlike you I am able to see the truth in madness.*"

"You were in Rhona's head," Varésh said. "How?"

His shadow twin grinned and tapped its nose. "*Truth from madness, Varésh Lúm-talé. See the truth in madness. Learn your greatest lie—only then will things become clear.*"

The shadow vanished, once more leaving Varésh alone to ponder the many lies his life had been built upon. Had any of that been real? The first dream and the last—it was possible they were real to some extent, but the fact of the matter, as it dawned on him, made Varésh cold to his bones:

Who were Rhona and Djen?

MOTHER WOE

Mɪʀᴋᴠᴀʜíʟ ᴇxᴜᴅᴇᴅ ᴡᴀʀᴍᴛʜ. Rhona could feel it even from the first floor of her tower. Felt it more profoundly as she ascended to the pinnacle atop which the Phoenix resided. It eased her mind, pushed away the worry and anxiety of the last few days and helped her keep composure. It wasn't everyday citizens of Banerowos were granted an audience with Mirkvahíl, prominence be damned.

Mirkvahíl's quarters were radiant. She was, after all, the Phoenix—why should her dwelling not serve to further cement that fact? Like many of the other towers in the city this one too was open to the sky, possessing windows without glass and a long balcony that ran the southern length of the tower. It was there the Phoenix stood, garbed in whites and golds that fell to gossamer threads of mist. Her great wings were furled about her like a cloak and her hair fell in loose, dark curls.

"You have questions," she said as Rhona neared. "You dream but do not sleep. Fear clings to you." She turned, boring into Rhona with her pitch-black eyes. "Tell me your thoughts,

Rhona. Tell me your fears. What makes you think that we were wrong to imprison Luminíl? To exact judgment on her followers as was necessary?"

Rhona frowned, joining Mirkvahíl on the balcony. "Nothing. I don't believe we were wrong. I just...want answers. Clarity. How could two people as strong-willed and logical as Djen Shy'eth and Sonja Lúm-talé fall prey to Luminíl's influence? How could they not see her unbounded power threatens the existence of this world?"

Mirkvahíl studied her, never once blinking, never once looking away. "Something deeper tugs at you, Rhona. You *do* seek answers to these questions—you have always had the best interests of this world in mind. But your heart aches. I can feel as much. 'Why Djen?' you ask yourself. 'How could I have gone through with hanging her?'"

Rhona wiped a few stray tears from her cheeks. It was the first time she had cried in who knew how long. It was a peculiar feeling. She felt vulnerable here before the Phoenix and she did not like the sensation.

Mirkvahíl took her in a gentle embrace, furling her wings around them both.

"It is normal to feel such things," the Phoenix said. "The hurt. The confusion. The guilt. I have felt them all more and more with each passing day, each passing week and month and year. I loved Luminíl more than anything. I have felt her absence for some time, but I have also felt her phantom rage slithering through the air, unbounded like a storm. Were we right to imprison her? Were we right to favor country over person? Was there anything—*is* there anything we can do to quell her rampant mirkúr?"

Rhona said nothing as Mirkvahíl spoke. She focused only on the Phoenix's self-admitted pain, the very same she was going through. If such a creature as powerful as Mirkvahíl was having doubts then perhaps it was normal Rhona was having them too. She was, after all, wrought from the combined power of Alerion, Mirkvahíl, and Luminíl. *Everyone* was save Varésh Lúm-talé, and what must he be feeling?

"Why now?" Rhona asked. "Why express regret now after all these years?"

Mirkvahíl sighed. "Power and authority are enticing. They are seductive and profoundly so. You have felt this—that is why you are here. You need someone to whom you can relate. Idealism is a double-sided coin, Rhona. With utopia comes darkness. Every candle lit is another shadow cast. Perfection is a lie. Law requires chaos. It is a vicious circle; one I fear we have realized far too late."

"Too late?" Rhona asked, pulling back. "Too late for what?"

Mirkvahíl closed her eyes. "There is no saving Banerowos. There is no saving Jémoon."

"You can't possible know that," Rhona said. "Where there is will, there stands a chance. Luminíl's power is not so wild that it cannot be contained."

"I wish that were so," Mirkvahíl said, turning to stare out into the night.

Rhona bared her teeth in a rictus of disgust. "How can you give up so easily? If we are truly responsible for this mess then we have to do what we can to rectify it!" Mirkvahíl was silent. "How can you abandon your people so easily?"

"Luminíl and Djen might ask the same of us," Mirkvahíl said softly. "They *did* ask the same, and with what did we reply? 'I do as the Raven wills.' What a shield to hide behind. What a lie to justify our actions."

The warmth of the tower vanished. With it went the light and brilliance of Mirkvahíl until she was little more than a winged silhouette. "You came to me hoping for something else and for that I am sorry. For many things I am sorry, most of all you, Rhona. Farewell."

Disgusted, Rhona fled the tower teary-eyed and wanting desperately to shove a knife down Mirkvahíl's throat. Did she dare speak to Alerion now? Might he echo the same sentiments? Might he too concede defeat? Rhona didn't care to find out and so withdrew from Banerowos to the solace of Hang-Dead Forest.

———

WHAT DID it say about Rhona that she felt more at ease amongst the corpses in the trees than she did the majesty of Banerowos? Until tonight she had never thought to question it. Until tonight she had never thought to question many things, and the one person to whom she thought she could relate had done more harm than good.

"*You are going to do something reckless,*" Fiel said.

Is that a question or a statement? Rhona asked.

"*A bit of both,*" Fiel said. "*What sort of recklessness are you resorting to?*"

The expensive kind, said Rhona. *Some think my reverence of the trees overzealous—I will prove them wrong. Every action has a purpose, realized or not; every purpose has a price. Tonight my scarlet coinage grants an audience with the dead.*

Fiel gasped. "*Such an act is forbidden.*"

A lot of things are forbidden, Rhona said. *That doesn't necessarily make them wrong.*

"*How desperate you must be to have strayed from your path, little rule-follower,*" Fiel hissed. "*Have you begun rewriting your articles of faith or are you simply grasping at straws?*"

Rhona came to the Lost Tree from which Djen and so many others hung. It groaned in a breeze; bodies danced their pendulum dance. For a moment she imagined holding Djen, the pair swaying on the shore of the lake.

You seek the hang-dead dream, said the Lost Tree.

Rhona knelt and bowed her head. "Blood paid is a debt owed."

Indeed, said the Lost Tree, *and you have given much. I will grant you access to the dream, but know that what is written cannot be erased.*

"I understand." Rhona closed her eyes.

Be still, now, said the tree. *Be as the souls you seek. And remember my words—*

This is more than a dream.

———

THE LOST TREE was not the first to relay to Rhona the notion dreams were sometimes more than what they seemed. Such a thought was a favorite of the being Equilibrium whom Rhona had conversed with many times before. Still, this time around she couldn't help but feel...different. As if the Silent Place—to which the Lost Tree had surely delivered her cognizance—had manifested from within and engulfed her. As if it were calling out, trying to become one.

She turned about the darkness she had woken to, each step reverberating softly, each movement leaving an ethereal echo in its wake. The way forward was not certain; Rhona wasn't remotely sure what she was looking for in this instant. Djen, Sonja, any of the Hang-Dead souls were whom she sought but the question now was how to find them.

"*Mirkvahíl always had a saying,*" said Fiel. "*Do you recall? 'In the darkest night the faintest light is blinding.' Draw upon your-self to illuminate the path. This is, after all, a conjuration of your mind. At least, as the Silent Place interprets what you seek."*

Rhona held an upturned palm out to the nothingness. Gradually small beads of light coalesced at her finger tips, braiding inward until they formed a sphere of pale blue illumination. It ascended and the darkness bled away in rivulets just as it had the last time she had come. Instead of a silver meadow she found herself before the ruin of a temple, the sky above a pallid swirl of clouds.

"What is this place?" Rhona asked, mostly to herself, but partly to the ruin.

Fiel hissed.

Do you know where we are? Rhona asked. She took a step toward the threshold; Fiel snarled. *Spit it out.*

"*This is* her *realm,*" said Fiel. "*They call her Mother Woe.*"

Rhona had never heard of Mother Woe. *Where did you learn that?*

"*Through exploration,*" said Fiel. "*You and I are one and the same. In the rarest of instances I* do *have autonomy.*"

Imagine my shock. Rhona rolled her eyes. *Explain to me this Mother Woe. Why are you so afraid of her? What is she?*

"*Dangerous,*" said Fiel. "*As was Luminíl to Alerion, as Chaos is to Balance, Mother Woe is to Equilibrium.*" The temple door creaked ajar. "*It seems she has been expecting you. Be vigilant. Be receptive to her words. As the Lost Tree said—this is more than just a dream.*"

Rhona crossed into the temple, overcome by the scent of old stone and dirt. Of rain.

Of mirkúr.

She thought to conjure a blade but the notion fled as quickly as it'd come. She knew it was purely out of fear, a means of a defense, but she doubted Mother Woe would see it that way. Best to come unarmed to such an amphitheater of uncertainty, especially if its mistress was as powerful as Fiel had said.

The anteroom was long and wide, its ceiling arched. It had once been beautiful. Beyond the crumbling stone and lichens, past the dust and mold, were faded, fragmented inlays illustrating winged beings numbering in the hundreds. What had this place been built in reverence to?

The anteroom yawned into a circular courtyard bordered by tall white-leaved trees. Motes of light and shadow wafted through the air like snowflakes. Had the temple itself not been so glum Rhona might have found the scene beautiful.

"And here I thought you found solace in death," Fiel jabbed.

Rhona ignored the voice.

A faint melody tickled her ears. She trained her hearing to the words—it was coming just beyond the trees. She marched through the courtyard and into the woods, the song growing louder, more intelligible all the while. It was infectiously sad. The nearer she grew the darker she felt. By the time she withdrew from the woods and found herself staring at a stone altar, her cheeks were stained with tears and her eyes were so pained from crying she was ready to gouge them out.

"Now, child. Keep your hands to your side." The voice was gentle yet imposing, physical yet at the same time trapped between the fabric of the world. *"You have need of sight for as long as you are here. How else will you trail your sins? How else will you behold the majesty of your monstrousness?"*

Rhona swallowed her pain. She stumbled, nearly tumbling forward, but managed to regain her balance as a lithe silhouette manifested in a swirl of smoke. She bore a black cloak and hood; tattered bird wings trailed behind her and her eyes were two full moons encircled by dark veins and peeling flesh.

Rhona fell to her knees. *"D-Djen?"*

The woman offered a melancholy smile. *"I have not used that name in...centuries. I am called mother woe and I am here to point you on your way."*

———

RHONA'S MIND was a jumble of confusion. Mother Woe was *Djen?* What did she mean she hadn't used that name in centuries? Rhona pushed herself to stand. She was dizzy as she rose to meet Mother Woe's eyes. This place felt a blur.

"You have questions to which you seek answers," Mother Woe said. *"I could posit my own but what good would that do you?"* She held a hand out to Rhona. *"The way ahead is treacherous for those unprepared."*

Rhona hesitated. "How do I know you aren't lying?"

"You don't," Mother Woe said plainly. *"But what choice do you have but to trust me, the warden of this place? I can give you what Mirkvahíl could not."*

There was venom in that last sentence, decades of subtext. But Rhona *needed* answers and she was sure lashing out physically at Mother Woe would lead nowhere good.

Rhona took her hand. It was frigid. There was not a modicum of warmth to be felt. Rhona's heart dropped at that but she couldn't bring herself to be angry at Mother Woe, at Djen. She felt only sadness and an inkling of regret.

"Where do we go from here?" Rhona asked.

"The Bone Garden," Mother Woe said.

They started for the trees, crossed the threshold into a dark wood illuminated by tiny motes of light. Normally such a place would have made Rhona feel at ease. The manifestation of corpses, wayward souls, and twisted trees would have made her feel as though she had done the right thing, what the Raven had willed. But here, beside Mother Woe, all it did was fill her with dread. What was this place? Who were these sorry, white-eyed corpses hanging from trees? Who and what were all these wailing, gossamer spirits?

"*You will learn,*" Mother Woe said as if she had read Rhona's thoughts. "*In time you will learn. For now, simply walk and ruminate on everything you have been, are, and want to be.*"

FATHER SKY

Then

R HONA HAD ALWAYS HAD a soft spot for Alerion. To all of Jémoon he was the Raven, a third of the great creators of Harthe. Secretly, to Rhona, he was Father Sky, a parental figure for a woman who had simply come to be, like so many others of her kind. Yet she found herself questioning his judgment. So many Jémoonites had voiced their opposition to his jailing of Luminíl; for that they now hung from the branches of the Raven's Wood.

You aided Alerion, Rhona thought to herself as she stared at the lake. *Don't forget that. You went along with his decision. You were a willing participant.* She looked at her hands, at her forearms, at the reflection of her face, all caked in dried blood. *Was it worth it? All that death... I do as the Raven wills but...*

Rhona sighed. She had never felt so conflicted before. She

loved Alerion, admired his character, but she had also been friends with Luminíl, with many of the Jémoonites who risen up against Alerion and Mirkvahíl and lost their lives.

Rhona turned at a soft breeze against her back. Alerion stood there, midnight-feathered wings furled around him like a cloak. His gray eyes shone even without the aid of the moonlight. He offered a small smile, one that seemed to suggest his sympathy.

Rhona stood to face him, arms wrapped around herself. She chewed her lower lip, eyes narrowed pensively. "I want to believe our course of action was the right one. I *need* to believe, to know that Luminíl's continued freedom would have left the world prey to unbounded mirkúr. That jailing her was the kindest thing we could have done."

"Child." Alerion neared her. He cupped her cheek; his hand was warm and it eased her mind. "So often I have found the right thing to be the hardest. It breaks my heart. I can scarcely imagine everything that might be running through Luminíl's mind, through the citizens of Banerowos...but I take solace knowing we have quelled the threat of complete annihilation."

Rhona couldn't ignore that fact. The cage in which Luminíl now resided kept her rampant energies at bay while still allowing the Jémoonites to draw from her mirkúr as they drew illum from Mirkvahíl.

That somehow makes this feel worse. Rhona felt sick at the thought of Luminíl being little more than a source from which parasites drew strength.

"Was there truly no other way?" she asked Alerion.

He shook his head and his face caught briefly in the moonlight. His cheeks were tear-stained and his eyes red. "Mirkvahíl and I could find no other solution. I pray one presents itself in time; I do not wish to see Luminíl imprisoned eternally."

Yet your tone suggests the possibility of such a thing is great, Rhona thought.

"You are covered in blood," Alerion noted. "Why have you not yet cleaned yourself?"

Rhona bowed her head. "Shame. Guilt, I suppose."

"Both are reasonable responses," Alerion said, "but I see no shame in defending the livelihood of your people, of your home. The dead knew what they were doing; they rose up in favor of Luminíl despite Mirkvahíl and myself wishing things to be as peaceful as possible."

"Maybe violence was the most peaceful option," Rhona said. "I hardly think a being so powerful as Luminíl would enjoy being locked away, even willingly."

Alerion's expression darkened. "She was not—Luminíl has always been a bit difficult. It saddens me to say I foresaw her response. She always favored power slightly more than she did the lives of her people." Alerion tensed his jaw. "...She tried to kill Mirkvahíl some time ago."

Rhona's eyes widened.

"Not purposely, not entirely," Alerion said. "It was years back, when her temperance first began to wane."

"What would have caused her to do such a thing?" Rhona asked. "She and Mirkvahíl..."

"Were lovers, yes," Alerion said. "Mirkvahíl and I have been fruitless in our attempts to find an answer to her illness. What little we know is that it makes her lose control. It...eats away at her compassion, at her control."

"Entropy destroying Entropy," said Rhona. "It would be ironic if it wasn't so horrible. How many others know?"

"The whole of Jémoon," Alerion said. "It would be foolish for Mirkvahíl and I to conceal something of such import. And yet..." He heaved a sigh. "I know it will not deter her acolytes from trying to free her. I laud them for their dedication to Luminíl—it is plain to see she meant a great deal to a great many people. But I curse their blind allegiance, too. Releasing the Vulture from her cage will do more harm than good."

They were both silent for a time, Rhona letting Alerion's words sink into her head. Jémoon and Banerowos were still in their infancy. Country and city had come so far in just decades yet peace and growth had devolved into civil war and the notion of utter and complete destruction. Rhona had never once dreamed things would crumble so dramatically, if at all. Never once had she dreamt of utopia and dystopia being one and the same.

"What would you have me do?" she asked finally.

"See the bigger picture," Alerion said softly. "Country over person, Rhona. As difficult a tenet as it seems, it is the one we must live by if Jémoon is to survive. Alf elo nor, nor elo alf. Do you understand?"

Alf elo nor—one for all. Nor elo alf—all for one.

Rhona nodded.

Then

"Twelve in a single evening," said Varésh. "A new record."

"A new post-war record," Rhona said as they watched the blood-stained corpses dance their pendulum dance. She dragged her blade across the palm of her hand and pressed it to the earth, whispering, "*Alf elo nor*." It was her twelfth cut of the night.

"You do that more than most," Varésh said. "Actually, you

might very well be the *only* one who does it. Giving blood to Hang-Dead Forest, I mean."

Rhona shrugged. "It might do you well to mimic me, Varésh. Reverence goes a long way in a place like this. Blood paid is a debt owed."

Varésh snorted. "What could the trees possibly have to give?"

"Whatever they deem worthy of my blood," Rhona said, bandaging her hand. "Who knows? My sanguine reverence may yet save Jémoon, and then would you be questioning my many scars?" They numbered in the hundreds. A cut for every corpse. The more that hung, the more Rhona bled; the more she bled, the closer she grew to complete exaltation with Hang-Dead Forest. Her gut told her this was right, that someday everything she had given would be repaid tenfold. She hoped it meant peace, harmony at last.

"What does Mirkvahíl think of you shedding blood so freely? Alerion?" Varésh asked. He was a bit green in the face.

"They agree with it," Rhona said. "In fact, it was Alerion who first suggested doing so."

"A bit...macabre," Varésh said. "The Raven, wise as he may be, has become a bit dark these last several years. A bit more... oh, shit—what's the phrase I'm looking for?" He snapped his fingers repeatedly. "Superstitious. I think."

Rhona cocked an eyebrow. "Superstitious?"

"Alerion never used to be this obsessed with death," Varésh said.

"I would hardly call putting Jémoon's best interests at heart 'superstitious,' Varésh," Rhona said. "We do as the Raven wills. If Luminíl's acolytes are going to continue threatening harmony with their individualistic nonsense then what better recourse is there than to snuff them out? Utopia is only attainable if everyone is working toward the same goal."

Varésh sighed. "I suppose you're right." He shuddered. "Can we go?"

"Fine," Rhona said, and they started back toward Banerowos.

Then

"IT HAD TO BE DONE, VARÉSH." Rhona squeezed his shoulder. "I'm to lead Djen to her end a fortnight from now. I...know how you feel. I hope."

Varésh said nothing as he watched his wife, Sonja, swing from the Lost Tree.

"She and Djen freed Luminíl from her prison," Rhona continued, not knowing what else to do but preach the sins of their beloveds. "They may have very well doomed Jémoon—Harthe, even—to its end."

"I know." Varésh was hoarse. He had clearly spent the previous night screaming. "We do..." He sniffled, then tense his jaw. "We do as the Raven wills. If only Sonja and Djen had seen sense to do the same." He bowed his head, muttering indiscernibly.

"Power corrupts," Rhona said. "If it was not plain to see before then it surely is now." The words were meant more for her than they were Varésh. Sonja had always been outspoken where Luminíl's imprisonment was concerned, but Rhona had never thought she would do something so rash as releasing the

Vulture. She had never once dreamed Djen would be swayed to such recklessness, either.

Fuck.

"I suppose...I suppose I never really knew Sonja as well as I thought. My own *wife*, conspiring to sentence Jémoon to its end." A guttural scream escaped his lips and Varésh sent a thread of illum javelining upward through the trees and into the night.

Rhona took his hand and squeezed. "Come on. A drink will do you some good."

It would do *her* some good as well. She had a fortnight to rid herself of her emotional attachment to Djen. It was best to start now.

Now

"*I* WONDER IF YOU REALLY KNOW..." Mother Woe said, snapping Rhona from her pensive trance.

"Know what?" Rhona asked.

Mother Woe smiled and said nothing else.

Rhona had no clue as to how long they had been walking through this awful, twisted forest. Fiel had been utterly silent, quelled by the presence of Mother Woe, of what had once been Djen...centuries ago, whatever that meant.

"*Time is complex,*" Mother Woe said. "*Memory is complex. Amalgamate them and you might very well lose your mind trying to put the pieces in the right order. no one ever said parables were harmless.*"

"Is that what this is? Some sort of lesson?" Rhona asked.

"In a manner of speaking," Mother Woe said. *"If you really think about it your entire existence has been a parable, Rhona. one could say the same of alerion as well, the fool. What a lie he is."*

Rhona refrained from asking what Mother Woe meant. She knew the response she'd get.

At length, the forest bled into a pitch black night. Before them a stone bridge stretched the length of a massive chasm. At its other side stood an old gate and a wall of mirkúr, bone, and stone.

"What is it?"

"The birth place of clarity," Mother Woe said. *"The bone garden."* She gestured toward the bridge. Her hood fell back and her dark hair whipped about her face in a gust of cold air. Amidst her ruin, in the depths of her eyes, Rhona could see a hint of the woman she had loved, the woman she had hung. Her heart twinged.

"Am I to go alone?"

Mother Woe nodded. *"Farewell."* She took a step back and dropped into the chasm below.

Rhona wrapped her arms around herself and swallowed.

"What a horrible place this is," Fiel said, startling Rhona.

I...I don't want to cross that bridge, Rhona thought.

"You must," Fiel said. Its dread was evident. *"You seek answers."*

Rhona heaved a sigh. *Oh, Djen... What the hell have I gotten myself into?*

She started across the bridge.

FOREST DARK

THere was a profound correlation between morality, truth, and the lies one told oneself. Varésh had spent the last few days ruminating in silence—thank the Celestials for *that*—on Rhona and Djen, on their significance in what he had seen in his dream. It was certainly within the realm of possibility they and the dream were mere conjurations of his shadow twin, an attempt to further unhinge Varésh. To further blur the line between reality and falsity.

But something in him told Varésh there was more to the women, that they were connected yet to the Phoenix Mirkvahíl. His shadow twin's claim of having infiltrated Rhona's dreams suggested as much, suggested, at the very least, Varésh and Rhona had fought for a common goal. The only problem was Varésh, long as his memory was, could not remember once having that conversation, let alone speaking with Rhona.

"Trees," said Varésh as he crossed the threshold into a dense wood. "Thank the Celestials for trees." He had seen nothing but grass and ruins the last few days; this was a welcome change of pace. Or would have been if not for the myriad bones protruding from and hanging from the trees. "Fuck."

Hang-Dead Forest had never been Varésh's favorite locale but that was something he was going to have to stomach if he wanted to reach Mirkvahíl. Her song had grown increasingly louder the last day or so, to the point it had become a low and constant ringing in his ears. Varésh sighed; reluctantly he took the path at a measured pace, conjuring a tiny mote of illum to guide his way. It had been a long time since last he had come to Hang-Dead Forest, longer yet since this place had been free of its ever-present darkness.

"Why the fuck..." Varésh didn't need to finish the question to know the answer. The lust for power and the idea of utopia pushed people to barbarism, to nationalistic atrocities. "How could we have ever thought it was right?"

He stopped before a trio of skeletons hanging from a lower branch. One of the skeletons was far smaller than the other two, not yet fully developed. Varésh swallowed the bile rising in his throat and cursed himself a thousand times over.

I have to fix this, he thought.

"*You have to do a lot of things,*" his shadow twin whispered. "*There is much to be done to achieve even a modicum of hope to right your wrongs, Varésh Lúm-talé.*"

Varésh's upper lip curled. *You are the most back and forth monstrosity I have ever had the misfortune of conversing with. Which is it—do you want me to succeed or do you want me to fail? It seems to me you would find more joy in the latter.*

"*On the contrary. Nothing would please me more than to see Harthe spared your idiocy,*" his shadow twin said. "*You will learn the truth of things in time, that much is known, but as your Sonja said: the way ahead is arduous.*"

And I suppose part of the experience of failure is dealing with my demons, guilt, and manifested falsities, thought Varésh. *All of which you seem to exacerbate.*

"*I must do* something *to pass the time in here,*" his shadow twin hissed. "*I have seen your every thought and dream a thousand times over. There is little else I can do but goad you on your way, Varésh Lúm-talé. For what it is worth, this is as much a learning experience for me as it is for you.*"

Varésh said nothing as he continued through Hang-Dead Forest.

———

"*Do you remember when you hung me here?*"

The voice pulled Varésh from a long and meandering recollection about Sonja. He looked about, spied her luminescent silhouette in a clearing several yards ahead. He swallowed, choking back tears as the memory took like a flame to paper.

"How could I forget?"

He had dreamt it every night in the years since Sonja's violent end. Since he had murdered her for having differing beliefs. It was penance for his actions, but not penance enough. Nothing would ever be punishment enough for what he had done to his wife.

"*You could have stopped this all, Vare,*" Sonja lamented. She danced away from him, winding through the trees like a leaf on a breeze. Varésh gave chase. "*You could have been great. We could have been such keepers of this planet...*"

Varésh came to a sliding halt as Sonja vanished.

"*But you could never deny your father,*" the trees taunted in her voice.

"*Always had to prove yourself.*"

"*Always had to fuck things up—didn't you?*"

"Didn't you?"

Dɪᴅɴ'ᴛ ʏᴏᴜ?

DIDN'T YOU?

Sonja manifested in a burst of shadow, a grating shriek erupting from elongated jowls, eyes like wan full moons. She swiped at him with taloned fingers and it was all Varésh could do to avoid her fury. He stumbled backward, nearly tripped over his own feet as he shaped his illum mote into a thin, radiant blade. Sonja hissed at its warmth; its light revealed the utter ruin of her countenance, peeling flesh and all.

"Celestials..." Varésh whimpered, feebly but successfully deflecting another enraged swipe, *"what have I done?"*

"Look at me," Sonja snarled. *"Look at me, Varésh. look upon the manifestation of your lies. You are a fool if you think finding Mirkvahíl can remedy this. You are a fool if you believe the lie you have sold yourself. Some things are simply set in stone."*

"I can redeem myself," Varésh said, brushing away his tears. "I *can.* I *must,* Sonja."

She struck again; this time the blow landed with force. Talons raked across Varésh's face and he fell to the ground in a daze. His blood was warm against his flesh, soothing as Hang-Dead Forest spun in and out of focus, as the specter of his beloved Sonja knelt and tugged upon his spirit. Her mirkúr wormed its way to the center of his chest, of his mind and he saw light.

———

Vᴀʀᴇ́sʜ ʙʟɪɴᴋᴇᴅ ᴀɴᴅ the world was still. He stood before a lake. Its surface collected starlight as a net would fish. It was beautiful and it made him feel at peace.

"This isn't right," he murmured, the image of Sonja's ruined corpse fresh in his mind. He had been in Hang-Dead Forest. Then he had seen a light far brighter than anything before him now. Sunlight? Moonlight?

"That is a very astute observation."

Varésh watched the lake manifest his shadow twin. There was something different about it this time, something more... whole and realized. The storm-gray eyes, the sharpness of its jawline, and...

"Shit."

The midnight, feathered wings he had seen so many times before. As they burst forth from his shadow twin's back so too did they sprout from Varésh, pushing through his flesh and procuring a shriek, completing his lie.

"You wear me sadly," said Alerion. "Like a cutthroat does a crown achieved by spilling blood." He smirked at Varésh's discomfort. "I told you clarity would come to you soon enough. And worry not—all is yet to be revealed."

Varésh had a long memory but none of this registered. How had he come to wear Alerion's guise? What had happened to Alerion?

"Is this another trick?" he asked. "What is this place? Why am I here?"

"No, not a trick," Alerion said. "I am not so cruel as that. I am not so cruel as you, Varésh Lúm-talé. As you are wont to ravage lives, I am sworn to save them—that is what I have done for you. Saved you from the product of your arrogance."

"Sonja."

"She is just one of many bent by death, by the touch of wild mirkúr," Alerion said. "A rusalk. A once preventable monstrosity now numbering in the hundreds of thousands." Alerion shook his head and heaved a sigh. "Power is fool's gold, Varésh. Do you see now what it does? The ruin of this world and its people is the very same that fate will deliver unto Indris, unto your father and your people."

Varésh bowed his head. "I have seen—I have known this for a time. It is why I *must* find Mirkvahíl. To make things right, to quell the destruction Luminíl has wrought. To save her. To... to..." He steeled himself and looked Alerion in the eyes. "To be better, *different from* my father. To be a *true* Architect. To rear and nurture worlds, not remake them in my image. Please."

Alerion frowned. "There is passion in your words, Varésh Lúm-talé. Sincerity wrought from guilt. But even if you are able to find Mirkvahíl I fear she will be of little use to your cause. I have seen her soul and it is shattered. Her mind is lost."

"Still, I have to try," Varésh said.

"I know. The way ahead is dangerous," Alerion said. "There are things you will learn that have the power to destroy you."

"Rightfully so," Varésh murmured.

"Indeed." Alerion held his hand out to Varésh. His expression softened and for a moment Varésh swore he saw a hint of sympathy in that gray stare. "When you are ready I will deliver you from sleep. Stay vigilant."

Varésh took Alerion's hand and the lake-world melted away in rivulets.

He awoke in Hang-Dead Forest with a gasp.

———

VARÉSH's face burned something fierce. He ran his fingers gingerly along the lacerations. They had closed of their own volition, scarred; Sonja's talons had also missed his eyes and he drank the darkness in. It was beautiful.

"*Stand,*" Alerion commanded, once more a voice in Varésh's head.

Varésh stood, ears trained to a distant song, that of the Phoenix Mirkvahíl. He was growing closer; his quarry, his destiny was perhaps only hours away on the other side of Hang-Dead Forest.

Where is Sonja? he asked of Alerion.

"*About,*" Alerion said. "*They* all *are.*"

A shiver crept up Varésh's spine. He had failed to quell Sonja's wrath—how did he expect to best *all* the rusalks? How many did *all* even mean? He supposed it didn't matter. He would either reach his destination or he would die trying. It was all part of the experience of failure. It was all part of redemption, and Celestials, did Varésh want to be redeemed.

He steeled his nerves and walked.

IMPOSTER SYNDROME

Then

Varésh Lúm-talé had never seen a planet so beautiful as Harthe, Harmony in the Celestial tongue. This celestial sphere in all its splendor—it was *his* to mold, his to remake in a manner of speaking. Some planets were little more than spherical scenery, devoid of any sentient life. Others were blooming. And then there were some, like Harthe, wrought from their own unique pillars of creation yet, for whatever reason, needing that extra nudge.

Varésh had always wanted to nudge and now he had the perfect opportunity—*if* the locals saw fit to accept his aid. He walked the grassland, hands behind his back, nose keen to the sweet perfume of myriad flowers riding on the wind. To his left sat a great lake, placid, like a mirror or a doorway to an inverse world.

"So much I could do here," he mused. "What a world I could make of Harmony. It could be the greatest restoration, the greatest maturation in Celestial history. Orchestrated by me, a novice Architect."

So many times Varésh had fantasized about getting his chance to prove himself to his people and their emperor, his father. There were many who believed Varésh had been given this responsibility simply because of his birthright, but if they *really* knew Ouran, really knew what made him tick, they would realize Varésh had been anything but his favored son. In fact, at times, Varésh had felt he *wasn't* Ouran's son. Ouran was a man of vision. Varésh had...pieces of visions, and that was about it. Ambition but without the wherewithal to capitalize on his intent.

Until now. His power surged at the notion. The energy, radich, swam through him like an eager serpent toward its prey. *So much possibility,* Varésh thought. What would his radich take the form of here? What energies did these great pillars of creation wield? Varésh salivated at the thought, at the anticipation. He *needed* to know. He burned to.

And yet... He couldn't ignore the tiny voice in the back of his mind, chiding the Celestials and the emulative nature of radich—*possibility* in the Celestial vernacular. There were, unfortunately, many a Celestial Architects through the history of Indris who had used their power for lesser, more...unconscionable things.

But I will not be one of them, Varésh thought, dropping to his knees and closing his eyes.

"I will not."

Now

. . .

Retrospection was both enlightening and frightening. Varésh remembered well the first time he had set foot on Harthe, the first time he had breathed its sweet air. The first time a vision for what this planet could be had manifested wholly in his mind. All of that seemed so very long ago. A dot of light in what had otherwise been a stumble through darkness and uncertainty.

"Do you know what I find most interesting?" Alerion asked. *"About you as you were then and you as you are now? A sense of hope, dedication wrought not from a hungering for control, but from the desire to make things better."*

I suppose it's good someone *sees that,* Varésh thought. *All I see is a fool.*

"We are all of us fools at some point in our lives," Alerion said. *"Myself included."*

Varésh wasn't sure what Alerion meant by that. He brushed it from his mind and continued through Hang-Dead Forest, vigilant to every sound, spooked by every cracking twig or gust of wind. He almost wished Sonja and the other rusalks would show themselves. Then, at the very least, he would know what pitiful things were watching him.

Do you recall ever knowing anyone named Rhona or Djen? Varésh asked. *You showed me a conversation with myself from Rhona's perspective but...*

"You still can't recall having ever met either of them," Alerion said. *"You can thank Luminíl's unbounded mirkúr for those gaps in your memory. It magnifies the guilt and that in turn magnifies repression."*

So how is it I have come to remember what I have on this journey? Varésh asked.

"*I am balance,*" Alerion said. "*I both destroy and preserve. Think of it as...removing mental blocks.*"

I suppose that makes sense, Varésh thought. He was more damaged than he had first thought. Rightfully so. After everything he had done why would he *want* to remember any of that? It was like Alerion said—truths were often times lies one told oneself. The Sonja he had first met in the meadow, her sweetness and confidence in him, had been a lie. Fuck, Varésh's very *guise* was a lie. How many more truths had he fabricated? What monstrosities yet awaited him?

At length he came to a small clearing. In its center was an effigy. He knew in his gut he should recognize it, knew it should make him feel *something*—but he could not, and it did not. He stood there, staring at the eldritch thing, little more than a hood and robe from which protruded six great wings.

"What have I forgotten?" he asked the effigy. "What shame have I repressed?"

The statue seemed to *shift* at his words. The forest dilated, leaving Varésh and the effigy in a void neither dark nor light but rather both at once. He felt dizzy, nauseous. What was this? Where was he? *What* was he?

Desolator. Woe Bringer, said the statue. *As we have epithets so too do you, Varésh Lúm-talé. you Are the very definition of your name—did your father never tell you what your name translates to? Falsity. You have always been a lie. From the time of your birth, until the day you die, and for eternity, you will always be a lie.*

Fragments of stone exploded outward from the effigy, revealing the towering monstrosity within. Dark as night, six feathered wings, and an orb of stark white light where a face should sit. It reached for Varésh and plucked him from where he stood with its thumb and index finger.

Like a carrion bird to a corpse, I will devour you, it said. I will eat your pretense. And you will know. Everything.

It held him over its luminescent face; the light dilated to reveal a cavernous void.

Varésh shrieked as he fell.

———

THIS WILL BE THE SECOND worst thing you learn of yourself.

You walk the streets of Banerowos with intent born of desire. You tell yourself you are doing this thing because you wish only to nurture Harthe to greatness, whatever that may be; that is not yet known to you. You tell yourself you do this thing because only you and you alone know how to save this infinitesimal world. You are an Architect. You were born for this —it is in your very blood.

The night is cold and your blood runs hot with anticipation. You tell yourself you were sent here for a reason. Alerion, Mirkvahíl, and Luminíl...they require guidance, they require molding. They must see things as you do lest they destroy this orb they call their home, their creation. Things have gone well enough but there is always room for error. if only they could see...

"The right thing is often times the hardest," you whisper to yourself. You urge yourself to believe it, though deep in the bowels of your existence, in that nook in which some semblance of your conscience still remains, you know that this is wrong. Why else would it be so difficult?

You come to the lake you so often times find yourself staring into. It is beautiful as always. It makes you think of home, of Indris in a way. So many stars collecting in that placid surface, so many possibilities.

"Varésh. well met," Alerion greets. He stands before the lake, hands clasped behind his back. His eyelids are heavy and he wears a soft smile; he has had a good day. "How are you this evening? What brings you here?"

"Well," you reply, mimicking his posture. "Just...admiring the lake as I am wont to do."

"She is a sight," Alerion says. His storm-gray eyes shine bright without the aid of light and his shoulder-length raven hair is pulled back behind his ears. His wings hang limply from his back, touching the grass beneath his feet. How beautiful they are. How beautiful a thing Alerion is.

"Harthe has come a way these years," you say. It is true. There has been great progress where the evolution of harmony is concerned. Banerowos is a jewel. Jémoon is...something you cannot put words to. But you love it dearly. "Still, I find myself fearful, wary. I dread the tipping of the scale."

"It is a necessary thing," Alerion says. "Without destruction there can be no evolution."

"Easy for you to say." You sigh. You feel a tickle in your throat. "You are balance made manifest. That all makes sense to you. I just..." You have seen so much destruction. You have seen worlds annihilated, you have seen people slaughtered, and for what? A witness to chaos without the power to prevent it. "I cannot let that be. It is possible to evolve without destroying what we have built. Preservation is always an option."

Your radich burns inside of you. Burns so hot it makes you cold. It hurts like nothing you have ever known, But it is a price you must pay. You concentrate, pushing the energy into the blade beneath your cloak. Urging your radich, willing it to shift, to manifest itself as mirkúr. Tears well in your eyes and you swallow the lump in your throat. You don't know if you are ready for this—but you must be. You must have strength.

You have never killed a god before.

Quick as lightning you draw the blade and thrust it into Alerion's chest, piercing bone and punching through his heart. He wears surprise as you bring him to the grass, as you cradle him in your lap.

"This is for the best," you whisper, you urge yourself to believe amidst the distant, muffled shriek from the abyss of your existence. "Forgive me."

Forgive you—for the blade you've buried in his chest and for the atrocity you have been conjuring this entire time. Alerion turns to ash without a word. You stand to admire your reflection in the lake and smile.

You will make a better god, a better creator than Alerion ever could.

You will make a better Alerion than he ever could.

———

VARÉSH FLAILED IN THE DARKNESS. Shrieked and tore at his eyes, at everything he was.

The worst is yet to come, the statue hissed. *I will break you a thousand times over. And when I am done, Varésh Lúm-talé...I will do it all again. Over and over. For as long as you may live.*

He was drowning, now. Liquid filled his lungs.

The darkness grew.

Then Varésh saw a man.

———

"NERÓSH."

You reach for the man. He puts a steadying hand on your arm. You are dying. He and the rest of your acolytes have done their best these last months but the end is inevitable. Your end is inevitable. The empire is on the brink of collapse; Indris wilts beneath a shroud of civil war and parasites unleashed from Celestials know where.

"Nerósh," you murmur. He has been your loyalist follower for as long as you can recall, the person whom you trust above all others; he is your friend. You have very few of those left, if you ever had any at all.

"Ouran'il will soon be overrun," Nerósh says. You notice the blood dripping down his face, the signs of battle on his garb. "But...we have found a way." The way he says those words, the glint in his orange eyes... "A way to ensure you carry on. It is untested but—"

"Do it," you say. If there is even a chance, you must take it. The empire must survive; the seeds of resurrection must be sown. "Whatever it is, whatever the cost, Nerósh...please." Such a foreign word, that. You have never pled for anything in your life."

Nerósh bows his head, touches his left shoulder in salute. "As you command, Majesty." He looks up, looks you dead in the eyes, bores into you with a stare that says more than words ever could. "It has been an honor, Ouran."

There is a burst of light, scalding, shrieking, horrible.

Chaos.

Muffled annihilation.

You are hurtling through...something. Through madness.

The velocity flays you.

You are screaming muscle.

You are howling bone.

You are...weightless. A ghost among the stars. A spectator above the pandemonium and ruin of Indris, of Ouran'il, the city you built so long ago. You cry phantom tears; they drip down phantom cheeks.

Your memories shift and crack. All fades to black.

A blackness unlike anything you have ever known.

Then, a light.

A lake. Your reflection gazes up at you. You are Nerósh, but you are not. You are Ouran, but you do not remember. You are something else, someone else, with memories from a childhood of yore.

You are Varésh Lúm-talé, son of Ouran.

You are the greatest lie of all.

VARÉSH HAD NEVER RETCHED SO MUCH in his life. This was surely a trick of the mind, this eldritch entity trying to break him with falsities. It had to be. He *needed it* to be. He was not his father, he was not and never *had been* Ouran, Celestial Emperor of Indris—right?

"R-R...*ight?*" he wheezed.

I told you I would break you, Varésh Lúm-talé. I told you the worst was yet to come and now you know, the entity said. *Now you know the extent of your lie. You were never meant to nurture Harthe to greatness—your past made it so. It is in your blood, your bones, your soul to conquer in your given name. You are vanity made manifest, arrogance in the flesh, and I am here to put you in your place. You will lose your mind.*

From the darkness came that awful, faceless orb of light. Blinding. Searing. Spellbinding.

See your lies, Varésh Lúm-talé, it hissed. *See the ruin you have caused. See them die—each and every one of them. See your Sonja as she flails from her noose—*

The entity shrieked. Its light dimmed and an ethereal figure took shape, threads of illum and mirkúr streaming outward from its feathered wings to quell the hostility.

Alerion...

"This is not the way," Alerion said.

The entity snarled, raging against its tethers. *You know well what imprisoning me does. Why stoke entropy to save this...this thing, this lie of a man?*

"Balance," Alerion said. The energies surged and the brilliance of his wings began to fade.

The darkness exploded with a howl. When the chaos cleared Varésh was kneeling before the effigy in the clearing in the woods.

"That...what—was that—?"

"Luminíl," Alerion confirmed. "A manifestation of her at least, tied to this sorry place. Stand, Varésh Lúm-talé. You must find Mirkvahíl. If we hope to have even the slightest chance of tempering Luminíl, of righting your atrocities, we must find the Phoenix before it is too late."

Varésh pushed himself to stand. His knees knocked together and his stomach threatened to empty itself further. He didn't know what to think anymore, of himself, of anything, of anything he had done. Was this quest, this undertaking to find the Phoenix even worth it? Was he worthy of being in the presence of Mirkvahíl or would the truth of his existence gradually, unconsciously force him to commit such a string of atrocities again?

Just...try, he urged himself. *Do something instead of standing here, wallowing in your failure.*

So he walked.

Mirkvahíl's song grew louder.

DEAR INSANITY

AT ONE POINT in her life Rhona would have found the Bone Garden a place of beauty. To sit amongst and converse with the ruined dead was a privilege, the peace provided by the garden second to none.

Now, here in *this* place? Every fiber of her being screamed to turn around, to flee through those gates of bone and mirkúr and hurry across the bridge, to never come back. Guilt was such a powerful thing and it was all Rhona could do to persevere, to continue into the garden depths as muffled cries and moans rang out around her like a song she once had known and loved.

"*Find strength,*" Fiel whimpered. "*You* must."

In what? From where? The Bone Garden was surely meant to do exactly what it was doing now, sapping will, instilling dread, making Rhona wonder why she had ever thought to come here. Why should she be so privileged as to speak with the dead, with the many souls for whom she, Alerion, Mirkvahíl, and so many others were responsible for sentencing to this awful place?

She started at a tug on her hand. Looked down and saw the spirit of a young girl. Realized it was pulling not on her hand but on her *illum*. "Please," it groaned, siphoning more of Rhona's illum. "I...I am so...*hungryyyyy*..."

Rhona tore her arm away. The spirit fell to mist with a rasp; more manifested in its wake. Silhouettes with stark white eyes and the slightest hints of facial features. Rhona ran. They followed. She sprinted blindly, purpose momentarily quelled in favor of safety, solitude, anywhere these things couldn't find her.

This must be what it feels like, what it looks like when guilt manifests, she thought, pushing back tears. Ghosts of yore, harbingers of sorrow, bannermen for a lady of woe. *They* were her legacy, and what an awful thing that was.

She stopped, turned to face the past. The spirits encircled her. They stood staring, little more than incorporeal effigies. What were they doing? What were they waiting for? Rhona opened her mouth—to say...what? To *ask* what?

"*I was a farmer,*" said one.

"*I was a nursemaid,*" said a second.

"*We all of us were something to someone,*" said a third, brighter-eyed than the rest. It approached Rhona, stopping just a foot or two away, boring into her with a full-moon stare. "*You stripped us of our futures. You mistook subjugation for harmony, mistook individuality and freedom of speech for sedition. You whom we adored, whom we looked to for guidance. You are a lie.*"

Rhona swallowed. The words stung more than she had ever thought they could. "Is this why I have come? Is this—are *you* what I was meant to find?" She felt another tug on her illum. It was greater than the first and this time Rhona did not flee. Despite Fiel's frantic pleas she stood her ground, watching her illum leave her flesh in wispy, luminescent threads.

Djen—Mother Woe said the Bone Garden is the birthplace of

clarity. Rhona faltered, dropped to one knee as the garden waxed and waned. *What...* Images flashed across her mind. They were little more than swirls of color. *What...am I... supposed to find...? Who—*

Who.

The wind howled and a shadow reared up before Rhona, more monstrous than anything she had ever seen. Her vision steadied, she went cold. Never before had she felt such dread. Lithe and winged, an orb of brilliant light where once a face had been or should have been. It plucked her from the earth with ease and held her to the blackened sky.

I will break you, it hissed, and its words were like the sea crashing against rock. *I will break you a thousand times. You are false. You are ruin.* A portion of the faceless orb dilated to reveal a maw, a pit of absolute and utter emptiness. *You are mine.*

Rhona wailed.

She fell.

———

Rhona bolted upright from the grass with a gasp. Before her stood the Lost Tree. Beside her, a familiar figure.

"I should like to tell you it gets easier," Equilibrium said. "So much of me wishes I could—but that would be a lie. Nothing will *ever* be easy for you. You saw to that long ago, my dear friend."

Long ago. It was a phrase of such simplicity, yet the way Equilibrium said it told her there was a deeper meaning. Rhona could feel it in every fiber of her being and it made her cold. If she could only see behind the curtain of it all...

"Before this I was somewhere else," Rhona said. "The Bone Garden. And before that, with Mother Woe—with Djen, a name she claimed she hadn't used in centuries." Her brow furrowed. "I think I've lost all sense of time. All sense of... everything."

"On the contrary," Equilibrium said. "You are regaining sense. Fantasies and falsities, memories and dreams—all have brought you to this point. Your existence is a parable of utmost import. It will shape the future of your world."

Rhona's frown persisted. "What does that mean? Mother Woe said the same thing, my existence being a parable." She punched the grass and growled. If she could only see what she was being pointed toward!

She blinked and Equilibrium was gone. Snow fell; the meadow was a blanket of white through which the Lost Tree rose. A familiar figure stood beneath its branches, staring directly at Rhona. She knew that white-eyed gaze intimately and stood, approaching hesitantly, trembling not from the cold but from the confusion of it all.

"Djen?"

"Memory is a complex thing," Djen said, walking to meet Rhona.

A ragged sigh escaped Rhona's lips. "Is...is that all this is? Is that all *you* are, here?"

Djen shrugged. "I...am many things everywhere."

"I just..." Rhona reached for Djen's hands, held them tightly. "I feel so lost."

"Such profound guilt has a way of doing that," Djen said sadly. "Just as power and authority dull one's sense of morality. One's compassion. Do you see the irony of it all?" She pulled Rhona to her, kissed her deeply. "The taste of regret is strong."

Rhona pulled back, tugged herself from Djen's grasp. Mother Woe stood staring back.

"*Hell is a place of one's own making,*" Mother Woe said,

holding her arms out to the side. *"And the irony? In seeking to create utopia you did the exact opposite, you and Varésh Lúm-talé alike. No perfect world—only entropy. Only the beginning of the end."*

The meadow darkened, melting away in rivulets to reveal the Bone Garden. Rhona's vision waxed and waned. Her equilibrium fluctuated violently. Had she ever left this place? Had she ever actually spoken to Equilibrium, to Djen, or had everything been a lie? She fell to the ground. All around her spirits moaned, tugging on her illum.

"As I said..." Mother Woe knelt beside Rhona, leaned in. Her breath was cold and sharp against Rhona's ear. *"I will break you."*

Then—

———

VELA and her prisoner were halfway through the woods.

It was cold here where the sun was silent, where the world was quieter still. Her mind was chaos. Why had her village chosen Vela for a task so horrible as this? How could they reasonably expect her to spill the blood of the woman she had known since childhood? The questions were rhetorical—Vela *knew* the answers.

"Are you going to kill me?" asked Djorev for what felt like the millionth time.

Vela was silent. How was she to answer? Sacrificing Djorev would keep their village and the land of Jémoon safe; it was Vela's duty as a Walker. But it would break her heart. To sacrifice Djorev was to betray their friendship. Vela tightened her grip on Djorev's leash, cursing *alf elo nor*. The Jémoon tenet decreeing *one for all* was a wretched thing.

"Are you ever going to answer me?"

"I don't know," Vela said finally.

"I wouldn't blame you if you did," said Djorev. "I'm spellscarred."

The word stung every time Djorev used it.

Curse you, Vela thought of the Raven, the deity warding Jémoon. *This is your fault.*

"You shouldn't blaspheme so loudly," said Djorev. "It's only going to make this worse."

Vela stopped and wheeled around. Djorev's stark white eyes gazed back from the depths of her hood. "How could this get any worse? Why should I care if the Raven hears what I say? It's that overgrown bird's fault you're tied to this leash. If it had done its duty to Jémoon and kept the Vulture quelled, you wouldn't be infected by wild Dusk."

"But the Raven didn't, and I am," said Djorev. "Now here we are in a dark forest, arguing as the wolves descend." Vela gave her a questioning look. "I heard them a mile back. Except for the obvious stigma, being spellscarred isn't *all* bad."

Vela drew her dagger, wondering how close the wolves were. "I wish you would take this a bit more seriously."

Djorev grinned. "Afraid the severity's slipped my mind?" She snapped her fingers and her bonds and tether turned to ash. "Hmm. Wonder what that little magic trick cost..."

Vela groaned. She didn't want to think about it. The price of a spellscarred's power was terribly unpredictable and unpredictably terrible. It was a small part of why Vela made no move to apprehend Djorev. The bigger part was *because* it was Djorev—Vela trusted her to stick by her side regardless of the circumstances.

"About four or five wolves half a mile behind us." Djorev grabbed Vela's hand and yanked her along. A bead of light bloomed overhead and proceeded to illuminate their way as they fled.

"We could take the wolves," said Vela.

"Or we could save our strength and run," said Djorev, and that really meant, "Or we could not risk me blowing us up."

Vela decided it was the right call.

———

THE TREES HAD THINNED by the time they stopped running.

Vela doubled over to catch her breath. Djorev leaned against a tree, singing softly, indiscernibly. How long had they fled? How long ago had they left the village? Had the sun still been up or had it been night?

"I wonder if I could kill the Vulture," Djorev said. "I wield what wrought it, after all."

Vela rose to her full height and frowned. "More likely than not, you would destroy Jémoon if you tried. Or, at the very least, yourself, and then what would I do?"

Djorev shrugged and pulled her cloak a bit tighter. "Find another spellscarred to love?"

That stung more than the word spellscarred did. Vela swallowed her rage and the lump in her throat. "Doubtful."

There was a long, cricket-filled silence between them.

"This is a really shit situation," said Djorev with a noticeable quiver in her words. Such evident fear was rare in her. It was often times masked by grins and forced jokes, much as she had been doing ever since they had set out on this wretched task.

"Djorev..." Vela pulled her into her arms and held her tight.

"What if I promised not to use my power?" Djorev whispered. "Could I go back? Could things go back to the way they were?"

Vela knew the answer. Village law was strict. To be spellscarred was to be a sacrifice, and sacrifices kept the Raven strong. The way Walkers saw it, bleeding a spellscarred dry took strength from the Vulture, especially if it was true the spellscarred were manifestations of the Vulture. She buried her face in Djorev's hood and sighed.

"Are you thirsty?" Djorev asked.

Vela chuckled softly. "Terribly." She pulled away from Djorev and knelt by the tree, digging half a foot into the earth. She pricked her finger with the tip of her dagger, intoning, "*Alf elo nor,*" as the blood dripped onto the roots and into the dirt. In return, the tree presented them with the means to quench their thirst. As it was in life, alf elo nor was the way of things in the woods.

"How far from the Nohl Waypoint do you think we are?" Djorev asked when they had finished.

"A day or two," said Vela. "Hopefully not longer." The Raven only came to the shrine once a month, and a missed sacrifice meant further catastrophe. The Vulture's strength would grow, the Raven's would wane. Rivers would dry up. Game would grow sparse. Plagues would spread and people would starve.

Vela stood and helped Djorev to her feet. "Come on. We can sleep when the longest yawns come."

———

It was still dark when those yawns came, but the darkness was peppered with stars as Vela and Djorev emerged from the woods. Before them stretched a meadow; the forest path had turned from dirt to a mottling of stones. A gentle breeze tousled the reeds and a perfume of vanilla and honey permeated the air. Vela breathed it in with a contented sigh. It had been at least a year since she had smelled it; it relaxed her mind.

She looked at Djorev, who beckoned to her from the grass.

"Promise I won't accidentally blow you up with a snore," said Djorev with a weary smile.

Vela chuckled and joined Djorev, pressing against her for warmth. She closed her eyes and sighed. The world could wait for a night.

———

VELA STARED AT the oak tree and she knew this was a dream. The tree was beautiful in its gnarled and twisted way, its white leaves like suspended snow. She had dreamt it many times before, though she could not say why. As she had the oak tree, she had dreamt this meadow too, its grass a golden sea.

The Raven stood before the tree. It was larger than a horse, with feathers dark as night and eyes like mid-month moons. Beside the Raven stood a man with feathered wings and charcoal eyes. He was called Varésh and she had dreamt him many times before.

"Child, you return." He took her in his arms. He was warm and smelled of cold nights and campfire smoke.

"I do not know why." Vela sighed into his chest.

"Don't you?" Varésh asked, and he pulled away to look her in the eyes.

She had seen that stare before, soft and knowing all at once. "I am scared."

"Tell me," said Varésh. "Tell me of your fear."

Vela eyed the Raven. Its wings leaked gossamer threads of Dusk. The meadow wilted and the oak tree fell to ashen rot.

The Raven met her gaze before it too was ravaged. In its wake a single night-black talon lay.

"Failure," said Varésh. "I am very intimate with failure."

"How do you face it?" Vela asked. "How do you face the fear of failure when your own morality holds you back?" Tears stung her eyes. "I never asked to Walk. I never asked to sacrifice my friend."

"And yet you know you must." He kissed her forehead. "Lest you doom Jémoon to rot."

"*Alf elo nor*," she whispered, and the world dissolved.

———

VELA WALKED with heavy legs and a crick in her neck. She had slept little the previous night and the dream still clung to her like a shawl, light but heavy enough to perceive. Her conscience was compromised and it put the people of Jémoon at risk. What was she to do?

You know, a side of her hissed.

It is not right, another argued. *It is not fair.*

Life is not meant to be, the first side said. *Everything dies; every soul is alf elo nor.*

And yet the notion of taking a life— Djorev's life—still felt wrong; it made her stomach churn. She balled her hands into fists and growled to herself. Why could they not simply pray to the Raven? Why could it not subsist simply on praise?

For the same reason courtship is more than handwritten letters and words, said the voice in her head. *Action says more than a word could ever convey.*

In most cases.

What would you have me do? Vela asked of nothing in particular.

Djorev was silent as they walked, and that was probably for the best.

———

THE EARLY MORNING sun beat down upon them, tempered by a mottling of clouds. Save a trio of snowjays, Vela and Djorev were alone. In a way it was nice. To be alone in the wilds was something Vela had dreamt of for years. The reflexive nature of home had grown to be gratingly dull.

But it was harrowing, too. Save Djorev, she was alone with a knife, her fears, and her thoughts—and that was a dangerous thing. The fate of Jémoon rested on her shoulders, and Vela was not sure it was a weight she could bear.

They kept on. The clouds devoured the sun and a gentle breeze swept across the meadow, tousling her hair. Even though they were alone Vela could not help feeling as though their steps were being watched. Spirits lurked in the plains, but they were rare and mostly kept to themselves.

Perhaps a jétjune, she thought. The fox-like sprites were notoriously drawn to Walkers.

Or maybe the feeling was nothing at all. Djorev had yet to notice anything, and her senses were greater than Vela's.

At length they came to a ruin through which a river ran south. It was the village of Yahn, marked by a crumbling tower of stone. Yahn was the precursor to Nohl, or had been at least. Now it was dead and guarding the forest passage to Nohl.

"Cheery," Djorev said.

"It was beautiful once," said Vela. "Or so I have read."

She walked the weed-covered streets in a daze, Djorev haunting her steps like a silent wraith. How long had it been since Yahn stood whole? No one could seem to recall. For that,

Vela was sad. How many names had been lost to time, never whispered again? The wild Dusk did terrible things and the very thought of Yahn's desolation filled her with fear. A cold sweat blossomed on her brow. Was this what fate had in store for her village if she failed to bleed Djen dry at the shrine?

They came to the village square. Djorev sat, massaging her legs while Vela wandered. Just north of the square was the tower. Vela approached it and ran her hand along the weathered white stone. She felt a connection, an attachment to Yahn born of study, stories, and dreams. So many times she had climbed to the top of this tower, so many times she had run through these streets chasing children or dogs.

She ducked beneath its crumbling archway. Inside it smelled collectively of dust and wet earth, of history. Even now, Vela could make out the remnants of inlays depicting the Raven, wide-winged and dark. She bowed her head to the image. It was a reflex born of reverent superstition, though this time it was meant as an apology for the previous night's blasphemy. Outwardly, she placed the brunt of the blame on the Raven, but in her heart she knew the Walkers of yore were equally to blame with their belated offerings. As important as alf elo nor was, the Jémoon tenet nor elo alf—all for one—was equally as significant.

"Want to have a deeper look?"

Vela started. "Must you always be so silent with your steps?"

Djorev poked Vela in the small of her back. "Is that a yes?"

"So long as we don't disturb anything."

"If we do, I shall be the first to know," said Djorev, tapping her skull. "Come on."

The tower bloomed with strange pastel light the deeper in they went. It was peaceful and brought a bit of majesty to a place ruled by utter desolation. How beautiful the tower must have been in Yahn's heyday, filled with scholars and mages dedicated to the wellbeing of Jémoon.

"I had a dream about Yahn last night," said Djorev. "At least, I think it was Yahn."

Vela had dreamt as well, though hers had be decidedly different. "I once read dreams are sometimes more than dreams." She wasn't sure how much stock she put in such a notion but it was fascinating to think about nonetheless. "What did you see in yours?"

"Yahn as it once had been." Djorev pulled her hood back. The extent of her spellscarred transformation was jarring even now. Pale flesh, cracked and mottled; stark white eyes encapsulated by dark circles. "You're staring again."

Vela averted her gaze. "Sorry."

"At least I know you aren't judging me for it," said Djorev. "Yahn was a garden once, at least in my dream. I saw colors I couldn't put names to. It was beautiful. *Everyone* was beautiful. And there were duskeels that swam through the sky, and dawneels."

No one ever talked about the Dawn, the inverse of the Dusk, for the simple reason it was little more than a myth. If the energy existed none could say when, not for certain. And if the Raven of Jémoon had ever wielded such a force it had all but forgotten how.

"I wish I could see what you see," Vela said. Her dreams of Yahn were different but beautiful in their own way. Still, she longed for something to share with Djorev besides this terrible journey.

"Maybe someday you will." Djorev took her hand and they pressed on.

The ruin grew more profound as they ascended a winding stairway. Sunlight streamed through cracks and holes in the wall. Several times the stairway itself threatened to collapse. Strangest of all was the dark membrane-like substance mottling the wall for as high as Vela could stare.

"What do you suppose this is?"

"Some form of Dusk." There was dark certainty in Djorev's reply, and the black mottling on her flesh seemed to react to the membrane, reshaping itself to various patterns as if ink dripped on parchment.

"We should leave," said Vela as they reached the second-floor landing. The Dusk's presence was prominent here. Gossamer threads twirled and twisted from the membrane, flittering through the air. It made Vela's skin crawl, made her forehead slick with cold sweat. "Djorev?"

"It's harmless." Djorev held her hand out to the wispy strands of Dusk and they came to her, coiling through her splayed fingers and up her arm. "Duskeels, see?"

And Vela *could*. Nearly indiscernible were a pair of white dots she suspected were eyes.

"I think this tower is their nest," Djorev said. "This stuff on the walls."

"What was your skin reacting to?"

Djorev shrugged. "Close proximity to anything made of Dusk? A lot of this spellscarred stuff I haven't figured out yet." She brought her arm before her eyes, smiling at the duskeel, chuckling as the creature mewed. "Gentle little things, these eels."

Her eye twitched and she cocked her head. "Did you hear that?"

"No." Vela tried to follow Djorev's gaze.

"Sounded like...crying, from the floor above." Djorev started up the stairs at a vigilant pace, Vela trailing with her dagger drawn.

Leave it to Djorev to find a ghost, she thought, though she wasn't entirely sure *what* Djorev had heard. It was certainly possible the tower was occupied by a hermit or a lost traveler, or that a jétjune was playing tricks as their kind were wont to do. Hopefully it wasn't anything more.

The third floor was little more than a writhing mass of Dusk, myriad eels flittering about. Djorev walked with certainty. Coldness emanated from her; in fact, Vela could discern a faint aura about her person—what was it?

"Are you all right, Djorev? You're glowing..."

Djorev said nothing as they wound deeper. Eels parted before her like grass in a breeze. Whether in reverence or fear, Vela was not certain. She *was* certain that she was a bit fearful of Djorev, of whatever they were searching for.

What a pathetic way to fail that would be. The very thought of dying here just a day removed from their village filled Vela with shame, enough she could hardly keep from snorting at the notion.

"Stop."

Vela nearly bumped into Djorev. Before them a worn wooden door stood ajar. Beyond the door, darkness, peppered with flittering motes of light. Here, at the threshold of uncertainty, Vela finally heard it—displaced crying, as if it existed on two planes at once.

"After me, I suppose," Djorev murmured. She pushed past the door and into the room.

Vela followed suit and the dreamlike attachment returned. There was an air of familiarity about this room and its inlayed floor, its meadow view and the figure standing several feet away. A woman garbed in white with a mane of fire-red hair. Behind her stood a tree, *the tree* from Vela's dream and—

Vela blinked. The room had dissolved; there was only a meadow, the woman, and the tree.

"So long," the woman murmured, looking Vela. "So long I have waited." Her yellow eyes were a mixture of fear and relief. She approached Vela and took her hands. "Thank the Raven you have come."

What is this? Where is Djorev? What was going on?

Vela tried to pull away but the woman's grasp was firm.

"Please, take me from this awful place." The woman's eyes were wet with desperation.

"Tell me who you are." Everything about this felt wrong.

"Please! Before it comes!" the woman cried.

Vela tried to pull away, again to no avail. "Before *what* comes? What is going on?"

A shriek ripped through the meadow. The grass wilted beneath the horrible sound and the tree's leaves turned to ash, falling from the branches like a pathetic snow. The woman screamed, falling to her knees, hands pressed to her ears.

"It comes! It comes! The Vulture!"

A great shadow darkened the meadow. Vela's hair stood on end, goosepimples rippled across her arms and neck. She looked to the sky as the shape came back around, long-necked and black with six great wings trailing into smoke. The Vulture screeched and Vela bled from her eyes, nose, and ears. She fell to the grass, writhing, watching as the horrible shadow swooped and took the woman in its beak. With a snap it halved her and the remnants fell to the ground with a thud.

Vela forced herself to stand; her legs trembled terribly as she approached the remains.

But there was nothing save swirls of smoke.

She started at a flap of wings and whisper in her ear and spun around.

Gasped as Djorev pulled a jagged blade from her chest with a squelch.

"So long I waited," she whispered as Vela spat blood, as the meadow waxed and waned. She pulled Vela close so their noses were just inches apart. "So long." Her bright eyes were narrowed, a swirl of triumph and emptiness. "Alf elo nor. Nor elo alf."

———

"Dreams are sometimes more than dreams," said Varésh. "One might choose to think of them as cries from the subconscious. But you already know that, of course. Tell me, child—save failure, what do your dreams bespeak?"

"Failure is all my dreams suggest," said Vela. She gestured at the oak tree and its leaves like winter snow. "So many times I have seen this wilt. So many times I have seen this meadow die." She wrapped her arms around herself, trembling. "And this time I saw it—the Vulture. I saw it kill. I saw its pestilent influence unbounded all because I failed my Walk. And..."—Vela shuddered—"I think the Vulture was *her*—Djorev. She stabbed me, Varésh."

"Peculiar things, these dreams we dream." Varésh stretched his great wings then furled them like a cloak. "Peculiar more, the things of which we dream."

Vela frowned. "What do you mean?"

Varésh reached forward, cupping her cheek. "You know well what I mean." His eyes bore into hers and Vela felt a fog dissolving from her mind. "There are no such things as Ravens and Walks."

———

"GLAD TO SEE YOU UP. Been out cold for a week."

Anja blinked. Remnants of a dream clung to her like mist and her head ached something fierce. A gray-eyed man with a hawkish face and dark hair pulled back behind his ears stared down at her. He wore a warm smile.

Anja returned it with a weary one of her own. "Varésh."

He leaned in and kissed her forehead. "How are you feeling?"

"Dazed." She wasn't sure if that was the proper word but it fit for the time being. "Like I drank far too much at the tavern. So many weird dreams... You were there and..." Anja frowned. "So was Djal Shy'eth."

"I would expect nothing less from the Dreamweaver who did this to you," said Varésh. "Quite a nasty reputation and a particular distaste for you. Not fond of being locked away in Misten Fahg either, it seems."

"Don't really blame her for that," said Anja. Misten Fahg, renowned tower college of magi, was an absolute lie. A beautiful lie but a lie nonetheless. It was a prison, the magi its guards.

She sat up and pushed a few loose strands of hair out of her face. She could see the moon out the window at the far end of the room, brilliant and full, boring into her like a knowing eye. Bits and pieces of her dream waltzed across her mind, dissolving as quickly as they appeared. What a strange thing it had been.

"Anything interesting happen while I was out?" Anja asked.

Varésh's expression darkened. "A day after your encounter with Djal something came out of the Old Wood."

Names and words carried weight. Some were said to have true power. It was this very belief, this very superstition, that kept most from calling the Old Wood by its given name, Hang-Dead Forest.

"What was it?" Anja asked.

"Hungry. A shadow of a man."

Had this shadow come from anywhere else, Anja would have simply rolled her eyes. But things emerging from Hang-Dead Forest were cause for concern, rare as they were. The last time—and many years before Anja's birth—a man had come to the village Nohl in the dark of night. When the sun rose the following morning the village was dead and the man was gone. All that remained were myriad corpses, rotted and swaddled in smoke.

"Any idea where it might have gone?"

Varésh was silent. His brow was etched with worry.

Anja frowned. "Out with it."

"Here," Varésh said. "It came here. You and I are the only ones left."

Anja looked him in the eyes. "What do you mean, we're the only ones left?"

"Everyone else in Misten Fahg is dead," Varésh said. "Magi, acolytes, prisoners, the whole lot. Dead and gone, and soon the college will be too. Whatever this shadow man is, its presence is deteriorating the structure. We're only alive, you and I, because I've kept this room warded the last week." He heaved a sigh and wiped his brow. "Quite exhausting."

Great. Was it wrong to wish she were still stuck in her dream? At least the scenery had been nice. Anja took a deep breath to compose herself, to reconnect with her illum and mirkúr, the innate power of magi. The energies returned to her gradually and she felt comfortably cold and warm all at once.

"Maybe you should have a rest," she said to Varésh.

"Or," he said, "maybe we should flee."

Anja frowned. "And leave this thing to eat the rest of Misten Fahg?"

"Precisely that." Varésh chuckled wryly. "It's not as if we can stop it here. The entire college of magi is dead. What chance do the two of us stand?"

He had a point. Somehow, he always had a point.

"Flee to where?" Anja asked.

"Below."

Gods, but she hated the finality of his tone. Below wasn't just *below*. It was a very specific below: Banerowos, the city under Misten Fahg, the vast ruin from which the college drew its power.

"Pray tell, what good would fleeing to Banerowos do us?"

"I know what lurks within," Varésh said. "In the very bowels of its ruin. I know what sleeps, I know how to awaken it, and I think it will help."

"This sounds like a horrible decision," said Anja. Misten Fahg shook and a grating shriek ripped through the otherwise silent night. "But I suppose it beats the alternatives." She slipped out of bed, garbed as she had been the day she'd fought Djal. "Drop the wards and lead the way."

———

For the first time in all her years at Misten Fahg, Anja was glad her room had been on the second floor of the tower. She stood in the hallway, looking up at the night sky and the massive chunks of stone. They were suspended and floating through the air, as if trapped in time. Tendrils of shadow trailed in their wake. Whatever this thing from Hang-Dead Forest was, it was terribly powerful. As she followed Varésh down the remnants of the stairs it occurred to her they had no idea where in Misten Fahg it was lurking. The notion made her spine tingle.

Varésh, tired as he had claimed to be, walked with a bounce to his step. Dropping the wards and reclaiming the illum he'd used to scrawl them seemed to have roused him a bit. For that, Anja was glad. She had no idea how to get to wherever in Banerowos they were headed, and two against one were much better odds, slim as they already were, should they run into the shadow.

"All the light in Misten Fahg is gone," she remarked.

"The shadow must have eaten the rest of the illum," Varésh said.

So *that* was what he'd meant by 'hungry.' What name, what word must have been invoked for a thing of such terrible power to have emerged from Hang-Dead Forest?

"Do you think there's any correlation between this shadow and the man who brought the plague to Nohl?" Anja asked.

Varésh shrugged. "Could be. But it's hard to know for sure."

The stairway leveled out into a large, circular vestibule. Threads of shadow flittered through the air. Anja swore they were whispering to her in a language she could not understand. She ignored the cold tickling in her ears as best she could, focusing on floor beneath their feet and the ruined inlay of the Raven God. It reminded her of the tower in her dream, of the dreams within her dreams—a winged Varésh and a Raven larger than a horse. Gods, but what the hell had Djal done to her?

"Do you think *all* the prisoners are dead?" she asked. Her thoughts were fixed on Djal, now, and she couldn't push the Dreamweaver from her mind.

"I'm not sure."

That meant there was a small chance they might find Djal.

And why would I want to do that? Anja cursed herself for having such a thought.

Answers, said a voice in her head.

What?

About your dream, the voice clarified. *Answers about the shadow. Who's to say she didn't call this thing here?*

You have a point, Anja conceded, *but recall Djal, mad as she is, has never been one for absolute destruction of life. She's never so much as killed a fly.*

Anja had known Djal for years; there was history between them, more than she cared to let Varésh and anyone else know about. She hadn't thought about their years together, their years as friends in a long time. The pain was still too much, her heart was raw even now.

They withdrew from the interior of Misten Fahg, headed south across the grounds. These too were dead. Trees were bare and twisted. Effigies were little more than rubble. As had been the case inside the tower, debris floated through the air, trailed by gossamer strands of smoke. It was reasonable to think the village of Nohl, which stood at the base of Misten Fahg, had once more succumbed to the destructive power of this thing from Hang-Dead Forest. History was wicked that way.

The desolation grew more profound the closer they drew to the archway leading into Banerowos. The Misten Fahg grounds were little more than shadowlands. Varésh conjured an illum wisp to light their way, but even it was little match for the darkness encircling them; within seconds the light was devoured.

"Can we even activate the archway?" Anja asked. "If this darkness so quickly consumes light are the glyphs in the pillars going to hold their illum?"

They stopped before the archway, grand and intricately wrought. It was older than Misten Fahg itself, a relic from the days of Banerowos. Its connection to the dead city was the only reason it stood, unsullied by the hungering darkness.

Varésh took a deep breath. He placed his hands atop the

glyphs in the right-side column; Anja did so on the left. "Ready?"

She nodded. Illum flowed through her body, warm and welcoming against the pervasive blackness of the world. Keeping the channel was difficult, strenuous, but Anja had expected it to be. Illumination left her fingertips in streams, twisting, conforming to the glyphs' designs. She held her breath, willing more of the energy into the pillars as the darkness—wild mirkúr, she'd decided—tried to wrest the light away.

"*Why struggle?*" something whispered in her mind. It was cold and serpentine. "*Why fight when the simpler thing, the easier thing, is to relent? What are you running from? What do you seek?*"

Anja screamed as the whisper's frigidity consumed her. She poured every ounce of illum she had into the glyphwork, and the archway exploded with light. A majestic ruin rippled into view. Without a second thought she grabbed Varésh and they leapt across the threshold.

———

It was dusk and the meadow smelled of fresh rain.

The oak tree bore no leaves for it was that time of year. Anja leaned against its trunk, the grass soft against her legs and feet. Djal sat beside her, chewing on a reed, and before them stood Varésh, head tilted high, wings spread wide in all their midnight glory as he basked in the warmth of the setting sun.

The Raven soared above them, gentle strands of shadow streaming in its wake. The great bird swooped down into the grass. It landed and approached Anja, nuzzling her with its beak. She had found the largest things were often times the gentlest and the Raven was no different.

"I heard something once," said Djal, looking at Anja.

"You've heard a lot of things."

"Yes, but nothing so profound as this—dreams are sometimes more than dreams."

"Profound, yes, but silly, too," said Anja. "Dreams are nothing more."

Djal tossed her reed away. "According to whom?"

"Everyone."

Djal crossed her arms. "Everyone, hmm?"

Anja nodded.

"And how do they know this for a fact?"

"Because it's always been a fact," said Anja. "What else would dreams be?"

"Cries from our subconscious," said Djal. She cupped Anja's cheek. "This is not the first time I have died."

She wilted, turned to ash as easily as parchment in a flame.

———

SUNLIGHT GREETED Yora's eyes and she shut them immediately. Her body ached horribly, her mind more so. She knew exactly what had happened and it frightened her. The blackouts were coming with increasing frequency—they had been since that night in Hang-Dead Forest. Whatever she had encountered there had done something to her physiology; she was losing control over her Dusk and Dawn.

"There you are! I've been scouring Banerowos for hours."

Yora opened her eyes at the voice. "Djema."

"You had me worried sick," said Djema, helping Yora to her feet. She brushed Yora's cheek. "It happened again, didn't it?"

Yora nodded wearily.

Djema took her hands. "You're trembling. Gods, what did this thing do to you?"

"I wish I knew." So many lucid dreams. An endless string of phantasmagoria stacked within each other. Was this another one? "This is going to sound crazy, but...I don't even know if I'm dreaming or awake right now, Djema."

Djema pulled her into a firm embrace. "You are most certainly awake right now."

"That sounds like something a player in a dream would say," whispered Yora. "Something I would *make* them say to maintain the illusion of truth." She shuddered. "So many false realities..."

"Have you spoken to anyone else about this?" Djema asked. "Any of the other Ravens?"

"No." Yora knew by look on Djema's face she should have told her, should have told Varésh. They were the keepers and guardians of Jémoon. If they were to fall then Jémoon would be lost to the wild Dusk.

"You need to. Today," said Djema. "Now, even. The wild Dusk is growing stronger, hungrier, and if even one of us is compromised it could very well spell the end of Jémoon." Her expression softened; her white eyes were glossy. "We have lost so much already."

So many cities, towns, and villages, devoured by the wild Dusk. Yora had lost track of the death toll. Worst of all was the fact she and the rest of the Ravens still had yet to uncover just how the Dusk had gone rogue. For centuries they had kept it tempered without issue, and for centuries they had used the converse powers of Dusk and Dawn to shape the land of Jémoon. What had gone wrong?

"Are you able to fly?" Djema asked, unfurling her wings.

Yora's own ached horribly. She could barely keep them furled. "I doubt it."

"I suppose a walk might help." Djema took her hand and they started through the barren streets of Banerowos. Even now the emptiness was eerie; only months ago the streets had been routinely filled with people going about their days. Now they all kept to their homes and the relative safety provided by their wards. Their fear was palpable and it broke Yora's heart, especially because she felt, *knew* she was partly responsible. What kind of Raven was she if should could not help her brethren protect their people from the encroaching end?

"It's so easy to forget how beautiful this place is," Djema murmured. "The cost of fighting to survive, I suppose. I'm scared, Yora. Things are getting worse. I know you've noticed."

Yora had, but for the life of her could not remember *how* they had gotten worse. It was hard to keep track of it all when she could barely keep track of herself.

"And yet the struggle perseveres."

Yora went cold at the voice in her head. It was the very same she had heard in her dream.

"What do you fear? Why not relent?" it hissed. *"Why not let the veil part?"*

You aren't real, Yora thought.

The voice chuckled. *"Aren't I? I am infinite. Reliably and consistently present."*

Yora swallowed. *Am I going mad?*

"A sane question." Yora couldn't tell if the voice was serious or if it was mocking her. *"What do you think?"*

I think, Yora replied, *I understand absolutely nothing anymore.*

"Sometimes we need to start from scratch in order to fully comprehend what we are dealing with," it said. *"As you have heard so many times before, dreams are sometimes more than dreams. There is truth to be found in madness. And regardless of*

whatever opinions of me you have already formed, know I am here to help you. We are, after all, twins of a sort."

Somehow that put Yora at ease. Not completely, but enough she could focus on the spires of the Raven's Perch rising up in the distant center of Banerowos. She let go of Djema's hand and rolled her shoulders. She stretched her wings, painful as it was, and gave a great flap. The streets grew smaller with every passing second as she ascended, Djema following in her wake as they soared over Banerowos and made for the Perch.

———

"You should have informed us immediately," said Varésh. His eyes flashed angrily in the sunlight pouring into the chamber. "We can ill afford to be compromised when the perseverance of Jémoon depends upon us."

Yora made no attempt to argue. He was right.

"Did you know of this?" Varésh asked Djema.

"Not until earlier today," she said. "Have we found any trace of whatever came out of Hang-Dead Forest? Perhaps *it* might be the key curing Yora's ailment."

"No. Orjem has yet to return," said Varésh, "and that could mean anything."

Yora wasn't even aware Orjem had left. "Where did he go?"

Varésh and Djema frowned.

"The lands surrounding the forest," Varésh said. "You were present when he left. *You* suggested we send a party to investigate the ruins at its center."

"Perhaps we should send another to search for Orjem," Yora said. Her flesh had turned to goosepimples at Varésh's revelation. "Or maybe..." She sighed and rubbed the bridge of her nose. "Is there anything else I should know? Anything I might have forgotten?"

Djema and Varésh looked at each other.

"Why flee?"

The sunlight went silent.

"What do you fear?"

Their flesh paled and cracked, peeled away to reveal mottlings of Dusk.

"Te Mirkvahíl!"

Yora screamed. She turned and leapt from the chamber window, taking flight over the Dusk-constricted corpse of Banerowos. Tendrils and tentacles of shadow felled the once majestic city, turned its streets black and devoured every bit of illumination for as far as Yora could see.

"Te Mirkvahíl." The voice was solid, near—it had escaped her mind. Her echo rose up to meet her. She gripped Yora by the throat and they hurtled toward the streets. "WHAT. DO. YOU. FEAR?"

———

Rhona was alone beneath the oak tree. It was night and the stars were asleep; the moon too refused to shine.

"And here we are." Her echo manifested in a swirl of smoke. "Again. You cannot flee forever. Your vultures will inevitably prevail. You will discover the truth buried in all of this madness. Trust me—I have seen it many times before." It knelt and looked Rhona in the eyes. "Hell is a place of our own making. If you continue down this path, you'll not come out alive."

Tears trickled down Rhona's cheeks. "You think I want this? To be stuck in these dreams, these horrible falsities?"

Her echo smiled sadly. "If you didn't, you would have let the truth find you. But instead you run. Run as you have run for years, dreaming your dreams, taking name after name. Part of it is fear, part of it is guilt, shame. But all of it, Te Mirkvahíl? All of it is self-inflicted penance."

"For what?" Rhona asked. "What could I have done to wish this...this madness on myself?"

Her echo stood and offered its hand. "Why not stand and see?"

A white portal swirled into existence several yards from the tree. Through it Rhona saw herself in the Bone Garden, that thing leering over her like—

"The Vulture," she whispered, taking her echo's hand.

"Indeed," her echo said.

It locked eyes with her again. Rhona felt cold, sick like she never had before. She started for the portal.

"Wake up," a distant voice said. "*Wake up.*"

"Wake up."

"Wake up."

WAKE. UP!

———

You wake, now, wide-eyed, ragged-winged and filched of light. What a sorry creature at my feet. A flightless bird, an introspective liar. A glutton for eternal penance. Lo, she whimpers. Lo, she shuts her eyes to the truth—the woebegotten land beneath the tower high. Lo, the Phoenix Mirkvahíl whispers:

"Oh gods...what have I done?"

Perception is fickle, dangerously so. Often times we see things as we wish they were; we see ourselves as something we are not. We dream to run from what we fear—but the truth is never far behind. The guilt will always call you back. Welcome, Mirkvahíl, to the ruin of your world.

LUMINÍL'S LAMENT

IRKVAHÍL PUSHED HERSELF TO STAND; she could not.
The atrophy kept her weighted to the ground, to the
weathered stone atop the pinnacle of Banerowos, what was left
of it at least. Before her stood Luminíl, flesh cracked and ruined
as had been the case for Djen and Mother Woe, for Djorev and
Djema. Mirkvahíl knew this was real. She knew she was finally
awake, Luminíl's words echoing in her mind like a throng of
buzzing flies.

"Look at you, Mirkvahíl." Luminíl's voice was bereft of its
previous otherworldly depth. She knelt before Mirkvahíl,
boring into her with a cold white stare, strands of platinum hair
falling out from behind her ears. "Look at what you've done."

Mirkvahíl craned her neck as best she could. Banerowos
was little more than a corpse of stone and snow, an amalgamation of every city she had seen in dreams. Somewhere north of
here stood Hang-Dead Forest and the myriad murdered souls
for whom she was to blame.

"Power corrupts," Luminíl said. "That is the way of it."

A ragged sigh escaped Mirkvahíl. "Parable." She held out a trembling, upturned palm. "This is what you meant when I met you as Mother Woe." Tears dripped down her cheeks. "My story, my existence..."

Luminíl nodded. Thus far she was less monstrous than she had been in Mirkvahíl's myriad dreams, both in mannerisms and appearance. There was a softness to her, a sadness, and it pained Mirkvahíl tremendously.

"I wonder how much of it all you truly remember," Luminíl said. "The Fall, and everything from which it grew. I'd venture little judging from your labyrinthine dreams. At the very least, some, though horrendously dissected and distorted."

She brushed a cold hand across Mirkvahíl's cheek, lingering for a half second before she pulled away. "Would that I could I would rewrite history and change this all." Her expression darkened. "I would change much."

Luminíl's words were calm, measured, but Mirkvahíl knew what the Vulture meant, and who was she to argue? She had done horrible things to Luminíl and her acolytes. "As would I," she whispered. She expected no sympathy from Luminíl. It just felt like the proper thing to say.

"I'm sorry." As did that.

"An apology..." Luminíl smiled wryly. "Were I you, I too would say the same, but expressed regret for your atrocities bears little weight a century and a half into ruin. Apologies will not remake the world. Apologies will not bring back the dead, nor will they mend my wounds."

Luminíl stood, and Mirkvahíl pushed herself to do the same a second time. She rose to her full height and stumbled forward into Luminíl like a newborn foal. The Vulture caught her, held her in her arms. For a moment, they stared into each other's eyes. For a moment, holding Luminíl and being held by her felt like a dream from which Mirkvahíl didn't want to wake. She clung to Luminíl, but the Vulture pulled away and Mirkvahíl fell to her knees, choking back tears.

"You'll gain no sympathy from me," said Luminíl. "You shame yourself, Mirkvahíl. Weeping and wallowing as if you've earned your tears." Shadow surged around her, enveloping Luminíl, shaping her into a lithe and monstrous silhouette with tattered wings and a glowing orb where once her face had been.

"I should end you," Luminíl hissed. In a twist of smoke she was before Mirkvahíl, taloned hand gripping her throat tight. "I should annihilate you for what you did to me, to Banerowos and Jémoon. I loved you more than anything—and you infected me, imprisoned me, and left me to rot. You destroyed everything."

Mirkvahíl clawed at Luminíl but the Vulture's grip held strong.

"I need you to see. I need you to remember, Mirkvahíl. I need you to remember as I rip your soul asunder. Hell is a place of one's own making, and I will send you back to walk yours for as long as you exist. No matter how many realities you dream, no matter how many different names you take, the guilt will always find you."

Mirkvahíl's vision waned. Planes of existence fluctuated manically.

"Abandon hope..."

———

Trees.

So many trees.

They whisper murderously.

———

Mɪʀᴋᴠᴀʜíʟ sʜʀɪᴇᴋᴇᴅ.

———

Sᴏ ᴍᴀɴʏ ᴛʀᴇᴇs. They call to you, whispering songs of yesteryears.

Rain. The heavens weep as you walk.

Tears touch your cheeks. Fear and desperation permeate your soul.

For Banerowos, you think. *For all Jémoon and Harmony.*

It pains you more than anything, that thought—but the worst is yet to come. So you walk and you listen to songs of the trees, listen to the madness pushing you along. Your illum showed you darkness not yet born. Your dreams of late serve only to cement your fear of encroaching desolation. They bring you here, to your favorite tree, the Lost Tree, to the girl beneath the tree.

I smile.

———

Iʟʟᴜᴍ ʟᴇᴀᴋᴇᴅ ꜰʀᴏᴍ Mɪʀᴋᴠᴀʜíʟ. Through her flesh, through every orifice as Luminíl tugged ravenously on her soul, on her sanity, on her tether to this plane. She kicked feebly at the Vulture, cried out louder than her strength should have allowed.

"Relent, Mirkvahíl,

for I am the way into woe,

the way into the labyrinth eternal,

the way into Hell.

As Hang-Dead Forest whispered long ago,

abandon hope all ye who enter here."

———

I TAKE YOU IN MY ARMS, Mirkvahíl, as you join me beneath the tree. It has been a week since last I felt your touch. Tending to this world we three created takes its toll. You smell of honey and vanilla as you always do.

You kiss me.

I melt.

You pull away. Fear is present in your pitch-black eyes, in the galaxies they hold. I touch your cheek, you pull away. The forest sings and you furl your wings about yourself, a barricade, a barrier between your flesh and mine.

"Mirkvahíl?" I approach you, and I fall.

You stand your ground.

The sky darkens and the forest wilts. It smells so horribly of rot. I reek so wretchedly of rot.

"What...did you...? What is happening to me?"

You stand unsullied in a barrier of light, crying softly. "I had to, dearest Luminíl. For the good of Harmony."

I retch, pull my knees to my chest and spew agony across dead grass. "What...what...?"

———

BLOOD POOLED BENEATH MIRKVAHÍL, streamed from myriad punctures in her flesh, from the corners of her mouth. "G...Gods..." she half-whimpered, half-gurgled. *"Please..."*

Mirkvahíl felt a snap so painful and profound she could not scream.

Luminíl gave a great tug, and from the depths of Mirkvahíl produced the brilliant, six-winged silhouette that was her truest form—the Phoenix. It screeched desperately, its luminescence waning, devoured by Luminíl's rage.

"You took this from me," Luminíl said. "That evening in the forest. Took my temperance for your own because your energy was running wild. You turned me into this! I became the Vulture when this fate was yours to face. I would have helped you. I would have done anything to keep you safe..."

Luminíl shrieked and drew the mirkúr Phoenix into herself. Her monstrousness dissolved and she was once more a woman cloaked and trembling. She knelt at Mirkvahíl's side. Tears fell freely.

"I should have never loved you," she whimpered. "I should have never..."

She sobbed uncontrollably into Mirkvahíl's bloodied chest.

YOU BRING MY UNCONSCIOUS BODY to Banerowos, to Alerion —the *false* Alerion. You erect my prison as I sleep, the pair of you plotting falsities in the name of unity, of utopia. Power is seductive. Fear feeds logic to the wolves, and madness runs amok.

You war with those who would oppose you.

You murder those who learn your lies.

Sonja frees me from my cage. You murder her.

I murder you and thus the cycle starts.

You dream your dreams, you take your names, but that voice inside your head does not relent. Subconsciously you know— you cannot run forever. The guilt will always call you back.

Luminíl pulled away from Mirkvahíl. "You made me this," she whispered. "Because of you I wear a monstrous form, but do you know what? *You* are the only monster here. Sometimes the most beautiful things are the most horrible—and what an eldritch thing you are, Mirkvahíl. What an ugly soul you have."

Luminíl stood. "I do not possess foresight, but my instincts tell me somehow, somewhere, in another life, we two shall meet again. But until then, may your Hell be horrible, and may your guilt devour you from the inside out."

She turned from Mirkvahíl,
strode to the edge of the tower,
and leapt.

WHERE THE SUN IS SILENT

B ANEROWOS WAS DEAD. Varésh knew in his mind and heart the great city had fallen years ago, but to see it once more for the corpse it was pained him terribly. Little more than snow-dusted black stone, crumbled spires rising like a throng of jagged teeth. Old bones littering the streets, and the agony of yore whispering on the wind.

"Welcome," Varésh whispered, "to a place where the sun is silent."

"A morosely poetic epithet," Alerion said, manifesting at his side.

"One that should have never come to be," Varésh said, bowing his head.

"But it did," Alerion said, "and you must live with that as you must live with many sins. If you buckle underneath the weight of your past, of your atrocities...if you abandon your search for Mirkvahíl then you shame yourself, Varésh Lúm-talé. You shame the dead you have made. Is that what you have come here for?"

"No," Varésh murmured. He took a deep breath, steeling his nerves. "No."

Alerion offered an approving nod.

They walked.

"I cannot help but wonder what horrible surprises await me here," Varésh said. "What else have I forgotten, what else yearns to ravage me from the inside out?"

"If you focus on that," said Alerion, "it will only distract you, and that is dangerous here. You have yet to run across Sonja and the other rusalks, and who knows what else lurks in this corpse of yesteryears?"

Alerion had a point. It had been some time since Varésh had seen Sonja. Should she return with the rest of her damned brethren, Varésh wasn't sure he would be able to hold her off, let alone all them, however many the rusalks numbered.

He hissed at a sharp pain in his ears and it nearly made him double over.

"Are you all right?" Alerion asked.

Her song..." Varésh hissed. "Such pain. I...can feel it, feel *her.*" He pressed himself to straighten up and looked about Banerowos. Its tallest spire still stood sadly, if not proudly in the center. *That* was where he would find Mirkvahíl.

Or whatever thing is mimicking her song. The thought raised goosepimples on the back of Varésh's neck. Until now he hadn't considered the possibility this song he'd been hearing for some time might not actually be Mirkvahíl but something else. Something...malevolent or vengeful. Luminíl, perhaps.

"The only way to know for certain is to climb," Alerion said.

Varésh nodded.

They pushed on.

———

WHAT HAVE I DONE...?

Trees.

So many trees.

Leering, laughing, knowing.

...Gods, what have I done?

Her heart beats yet. My beloved Luminíl.

Gods...what have I done?

...Shut up. Just shut up!

...Trees. Whispering to me. "What a way to end the world, with false hope in a false god."

They know. They all know.

...But what?

What

do

they

know?

———

VARÉSH BLINKED. He stood in the anteroom of the spire, mind swirling, buzzing with a frantic memory that...wasn't his.

"Did...you see that, hear that?" he asked Alerion.

Alerion nodded. "Energy runs amok here. Threads and fragments of the past. The destruction of Banerowos, the conflict between Mirkvahíl and Luminíl left pockets to the illum network open. Illum can, to those who possess the innate talent, provide glimpses into memory, into time itself."

Varésh was aware of illum's capabilities. "That memory..."

"Mirkvahíl's." Alerion's expression softened, saddened. "This tower holds great sorrow."

Varésh didn't need the memories of someone else to tell him

that. He had been party to much of what had transpired in this place. So much judgment. So much death. So much arrogance and ignorance.

They ascended, the occasional snap of memory assaulting them, though not enough to disorient Varésh as badly as Mirkvahíl's had. What further bits and pieces of that moment in time would he be witness to? His curiosity came partly from simply wanting to peek into the head of a goddess, but mostly it was born of fear. The fear of seeing what he might have driven Mirkvahíl to. Guilt—

———

Luminíl rages in her cage. This...this is for the best.

Right?

"The guilt will always call you back," she hisses. "No matter what you do, Mirkvahíl, it will always call you back. Hell is a place of one's own making and you've just dug your way into the first circle!"

Tears stream from her eyes, swimming in rivulets through the black cracks in her ashen flesh.

Gods, what have I done?

It was necessary.

You were...compromised. You would have killed them all.

You should still kill them all.

I look at the acolytes. I wonder

if they know

how absolutely sane I am.

Stop it!

I had to ...

alter memories...

Everyone...
Rewrite history...
I had to
take
my Luminíl.
Her form.
Her power.
Had
to...
Dying.
...am the Vulture.
Always.

———

Varésh sat for a time, dazed. Horrified, even.

"Did you know?" he asked Alerion.

Alerion shook his head. Varésh had never seen the Raven god shocked but there he was, wide-eyed and trembling. Trembling still, an hour or so after the memory had left them.

"I...don't understand," Varésh said, trying to comprehend the madness he'd been witness to. "Mirkvahíl is...—*was?*—the true Vulture goddess, and Luminíl was the Phoenix?" He massaged his forehead, then rubbed the space between his eyes.

"It should have been Mirkvahíl inside the cage," Alerion *said. "For so many reasons."*

His form dissolved, leaving Varésh to his own devices in the ruined spire.

Am I to blame for this? He had no recollection, had seen nothing to suggest he had swayed Mirkvahíl to such an atrocity, not that he was anyone to judge.

He pressed on, finally emerging from the darkness, greeted by a cold, gray sky and a figure curled into a ball.

"Mirkvahíl." Varésh was certain of it.

Despite being—no, *masquerading* as the embodiment of preservation, renewal, and creation, Mirkvahíl looked closer to death than rebirth. What had happened to her? How long had she been here?

"Hell is a place of our own making," Mirkvahíl murmured.

"I know."

Her eyes were the darkest shade of black Varésh had ever seen. He studied her, gazed past the sorrow and ruin, and realized

She is Rhona, which means Luminíl is Djen. It made sense in the way a parable should, especially given what piece of Mirkvahíl's dream Alerion had shown him several nights ago. Her conversation with Varésh in his home.

Mirkvahíl gripped his arm and pulled herself upright. "Hell is a place of lies, a thing we dream to escape our deepest fear. But the truth is never far behind; the guilt will always call us back."

She looked at Varésh, tears streaming down her cheeks. Did she recognize him as the lie he was or did she think him Alerion?

"I should never have... I should have died. It should have been absolute. My Luminíl..."

Varésh knew how that felt. He had condemned Sonja to her end. Gods, what a pair he and Mirkvahíl were. Two vultures playing at gods. What a way to end the world, with false hope in false gods...

"I wish I had stayed dead," Mirkvahíl said. "It would be the very least I deserve. So much death...on my hands." She coughed, spitting blood. "I wish...I wish I would stay dead this time."

Varésh took her hands in his. "*Our* hands, Mirkvahíl." He paused. "But we are here, and...there is a chance to set things right, but it will not be easy by any means."

"What do...you mean?"

He cradled the false Phoenix in his lap. She was beginning to fade, her body turning to ash. "Luminíl runs wild. Her entropic power is unbounded by our doing and I know not whether she is in control of the mirkúr; she may be a slave to herself. For now the best thing we can do is temper the entropy, keep it from wholly devouring Harthe."

Mirkvahíl groaned. "And how will you—we—do that...?"

"The past informs the present. I have begun to sow the seeds," Varésh said. "In a place far from this ruin and decay. They are an incipient race, but in time they will help us right our wrongs. They will help us reshape Harthe. Will you help me, Mirkvahíl? Will you take this chance at reclamation with me?"

She was silent a while. As the minutes passed, as she waned, Varésh was increasingly sure she would leave him without an answer. But she did not.

"Without preservation, entropy erodes," murmured Mirkvahíl. "A...world will only survive...if there is balance." She looked Varésh in the eyes and it was like being addressed by a gathering storm. "We will rebuild. We will rectify. We will reshape. But for now..."

She closed her eyes. "With every life, another name. With every life, a memory...entombed."

Mirkvahíl fell to ash, leaving only a brilliant white-gold feather in her wake. Varésh took it lightly in his hand, gazing out across the ruin they had made. "Who," he wondered of the false Phoenix, "will you be when next we meet?"

When would they meet?

Varésh heaved a sigh.

Snow fell,

and the world

was

still.

THE WORLD BREAKER REQUIEM

BEING THE SECOND NIGHTMARE

"But the stars that marked our starting fall away. We must go deeper into greater pain, for it is not permitted that we stay."
— Dante Alighieri, *The Inferno*

PROLOGUE
RACH NA'SCHUUL

I am timeless, though my soul has felt the wax and wane of millennia as I watch realities rise and fall.

The stars shine high above my city Rach Na'Schuul as they have done for years; memories and hopes, for my beloved home is dead, cast to ruin by the god-things of Jémoon. By the madness of the god-things by whom I and all my corpse-kin were designed.

The stars shine high above my Rach Na'Schuul as they have done for years, for like this ruin they are slaves to perpetuity. They call these pockets of eternity Arcadia—but idylls they are not, for what is peace when I sleep circled by the dead, my Listener brethren of yore?

I shan't abandon Rach Na'Schuul; I *can't* abandon Rach Na'Schuul for I am bound to ruin by a quietus the hands of time would surely gift me if I did.

I sit, now, in the courtyard of a spire-keep and do as I have done for years—

I Listen. To a prelude long and dark.
A herald to a symphony of broken dreams.

ACT I

DESOLATE VIGNETTES

HOUNDS

Avaria Norrith was dead. Or dreaming. For how else could he have come here to this meadow with its silver trees and ocean-colored grass? He looked down at Geph, his faithful longhound companion, and the gray-furred creature simply shrugged.

"Have you considered that you might be stoned beyond all comprehension?" Geph inquired. He did that a lot. Talking. Most longhounds retained some manner of silence even after they had learned to speak but Geph was the chatty exception. "Avaria?"

"You know I don't partake," Avaria said, starting slowly through the grass.

"Then why the hell am I talking?" the longhound asked.

"It's what you do."

"Well, if *you're* dead," Geph said, "then why am I here? Am I dead too?"

"Maybe?"

The longhound heaved a sigh that fell into a yawn. "Fuck it all, Avaria, what have you gotten us into this time?"

Avaria glared at him.

"I'm just saying."

"If you're talking about the time we were interned for defacing Virtuoso Khora's effigy," Avaria said, "let me please remind you it was *you* who climbed atop and took a massive, runny—"

"I was *drunk*," the longhound grumbled. "And the statue called my mother a bitch. What would you have done?"

Avaria rolled his eyes. "The effigies are incapable of speech, Geph. And your mother is a bitch. It's the proper term for a female hound."

"You keep saying that," Geph said, "and every time I believe you less."

Avaria shrugged. "Not my concern."

"It should be." Geph let out a hacking cough. "Where do you suppose we are?"

"If I were to venture a guess? The In Between," Avaria said.

"Then where hell is Equilibrium? I have a question."

"I can guarantee you, Geph, that Equilibrium remains incapable of manifesting you a jar of peanut butter," said Avaria, drawing a whine from the longhound. "Though I'm sure he'll oblige you with an ear scratch."

Geph gave a toothy grin.

They walked.

"It all feels the same," said Geph. "Have we actually gotten anywhere?"

"Not yet," said Avaria. He had come to this place enough to know the straightforward path was never as apparent as it seemed. "But we will."

You won't.

Avaria started at the words.

Geph cocked an eyebrow. "Are you okay?"

"You didn't hear that?" Avaria asked.

Geph tilted his head. "Because I'm a hound I'm supposed to have spectacular hearing, is that it? Well—"

How long have you been on this path, Avaria? How many years now? Days, weeks, and months spent trying to win the affections of a woman who could give two shits about you, hmm? And she had the gall to call herself your mother!

Avaria whirled around but there was no one there.

Search, but you'll not find me in the grass, hissed the voice. *I'm where I've always been—here, inside your head. Comfy, cozy in this prison that you've built. No—that your mother built. If she had loved you, where would you be now?*

Avaria shrieked. The meadow fell to ash, and from its ruin rose a silhouette of smoke and flame.

"*I told you all those years ago,*" the figure said, "*that she would set me free.*" It beckoned with an upturned palm and Geph obeyed, each step leaving gossamer threads of smoke. "*Faithful as always.*"

Geph grinned at Avaria, green eyes glowing white, teeth like needles dripping blood.

Avaria retreated several steps. The figure and the hound advanced.

"*You'll not escape, Avaria,*" the figure said.

Avaria turned—

"*For I am legion here inside your head.*"

—sputtered, looking at the blade protruding from his chest.

"*And there is nowhere you can hide that I can't find.*"

Crying now. He tasted blood and tears.

"*For then what kind of vulture would I be?*"

Darkness.

———

IT WAS cold this night as Avaria walked the streets of Helveden, Geph beside him as he always was. His brow was slick with sweat, and his head stung something fierce. He'd had the dream again, stoked by vultures of his own design. Woken up retching in his chamber at the Hall, Geph whining on the other side of the door.

"Was it Wrath or Envy in the grass this time?" inquired Geph.

"An amalgamation of the two," Avaria said, fingering his chest. It was tender to the touch; he winced.

"Theories?"

"An answer," said Avaria. "The Virtuosos passed on me again the other night."

Geph nudged Avaria with his nose.

"Honestly... why'd she put me here if I'm never going to leave?"

"Your mother wants what's best for you, Avaria," said Geph.

"She's got a strange way of showing it," Avaria snapped. "Shoving me off to apprentice while Avaness and Maryn took up arms and went to war for Ariath. I've been here half my life, a slave to erudition and abused by my own mind while they found glory in the heat of war. While *they* made mother proud."

"And you think swinging arms is all that draws your mother's praise?" Geph asked. "You think to her that mastering a blade is the be-all and end-all to life?"

Avaria scoffed. "In Ariath? Yes."

"I think you focus too much on the glory of war," said Geph. "Look around, Avaria. War destroys physically and mentally. Helveden stands half-erect, awaiting its resurrection by the Lightweavers who have drunk themselves into uselessness. The thought of facing vultures breeds fear, and that fear instills the urge to drink. It festers even now, an indomitable infection that has all but smothered Helveden's glow. Is that what you really want of yourself? To go off and come back like...that?"

"If it would make her proud..."

Geph sighed. "Oh, Avaria..."

They walked the rest of the way to the Bastion in silence, Geph stopping to sniff the occasional tree and Avaria brooding all the while. He fingered the summons in his coat pocket as they crossed a tree-lined courtyard wrought of white and scarlet stones arrayed in varying designs. What could the queen possibly need of him this late?

A frowning stewardess awaited their arrival. "You're an hour late."

Avaria shrugged. "I got lost along the way."

Geph nudged him firmly in the leg with his nose.

"Fine," Avaria sighed. "I was drunk in bed and dreaming of the end."

The stewardess curled her upper lip and rolled her eyes. "Follow me."

She led them through the Bastion, glorious in its whites and reds and various depictions of the raven god to whom they all implored. It was paradise where the Hall of Lightweavers was eternal hell.

Further and further, they went. The walls, ceiling, and floor fell to a deep red. Avaria had never been to this part of the Bastion before, which was saying a lot. As a child he'd wandered where his legs and the Bastion staff would allow.

They came to a circular stark white door inlaid with glyphs and grooves. The stewardess extended a glowing index finger and traced the innermost glyph. Illumination swam through the grooves and into the outlying glyphs. The door dilated, revealing the chamber beyond. The stewardess dragged him inside. Geph stayed put.

Avaria eyed three women sitting at the far end of the room. *Shit.*

"Ah. We were wondering if and when you might arrive," said Virtuoso Khal.

"I was not so confident as Virtuoso Khal and Queen Ahnil," said Norema Sel, the shortest of the three. She dismissed the stewardess with a nod, leaving Avaria to the wolves.

Wolf, really.

He eyed the queen. "Hello, mother."

———

AVARIA STARED AT THE QUEEN. He hadn't seen her in at least a half-dozen years. She looked older in the eyes though no less hawkish and intimidating. Reluctantly, if not slightly mockingly, he touched his right hand to his left shoulder in the formal salute.

"How may I be of service?"

Norema Sel gestured to an open chair at the table. "Sit."

Avaria gave her a prolonged stare before accommodating her request. He hadn't seen *her* in a while either. His heart fluttered momentarily. They'd been a pair at one time. A secret kept in shadows, for what would people think if they knew General Sel had shared her bed with *him,* the Norrith family castoff?

"Virtuoso Khal says you're developing well," Norema said.

"*Have developed,*" his mother said. "You're able to wield mirkúr as I understand it."

"Have been for ages," Avaria said, picking at a loose fingernail.

The queen drew her lips to a thin line.

"You say that with such nonchalance, Avaria, that it suggests ignorance on your part," Norema said. "There are very few left who can do what you do, let alone as an apprentice."

Avaria considered her words. "It isn't ignorance Nor—*General.* I'm simply indifferent. What does it matter if I'm able to wield The Raven's Wings? Mastering illum and mirkúr has gotten me nowhere. I'm almost thirty years of age and the Hall sees fit to keep me there until I die."

An exaggeration, but it often felt like he would never leave.

Virtuoso Khal offered a sympathetic nod. "Apprenticeships at the Hall are notoriously demanding, but they can ill afford to be otherwise." She passed him a slip of parchment. "We have need of you, Avaria."

"It's time for you to spread your wings, so to speak," Norema said.

Avaria scanned the parchment. His eyes went wide.

"A simple yes will do," his mother said.

Avaria looked at the women. "I—"

"Unless you aren't up to it," Norema said. There was a glint in her red eyes.

Avaria slipped the parchment into his pocket. "Of course, I am."

"Excellent." Norema gestured toward the door. "We'll be in touch."

Avaria stood and gave the formal salute. Then he withdrew.

———

"You haven't said a word since we left the Bastion," Geph said.

Avaria nodded. He was prone to withdrawing into himself in times of stress.

"Avaria?" Geph poked him in the leg with his nose. "What is it?"

"Have you heard of The Raven's Rage?" Avaria asked.

"In passing," Geph said. "What of it?"

"They, um..." Avaria swallowed. "They want me to forge it."

Geph gaped. "A weapon? *That* weapon? Why?"

"I don't know."

"Are you going to?" Geph asked.

A light snow fell, dusting Avaria's hair and shoulders as he walked. "Maybe."

Geph whined. "You already told them you would. I know you did, Avaria. I can smell the truth on you a mile away." He snapped at a snowflake. "It's personal, isn't it? Of course it is. Avaria, your mother—"

"She needs to see!" Avaria snapped. "I need her to see in me what she saw in Avaness and Maryn. I want to do something she'll be proud of, Geph. I just..." Avaria heaved a sigh into the frosty night. "I want her to want me like she did them."

Geph licked Avaria's hand.

"You head on back to the Hall," Avaria said. "I need some time to think."

———

Avaria had always found solace in the woods, in the trees beneath the sway of night. Unlike Helveden they enfolded him in silence and allowed him peace enough to think. To brood as he was wont to do. To waltz with the monsters of his mind as they made manifest at his side.

"Envy, Pride, and Wrath," Avaria greeted. They followed him as hounds, threads of mirkúr trailing their wake. He made no move to banish them but held his arms out wide. "What do you think? Should I oblige them, forge this weapon they so *desperately* desire?"

Wrath snarled.

"It *would* make them see," Avaria agreed.

Pride snapped its teeth.

"True. I *am* the utmost of apprentices."

Envy whined.

"Swallow your fear," Avaria hissed. If he were to fail... "I need to be worthy. She needs to see me as more than just a thing she found in the woods. If I were to perish, would she care? Would—"

Pride growled. Wrath and Envy bared their teeth-like-knives as a distant-growing-nearer shriek destroyed the forest calm. Avaria formed a thread of mirkúr to a blade; he advanced behind the hounds.

At length the trees fell to ruin, and they entered a glade. At the center stood a shrine; before the shrine there knelt a girl. Avaria and the hounds approached with heed. His mirkúr pulsed with every step; the hounds dripped ichor from their mouths.

"Who are you?" Avaria asked.

The girl turned. Her eyes were dead moons, and her flesh was burnt paper; her hair hung in silver strands. She cocked her head.

Avaria held his blade between them. "I asked—"

"We in this moment depart," the girl rasped, "replacing all that we are."

She stood and took a step toward Avaria, dark energy enfolding her from head to toe. Where once her face had been now hung a snow-white shroud; and from her back, six wings of black.

The hounds dissolved in her presence.

Avaria fell to his knees beneath her sway, cold in his bones. What was she?

"Are you going to kill me?"

She approached and pulled him up into a cold embrace, whispering, "Listen to your dreams, for things are never as they seem. We in this moment depart, replacing all that we are...."

She was gone, and Avaria was holding mist.

SHE

The meadow.

Avaria was alone save a bird in a tree. A raven. It blinked its beady eyes and squawked.

"Am I supposed to understand any of that?" Avaria asked.

The raven clucked. It abandoned its perch in favor of Avaria's shoulder, digging its talons into his flesh. Avaria cursed and the bird snapped its beak. He shooed the stupid thing but that only served to tighten its grip. Avaria hissed.

"Ease up, all right? What do you want of me?"

The raven gestured with its wing.

"A tree," Avaria said. "What about it?"

More talons. An authoritative squawk.

"Okay, okay!" Avaria approached the tree in all its silver majesty. He felt a sense of peace beneath its branches. Peace, with undertones of... something. He couldn't quite put his finger on it.

The raven offered a soft cluck.

"Did something happen here?" Avaria asked.

"More than you know," the raven said, and Avaria jumped. *"Compose yourself."*

Avaria massaged the spot between his eyes. Talking birds. Had he gotten drunk before bed again?

"We in this moment depart," the raven said, *"replacing all that we are. It would do you well to remember that. Lest she leads you through a forest dark."*

"Lest who?" Avaria asked. "The girl from the woods? That... thing?"

"Stay vigilant, Avaria Norrith, for things aren't always what they seem."

The raven gave a great flap, ascending as The In Between was cloaked in flames.

———

Midmorning.

Avaria sipped of his flask. He'd gotten fuck-all for sleep; had sat awake in bed pondering the girl-thing in the woods and the raven in his dream—his *new* dream. Word for word, they had said the exact same thing.

"We in this moment depart...replacing all that we are."

"Cryptic," offered Geph as they strolled the western grounds. The Hall was the city's pride and joy, though its occupants were often devoid of both. Fifty weeks of intellectual abuse quelled even the strongest of wills.

"Hmm."

"Are you *sure* you weren't—"

"Stoned beyond belief? No, Geph, I'm *quite sure* I wasn't."

Geph yawned. "What do you think it—er, *she* was? Demon of some sort?"

"Doubt it," Avaria said. "Haven't seen vultures in these parts for years."

War and extinction had a very intimate relationship.

"Spirit?" Geph asked.

"Maybe." Avaria stroked his chin. "Though it's been at least a dozen years since I encountered one, and it looked nothing like the girl I saw last night. And the way she..." He trailed off. He'd neglected telling Geph about his hounds.

The longhound cocked an eyebrow.

Avaria sighed. "The way she dispersed my hounds with her sheer presence"—Geph barked objectionably—"put fear in me like I've never felt before. Have you ever been cold in your bones?"

"I can't say that I have," said Geph, "but more importantly—"

"I was a mix of things last night," Avaria said. "I didn't mean to let them come—"

"But you made no try to hold them back," said Geph. "I know you better than you know yourself sometimes, Avaria. I'm one-hundred and fifty years old—I can *literally* smell bullshit a mile away."

"Does it help if I tell you they were leashed?"

Geph narrowed his eyes. "How the fuck does one *leash* a sinhound?"

Avaria tapped his head. "In all the time you've known me, Geph, have I ever—*ever*—let them run amok? Have I ever hurt anyone beneath their sway?"

"No," the longhound muttered. "But you *have* let them influence the way you live your life. Holding onto all that rage, all that pent up frustration and jealousy—you're only making them stronger, Avaria, and that's the part that frightens me the most. One day you'll lose control, and the hounds will sow slaughter unlike anything you've seen before."

"And how—"

"I've fucking *seen* unbounded sinhounds in my time. *Long before* I came to be your friend. *Long before* your mother came to be." Geph sighed, a faraway look manifesting in his eyes. "She was a good girl. But she couldn't quell them in the end."

"Geph—"

"I've a thing or two to take care of," Geph said, breaking from Avaria.

Avaria stopped and watched the longhound trot the opposite direction.

Rain fell.

It was going to be a long day.

————

"I'LL DO IT," said Avaria. "On the condition that you tell me what it's for."

"Temporal alteration," said Norema. "The chance to rewrite history and prevent the vultures' wrath." She leaned across the table so their noses nearly touched. "To bring back those we've lost."

Avaria blinked. He hadn't expected such a forthcoming, if not ludicrous response. "Is... is that even possible?"

"Anything is possible," said Virtuoso Khal, "when one possesses possibility itself."

Maybe *they* were stoned.

"The Raven's Rage is more than just a weapon," said the queen. "It is a key."

"*The* key," Norema said.

Avaria paused for a breath. "How does it work? How do you intend to rewrite time?"

"With enough energy it will open a way to the Temporal

Sea," said Virtuoso Khal. "And through the Sea we'll sail to where it all went wrong, and the darkness roused from sleep. We'll slay the beast before it wakes."

Now they *really* sounded stoned—but Avaria was intrigued. *Avaness. Maryn.* Could he bring them back? So many years alone. So many years reliving the news of their demise. Confined to the darkness of the Hall. Not even his mother had come.

"Your life could be different," said Wrath.

"You could be with your blood," Envy hissed.

"You could be free," suggested Pride.

Free. Of these chains. Of this loneliness. Of this loveless life to which he'd been condemned. Better to have to died in the snow that fateful night than to have wound up here.

"I'll do it," Avaria reaffirmed. "Just point me on my way."

———

AVARIA WALKED the Bastion courtyard at a measured pace, burdened with purpose for the first time in his life. In the depths and darkness of the Peaks of Dren, he would find the fragments of that old and ill-used sword, and with them forge a life worth living.

"Even when your steps are slow, you're faster than most."

Avaria turned to the voice, waited as the queen approached.

"Quick when silent," said Avaria. "Lest the Virtuosos beat you."

His mother winced.

"You seem surprised," Avaria said. "Or is that guilt?"

She said nothing. Avaria walked and she attended him.

"What we ask of you... it will be arduous."

"I know," Avaria said. "And I can handle it. I've trained and studied far too long to fail. But you only know that secondhand. Because you ordered Virtuoso Khal to keep you up to speed. Do I embarrass you? Does it make you ill to pay me mind? It seems to me we only speak when it's convenient."

The queen frowned. "You know you don't, Avaria. You could never—"

"Then why the distance all these years?" Avaria hissed. "Fifteen years, mother. Fifteen years of torment in the form of erudition while Avaness and Maryn reaped glory and affection here at home!"

Avaria yelped; his cheek stung. His mother held her left hand firm and ready for another go. "How dare you... How dare you speak ill of the dead. Of your broth—"

"You struck me..." The words felt strange as they left his tongue. In all his years she had never hit him once. He touched his cheek and turned away, left his mother standing in the courtyard as the shock withered and the pain bloomed.

Walked.

Walked until he reached the Hall.

Until he reached his favorite tree at the northmost end of the grounds.

He cried.

———

An old city.

A grand city.

A *dead* city.

Avaria blinked. He was dreaming, but he had never dreamt this place before. A necropolis beneath a sky that threatened rain, the skeletons of spires rising as if the ruin were the maw of something monstrous. Instinct drew him inward, and he walked with measured steps, the stillness sending shivers up his spine.

At the center of the city stood the greatest spire of them all. Despite the ruination it was mostly intact. Avaria touched the wall; whispers kissed his ears, and a feeling of dread entombed his heart. There was sorrow here inside the stones; fear and fury warred for rule.

"This place was beautiful once."

Avaria turned to the voice and met a man with midnight-feathered wings. There was a gentle melancholy to his face; his eyes were two gray pools of woe.

"They call me Ruin King. They call me Alerésh the Dread." He held his arms out wide. "I have done horrible things."

Avaria frowned. "I—"

"What do you mean?" a second softer voice inquired. "Why are we here?"

Avaria started as a figure passed through him; he realized he was little more than a ghost.

"We were rotten, she and I." Alerésh closed his eyes. "We envisioned life, yet from our hubris we birthed only ash. Ash—and annihilation like this world has never known." He opened his eyes. "He quelled the malediction once, but you will not do so again. The hounds hunger—and they are near."

"*She* is near."

———

SCREAM.

Like an infant kissed by flames.

Scream.

Scream.

SCREAM.

———

She left him by the tree beneath which he slept.

Her wings trailed behind her like the train of a tattered gown.

"So much ruin." Her voice was ash in the wind; it ached to speak.

She walked—through the darkness, kissed by shadows she had mothered for millennia.

She dwelled—in thoughts of geneses and ends, of hounds and fowl.

She died—

and was reborn.

No sleep.

ANATHEMA

One life lost this night. One friend.

Erath spat into the snow, jaw quivering. Tears streaked her cheeks. How could this have happened? How could a simple walk have ended like... like *this*? Sinhounds. Fucking sinhounds. Fucking *demons*. There hadn't been demons in the Peaks of Dren for decades. So why now, of all days? Leru's birthday—the queen's *youngest daughter's* birthday. She grabbed a fistful of snow and hurled it into the night.

Footsteps.

Erath glanced at the source, sighing. "Serenae."

She regarded Erath with eyes the color of moonlit snow. Had they been darker, she and Erath might very well have been twins. They had always been of similar guise.

"They're going to light the pyres soon," said Serenae.

Erath closed her eyes. "What must Queen Silith think of me..."

Serenae wrapped her arms around Erath. "Nothing so ill as you might concoct. You were ambushed, Erath. You were preyed upon by nightmares come to life. How could you—how could *anyone* have foreseen such a monstrous thing?"

"Illumancy?" said Erath.

"You know that isn't how it works," Serenae said. "Not anymore..."

"I know," Erath whispered. "But... demons. After all this time."

"There *is* something wrong—of that I have no doubt." Serenae pulled Erath to her feet. "But for the moment it can wait. We need to say goodbye."

Goodbye. Such a horribly finite word. In this moment Erath loathed it as the sunlight loathed her flesh. She trailed Serenae with sullen steps. She sensed tonight was just the beginning.

———

ERATH HATED songs for the simple fact the only songs her people sung were requiems and the last two songs she'd heard were requiems for friends.

Fire danced; shadows waltzed. They consumed Leru, devoured flesh made dead by demons so her spirit could ascend. *Ascend to what?* Erath watched, hands clasped behind her back, as drenarian throngs paid reverence to Leru. Tears. Prayers. Recollections of a fabricated friendship and a countless many men proclaiming their undying love. *Fucking idiots. Fucking frauds.* A show to curry favor with the king and queen.

She sought them out beside the blaze. Fenrin, silver-eyed and wolfish in the face. Silith, yellow-eyed and hawkish. It made sense considering the bestial shapes they took. They regarded her with solemn stares; Erath bowed her head in reverent guilt. She continued to the altar, spellbound by the azure flames in which the princess burned.

"Why did she have to die?" Erath started at the inquiry, at Silith's hand upon her own. "My youngest, Erath—why?" Erath sensed no accusation in her tone, yet still she felt the phantom strings of culpability tugging on her soul.

"...My fault," she whispered to the queen. To no one. To the night.

"Erath..."

"There were so many... and I couldn't—"

She pulled away from the queen. Ran from the flames. Through snow and darkness like the coward that she was.

———

THE WISPLANDS LAY southeast of Nil-Illúm. They were a haven, a remnant of her life before the Burn. Cloaked in wisplight, they were sheltered from the sun; *she* was sheltered from the sun.

Erath strolled through wisplit snow, enfolded in a black cloak the queen's eldest daughter, Alor, had gifted to her some years back; Alor was dead. Erath wore the garment when the weight of life seemed its heaviest.

At length she came to a henge of midnight-colored stones. Three total, each depicting a figure cloaked and winged. They had been a source of intrigue for years; encircled in their primordial majesty she felt a sense of peace unique unto the Wisplands and the henge. She sat now in the snow, legs crossed, hands resting on her knees. Body trembling, breathing soft. Eyes closed and swathed in the darkness of her mind.

Think, she urged, *of something bright. Soft and bright like illum on a summer night. Like wisplight in the darkness of the trees.* Like Alor holding baby Leru. Like Leru holding a fox in the days before the Burn. Like the days before the Burn.

Blood on her tongue. Erath cursed and opened her eyes. Spat red in the snow. "Why?" she hissed. "How?" That was the utmost of questions, the ghost of yesteryears that trailed her like a hungry dog. How had a sword managed the Burn? She gnashed her teeth at the memory of a nameless man, the wielder of The Raven's Rage. Long dead, buried in the ashes of his folly, yet anathema to Erath even now.

"Erath."

She started at her name. Turned to see a young woman. Eyes like fire, black of hair. Pale—paler than Erath who was paler than snow. Pack on her shoulder, blade on her waist.

"Rowe." She approached her friend.

"Been a while," said Rowe. "Little less than seven years. How've you been?"

Erath cackled. Clapped a hand to her mouth. Eyes narrowed; vision obstructed by tears. Weakness. Disgusted by the cracks. What a fragile, ugly thing. What an ugly thing fragility was...

"Erath..." Rowe took her hand.

"Leru is dead," said Erath. "And..." Nothing—and nothing. What else was there?

Rowe pulled her into a tight embrace; Erath melted. "I'm so sorry."

"...Feels like things are..." Were what? "It feels like all those years ago." The lead-up to the Burn. Madness, monsters. "Why are they back, Rowe? Sinhounds. Why the *fuck* are they back— and why did they have to take Leru?" She pulled away from Rowe. "Why are *you* back?"

"Questions," Rowe said. "Questions that need answering." She pulled her collar down to reveal black mottling encircling her neck. "It should have faded, but it's the angriest it's been."

The words chilled Erath. It was the mark of Te Mirkvahíl.

She brushed the blighted skin; Rowe winced but made no move to push her hand away. "You killed Te Mirkvahíl."

"Did I?" Rowe took a seat in the snow; Erath joined her. "I've been having nightmares. Dreams that feel like something more. Like..." She shook her head. "Like what I see has happened once before, one way or another. I can feel it in my bones."

"And what do you dream?" Erath asked.

"Of hounds and fowl and a sword that shouldn't be."

A memory of light; a memory of pain. "The Raven's Rage."

Rowe looked her in the eyes. "It's somewhere in the Peaks. Every nightmare leads me closer, Erath. It whispers in my sleep. It..." She looked away. "You must think I'm mad."

Erath took her hand. "Never."

Silence. Wisplit solace. It was easier to breathe.

"Rowe?"

"Hmm?"

"I missed you."

Squeeze of the hand.

Dancing wisps and memories of sunsets in the fall.

"Will you come with me, Erath?"

To chase a whispering dream? To find the blade anathema?

"Yes." Erath wanted answers—and she wanted them in blood.

———

Screams—Aveline heard them even now, millennia removed.

Ash—she felt it even now, their remnants tickling her face.

How many years? How many centuries more of suffering would she endure? She cared little for this wasteland she had wrought; little for the people she had met and even less for the people she had killed. This reality was a flaw, and yet—she wrestled. With herself. With the voices in her head. With her hounds and fowl of smoke. She wrestled, and her skull ached every moment of the day, every moment of the night. Ached with the coldness of regret, with the fire of intent.

With the numbness borne of weariness, uncertainty, and grief.

"I will save you," she uttered to dead people from dead days, and her words were children looking on the corpses of their kin —wishful but unsure.

"Rowe?"

She looked at the girl called Erath; for a moment, felt the misery in her stare. Knives of sorrow biting through her flesh at the loss of sweet Leru. For once, a death *not* on Aveline's conscience. What, then, had slain the girl?

Again, Erath beckoned to her guise. "Not much further— come."

Aveline smiled wearily and walked.

The sky hemorrhaged. Beads of crimson kissed her face— softly, as Alor had long ago. Before the Burn. Before the soldiers gut her in the snow and left her in the sunlight for the carrion birds and flies.

Still, Aveline walked.

Still, history screamed.

HUSH

Gil'an Mor, City of Hounds, was dead. Had been for millennia, since before the time of Dren. High-walled, guarded by statues of Ybot, Mother of Hounds, Reader of Time, First of Her Kind.

Mother of Geph.

"You called me here," he whispered to the ruin, to the memories roiling in his head. "I forsook my friend to walk your streets, to see what secrets you still keep. Please—come to me. Lead me on my way." The hush of Gil'an Mor endured; Geph shivered. "So be it."

He would go it alone.

———

AZURE STREETS INFECTED WITH GEODES. Windows void of light.

A million Threads adrift, like corpses in the sea. Dead and bloated with the history of Gil'an Mor. Ghosts of longhounds past. Geph whimpered at their touch, for every kiss invoked its master's doom, put voice to something old. Words like wind-churned ash and gutted crows.

"You..." he whispered to the hush of Gil'an Mor. "Are you here?"

Threads of memory licked his ears—the Quietus of All. Crystal corpses crumbling in Her wake. Her She It—The Demoness of Down Below; The Beast of Underlight; this *thing* that they had leashed 'neath moons of yore.

A hand of Threads to lead him on. A curling finger beckoned. Geph obliged.

To the Angelarium he went.

———

A HALL OF EFFIGIES, tall and dead. Hounds of feathered wings and halos wrought from stars. So much time had Geph spent here, wishing he were of their ilk. That he could sail the skies as Ybot, Ykoms, and Ymmas had done. He was Geph, son of Ybot —but of her majesty, his blood was filled with none. He had been the weakest of them all, and yet—he and he alone remained.

"We were great once," Geph said. "The future. Greater than the Reshapers, even. We could have changed the world—literally. But with you went the science of revision; we cannot rewrite our ills."

And that was why this business with The Raven's Rage disturbed him so. How did they expect to *literally* rewrite time with *that*—this blade of old which, last time used, had seen the drenarians devoured by the sun?

'*Thus the Peaks of Dren do dwell in night etern,*' recited Geph. Many a tragedy chronicled the drenarians' cruel demise

—were they players in this new game too? Geph urged his dreams to show him something more. Threads of distant memories, condemned to Underlight millennia ago, acknowledged him with whispers in the tongue of Mor:

"Descend and see—seek relics 'neath expired light, O Child of Ybot."

Through ruined halls they went, every pawstep arousing pastel echoes of the past. They regarded Geph and his Thread-wrought guide with idle stares, uniform in quietus; faded back to whence they'd come. He longed to free them from this place; he longed to free Gil'an Mor of itself—but such a thing was difficult and required answers from below.

They descended.

Memories screamed.

———

THEY WHISPER OF ME.

They whisper and they stare.

Things. Hound-things. Graceful beasts beguiled by the ills of all.

Kismet. This place called Gil'an Mor—this realm of Underlight. That I should rouse here 'mongst these lesser things, these hounds of sin. That I should rouse here after burning for millennia in tortured sleep.

Kismet, that I should catch her

staring through

the dark.

Staring.

Burning.

Gods, I'm burning.

She is ash.

Gone.
Memory.
Dead. Just...
Dead.
Kismet.
LET.
ME.
OUT.

———

Sᴄʀᴇᴀᴍs.
They burn.

———

Sᴄʀᴇᴀᴍs.
They cower.
Cower like the beasts, the noble hounds they are.
Mine.

———

Hᴜsʜ.
Kismet. Dead place. Dead place full of hush.
Hush
Hush.
HUSH.
An epithet.
I am Hush.
Free.

———

GEPH FLED the corpse of Gil'an Mor. Crashed through trees. Smacked streams. Itched—itched like hell. Sin crawling in his flesh—the touch of that *thing*. His leash. Tripped, rolled. Swathed in mud. Smelled the rot of yore, escaping memories of Gil'an Mor, strong like sunbaked corpses cloaked in shit.

Voice like fly-kissed salted honey in his ears.

Yelped, howled, whimpered like the pup he hadn't been for years. Mother—mama, mama, mama. Nothing else and no one else he wanted more. To hold him, clean his fur and tell him all was well and right.

Voice like dying in his ears. Crooning of a carrion thing.

Geph pushed himself to stand. To see this nightmare that had come, this thing that'd found him in the dead and dark and sorrow of the woods surrounding Gil'an Mor. Eyes like coins alight and feathered wings that fell to smoke. Tattered flesh of flame and Thread, of time and stars.

Voice like virgin snowfall in the dead of winter night in his ears.

"Quietus," whispered Geph.

"Hush."

She beckoned.

He obliged. She reeked of memory, stoked his gluttony, his need to feed—to drink of yesteryears and feel the brilliant warmth of Gil'an Mor as once she'd stood.

To see his mother. Hear her. Kiss her.

Voice like feathers, leaves enraptured by a breeze in his ears.

They went.

CACOPHONY

S now.
 Silence.

Avaria departed Helveden draped in both. He walked alone; Geph had business elsewhere. So be it. Avaria was used to solitude—it ruled his life. He pulled his cloak tighter. Retreated further into the dark of his hood and breathed. Tension dripped away like rivulets of sweat; purpose bloomed— find the sword. Find the fragments with which freedom would be forged.

He gazed south through darkness fleeting at the touch of infant dawn. South toward peaks of ruin in which ruined people dwelled. The drenarians—he could fix them if he tried. If he wrought The Raven's Rage, he could slaughter misery and mend mistakes. Find freedom in a world renewed. Genesis in restoration.

If there was any truth. Who but the gods could rewrite history—and even then, to what extent? Here they were—here *he* was seeking fragments of a madman's folly for a gambit predicated on a hope. A desperate dream the ink of yore could be erased, replaced with something better than before.

He walked.

Clouds hemorrhaged.

Still, he walked.

———

Night like the snow-choked abyss.

A road of blood and screaming trees.

The trek to Ulm had been a joyless blur of his design. Misery was motivation. Avaria clung to dreams of ruin like a leech to flesh. Lingered on the sting of his mother's hand across his face. He'd thought of nothing else for the past two days; he'd slept for less than half.

Ulm was dead; had been since the war. A dead place filled with dead things. A sepulcher abandoned to the hands of time, as was much of Ariath in the wake of bladed dread. He trekked with idle hands; the sinhounds roused inside his mind. Hissed. Snarled. Unintelligible yet persuasive all the same. They came like smoke. Whimpered at the stench of dead Ulm. Disappeared.

What, Avaria asked them, *do you fear?*

"Mother Sin," said Wrath.

"Leave Ulm lest she leash us to her will," begged Pride.

"Lest she leash you, *Avaria,"* said Envy.

A cacophony of fear. His skull ached.

He left. East. North.

A tree in the shadow of the Peaks. Gnarled and twisted like the tentacle of something old. Eldritch whispers tickling memories awake; soothing him to sleep. He sheltered in its oaken void, enfolded in the dark and silence of his cloak. Slept. Dreamt. Awoke.

Walked.

Dawn wept silent snow.

Still, he walked.

Turn, the daylight whispered.

Turn, his instincts hissed.

So, he did.

The sinhounds shrieked.

Still, he walked

Ulm called.

———

In the dead and dark he found her corpse—that girl of burnt paper flesh. In the dead and dark of Ulm she did remain, ravaged by the claws of something bestial and mad. Avaria walked to the center of the necropolis, sinhounds screaming all the while. What had brought him here? What had turned him from his path?

He trekked through weathered gore and rock, through streets of ash and bone, old mirkúr slick and thick like rain-borne mud. The rib-cage remnants of the church appeared, a sullen beacon in the wake of war. The jagged ruin called to him; the sinhounds howled; his skull ached.

Still, he walked.

Once, as a boy, he had come to Ulm. And once, as a boy, the city had been beautiful—a stone-wrought tapestry of reds and whites where dead kings slept, and warriors were born. Dawn-bringers, Aegises, and in between.

"You called me here," he said. "Why?"

Whispers slithered from the church; kissed his ears like sirens.

Avaria held his ground. "Come to me. Whatever you are, come to me."

Whimpering. Sorrow. Trapped inside—the way was shut.

Avaria tensed his jaw, formed a mirkúr blade. Curiosity pushed him toward the church. Inside. Further yet, within the bowels of ruined sanctification. Inlays, effigies—laid waste by war and time.

He came to a chamber guarded by a door inlaid with wards —dying glyphs that thirsted for his light. He pressed his palm to the door; illum streamed from his fingertips, filling the patterned grooves. The door groaned, dilated to reveal a room— and a floating head, preserved in twisting energy the color of a cloudless midday sky.

Avaria arched his brow. He entered at a measured pace, arm and blade extended fully. Whispers. Shards of shadowed recollections emanating from the head. Avaria winced at the onslaught, staggered. Pressed himself against the wall to keep from falling.

Bright eyes. Like the roiling sea beneath the sun, a swirl of greens and grays and blues. Bright, but weary. They regarded him with... what? Curiosity? Ragged desperation? Either way, Avaria felt compelled to push the crashing memories back and pluck the head from rest. It called to him in a way he could not yet define. He steeled himself and grasped it by its gnarled and braided hair.

It gasped; Avaria yelped, nearly dropped the fucking thing. Garbled language trickled from its mouth; threads of pale blue luminescence clung to strands of hair. Its eyes rolled independent of the other.

Avaria grimaced, held it level with his own. "What... who—"

"Ssswwwooorrrd..." Panting. Gasping. *"SsssswooOrd."*

Avaria narrowed his eyes. "Do you mean The Raven's Rage —*that* sword?"

Rictus, wheezing like the dead—the maybe sort of who-the-fuck-knew what. *"Ffﬁiinnnd... ssswwwooorrrddd... Sssaaave..."*

Silence. Sleeping—dead? Avaria sighed, tucked the head away inside his pack.

The sinhounds wailed yet.

He retreated from the church. Past her corpse—that girl of burnt paper flesh. Fled the dark and dead of Ulm, half-relieved, half-disappointed to have not encountered Mother Sin, this thing his hounds so passionately feared.

It snowed—and he walked.

Still, he walked.

MELANCHOLIA

"I found myself by losing hope."

Erath could not remember where she had read that, but it stuck with her as she and Rowe traversed the Wisplands. Enfolded in the cloak Alor had gifted her some years ago, never had she felt more lost.

"Was this what the Peaks were like?" Rowe asked. "Before the Burn?"

Sunshine just beyond the wisplight ward. Erath took a deep breath, exhaled slowly through her teeth. "Yes. The Wisplands are a remnant of better days."

"Is there no way to harness the wisplight?"

Erath smiled sadly. "If there is, we've yet to find it." She looked at Rowe. "You dreamt again last night."

Rowe nodded. Ring-eyed, red-eyed, sunken like a ghoul. Looked as though she'd aged a year or two in sleep. "An isle in the clouds. A dead city."

"How does that relate to the sword?" Erath asked. "You said it was here in the Peaks."

Rowe shrugged. "Could be that the isle is above the Peaks. I'm not sure; I only know of what I dreamt—and what I dreamt begs that I ascend. That *we* ascend."

Silence.

They walked; wisplight danced.

"It all goes downhill so fast, doesn't it?" Erath asked. "One day everything is all and well and the next it's just... not. And the ills of the world begin to bleed into one another and soon enough it's hard to remember the moments of peace because the darkness is so overwhelmingly profound."

She flashed pale skin. "I haven't seen the world in years, Rowe—*truly* seen it. How could I when the Burn confined me to a rock? Too long beneath the sun and my fate is the same as Alor's—just... ash."

"The world is an unkind place full of unkind people and unkind things." There was a bitterness to Rowe's words, as unfamiliar as it was intense. She flexed her jaw. "I saw things while I was gone. Things that made me wonder whether revising history would be the proper thing to do if it were possible. Rewrite everything—start from scratch..."

She looked at Erath and her eyes were wet. "I loved someone. We had a child, and everything was nice, and the world was beautiful across the sea. And then..."

Erath stopped, pulled Rowe into a firm embrace; held her as she shook, and fresh snowfall kissed their hair and cheeks.

"The world is dying," Rowe whispered, "and I want to fix it. Right wrongs, put families back together, raise the dead who died before their time—*just fucking fix it all.*"

"Me too," Erath murmured. "Me too." Would that she could —*You would rewrite history?* she asked herself. *Just like that— without a second thought?*

Yes. The reply came with far more certainty than Erath had expected, but how else should she have answered? How else could she have responded to a question so direct?

"What do you think it means," she started, pulling away from Rowe, "to find oneself by losing hope?"

For as long as Erath had known her, Rowe had enjoyed philosophical inquiries and commentaries. Something soothing about them.

"There are infinite interpretations," Rowe said, "but to me it means dwelling in darkness so profound we learn how intense our resolve is; we see our character at its most vulnerable and honest."

"To me as well," Erath said.

Rowe gave Erath's cheek a light caress. "We should keep on."

Erath nodded.

They walked.

———

AVELINE THIRSTED for The Raven's Rage in the way she longed to hold her husband, Beht, and her son Jor; to kiss Alor—desperately, enough so she would raze this world to see them, feel them, hear them.

She urged her dreams to lead her on, to point her toward this cloud-swathed, sky-bound isle she had seen. It was there—she could feel it in her borrowed bones. The means to reclamation.

She snuck a backward glance at Erath, the sweet young woman. She reeked of melancholia in a way that few could understand—but Aveline did, and she yearned to ease her pain for simple fact she bore Erath and her people no ill will. They had accepted her as one of their own those years before the Burn. Save Alor, it was *Erath* who had been her closest friend.

But she couldn't know what Aveline had become. She couldn't know what monster hopelessness had made her. What her monstrousness had made her do to Rowe.

She clutched a silver pendant around her neck—a gift of yore from Beht. *You would do the same, would you not?* She paused, as if waiting for the silence to reply. *I know you would. Please tell me you would...*

She heaved a sigh to the mountain wind and thought.

Dreamt.

Just...

Dreamt.

————

THEY COME. They seek this thing of misery and wrath, of possibility and hope. I am duty-sworn to keep it... yet I know not if I can. The songs of old, the symphonies of Rach Na'Schuul do not resound as once they did; the crystals have run dry—I am weak. Finite. The last of the Etheri kind.

I dream of snow and stars, of nights beside the lake.

I dream of Banerowos as she stood before the cull, before the gods went mad and killed us all.

I dream of Sonja, my beloved daughter murdered in the sorrow of the woods. Hung by the man to whom she gave her heart, from whom she gained a name.

I dream of worlds. Realities not my own, yet from mine they were born. From the Fountainhead they came, myriad conjurings of desperation, woe, and might. Might—for the mad ones who discern the means to rewrite time are mighty things indeed.

I dream here in this Pocket of Arcadia, this place beyond the rules of time. I dream here of the Fountainhead and the day it all went wrong—the day that wrought a million times a million realities and worlds.

I dream here and I know—

the cycle never ends.

NAMELESS

A cave somewhere in the Peaks.

Darkness save a single wisp of illum.

Two days up through rock and snow. In mountain-manufactured gloom. In silence and in pain. Rolled ankle, sprained neck—lucky it wasn't worse, that fall. Avaria leaned against the wall, weary but well-fed; fuck, but he'd had a lot of dried meat since leaving Helveden. Dried meat and water smelling mildly of maybe still ripe lemon. What luxury, this princely life he led...

He sat there, looking at the severed head his trek through Ulm had gifted him. Silent, dead-eyed, pale as death, leaking energy in threads—what was this thing? *Who* was this thing—this thing that clearly knew about the sword? Not a peep since then, since emerging from the dead and dark of Ulm—was that it, then? Avaria nudged it lightly with the toe of his boot.

"Going to say something? *Do* something?"

Cough. Ash-dust in the air. Avaria jumped. It regarded him with... what?

"...*uuuggg...*" it moaned. Cough. More ash-dust, motes of

infant light; dull like dying eyes, but brilliant in the gloom. "...*UUUGG*..." Hack-cough. Something like bile but... not. "*FUUUUCK*."

Avaria pressed against the wall. "Fuck is right!"

The head rose several feet, propelled by threads of light. Bright eyes, like the roiling sea beneath the sun. Hawkish in the face. It blew a loose strand of hair out of its eyes. "Who the fuck," it rasped, "are you?"

Avaria cocked an eyebrow, keen to draw a blade. "Who the fuck are *you?*"

"I..."—hack-cough, ash-dust—"asked you first?"

"I saved you," said Avaria. "Think that counts for something, hmm?"

Faraway look in those beautiful maelstrom eyes. "Saved me..." Soft voice. Puzzled. Disoriented—eyes betrayed as such. Horribly so. "Saved me from... what? Where?"

Avaria swallowed, took a deep breath. Eased his blood. "The church. Beneath Ulm. Not sure from what, if anything at all." A lie? Maybe. Maybe there'd been something there, this Mother Sin the hounds so passionately feared. "Where's the rest of you?"

Glazed eyes. "The rest of me..." Cough. Cleared throat, not sure how seeing as there was nothing below the neck to give it wind. Magic, he supposed. Whatever the hell kind of magic this thing swung. "I don't know."

"Awkward." Avaria crossed his arms to his chest. "Do you have a name?"

A smile that said, "You know the answer—why'd you ask?"

Avaria sighed, rolled his eyes. "Right." Stuck in a cave in the Peaks with a head. Stuck in a cave in the Peaks with a head without a body and a name. Had someone told Avaria a week ago where he would be today he would have laughed until it hurt. But—in a wasteland world of demon hounds and demon fowl, who was he to nix the possibility of something this farfetched? "What do you know about the sword?"

Nameless Head perked up. "The sword." Glint in his eyes. "The sword."

Avaria frowned. "Yes—the fucking sword. The Raven's Rage —that thing you begged I find and save not two days ago. What. Do you know. About the sword?"

Nameless Head sneered. "Impatient."

"Things to do," Avaria said. He was not opposed to boxing it across the cave.

"Best do them right," said Nameless Head. "Lest you end up like me."

Clenched teeth. Hiss-sigh. Cough; cold as shit despite the cloak. "Fine."

Nameless Head nodded. "Fine. Where to start...—shut the fuck up. Rhetorical." Fixed its eyes on the ceiling. Threads of... something trailing from its hair. Like a midday sky in summer; not illum, not mirkúr. Just... something else. Strong, old. Avaria hadn't felt it then, back in Ulm. Put a mote of fear in him. Not like that girl of burnt paper flesh, but enough to give him pause. To eke out a fragment of respect.

"Maybe..." Nameless Head fixed its eyes on Avaria. Intent. Hungry. Like a famished wolf. Extended threads of pastel light, caressed his cheeks; grinned. "Maybe I could show you."

Avaria recoiled. Narrowed eyes. "How?"

"Illumancy," said Nameless Head.

Maybe it is illum. "My head or yours?"

"I expect implanting... *things* inside your head will be much easier than it is to bring you into mine," said Nameless Head. "As you can see, I'm not entirely here, and it's best to do these things on solid ground."

Avaria sat, crossed his legs. Illumancy. Divination. Not his favorite thing in which to partake; too invasive. But maybe this, whatever Nameless Head was going to show him, might help him make sense of his dreams, whatever it was they were trying to tell him.

"Just... close your eyes." Soft threads against his cheeks. Light kissing his eyelids.

Darkness neither cold nor warm. Just... there. Existent. Sentient?

Whispers, like a million distant, dying screams. Dug his nails into his thighs.

Breathe. Breathe. Breathe...

Silence. The rise and the fall of lungs. Lungs from which the world drew breath.

Light. Light. So much light! Smell of seared flesh—pungent, like ash. Yet sweet like hot honey. What the fuck...

Beach. Starlit ocean and a breeze of salt and sand. Sweet. Cold.

Full-bodied Nameless Head adorned in rags. Looks like him, at least. A second, parallel and draped in red. Regal in a way. Beautiful where Nameless-Head Premier is gnarled and rough. Both bears feathered wings the color of a starless night. The second wields a blade in which infinity exists in tendrils of entwining white and azure light. Beyond them lurks a third thread, faint and dark like coming dusk.

"...You said..." Nameless Head sounds... afraid.

"I said many things," his twin replies. The words are cold.

"You would destroy them," says Nameless Head. "And for what?"

"Reclamation," says his twin. "The only thing that matters. The only thing that *ever* mattered." He draws the blade level with Nameless Head's eyes. "If only you could see..." He heaves a sigh to the salt and sand. "*You will.*"

The blade sings.

There is darkness. Foul, like rot and wet earth.

There are screams. Somewhere. Above, below.

His head is empty where it once was not; memories are lost. Somewhere.

Avaria gasped; the cave bloomed.

Nameless Head hovered above him, brow furrowed. "Are you all right?"

"I..." Avaria massaged the spot between his eyes. "He looked like you—*was* you. A different you... Who...?" Or what. A beautiful man with wings and a blade—*the* blade. What a sight, The Raven's Rage. Gorgeous. Monstrous. "Help me understand."

Nameless Head frowned. "I was hoping *you* might help *me*."

"And how would I do that?" Avaria asked.

"The sword," said Nameless Head. "We find the sword..."

"We find your memories?"

"Something like that—the pertinent ones. I'm not *entirely* void of recollections."

"Great." Avaria coughed. "Fucking thing is supposed to be here in the Peaks, just not sure where. I mean, I have an inkling—I just hope I'm right." Or wrong given everything he'd read, everything he'd eked out of the Virtuoso Archives in the Hall back home. "I don't suppose Rach Na'Schuul rings any bells?"

Another glint in those gray eyes. Wonder. Sorrow. Trepidation.

Knowing.

Avaria sighed. "Fuck."

———

I WONDER if they comprehend the nature of this monstrous

thing they seek. If they could see what I have seen, see what horrors of memory lurk inside this blade—they would turn back.

If they were sane. If they were not saturated with despair and desperation—they would turn back. But they are all of them broken things. I will intervene. I will speak reason—but it will fall upon deaf ears.

I know—because I have seen this before. Crossed worlds through Pockets, clung to desperation all my own before the terrible truth of everything emerged.

Reclamation is a hydra.

There is no going back.

Only chaos.

———

Sleep—how many centuries since last she'd slept? How long had she been tethered to this leash, this cross-world tug of war? Cat and mouse, hide and seek—stars above, but she wished the game would end. *Knew* that it would end—but where and when and how?

The chill of the Peaks was warm against her flesh, relative to her flesh in the way her lover's hand against her cheek had been so very long ago. It soothed her, gave her pause enough to scent the mountain air—they, all of them, were near. The sad boy and his hounds. The sad girl and her... friend.

She narrowed her eyes. Something more than hounds accompanied the boy—something old and plucked from ruins where her body last had lain. She had an inkling as to what— and it made her seethe.

God-things were deceitful things.

God-things slew their wives.

God-things... had to die.

No—she had left that life behind. In the ruin of a city in the center of a forest dark and dead she had cast aside that guise called Mother Woe. Now, she was nothing—nameless. Free, for nameless things could not be leashed.

"Except," her conscience hissed, *"You are not a nameless thing. You are a thing that fears its name and all that comes attached. The horror and the pain. There is no freedom in ignorance—that is a lie, your lie. Run all you wish but remember this: the truth is never far behind; the guilt will always call you back."*

"I know," she whispered. She closed her eyes; saw not darkness, but the world—violent, cold, and cruel.

Blood rain.

Chest ache.

Ash.

Quietus in red and white.

———

"Rach Na'Schuul is dead," said Nameless Floating Head.

"No shit," Avaria said.

"More than just a ruin," Nameless said as they crossed through snow and gloom. No light in the Peaks of Dren. Not anymore. "A... monument."

"Are not most ruins also monuments?" Avaria asked.

"Not the right word, I suppose. More like..."

"An open wound," Avaria said.

"A fissure of regret and shame," said Nameless. "I just can't remember why."

"You will," Avaria said. "I had a dream once years ago. A nightmare, really. In it, something from the darkness spoke: 'The guilt will always call you back.'"

"Profound." Nameless eyed him. "Pray tell, O Savior Mine—what do you flee?"

Avaria's left eye twitched. "None of your concern."

Nameless smiled wryly; squinted. "We're not alone. Look."

Figures, cloaked and hooded, bearing arms. Avaria formed a mirkúr blade and willed his illum wisp to bloom. Eased at faces he'd not seen in years. Rowe, older in the eyes for having danced with and destroyed Te Mirkvahíl; Erath... just Erath.

He trudged ahead, allowed himself a grin—

The world collapsed.

Darkness.

Pain.

———

Snow. Cold. Cold like death.

Darkness in the forest save a thread of moonlight.

A body. Small. Shivering. Almost blue. So cold.

Tiny hands clutch snow. Whimper. Weak.

Chaos.

Warmth. Faint. Stronger. Blankets. Swathed in furs to ward away the chill and touch of death. Warmth against his cheek—a hand.

A voice. Incoherent. Calming.

"Breathe, little one. Breathe."

Lungs are weak; wills himself to breathe.

Tiny hand. Fingers searching, clutching. Warm—her hand is warm.

He does not know yet; he drifts between.

He does not know—but *she* knows, knew it when she found him trembling half-dead in the snow.

She pulls him close.

Her baby boy.

———

"Alone," said a voice. Soft, tired. "You are alone."

"Why?"

"The mountain consumed you," the voice said. "I watched you fall. You broke your neck and died; they left you there, a royal corpse entombed in gloom—now, here you are."

Died. Died? *I'm dead—dead. Fucking dead.* "Where am I?" Darkness. "Who are you?"

"Alone," it whispered. A statement. "Alone..."

Blink.

The world. *A world.* Something. Someplace. Ruin. A city gray and kissed with ice.

"Come."

"Where?"

"She calls. She aches."

"What are you talking about? What is this?"

"Save..." Whimper. Weeping. "Just... save."

Starlight. Air like wet leaves in a winter breeze.

"Save what—who?"

"Mother." Whispers like a song-kissed dying breath, tickling and nipping at his ears. "In the dark of memory... find her."

———

Tattered flesh of flame and Thread, of time and stars. She is infinite and everywhere, shadow, shade, and silhouette. Her ghoul voice whispers, "Find her."

The darkness screams.

MAUSOLEUM

Erath wasn't sure how far or long she and Rowe and now this floating head had walked. They'd left the latter's corpse companion for the earth; no point dragging dead weight, whoever the hell it'd been. Grim? Sure. Callous? Probably. But such was life—and right now Erath was intent on finding a way out of wherever it was they were.

But curiosity hissed. "Your companion, Head—who was he? Who are you?"

"Haven't the faintest idea," said Head. "In regard to both. People of importance, maybe—he and I both sought a sword, you see."

Erath stopped. Looked at Head. "Sword?"

"Yes," said Head. "Used for stabbing and slicing and—"

"I know what a sword is for. What I'm intrigued by, Head, is the actual sword itself."

Head narrowed his eyes. "You *both* seek The Raven's Rage as well—why?"

"Dreams," said Rowe. "Nightmares. Somehow, the sword is connected."

"I see." They started on. "I have dreams as well. Memories—an itching where they once were. The blade calls to me. My companion theorized it dwells here in the Peaks. In the ruins of Rach Na'Schuul."

"Isle in the clouds..." Rowe murmured. "A cursed place. Here, somewhere."

Another city in the Peaks of Dren? Erath had never heard of Rach Na'Schuul but she supposed it was possible. The mountains were vast, and nothing really made a lick of sense. Though the way Rowe said an isle in the clouds...

"Did the city... *float* at one time? Sail the skies?"

"It did," said Head. "Until it did not." He sighed, muttered indiscernibly. "Gods fall. Things fall. Inevitable, really."

A city of gods? Fascinating, if such things as gods existed. Erath was skeptical. They called Dren a god, *the* god, *her* god for the simple fact her people bore his name—but there was little if any proof the drenarians were of his hand.

"What makes a god?" she asked. "Or a goddess? Truly, do such things exist or are they merely mortals placed atop pedestals for doing wondrous things?"

"In my experience gods are falsities," Rowe muttered. "Little people adorned in large lies. The most monstrous of things. Gods bring only death."

"A compelling opinion," said Head. "If not mutual. I can't put names to faces, time, nor places but I too have had my share of run-ins with these people playing at goddesses and gods. So much sorrow..."

"Falsities," said Erath, "yet silver-tongued enough to sway the many minds of Harthe." It both disgusted and intrigued her. Words were powerful.

They kept on for a time in silence. Walls of ice and rock grew smooth and etched with symbols unfamiliar to Erath. Symbols which appeared to feast on the pale blue luminescence bleeding from Head. He seemed not to notice, nor did Rowe; or, if they did, neither one said a thing. And what was the essence streaming from Head? Not illum. Not mirkúr.

"What is this place?" Rowe asked.

Erath fell from thought. Before them stood... something. A ruin carved into the whole of a massive cavern with a ceiling through which threads of light crept in. It spanned far and wide; there was no telling how large the ruin was.

"This..." Head hovered, eyes fixed in the ceiling. "This place did not originate within the rock, within the belly of these peaks."

Rowe wrapped her arms around herself, trembling. "This is it," she whispered. She looked at Erath. Fear. Urgency. Realization. "I can feel it tugging at my dreams."

"Rach Na'Schuul," said Head. "A mausoleum where once beauty stood." He floated inward. "Come."

They followed.

———

THIS STARLIT ruin kissed with ice evoked a sense of wondrous dread. It was beautiful and horrible; Avaria longed to know it, *ached* to—there was something familiar to this place. This world beyond physicality. Was this The In Between? Where was Equilibrium? Something else, perhaps—but what?

"Mother," he whispered. In the dark of memory, find her. He frowned, trying to riddle out the words, never mind the fact that he was dead. Maybe this was part of the game, the sword testing him—the *world* and *fate* testing him. He passed faceless effigies of winged crystal things, walked beneath archways through which history had come and gone, archways that were history themselves. Directionless but with intent.

"Mother."

Streets like ash-dusted snow. Crystal spires like needles. Death—so beautiful. Lonely.

"You are death." A new voice. Familiar in the way so many unfamiliar things tend to be. Soft. Warm. "Do you see me? Here —just beyond the bridge ahead."

A luminescent silhouette. Tall. Lithe. Beckoning. Avaria made his way; crossed the bridge beneath which rock and water clashed, a violent dance of gray and blue and black. He stopped a sword's length from the master of the voice. Faceless save for eyes like eclipses.

"Who are you? What are you? Where am I?"

"Something. Somewhere," said the silhouette. "Malleable to whatever shape your mind desires—a canvas of radich."

"Radich." A familiar word. Like a memory from a dream. "Possibility."

The silhouette nodded.

"Show me," Avaria said—*willed*. "Show me the truth of things inside my head. Show me the seed from which this all was sown."

The silhouette bowed its head. Snapped its fingers.

Blue sky, sunlight blooming like a wide-eyed babe. A spire in a city in the center of the woods.

She beckoned.

He chased.

———

Hush strokes the dead boy's cheek. Such broken thoughts. Such a mental massacre—so beautiful. The pain is glorious; it stokes her flames, and she pulls him close.

She whispers—"Find her."

She whispers—"Please..."

She can smell that old scent clinging to his flesh, subtle yet profound, the creeping cold of dark and gloom and woe. The perfume of a broken heart. Hush aches to know.

"Find her."

The darkness of her being thirsts like dying things in a desert. She relents; it consumes the dead boy's flesh and soul, sucks the marrow from his bones and drinks of mirkúr and illum. They are one—the darkness swathes his spirit like a babe; Hush feels... something. His memories bleed, drip through her cognizance like drops of rain—refreshing, slow, so agonizingly slow.

She walks. His task appeals.

Hush hears the sword.

What a song it sings.

————

What must this place have looked like once? Before it fell, before the rock and snow consumed it for their own. Erath assumed it had been beautiful; in her experience the most beautiful of things were often fated for horrible ends—her people were proof. Rowe was proof. Steadfast, yet robbed of verve. Of solace by nightmarish dreams—dreams that'd led them here to the corpse of Rach Na'Schuul. Her fingers brushed the wall of a small structure; she winced—a distant wail kissed the depths of her mind. Touched the wall again, longer this time; the wail turned to shrieks and Erath leapt away from the building to the center of the street. What had happened here?

"Don't touch anything," she said to Rowe and Head. "Just… don't, unless you want to hear the dead scream."

Rowe grimaced. "I don't need to touch anything to hear that." She tugged at the collar of her shirt, itched the mark her dance with Te Mirkvahíl had left. "Some days it was bad enough I considered knifing myself." She growled low, pushed her collar into place. "What a life…"

They continued inward. Large crystals bloomed with momentary life, rejuvenated by the luminescence Head left in his wake. Rowe clutched the hilt of her blade with a trembling hand and a grip so tight it made her knuckles white. Erath drew a dagger of her own. Simple steel—the Burn had robbed her of the ability to wield Illum despite the fact it still flowed through her like a constant stream.

"It tugs at me as well," said Head, turning to look at Rowe. "At memories entombed in fog. I have been here before. Many times. Before it fell." A faraway look in his eyes. "This city hates me."

"Why?" Erath asked.

"It just does," said Head. "The why is not yet clear, but the further in we go, the less dammed my recollections are. Answers await in the darkness of this place."

Deep. Deeper yet through the jagged stone and crystal corpse they went. Through the cracks in the cavern ceiling came the distant howl of wind, dulled to a low whistle. They came to rest before the archway of what Erath guessed was once a temple. Weathered, winged effigies yet stood guard, and the jewel in the center of the archway bloomed with faint light.

She looked at Head, at Rowe. "Here?" They nodded. Erath steeled herself, clutched her dagger tighter. "The sword?"

"Something," Rowe said. "Powerful—feel the energy in the air."

"Odd..." murmured Head. He furrowed his brow, sniffed. He said nothing more, but his expression betrayed intrigue. Memories or not, Erath sensed he knew more about this place than he was letting on—and that did not sit well with her.

They crossed the threshold into the temple; the hair on the back of Erath's neck stood on end; goose pimples rippled down her spine. For the first time since setting off impulsively with Rowe she wondered if she had made a mistake. Maybe it would have been better if she had stayed and moped and mourned in the pale brilliance of the Wisplands. Sure, she would have been lonely, sad, but at least... at least she would have felt... safe.

You idiot, she scolded. *What the hell are you doing here— with Rowe, who looks... not herself, and this melancholy floating head whose every word seems vaguer than the last?* She could practically hear Alor and Leru rolling their dead eyes. Could feel their phantom judgment in the coldness of this place.

"You seek reclamation," said a voice, soft yet resolute. "But there is none here to be found. Only suffering. Only madness." At the far end of the temple stood a figure shimmering in the gloom. It's tattered, feathered wings were furled against its chest and its eyes shone blue-black like a pair of luminescent bruises. "More than motes have any right to comprehend, for why should suffering be so liberal in its applications?"

Rowe approached, hand still clutched around the hilt of her blade, which she looked increasingly less likely to use the closer she drew to the winged being, whether out of reverence, fear, or something else.

"I've had dreams," Rowe said. "Nightmares, all leading to this ruin buried under rock and snow and ice." She yanked her collar down, flashed the mark around her neck. "I felled the beast who gave me this—why does it yet burn?"

Did Rowe truly believe this thing would know? That it was some sort of all-seer? She stood there, small and insignificant in the shadow of its broken majesty. It unfurled its wings; reached for Rowe and cupped her cheeks with taloned hands.

"Such sorrow."

Rowe touched a taloned hand. "Please..."

Erath started, let out a muffled yelp at a hand on her mouth. A strong arm pulled her into the shadow of the archway. "Quiet," said a male voice, "otherwise she'll hear."

The speaker released her. Erath turned. A familiar face she hadn't seen in years. "Avaria?" Images flashed; Erath's eyes went wide. "Wait... I saw—you were..." She felt dizzy. "You were *dead*."

Avaria shook his head. "No."

"Your neck was broken."

He shrugged. "Illum and mirkúr. I saw darkness, then... I was looking up at the stars from my back." He rubbed his neck. "I *should* be dead but..." Another shrug.

He seemed different than she remembered, but she couldn't say why. The cold of death clung to him—she could feel it standing this close to him, could see it in his blue-tinged flesh.

"You were with that floating head," she said. "Searching for a sword. *The* sword."

"You and Rowe as well by the look of it. Why else would you be in this forsaken hole?" He leaned in. "I know where it is. I don't know why or how, but I can *feel* it, *hear* it. Help me retrieve it, what's left of it, at least."

The Raven's Rage. The blade anathema. She loathed it and its wielder more than anything. Yet she had followed Rowe this far to find the wretched thing. Had thought of reclamation, of the days of yore long before the Burn had ever come to pass. If Rowe, then why not Avaria as well? She'd known him going on a decade after all; they were letter friends as was the term.

"For what do you seek it?" she inquired.

"A chance," he said. "To change everything. Fix things." He hesitated. "Rewrite history itself..."

There it was. "You think that's possible?"

He led her away from the archway. Away from their companions and into the labyrinthine arrangement of the ruin Rach Na'Schuul. Deep, until the city center rose up like a jaw of jagged teeth and the only thing she felt was cold and moderately circumspect about the choices that had brought her here.

Avaria held his arms out wide; a mote of illum bloomed atop his right palm, ascending to illuminate the innards of the stone and crystal corpse. "Rach Na'Schuul was once beautiful," he said. "A utopia. A roost for god-things, kept and hidden by the sky." His expression darkened. "Now it's dead. A mausoleum, as is the fate of all great cities; time waits for nothing. Time is silent vengeance."

"But you think it's possible to alter time?" Erath asked again. "With The Raven's Rage?" She tried to wrap her mind around the idea. "How... would you even go about doing that? Never mind with the sword—how does one rewrite history?"

"You'd have to ask my mother, General Sel, and Virtuoso Khal. I'm just the errand boy," he sneered, "sent to gather fragments of the blade anathema in hopes reforging it and subsequently wielding it might lead to greener pastures."

Erath smiled sadly, meekly. How to respond? It seemed old habits die hard, old problems lingered like a throng of carrion creatures near a corpse. She reached for his hand, squeezed it gently. "Not much better in my neck of the woods, for what it's worth," she said, and relayed Leru's demise.

"I'm sorry," Avaria said. They walked with measured steps, aimless to the naked eye, but there was obviously intent; the intermittent twitching of Avaria's nose betrayed as such. Could he *smell* the sword or what remained of it, its energy perhaps?

A structure—a tower.

Dark inside; walls infected with a mottling of... sick. Mirkúr, maybe. An inlay in the center of the room—winged things, glorious and talon-handed like the figure whom they'd been confronted by. Beautiful, angelic.

"Dead." The word slipped from Erath's mouth, little more than a hoarse whisper as she noticed, for the first time, the myriad corpses strewn about the room, all preserved in varying states of the decay by the coldness and the gloom. "What happened here?"

"Time," Avaria murmured. He paused, nose to the sky. "The pinnacle. It awaits."

They ascended.

———

AVELINE KNEW ERATH HAD WITHDRAWN, stolen away by a dark thing with a silver tongue; she would see to them later. She dropped all pretense of madness and kicked the winged figure away.

"Where is it?" she asked. "The sword. The blade anathema."

The creature smiled wearily. "Your guise might have fooled most, Te Mirkvahíl, but I am not most." The creature tapped its skull lightly. "I know what you are and what you seek." It pointed to Head. "I know what and whom that wretched remnant is as well."

Aveline held her right arm to the side; a mirkúr blade took shape. She placed its length between them. "Then you know I am relentless in my pursuit," she said. "I have felled queens and kings, razed empires old and new, and this"—she gestured with her free hand—"is but a minor inconvenience. A momentary itch. Where is The Raven's Rage?"

"I too would like to know," said Head. "I don't doubt your claims I'm wretched, not for a moment, for I can feel I am—I *know* I am. But you see, I don't... well, how to put this simply? I don't remember who or what I am."

The creature approached, careful to keep its distance from Aveline. "Do you know who *I* am?" it inquired of Head. It held out its hand. Beads of light streamed outward from its talons, twisting, braiding, blooming to reveal a woman's face. "Do you know who *she* was?" Head trembled. The creature snarled, gripped Head by his hair. "Search your mind, wretch. The answer is there—the guilt will always call you back."

Head whispered indiscernibly. The creature shook him. He murmured, "Sonja."

"*Memoria,*" the creature sung, and tendrils of illumination pressed on Head, on the space between his eyes. He howled; Aveline shielded her eyes as the brilliance intensified, grew to a near blinding white light.

Stillness.

Whimpering. A man on his knees, face buried in his hands. "Oh, Sonja..."

Something familiar about him. "Stand," Aveline ordered. "Head—stand."

He obeyed, turned and looked her in the eyes. "What a terrible thing I am," he murmured. "What a parent. Ruination thrice." He reached for Aveline with a quaking hand; his tattered wings hung heavy from his back. "Yet you remain... somehow. The last of the Reshapers."

Aveline curled her lip in a rictus of disgust, placed the blade's length between herself and him. "You abandoned us—"

"He has always been proficient in that respect," the creature said.

Avaline yanked her collar down to reveal the mottling of mirkúr. "Left us at the mercy of this... this..." Memories flashed. Not just a plague envisioned by a random twist of fate. That figure, that face at the far end of a dark hallway the night her beloved Beht fell to ash... *Monster.* Her blade hand trembled at the coldness of the memory. Bile churned in her gut. "It was born of you—*admit it*. Master of a monstrous thing."

He bowed his head. "Nothing could be more monstrous than I, my dearest Aveline, not even the atrocities my arrogance made manifest. There is a reason they call me Alerésh the Dread."

Aveline narrowed her eyes. "Alerésh? No—you are Varésh Lúm-talé."

Alerésh shook his head. "In another time, on another world, perhaps—but here I am who I am."

Aveline withdrew a step.

"He speaks the truth," the winged thing said—Aveline still was clueless to its name. "He is Varésh Lúm-talé, yet he is not. The being Dren, the first wielder of The Raven's Rage, was once called Varésh too—but it is complicated, maddening to those who fail to comprehend the mechanics of it all. Temporal alteration is so much more than you know—and that is why you will fail."

"Ever the optimist, Oura," Alerésh said. A pep to his words. An edge. "You are no stranger to failure either." He sighed. "What a falsity I am... Did you know, Aveline, the name Varésh

Lúm-talé means 'Great Lie?' Of course not—why would you?" A melancholy chuckle as he looked about. "Where is your companion. Where is Erath?"

Oura sniffed the air. Looked at Alerésh and Aveline.

"Sin."

MARTYRS

Alf elo nor. One for all.
Nor elo alf. All for one.

Fate was monstrous. Cruel. His mistress. Fate was understanding what he was and always had been at the core. Geph stood atop the hill, overlooking distant Helveden as a midday rain fell heavy, red. His breath clouded, hot with fury, cold with envy. What a wretched engine of destruction he was. He flexed his paws, felt the wet earth; keened his ears, heard the sin buried in the atmosphere. Tasted it.

"One to fall," he whispered. "All to rise." All to fall, one to rise. *She promised.*

How he longed to see his mother.

Geph bayed and the midday trembled 'neath his cry. He waited.

They were coming.

They were hungry.

"Forgive me," he whispered to no one and everyone. "This is requisite." *She* was requisite. *He* was requisite. From entropy, law. From both, balance. He thought of Avaria; they'd not parted well. Geph had chastised his manifesting sinhounds and he saw now he'd been wrong. So *absolutely wrong*. Why leash sin, why keep such beasts at bay when they were a means to peace?

"*How very introspective,*" said a voice in his head. "*It pleases me to know you've seen the error of your ways.*" It manifested at his side, an echo of his darkest self—his shadow twin. "*Entombing sin, denying it... that leads only to the manifestation of excessiveness. Of unbounded sin—false sin.*" It sat back on its haunches, shape billowing in the rain and breeze. "*True sin, Gephorax, is not, contrary to belief, evil—and it is vital you remember that. Existence is not black and white, but shades of gray, and only the ignorant believe otherwise. The key is temperance. Be free but understand that everything has limits.*"

His shadow twin dispersed.

Geph closed his eyes. *If this is right,* he thought, *then why does it feel so wrong?* He opened his eyes, watched the blood rain soak the distant city like the omen of atrocities it was. His neck prickled with anticipation. The path to peace, to reclamation, he understood, meant sometimes your heart would break; sometimes the right decisions were the hardest ones to make.

"Forgive me," he whispered again, this time to Avaria—and Ahnil. Geph had been there in the woods the night she'd found Avaria as a babe. Even now, despite the rift between them, he could say with all the certainty in his wretched bones that never had he seen a mother more in love.

A change in the wind, a shift in the atmosphere—it was time.

They were hungry.

They were here.

———

AVARIA HAD BEEN HERE before in dreams. But the city then had been a ruin. Now? It was a jewel, dark and shimmering, its black streets like deep pools of water swallowing the sky. Towers of midnight kissing the sky like needles drawing thread. He walked, alone, every step suggesting otherwise. He could not see it, smell, nor hear it, but he knew, *felt* there was something in this place. Watching. Waiting. Was it *her*, this figure he had chased here? Something else?

His own words drifted through the air, whispered to him by the wind. "*Show me the truth of things inside my head. Show me the seed from which this all was sown.*" This—what was *this*? What had he meant by that? His dreams, or something more—reality; all of it?

"You return," said a distant silhouette. Nearer, near. Alerésh the Dread. "Again."

Avaria looked about but there was no one save himself for Alerésh to address. "Again... You say that as if we've spoken to one another before." Alerésh did not blink; his stare made the hair on the back of Avaria's neck stand. "Because we *have* spoken to one another before..." He massaged the spot between his eyes. He could feel it was true, yet... "I don't remember doing so. Can't remember where or when or why." He approached Alerésh, stopped and arm's length away. "Are you a memory or something else? Is this The In Between or am I trapped in my own head?"

"We are all of us trapped in our own heads," said Alerésh.

Avaria frowned. "I remember you being vexing. I see that hasn't changed."

Alerésh quirked a smile. "I am, dear boy, what you require

me to be. Whether a memory or something more, only time will tell." He gestured to the city. "Banerowos calls you home."

"That city is a lie," Avaria said. "Nothing but the subject of ghost stories. Decidedly *not* my home, whatever you mean by that."

"I mean *exactly* that," said Alerésh, pushing Avaria along. "And Banerowos, for all its mystery and horror, is, I swear to you, decidedly *real*."

"No." Avaria increased his pace into Banerowos as Alerésh trailed. "No. This is just the product of my own loneliness, my fantasizing an adventure while being constantly bound to the Hall. In fact—I'm probably there now, dreaming all of this."

Like smoke, Alerésh was before him. He placed his hands on Avaria's shoulders. "I want you to listen to me carefully," he said. "You, Avaria Norrith, are *physically* dead—your conscious yet remains, but"—a phantom shriek; black lightening snapped across the sky—"time is running out. You need to find an egress from this place."

"Am I stoned beyond all fucking belief?" Avaria asked. "Is that what this is?"

Alerésh growled. "Always were a bit mouthy, weren't you?" He gave Avaria a shake. "This is *real*—as real as Banerowos once was, as real as Ouran'an once was, as real as Helveden is and *will be* if you flee this... this... cognizant collapse. If this is all in your head, Avaria, that means that I am a part of you—what reason would I have to lie?"

A good question. Logical. More lightning. Another shriek and a boom of thunder like a thousand sinhounds howling.

Sinhounds—Avaria hadn't heard from his in... it'd been a few days at least, since the ruins of Ulm, if his journey to that place had actually been real. If floating Nameless Head had been real. If Erath and Rowe and the collapsing earth beneath his feet had been real and he had, in fact, broken his neck and—

Myriad distorted images flashed across his mind. Erath? A ruin deep in the earth. Distorted voices and a tugging sensation at the center of his chest—the sword, The Raven's Rage—

"Fuck." Fuck, fuck fuck. "FUCK." He pushed Alerésh's hands away. "How do I get out of here?" Shit, how was he supposed to— "How do I—my body? What do I do?"

Alerésh pointed to the center of the city. "There. You found the key once before; you can do it again."

Memories, dreams... always so absolutely, irritatingly vague, Avaria growled to himself. Why could they never be direct? Why was there always an air of mystery? This wasn't fiction meant to entertain—this was his existence! He ran for the center of Banerowos, toward the largest of its midnight spires, that tugging sensation in his chest having returned, neither cold nor warm, just simply... there. All of this felt oddly familiar, but there was no way he had lived this all before. No way he had experienced this to some degree at some point in time—was there?

The sky fell dark the closer he grew; gray and purple clouds bloomed like fresh bruises and a throng of shrieks ripped through the silence. So much agony. Was this hell? Had he dreamt himself into an underworld of his own design?

He reached the tower. Broken, weathered by age and rain. He pushed the old doors ajar and slipped inside. Threads of mirkúr clung to the ceiling, walls, and floor like tentacles of something monstrous reaching inward from another world. What had happened here? Fissures in the floor; a shattered floor. Wails and whispers swimming through the air, biting at his ears like hungry flies. *Flee. Save. DIE.*

Avaria started; goose pimples rippled along his flesh and a

cold sweat trickled down his brow and cheeks. He stopped in the center of the large anteroom. Alerésh stood beside him, wings yet furled against his chest like a cloak; the feathers though teemed with brilliant light.

"She cannot be allowed in," he said. "She nor her hounds. This is where we part."

Avaria looked at him. "I—"

The tower quaked. "Go!" Alerésh unfurled his wings; a blade of light and darkness formed in one hand. "Please—go! This cannot be for naught. Go!"

Avaria whirled around and bolted down the hallway at the far end of the room. Into the darkness, body trembling; an explosion of light whence he had come. A cacophony of rage and woe. A song, a symphony of sin arrived.

Follow your heart, he chanted mentally; he clung to it like a mantra, the sensation at the center of his chest growing more profound with every step he took, to the point it hurt to breathe. Deeper he ran; deeper he descended, finally coming to a circular chamber illuminated by a single wisp of pale blue light.

"Radich." Was this what he was meant to find? He approached the wisp, reached for it with a trembling hand... hesitated. Pulled away. Withdrew from the chamber and down the hallway to his left. Something about that had seemed far too simple; his proximity to it, the touch of its light had felt wrong.

Inward, downward—when would this all end?

———

THEY NEAR THE blade for which she thirsts—Hush can feel it with the body not her own. She can feel the dead boy struggle in his mind, feel him flee—he yet resists. She snarls to herself with lips that are not hers. *Breathe,* she urges. Things are as fate wills.

"Come," she calls to Erath. She hungers for the darkness of the woman's soul. Once she has the blade, once she holds The Raven's Rage, Hush decides that she will feed—on everything and everyone. She has never felt such hunger.

She salivates.

They descend.

She can smell the secrets kept by Rach Na'Schuul.

Her stomach roars.

———

WHAT DOES it matter if this thing kills her? Aveline thought of Erath's disappearance. *I would have done it myself; I would see her born anew—I would see them all returned once I possess The Raven's Rage and rewrite time.* She sighed; inner voices scolded her. She chastised herself mentally and could practically feel Alor whacking her in the back of the head for such a thought. *For you, Alor. For you, I will save her from this thing that stole her from my sight. For you, I will give her a choice.*

She followed Alerésh and Oura as the latter tracked their quarry's scent. Through the corpse of Rach Na'Schuul they went. Ruined houses, broken shops, dead groves peppered all about, now ruled only by dead crystals void of color. Nothing here, Aveline realized, held color. Not the colors of life nor the colors of death and everything that followed. Just endless grays that saw fit to trick the eye. Strange. Unnerving. As if this place were somehow trapped in time. Aveline cocked an eyebrow pensively—was that even possible?

She held her thought as Rach Na'Schuul trembled. The cavern ceiling cracked, sending shards of ice and rock hurtling toward the city. Aveline, Alerésh, and Oura charged ahead, dodging debris as best they could, finally coming to a maw in the street in which they would take shelter.

"It stirs the city," Oura said. "The sin that stole your friend—look."

Aveline peeked out at the city. Gossamer threads of energy swam about; spirits manifested. Rach Na'Schuul moaned. She ducked back into hiding. "What is this? What is happening?"

"Unwilling martyrs rise to keep their tomb," Alerésh murmured. He closed his eyes and sighed. "I remember this moment as if it happened yesterday." He gripped Oura's hand; she yanked it free. "This is The Fall."

"We must hurry," Oura said. She motioned they withdraw.

Aveline first, then the other two. Through ghosts and gray they went. So many screams; Aveline's skull ached, longed to explode. She could hear their rage and suffering in her mind, could feel it in her bones and it made her want to die for it reminded her of home—of the fall of Ouran'an. Of Beht and Jor. Of everyone and everything that she had ever known and loved.

They pushed into the city center, found themselves surrounded, set upon by spears of twisting light and dark. Aveline parried with her mirkúr blade, sent the blast of energy upward, watched it take a spirit in the chest. It stung in her heart to have done so; things dead should not have to suffer the living.

"Can't you reason with them?" she asked of Alerésh and Oura. "They're your people, are they not?"

Oura's wings shimmered with light; a barrier pushed back against the onslaught. "The dead cannot be reasoned with," she said, "especially not those twisted by her song." A glint in her eyes. "Songs... Sing with me, Alerésh. Sing as once our people sung to Mother Moon and Father Sky."

"We will give you time enough to run," Alerésh said to Aveline. He pointed to the remnant of a large tower infected with shattered crystals. "There."

"High above," Oura added. "In the heart of Rach Na'Schuul." She gripped Aveline's arm, pulled her close so that their noses nearly touched. "Do what is right. Fight your selfishness—break the cycle."

Aveline pulled away. "I will do what I must."

Their wings shimmered; they began to sing. The spirits shrieked. *Just wait. Just wait.* So many ghosts. Endless. Hungry. The barrier faltered; threads of light fell like shards of glass.

She ran as the spirits converged. Felt the mirkúr flowing through her, cold, desperate; she called the shadows of this place and they accepted her. Like smoke, she stood before the tower archway, away from the chaos. She gave a half-second glance back at the mass of wailing energy. Then, she stepped inside.

———

AVARIA TOUCHED DOWN IN... an anteroom? He looked about—surely he had been running *down* the stairs, but this... felt like he was back to where he started. He conjured a wisp of light. The chamber was dark, but his light offered a modicum of clarity, enough that he could walk without tripping. The air smelled of dust and dirt and was thick enough Avaria could almost imagine it parting around him as he went.

"What the..."

This place was massive.

"It might behoove us to split up and explore."

Avaria started at the voice, whipped around. "Alerésh?"

"Maybe?" said Maybe-Not-Alerésh. *Definitely* not Alerésh. He was garbed in black, and his flesh bore tattoos that shone with the same blue light—radich—that'd come from the wisp in the chamber somewhere upstairs. From the tattoos manifested three wisps of illumination. "Considering the size of the spire and the clock we're running against would you not agree we should split up?"

Clock? Avaria smacked his forehead. "Right. Clock—are we talking about the same clock? Are *you* talking about the same thing as the, uh...—your *twin* was talking about?"

Definitely-Not-Alerésh shrugged. "The mind tends to—oh, what's the phrase? Fuck things up on occasion. Especially when one—such as yourself—is in a bad way." He narrowed his eyes. "What did you do?"

"I died," Avaria snapped. "I *fucking died* and now I'm trying to keep my mind from being devoured by some... thing. I have no idea what's going on; I need to escape. Somehow."

"Sure," Definitely-Not-Alerésh said. "Sure. Look. I'll take the third and fourth floors, you take the second. We'll meet back here once we're done and relay our findings. There should be something here that can help."

"Right. Fine." Avaria watched Definitely-Not-Alerésh ascend the corkscrew. He manifested a mirkúr blade and followed suit, his newish companion becoming little more than a glowing dot as Avaria reached the second-floor landing and started into the chamber on his left. His own wisp ascended to the ceiling, casting its brilliance over the room. It was adorned with myriad bookshelves, each packed to capacity with leather-bound tomes, and in the corner was a desk, it, too, overflowing with various texts. It was the engraving on the wall at the far end of the room, though, that drew Avaria further in.

"A raven," he murmured. This memory or dream or what-ever of his, these ruined cities and winged people... there was something more to it than that which currently met his eyes.

He pressed into the adjoining chamber, at the center of which stood the stone effigy of a giant bird, its feathers fluctu-ating midnight to snow white and back. It was beautifully hypnotic, so much so Avaria almost failed to notice the body lying limp at the statue's base. He rushed to its side. He wasn't sure who it was or what had happened to them, but they were still alive, though barely just, their breathing labored. Avaria rolled them gently onto their back and gasped.

"You're... me?"

His twin replied weakly in a language Avaria once again could not understand and allowed Avaria to help him to his feet. They were twins only in the face. Everything else was different. Tattoos not unlike Definitely-Not-Alerésh's peeked out from the sleeves and collar of his robe, glowing faintly, and his dark hair was pulled back into a series of thin braids. He rolled his shoulders back, then motioned for Avaria to follow him back the way he'd had come.

They were silent as the newcomer led Avaria back to and up the corkscrew stairway. For a man who'd looked near death just minutes ago he was unnaturally alert, his movements fluid, graceful. There was purpose in his steps and Avaria wondered where they were going, who the stranger was if not an echo of himself.

"Nothing atop," Definitely-Not-Alerésh said, descending toward them. "Silent as the..." He rushed to the man, embracing him. The gesture was returned with enthusiasm and the two conversed in their strange language.

"Who is he?" Avaria asked.

"A friend," Definitely-Not-Alerésh said. There was a sadness underneath his smile. "A friend long dead but ever present in this place of memory. Please meet Jor Dov'an."

The man, Jor, bowed his head to Avaria and he did the same in return. Jor tensed his jaw, looked toward the chamber on their right. There was apprehension dancing in those purple eyes. Fear, too, and... was it anger?

"Is he all right?" Avaria asked.

"He will be." Definitely-Not-Alerésh started toward the chamber. "Come."

Avaria trailed them, blade extended. He hadn't liked the look on Jor's face and had liked Definitely-Not-Alerésh's reply even less. He hoped they were going in the right direction, that he would soon find the key to his egress from his labyrinthine mind, but who could tell in a place like this, in the twisted dreams and maybe-memories of a man so desperate for adventure, for escape, and—

Avaria's breath caught in his throat as the wisp light revealed a dozen or so corpses strewn about the room. Blood stained the polished floor. The corpses' eyes were a sickly white with threads of what Avaria guessed was mirkúr twisting aimlessly about. He swallowed, clutched his blade tighter. What was this horrible place he had fallen into?

I died, he recalled. *And my body...* Dread crept through him as the realization dawned—his dreams and memories were bleeding together with whatever *thing* now wore him like a suit. This phantasmagoria would not release him unless he fought.

They crossed to the other end of the chamber and into the room beyond. More corpses. More blood. Walls and pillars infested with wispy tendrils of mirkúr, with a pulsating, thickening membrane. Mirkúr, too? Avaria swallowed the urge to retch—at everything.

"Slow," Definitely-Not-Alerésh said. There was worry in his tone, in the crease of his brow. He asked something of Jor—at least, Avaria thought it was a question—and Jor offered only a tiny nod. "Be on your guard."

As if Avaria had needed instructing in that regard. They continued through a network of hallways, their steps hastening as they went, before they finally came to rest in what looked to be a bedroom. At the far end of the room stood a red-haired woman and a blond-haired man, back-to-back, eyes darting about. Repressed instinct—Avaria wasn't sure if it was his—bid he run to them, but Jor blocked his path with his arm.

Jor shook his head and pointed to the shadows on the wall, cast by the wisp light.

"Vultures?" Avaria asked. "Sinhounds?"

Jor nodded. His tattoos bloomed beneath his robe and an illum longsword took shape in his hand. Definitely-Not Alerésh did the same and the pair advanced into the room at a walk, Avaria at their heels, itching to imbed his dagger in whatever thing saw fit to provoke him. They reached the man and woman and the shadows struck. Avaria sidestepped, thrusting his dagger clumsily into the demon nearest him, but the blade had no effect and simply passed through his quarry's smokey form.

"Run!" Definitely-Not-Alerésh ushered Avaria out of the chamber. Avaria obeyed, but not without a prolonged glance at Jor, who shouted in his foreign tongue.

They sprinted back the way they had come, their steps haunted by the distant shrieks of demons as Jor gave them time to flee. They descended to the base of the tower and burst out into the night in time to see the fog encroaching from the woods. Without hesitation they turned tail and bolted for the trees beyond.

Avaria was not sure how long they had been running when

they finally stopped to catch their breaths. He looked at Definitely-Not-Alerésh. "Your name—what is it?"

"Now? Varésh," he said. "Why do you ask?"

Avaria frowned. "Just curious." He cracked his neck. "I don't understand anything that's going on. All of this is..." He gestured wildly. "I've walked The In Between before, and this—this is something more."

"The mind is a dangerous place. Quite disordered, as you can see." His expression darkened. "Especially when your dreams and memories braid together with those belonging to a monster."

That was an understatement if ever Avaria had heard one, and it only served to chill him further—he had confirmation. Disordered didn't begin to describe the situation. His thoughts returned to Jor. "Your friend—"

Varésh shook his head sadly and Avaria understood. But what had he witnessed? His heart stung despite his best effort to remain indifferent. *Why* did it hurt? He massaged the spot between his eyes. Hopeless. Desperate. Confused. He looked at Varésh. "Am I going to escape this place?"

Varésh pointed straight at the darkness of the wood. "The key. You found it once before. You'll find it again—you'll know it when you do."

So Avaria went. Alone. Cold. Through a dark wood of error. Screaming trees. Bleeding earth. Whispers kissed his ears, promised death, begged for torture. Ached for release. Trembled. Still, he walked, hugged himself tight. Thought of nothing but freedom from this hell. Followed his heart.

A clearing. A tree greater than all others. Corpses swung, danced the dance of death. Gods, so many bodies. He looked about—withered waltzers by the hundreds. More. Oh, gods...

Back to the great tree. To the figure standing at its base.

Garbed in black. Eyes black as night. Skin pale and cracked. Like that girl of burnt paper flesh; not her. Different. Cold, but... cold in the way intense heat feels on one's skin. He wilted underneath her stare.

"This place is mine," she said. Voice like serpents hissing rain. Angry. Scared.

Stomach churned bile. Sour taste on his tongue. Hand shook, still clutched his blade. He placed its length between them. "This place is *mine*—let me out." He took one step toward her. Furrowed his brow. Rictus. Growl. "Let. Me. *Out.*" Called out with his mind. *Envy. Pride. Wrath.*

"They'll not come," she said. "They are not yours."

"My head, my hounds," Avaria said. Hot with rage, with desperate intent. Distant howls. He grinned. "See?"

She swallowed, pressed her back to the trunk of the massive tree. "*Please.*"

Like smoke, Avaria was before her, blade to her chest.

"You will doom them all," she whispered. Tears streamed from her abyssal eyes. "If you leave. If you leave the temperance disappears. *Please!*" She grabbed him by his shirt. "*Please... I just...*" She sunk into the blade, wept into his chest. "So tired..."

The forest shrieked.

"Again." Her speech was soft. "Here we go... again."

Light exploded.

Burned. Gods, it burned.

Avaria screamed.

———

Hush screams. Something in the depths of her being has been violated. Desecrated. She falls to the floor, writhes in the body not her own. Erath tends to her frantically. All Hush can do is weep. Howl as the body not her own rends itself from the inside out and energies bleed and flee. Twist and braid and slither through the ruined ceiling of this place.

She lays there, dying. This was not foreseen—but this is fate, and Hush does as fate wills.

She dies.

———

AVELINE FOUND them on the topmost floor of the tower. She dispersed her blade; she breathed a sigh of relief at Erath, hands covered in blood but otherwise fine. She glanced at the corpse, her right eye twitched. It was Alerésh's companion, the one they had left behind. She shouldn't have been disturbed by it considering the numbers of bodies her vultures had stolen and worn, and yet she could not stomach the mess. She doubled over and retched.

"Are you all right?" Erath asked.

Aveline stood tall, wiped the bile from her mouth. "Fine. Could ask the same of you." She nudged the corpse with her foot. "Wasn't actually him, whoever this *thing* claimed to be. It was..." She shook her head. "I don't know what it was. Dangerous."

"Avaria Norrith," Erath said. Her voice trembled. "Prince of Ariath. A friend."

Aveline sighed, pulled Erath into an embrace. How many more people would this poor girl lose before all was said and done? "Shit," she whispered. Half to play the part, half to actually... mourn? "How could we have not noticed? The *Prince of Ariath*. What a wretched journey this has been..."

Truly—what a wretched journey, what a wretched life these last however many thousand years, however many centuries

Aveline had walked this world alone. Was Oura right—was failure all fate had in store for her? She glanced past Erath to a shattered blade encased in brilliant pale blue light. There it was. She pulled away from Erath and approached the sword.

"The Raven's Rage," she said. "As I dreamt." She held her hand to the light, manipulating it with her fingers. "So much possibility." She'd not tasted of radich in ages; it was sweet, its phantom vapors like honey on her tongue. "Rewrite history with the blade anathema—what do you think?" She had given her word—a choice. "Erath?"

The drenarian approached, stopped a few feet from Aveline.

"I don't know."

Somehow, Aveline had expected that. She smiled softly. Thought of Alor. Of Beht and Jor. A lump formed in her throat. Urgency and desperation gradually melted away, replaced instead with sorrow. How absolutely bittersweet. "Me neither. In fact..." She heaved a ragged sigh, fought back tears. "We should destroy it—once and for all. Such power should not exist. It is far too dangerous, far too tempting, and I have seen what sin does because..." She trailed off. "War does terrible things." Truth to hide her lie.

Erath nodded. "How?"

"The same way it was wrought," Aveline said. She placed a hand on Erath's shoulder. "We take it to Dren."

———

"To... Dren." Erath felt dizzy among other things. "To Dren because..."

"He wrought The Raven's Rage," said Rowe. She chewed her lip; Erath could sense she was keeping something from her.

"He... fuck. Dren is the one responsible for the Burn, Erath. He was the wielder of the blade."

"No." Erath shook her head. "No, why would he—*no*. Who told you this?"

Rowe explained what had transpired down below after Erath had left. She felt sick. Betrayed. Was that all her people had ever been—martyrs for a madman's desires? She tensed her jaw. "*If* Dren is even still alive, how do we find him—and can I kill him once The Raven's Rage is dust?"

"The Wisplands," Rowe said. So much guilt drawn across her face.

"You and I are going to have a *long* talk once this is all said and done," Erath snarled. She looked to Avaria's corpse. Just ash and a twist of mirkúr. Was that what happened to his kind, those able to wield mirkúr, when they died? She wasn't sure.

"Let's go."

GEPH WEPT AT HER FEET. She had died peacefully—they all had, with grins stretched wide across their faces. It horrified him; the joy of corpses wormed its way inside his mind, tattooed itself to Geph so he would never forget what had transpired here this day—what *he had done* this day.

At least, he thought, *her end was not my doing.* He could never have lived with that—murdering Queen Ahnil. Everyone else? His soul would bear the weight, the guilt, profound as it already was. He had no other choice.

"*You did well, Gephorax,*" his shadow twin whispered.

If by 'well' you mean I destroyed a city, Geph thought, *then yes—I did.*

"*From entropy, law. From both, balance. Stick to the path, Gephorax.*"

Geph pressed his nose to Ahnil's cold cheek. "Forgive me..."

He withdrew from Helveden. The city burned. The dying sang.

But Geph sang louder.

TIME

Time was cruel. She found them in the corpse of Rach Na'Schuul; their final song hung heavy in the stunted air. Dead air. Oura had been good, always good; Varésh Lúm-talé had been a lie, always a lie. "Alerésh," she sneered. "As if you could ever have lived up to his stolen name. As if you could ever have been Alerion." She took his light, took his radich for her own. So delicious. She wreathed Oura in darkness, swaddled her in shadows; delivered her from hell, for such a timeless place as this could only be described as eternal damnation.

"Hell is a place of one's own making," she whispered. An echo out of time, those words. She breathed the stale air. "I see. Hush is what you call yourself now. What do you seek? What madness drives you?"

Shift in the atmosphere. Breath on her neck. She turned.

"You're here." Horror of shadow, flame, and stars. Limp wings trailing like a tattered cloak. It reached for her with a quivering hand, bore into her with eyes like tarnished coins alight. "Luminíl..."

Luminíl furled her wings against her chest and hissed. "Monster."

Hush recoiled, whimpered. "Monster... yes, but..." Ragged breath. "For you, Luminíl. All for you. No—" Scratched her eyes, snarled, wailed. "For them. For all. Deliverance. I need you." Absolute certainty. "Badly. So... *badly*."

"No one *needs* anything," murmured Luminíl. Half a lie—right? "But you—you need sleep." Eternal. Dreamless. "*I* want to sleep. So long since last the darkness kissed my eyes. Every death, a lie. Every life, perpetual agony—and *you* are to blame."

She raised a hand to Hush—

Fire in her chest. Burning.

Cold. So cold.

Not again.

Hush screamed. Reached for Luminíl.

Quietus in ruin.

Hell.

———

Snow.

Silence.

Helveden was a corpse. The clouds hemorrhaged; Avaria walked the dead streets. Crows picked at lifeless flesh, pulled eyes from sockets, tongues from mouths. Spires stood like jagged teeth. None of this was right—how long had he been gone? What had happened here? Was any of this real? He pressed himself to think, to remember—a dark forest, girl of black and woe.

"Hello?" An echo in the stillness of death.

He remembered dying in the Peaks. Sort of. Remembered

learning he had died. Traversed his labyrinthine mind. Walked ruins, fled monsters. Any of this—what was *any* of this?

"HELLO?"

Shimmers. Twists of light and shadow. Avaria cocked an eyebrow. Distant screams kissed his ears. Distant, yet so very near. He frowned; fear crept through him like a frozen river thawing. Slow, rushing. He pushed through Helveden, what was left. Raced for the Bastion. *Dream*, he urged. *Just let this be a dream.*

A nightmare. Had someone else made it to The Raven's Rage before him? Fuck, had *he* obtained the blade and done something catastrophic, so profound he couldn't remember? *Wish you were here, Geph.* Longhound could always make sense of madness.

Figures in the distance. City draped in fog. Whispers on the wind. Avaria gave chase, called to the phantoms—no answer. Through charred groves and splintered courtyards. Thick rain, snaps of light. To the Bastion, through defiled gates. Streaks of... blood. Threads of mirkúr twisting, tickling ruined stone, drifting.

They beckoned from the egress.

Avaria indulged.

———

TIME WAS A PECULIAR THING. Abhorrent, really. Time disgusted Dren; he disgusted himself. He deserved worse than this, jailed within the Wisplands of the peaks that bore his name. So much worse than luxury when his children dwelled in woe, forsaken by the sunlight—forsaken by their father. Intent was blinding. Intent was fueled by arrogance, and arrogance by intent. He sighed.

"What a thing," he mused. "What a lie I am. Living whilst my children think me dead. I *should* be dead—worse than dead. Yet here I am..." He sighed. Waited for the myriad voices in his head to snicker, snarl, and whine. That was the thing about imprisonment—it drove the mind insane. Snuck in pictures of a previous life, a twisted knife in a rotting wound. Dren had been someone else once. Better by the looks of it, though "better" was subjective. Relative, rather; the person he *had been* was prickish in his own right—just not to the genocidal degree for which Dren dwelled in shame.

He withdrew from the darkness of his cave, the ruin of a temple crafted in his name. Wisplight kissed his flesh; it stung his eyes and he looked away to a copse of trees, leafless, dead. Dead, like so many of his children. He narrowed his eyes, watched two silhouettes emerge. Emotion roiled through the air, anger, fear, and grief. Confusion. They were coming toward him, coming *for* him—a drenarian and the creature called Te Mirkvahíl.

And they were wielding something monstrous. Dren felt sick; his stomach gurgled. The Raven's Rage had come home to roost. He sucked in his breath, steeled himself as best he could, and greeted them with open arms. They stopped at the base of the crumbling, snow-covered stairs. In Te Mirkvahíl's eyes he saw guilt and sorrow. In the drenarian's, rage. Hatred. She knew.

"Rowe." He nodded to Te Mirkvahíl. To the drenarian, he bowed his head. "Erath." He was lost for words, and his breath caught in his throat. Unexpected. "Erath, I..."

"Alive," Erath hissed. "Alive all this time..." Dren could practically feel the heat of her fury in her words. "Rowe told me something interesting. She told me *you're* responsible for the Burn. That *you* wrought this cursed fucking blade..."

No words. What was Dren to say? What could he say that would erase years of pain? That would rectify the monstrous consequences of the Burn? He heaved a sigh, and his guilt felt like a thousand thorns biting his heart. "Yes."

Cold wind and silence. Te Mirkvahíl looked from Dren to Erath and back. Ironic such a monstrous thing as her would mediate whatever conversation was to take place, though maybe not considering what a monstrous thing it was that Dren had done. *We are monsters,* he thought. He looked at Erath, surprised she hadn't tried to kill him yet; she deserved to, and he sensed she longed to.

"Why?" she asked. "All of it—why?"

Truth. No sense in lies. Look where those had gotten him. Look where those had *always* gotten him. "Reclamation is a complicated thing. An undertaking often fueled by desperation." Again, he sighed. He approached them, dragging his dead wings through the snow. "The blade was to be the key, the means to unlock the doors to the Temporal Sea."

"Temporal alteration..." Erath murmured. "It's *possible?*"

Dren nodded. "Very much so—but dangerous. Destructive. The price is often far too high, so it took the Burn for me to learn. To save what has been lost, one first must destroy what is yet to be lost, do you understand?" He searched her eyes. "To save this world, I was going to destroy it—but I failed."

Silence reigned. Dren waited for either of the women to respond, though he doubted Te Mirkvahíl would lest she betray her lie.

"There is hope, however small it may be, to reverse the Burn," Dren said, "and the key lies here"—he held his arms out wide—"in the Wisplands. I know because there is one amongst you who was spared that day. He never made mention of it, walked as the rest of you walked in solidarity.

His character kept his freedom secret. Fenrin was and is the king of kings."

"He was here that day..." Erath looked about. "Something about the wisplight."

Dren nodded. "Speak with him if you wish." He eyed the blade at Te Mirkvahíl's waist. "What will you do with it?"

"Destroy it," she said. "As you made it, so must you *unmake* it."

"Gladly." Did he mean that? Such power in The Raven's Rage, such potential... He shuddered. Gestured to Te Mirkvahíl to bring the blade. She approached; he took it from her, felt the energies permeate his flesh, the entirety of his being. He felt *awake* as images flashed across his mind—The Raven's Rage had indeed come home to roost.

Memories across the span of time. Across realities not yet always mine. So many worlds. The illum network was a wondrous thing. Mysterious in its full potential, but clear enough to Dren to understand what he had seen. To remember who he had been, was, and always would be—and it made him sick. With guilt. With possibility. *Radich, my old friend...* The sword rose from Dren's hand, hovered as he wreathed it in mirkúr and radich. Soft threads of energy streamed along the blade—and gradually it fell to mist. Gone. Dead.

And Dren felt weak. Tired. He sat down in the snow and closed his eyes.

"It is done," he said. "Go. Leave me to my end—it *is* coming."

"We loved you," Erath said. Such sorrow, such pain. "But we were wrong."

Dren said nothing, only listened to the screaming silence as Te Mirkvahíl and Erath turned and walked away.

Please, he thought, *let this have been the right thing to do.*

He opened his eyes to the barren, snow-draped waste...

and conjured The Raven's Rage.

———

So. That had been it. Dren was alive and The Raven's Rage had been destroyed far more easily than Erath would have imagined possible given the mystique behind the blade anathema. Somehow it all seemed... anticlimactic.

She eyed Rowe as they trekked through snow and trees. Neither had said a word since leaving Dren to perish in his ruin. Erath wasn't sure what she wanted to say. What she was sure of, however, was that she wanted an explanation from Rowe—about everything. How had she known Dren was alive? What about Rach Na'Schuul? The more she thought on everything, the more she felt like there was far more that Rowe was keeping from her. Where had she gone after the war, after felling Te Mirkvahíl, and if the demon was well and truly dead then why did vultures and hounds still run amok? Why was Leru dead?

Rowe halted. She looked exhausted, and if anything, the mark around her neck had grown worse. Threads of mirkúr webbed out of her garb and up her neck.

"Over..." she murmured. "All of it—over..." She leaned against a tree, slid down the trunk and sat in the snow. Silent tears streamed down her cheeks. "You deserve the truth..."

———

Rowe was dead. Had been all this time. Erath was numb. She looked at this *thing*, this monstrous *thing* that wore the image of her friend, wore her flesh as if it were a coat in and out of which she slipped with ease. Her chest was heavy, and her thoughts were shrieking.

"I loved her, you know," Te Mirkvahíl said softly.

"Who?" Erath asked. "Rowe?"

"Alor," said Te Mirkvahíl. Shadows twisted round her form; reshaped her into someone Erath swore she'd seen before, had known a time ago.

"..." Erath clapped a hand to her mouth. "*Aveline...?*" What was going on? So many names within names. It was getting hard to keep up. "You—you're Te Mirkvahíl." A statement she had meant as a question, though she supposed it didn't matter; the truth stood before her, broken, sad. She thought back to Alor, to her death at the hands of Ariathan soldiers and their blades. Something in her ticked, clicked, snapped—everything made sense. "Your war was in her name."

Aveline nodded. "I felt at peace with Alor. At ease, so much so the import of my undertaking waned. I..." She breathed deeply, heaved a sigh. "Felt I could finally let go of what had come to pass; I had accepted my people were gone. That my husband and son were gone." She reached for Erath's hand, squeezed it tightly. "You were a tremendous part of that. You were my friend, Erath..."

Erath let the words sink in, let them swim and slosh and permeate her soul. Friend. What a strange word, that. Friend. Friends. So foreign after all these years, coming from the mouth of... this. Aveline. "Time is monstrous."

"People are more so," Aveline murmured. Erath could practically taste the shame, the regret in her words. What a sorry, lost creature. What sorry, lost creatures they both were. "Do you recall what you asked me on our ascent? To find oneself by losing hope?"

Erath nodded. "Having an epiphany?"

Aveline nodded.

"Don't need you to tell me," Erath said. She thought she

understood well enough by looking upon Aveline—Aveline as she truly was. In doing so, Erath realized she had never felt more lost. More... fragmented.

"Will you walk with me?" Aveline asked.

"No," Erath said. "I..." She what? "I'm going to speak with Dren." What a stupid idea. What a stupid instinct. "Just... something."

She pulled her hand from Aveline, turned to walk away. Paused. Turned back and pulled Aveline to her. There was a lot to work through, but... "Come find me in Nil-Illúm. We'll figure things out, somehow."

Aveline pulled back, flashed a melancholy smile. It faded; her eyes darkened. "I need you to know, Erath. Leru's death— that wasn't me."

Erath nodded; a chill crept through her. If not Aveline, then who? What?

"Be safe."

"You, too."

They turned from one another
and went their separate ways.

————

THROUGH THE BASTION COURTYARD, where for every corpse there buzzed a thousand flies, or the deafening sound implied. Avaria swallowed the urge to retch and continued inward, measured steps hastening with every lifeless face he passed. Eyes burnt out; flesh charred. Dying breaths lingering in the foul air, as if spirits struggling for release but tethered to this hell. Was this a nightmare? An alternate reality? What had happened in the Peaks? What had happened in *his own mind*?

He pushed the battered Bastion doors ajar; the anteroom

was cold and ruined, stained with gore and kissed with wispy threads of mirkúr rippling in the air like tentacles.

"Hello?" Stupid. Foolish. Whatever had done this might still be lurking—but he needed answers. He needed *someone, something* to answer, to let him know if he was dreaming or awake.

Were you sleeping, boy, what then? Would you will yourself awake? Would you will yourself awake to find you'd actually been awake this whole time? What then?

The voice sent a chill up Avaria's spine; goose pimples rippled along his flesh. The voice sounded distant yet so very near, ethereal yet whole. Something in between.

"Show yourself and find out," Avaria said. He willed a blade to take form... but neither light nor shadow granted his request. What was going on?

Laughter. Hissing. Giggling cackle shriek. The song of a dying bird. The horrible sound pierced his ears; he felt blood trickling, creeping down his jaw. Heard the cacophony in the depths of his mind like a symphony of dead and dying monstrous things. Avaria clutched his ears and screamed.

Silence. Fog and a Bastion anteroom devoid of gore. Pristine, as beautiful as Avaria had ever seen it. A silhouette atop the raven inlay, lithe and cloaked in feathered wings. It neared— Avaria had seen this thing before.

"Floating Head..." he murmured.

The figure smirked. "One of many names bestowed upon me, yes. Call me BzZzzzz." He unfurled his wings, feathers shining like a cloudless midnight sky. "Time is a peculiar thing. A wretched thing. A peculiarly wretched thing, dear boy, as can be the mind. Wondrous and terrible."

"What is this?" asked Avaria. Was he going mad? Was this hell?

"The calm before the storm," said BzZzzz. "Monsters walk the earth and sing their songs of ruin. The world falls in tempo with their stride. Or will. But you must wake. Push through memory and take the hands of Time."

Avaria massaged the spot between his eyes. "None of that makes sense." He looked about the anteroom. "Where did all the bodies go?"

"Like I said, time is peculiarly wretched." Such melancholy in those words, in that stormy stare.

Avaria felt his stomach drop. "All of... that..." He gestured at the vacancy. "It was real, wasn't it? Something happened to Helveden. To..." Urgency erupted; he pushed past BzZzzz. "Mother! Norema?" Adrenaline like a gushing wound. "Virtuoso Khal?"

He charged through the fog. Screams and whispers rose from nothingness to omnipotence. Stumbled. Vision blurred. Bile churning in his gut, mind waxing and waning.

Emptiness dilating. Throne room of horror. Monsters ripping limbs and rending flesh. Hounds of sin and flame and nightmare grins.

"Mother!"

Maddened grin ripped wide across her face; eyes like burning coals. She cleaved her acolytes—

Then by Norema's blade she fell.

And by the hounds, Norema's head was severed at the neck and her body fell limp and flopping with whatever dark power the hounds possessed.

So much agony. So much screaming. Heartache. Betrayal— by the throne stood Geph. Watching. Silent. Eyes alight with flames the color of a midday summer sky.

"Forgive me," the longhound *sinhound bastard fucking monster* mouthed, the cadence of his sorrow and regret muffled, almost choked to silence as the fog returned and everything went dark.

———

Hush loves streams. They remind her of the illum she brandished long ago. Gentle, beautiful, but dangerous when provoked. Much like someone she loved so long ago.

She senses a woman, the Reshaper, so she turns.

"I knew you would be here," said Aveline. "You reek of mirkúr. Of temporal rot. What are you?" The trees moan. "Hold that thought—those would be the hounds."

Hush gives a weary smile. "They are coming for you—but not in the way you think. Hubris... is amusing when it comes from things who play at god." A dark blade takes shape in her hand. It holds form as the hounds erupt from the trees—a good sign.

Aveline drinks them in. Hush can see it in her eyes—she has caught her unprepared. Dilated pupils unmask fear.

"You haunted us in Rach Na'Schuul," says Aveline. "Hunted. What are you?"

"Timeless." Hush strokes the ears of the hound nearest her. "Some have called me Mother Sin. Others, Devourer of Vice. Even a small handful have called me goddess... It's a matter of perspective, really. But the simplest of answers is—I'm the greatest quisling of them all."

Aveline arches an eyebrow at that.

Hush takes one step toward her—and Aveline flinches. "How weary you must be... Lonely. To have walked the world alone for all these years... I expect it all begins to blur." The hounds entomb her with their size. Hush holds her dagger toward Aveline. "I can help you though—and helping you, helps me. Do you understand?"

Aveline's eyes are white beneath her sway. Hush wonders if she feels it on her neck, the breathing of the hounds—the flimsy barrier between their hunger and her flesh. Or perhaps the dagger entering her chest, or the grass beneath her back as Hush lays her gently by the stream.

"Forgive me." Hush isn't sure to whom she is appealing; it simply sounds like the proper thing to say for having a killed a woman entranced.

She rips the blade from Aveline's silent heart. "They told me, whispered through the shadows you would come. Hounds are loyal beasts—especially to the cloth from which they all were cut. They call me mother and I love them so."

She places a hand atop Aveline's chest and draws her mirkúr through the wound. Imbibes her memories and dreams, her sorrow and her joy. She had a family once, a husband and a boy.

A tear streams from Hush's eye. It's been millennia since last she's cried. She leans in close, whispering, "I will save you all."

Hush rises; from the glade she goes—she has a blade to steal. The hounds bay.

INTERLUDE
LEGACY

Reshaper Year 1895

O uran'an, once great city of the Reshapers, was a ruin. A necropolis of hoarfrost spires like the jagged teeth of dragons. A sick, black essence webbed its way along the streets; it crept up buildings like vines. Its gossamer threads extended from the rotted corpses strewn about. It had left none untouched.

Varésh Lúm-talé stood beneath the archway of the city gate and wept, consumed by memories. This was not the first metropolis or people he had failed. He crept inward despairingly—just one more look. A moment in another monument to his failure, this stain of a legacy.

He wrapped his midnight, feathered wings around himself, though it did little to ward away the early morning chill. There was something angry to the cold, something... old. Familiar.

Varésh closed his eyes and held his nose to the sky. Being the creature, the abomination that he was, he could discern the various energies in the air—arcane or otherwise—with but a sniff. They were more or less of him, after all.

"Mirkúr." But different than the black essence tattooed to the city and the dead. Less a plague. He opened his eyes and trained them on the tallest spire. Even here, perhaps a mile or two away, he could feel the mirkúr's urgency. He unfurled his wings and, with a great flap, took flight.

———

MIRKÚR CHOKED the interior of the spire. Every now and then the energy seemed to hiss, its discontent provoked by the illumination streaming from Varésh's wings. He descended from the topmost balcony, heart thumping, skin like gooseflesh underneath his garb.

There were bodies here, what remained of them at least. The gore had left no ceiling, wall, nor floor untouched. This was where the slaughter had begun, in the halls and chambers of the Reshaperate Spire. Or, at the very least, where the savagery had reached its peak. Varésh pressed on, through the catacombs, and into the depths below.

He touched down in the anteroom; his equilibrium faltered. The world spun in and out of focus momentarily before Varésh was able to steady himself. He took a deep, ragged breath and pressed ahead, crossing overtop the inlay of a black and white raven. Trickster, most believed. Wisdom bringer, Varésh sought to make them see.

Had sought.

The Reshaperate Vaults stood in a hallway wide enough for six to stand abreast. There were nine doors total, the first eight of which stood parallel to one another; the last was further on. Each bore a labyrinth of grooves extending outward from a unique symbol carved in the center of the door. The crests of the eight Reshaperate families. Though they bloomed with light as Varésh passed them by, they remained sealed.

He reached the final door, engraved with the symbol of a raven, wings outstretched. He mimicked the depiction, wispy tendrils of brilliant light—illum—extending from the tips of his wings. The illumination permeated the engraving and the grooves. The door dilated with a groan.

Varésh furled his wings around him like a cloak, light streaming from his feathers to erect a barrier that pushed against the wall of darkness that'd erupted from the vault. Smoke shrieked and crashed against the barricade, forcing Varésh to expend more illum than he would have liked. The onslaught faltered after a minute or two, leaving silence and a white-eyed silhouette.

Varésh approached at a measured pace. He sensed whatever this creature before him was, it would not hurt him. This was just as well because he'd used up an entire wing's worth of illum.

The silhouette hissed bits and pieces of the old Reshaper tongue, though the words were too distorted to discern.

Varésh shook his head. "I do not understand. I am sorry."

The silhouette swirled and, in a rush of smoke, retreated to the back end of the vault. Varésh followed. The silhouette moaned, and he realized its tether to this plane was growing weak; its form was collapsing. He knelt before it, staring into those white eyes, searching for something, someone—a sign, anything. It mewed again and gestured with a wispy thread of a hand to a grimy leather book.

Varésh picked it up. His heart stopped.

A journal. The journal of a friend, of one whom he'd considered a true son.

The silhouette wailed and, in a burst of mirkúr, ceased to be.

Varésh clutched the leather keepsake to his chest, trembling. He opened the journal and read by the light of his wing. Read until he was numb, and the prospect of death seemed to entice him more than did life. His creations, his *children,* were dead. Some worse than dead, puppets dancing to the tune this tainted mirkúr sang.

He looked at the journal. Where ink related fear and the fall of Ouran'an, it also offered hope, desperate as it was, to quell the plague that entropy had wrought. But for this minuscule chance at reclamation, at redemption, to help see the hope in this journal come to fruition, Varésh was going to have to do the eighteenth most moronic thing he had ever done.

But do I have the strength?

A dead voice, a familiar voice, whispered from the shadow of his mind.

Varésh acknowledged the voice with a tiny nod. As always, it was right.

Journal tucked away, he withdrew from the vaults and the city he had failed.

It was time to swim the Temporal Sea.

ACT II

SO MUCH WEIGHT

DEAD

Names held power.

Blood was memory.

Dreams were history made manifest.

Avaria blinked. Before him stood a man. Beyond the man, a tree. Beyond the tree, atop a distant hill, the ruin of a city old.

Brightness—soft and warm. Foreign whispers on the wind and a feeling he had seen this all before. Beside him—hounds composed from threads of light. Three hounds, four now five now six—and a seventh near the tree. Seven, then a single beast beside him, the utmost of its kind.

"You've been asleep," the man said. Wings protruded from his back; midnight feathers tapered into mist. Eyes were placid storms. "Do you know me, boy? Do you know me by name?"

Avaria nodded.

"Speak it," said the man. "Speak it now and give me strength."

"Alerion."

Eyes like storm clouds come alive. Illum snaps like lightning in the night. Blood trickling from his eyes. "I have seen this all before."

"Seen what?"

Alerion beckoned with an outstretched hand. "Drink of me and see."

Avaria held his ground. "Show me here."

"I cannot." Alerion advanced. "This place is but a moment in a time long dead and we are naught but ghosts." He stopped short of the snarling hound. "Please—drink of me and *see*."

So Avaria did,

and the meadow

turned

to

ash—but the tree *endured*.

Come, it beckoned with a groaning branch.

Avaria indulged the ancient tree. The sky rained blood; he was alone now in the ruin of this place.

There were trees here once, the lone tree said. *They called me Lost.*

And now? Avaria ran his hand along the gnarled bark.

Memory, said the tree. *Sometimes Sorrow, sometimes Thorn.*

Avaria pressed his forehead to the tree. *And what do you prefer?*

The tree thrummed. *No one... has ever asked me that.* It caressed Avaria with a gentle branch. *Call me... Bringer. Yes, I would like that very much. Bringer...* The name lingered in the bloody air. It held benevolent mystique; it served to ease Avaria's mind as he melded with the tree

and woke with ringing in his ears,

black fire in his chest,

red snow beneath his back.

Find me, Bringer whispered on the wind.

Find her, Alerion whispered in his mind.

"Find *you...*" Avaria uttered to the night,

to the white eyes

gleaming in the gloom.

———

THERE WAS a warmth to the darkness enfolding the Peaks of Dren. To the cold blanketing Nil-Illúm. Avaria couldn't say what, but it served to his ease his blood, to help him focus on the fact he wasn't dead—not anymore. Not anymore. He was alive. No longer dead—alive like the wisps in the lamps that lit the street. Alive, with breath in his lungs and pain in his heart. Pain —So. Much. Pain.

"Your steps are confident for a man returned from death."

Avaria looked at Erath. "Tell me again—how long?"

"Two months."

"Two months..." Avaria massaged the spot between his eyes. "How...?"

"I was hoping you might tell me," Erath said.

Avaria shrugged. They walked. It snowed. The lamps fell blue from green and the world was silent.

"How did you find me?"

Erath shrugged. "Just... a feeling?" She looked more uncertain than she sounded. She frowned. "Feeling—how are you feeling?"

Three days since she'd found him in the snow.

"Like..." His throat itched with thirst. His mind buzzed like summer flies. Find me. Find her. Find you. "A fragment of a puzzle searching for its kin." Alerion. Blood rain. Bringer—

Hand to his chest. Scar, screaming, pain like needles kissing eyes. Madness grinning in his mind. His mother grinning like the dead—grinning like the dead and laughing like a storm. His mother—dead.

Dead.

Dead.

DEAD.

"She's dead..." he whispered. Felt a hand on his. "My mother."

Dead like all the light in Ulm.

Dead like all the light in Helveden.

Dead.

"We lost a lot that night," said Erath. "Flesh and blood and brick and stone."

"Where is it now—where are *they* now?" Sinhounds. Geph. Avaria ached to rip the beast to bits, tear them all to shreds. Abominations like a fucking cancer in the mouth. Bile at the memory of that grin stretched across his mother's face—Avaria retched. A knot of agony in his head—had she ever really *been?* Retched sour blood. Sickness—this was what it tasted like to be alive. Pungent iron.

"Te Mirkvahíl," Avaria growled.

"Is dead," Erath said.

"Can't be. Sinhounds running wild..."

"Te Mirkvahíl *is dead*," Erath said. "Trust me. This... this is something else."

Avaria processed what she'd said. "What is it?"

"You need to rest," said Erath, but Avaria waved her off.

"*You need,*" said a measured voice inside his head, "*to take a breath and grieve. Acting on emotion, on the numbness and the shock, will lead you anywhere but straight.*"

Half-mechanically, Avaria forsook the streets of Nil-Illúm for trees. Trees and weeping shadows, Erath following like a woman dragged along by a crazed longhound on a leash.

"Where"—she yelped, tripping over the log Avaria had leapt; kept her balance—"are you going?"

To scream at dead stars. "To grieve."

Leave him be. Leave him to his misery and his rage.

A flash of light. Spectral baying in his wake.

Erath cursed.

Avaria ran.

———

SHE STOOD there in the glade. The girl of burnt paper flesh and dead moon eyes. Hair like strands of snow and moonlight. Expecting him. Seeking him. Avaria could feel it in his blood, that coldness bonding them. Swaying him, much as it had those months ago in the woods.

"You live." She beckoned with an outstretched hand.

He approached. Stopped. "My mother's dead."

"I know. I can feel it, see it in your memories. I am sorry."

"If you can see my memories—"

"I can see what you experienced in The In Between before you woke," said the girl. "I would ask about Alerion, but your words would be of little help. I would ask about the tree—"

"But my words would be of little help." Avaria narrowed his eyes. "They're familiar to you, aren't they? Bringer and Alerion?" A hint of courage blossomed in his chest. "Am *I* familiar to you? Were we predestined for this meeting, and the last?"

She touched his cheek. Her hand was ice. "Yes."

"Is Te Mirkvahíl dead?"

"Yes."

She was mist and shadow, whispers on the wind.

Gone—as everything he'd known was gone. Desperate questions in the wake of ruin. Who was she? What was she? What was *he*? That knot inside his head—had has mother ever really *been* or had he been the plaything for monstrosities and horror from the start? What was anything—what was the point? What was the point when everything was gone and fucking...

dead.

He fell to his knees. Punched the ground, punched through snow until his hand was numb with cold and maybe pain. Wept a thousand tears of rage and woe, a thousand more for spirits lost, dead and gone. Dead and gone, just like his mother.

Dead.

Gone.

SPELL

Time was still. To Erath, at least. Had been for the past two months. So much lost, so many questions raised. She stared into the night sky, at the vast sea of stars, wondering if perhaps they might be the eyes of something monstrous, watching the chaos unfold. Were they naught but playthings?

Two months. No sign of Aveline since they'd gone their separate ways. Avaria Norrith, returned from the dead. Dren, *finally* dead; Erath had seen to that herself. It tugged at her even now, had every day for the past two months. It'd been surprisingly easy to kill him, maybe even a bit... satisfying. What a wretched thought—but what a wretched, twisted thing he'd been. She closed her eyes and breathed deep the chill air, falling into memory.

Wisplit snow and dead trees.

Stillness in the air.

Dren, hands clasped behind his back, dragging limp wings. A ruin rearing up behind him. "You return," he said. "Why?"

"I'm not satisfied with simplicities," Erath said. "You would sacrifice a world to save it, as you said—why? What was so broken about this world that it required saving, *destruction*? I want the truth, Dren. The *entire* truth."

"We are but motes of dust," Dren said. "Grains of sand on a vast beach. Insignificant." He sighed. "I can show you, but you'll not like what you learn. It might even break you."

"I'm already broken," Erath said.

"Aren't we all?" Dren motioned with his hand. "Come."

He led her into the ruin. Deeper yet, to a chamber with the tarnished inlay of a winged trio on the floor. Each was cloaked. Curiosity bloomed in Erath—she had seen these figures before, on the henges in the Wisplands. At the center of the chamber hovered a sphere. Dren touched it with his index finger and a brilliant blue light bloomed within, growing brighter.

"This," he said, "is the Fountainhead, the world from which all others are born." He traced the air; smaller spheres manifested, each connected to the Fountainhead by a strand of light. From those smaller spheres grew orbs of lesser size, tethered to their origins by luminescent threads. "These are the Nexuses and their respective Scions. From the Fountainhead, Nexus worlds; from the Nexuses, Scions—do you understand?"

"A multiverse," said Erath. "You're saying we exist in a multiverse."

Dren nodded.

"But how does any of this relate to temporal alteration?"

"Temporal alteration is the manner by which each new world is created. Every world is a variation of another," Dren said. "You wonder how I could possibly know this..." He closed his eyes. "I have tried many times before—and each time, I have failed. So many names. So many children. So much *death*. My legacy, my child, is destruction, failure."

"You still haven't answered my question," Erath said. "What was so broken about this world that it required your definition of saving?"

Dren opened his eyes. "Not just this world—*all* worlds. I thought if I could return to the Fountainhead—no... travel *beyond* the Fountainhead—I might be able to prevent any of this from ever happening. Fold the worlds, as it were, by quelling madness."

Erath glanced at the inlay, then back at Dren. "Does it have anything to do with them? Those figures?"

"Everything," Dren uttered. He waved his hand and, to Erath's horror and disgust, manifested The Raven's Rage. "I was a fool, my child. I cannot be trusted; I am weak." He waved his hand again and the blade shattered, leaving a silhouette of energy. "She will come for me. Come for *this*. The blade itself is useless—it's the energy she wants. Take it."

Erath took a step back. "Who is *she*? I... why give this to me?" What did Dren expect *her* to do with... with whatever power this was? "I'm nothing. I'm useless."

Dren waved his hand a third time and the energy—*energies* —wreathed Erath, embraced her. "You, dear child, are *not* useless. You are everything. This will help you see. Take it. Kill me. Flee."

The memory fizzled; Erath found herself looking up at the stars. Two months and she still hadn't a clue what anything meant. Hadn't an inkling as to how to use the energies Dren had gifted her, let alone who "She" was.

Tickle in her ear. Stupid buzzing. Smacked at the phantom bug thing, whatever it was. More buzzing. Whispers. She was going mad, fuck it all. Made sense. World had gone to shit—why shouldn't she?

"*Help.*"

Erath started. She'd heard that clearly, hadn't she? A voice asking for help. She looked about. Snow, trees, darkness. Not a soul to be seen.

"*Help... me.*"

Okay. She had *definitely* heard that. In her head? Somewhere nearby? A shift in the atmosphere, a twinkle, a fold of light. She grasped at it, catching only air. Another blink—southward. She followed. Through a frosted copse to a clearing and an overlook below which stretched a meadow vast. For a moment Erath wondered what it might be like to walk the grass, to feel the sunlight kiss her flesh. So many years... She could scarcely recall the sensation.

"*Help.*"

The voice snapped her from her trance. It had grown louder without a doubt, but still there was nothing and no one to whom the phantom voice belonged. She frowned, eyes narrowed, and swiped at the air with her index finger. A twist of light, a throng of screams, gone as quickly as they'd come. Erath stood motionless, mouth agape, adrenaline rushing through her like a spring stream. Again—more screams, distant, disembodied, indiscernible cries. What in the Raven's name had she stumbled across? Erath had long lost her ability to wield illum—what was this?

"Dren," she whispered. Those energies with which he'd wreathed her... She traced the air a third time, forming the letter S. Myriad pictures snapped across her mind, too quickly for Erath to make any sense of what she saw. Maybe there was a method to all this madness. Seeing things, hearing distant voices —had she tore through the seams which kept the worlds apart? A crazy thought, and yet...

"Show me, uh..." Gods, what did she want to see? "Spring. A century and a half ago." She traced the letter S once more—and rivulets of color dripped from the sky, as if to erase the present and manifest the past. Gone was night, were snow and darkness; here bloomed blades of green and rainbow flowers. A blue sky and sunlight. Erath looked at her hands—they retained their paleness, but the world around her was so much more. She stared, wide-eyed, body tingling, warmth blooming in her chest, just atop her heart. She'd all but forgotten what *this* looked like.

And then it was gone, in a flash of light, and motes of luminescence scattered to the wind, leaving Erath alone with the snow and the stars and her thoughts. If only Aveline were here. Maybe she'd have an idea of what any of this was. Fuck it all, if only Dren had *told her what it was...* Miserable winged bastard. She chewed her lip. There *was* one other she might ask, and he was the wisest man Erath knew, had ever known.

———

ALMOST THREE MONTHS since Leru's death. How slow time seemed to have moved since then. Agonizing. Cold. Like Fenrin's memories. Leru, spirit dwelling somewhere with her sister, Alor. Fenrin heaved a sigh to the lamplit streets; he walked them every night in thought, had for years, so many he'd lost count. Shortly before Alor's death. Murder. He thought of his daughters in their infancy, of the days they were born, and longed for the innocence of such moments. The world was a dark place. Sad. Sorry. Fenrin was the utmost of his kind in this regard, walking cloaked in darkness, in the knowledge he and he alone had been untouched by the Burn. Unsullied while his people were confined to rock and snow and shadow. What a wretched life.

Nil-Illúm was still and silent save his footsteps and his clouded breath. Save the occasional rustling of leaves or the crowing of night fowl. Eerie, that. The world. On edge these last two months since Helveden's fall. Sinhounds. Fenrin shook his head; they'd left none alive. A city so large, yet not a soul had survived.

Unless, he thought, *one counts the prince.* Strange prince. Prince of Misery he was known as here in Nil-Illúm. Lord of Sorrow, Prince of Woe, the list went on and on. Not a slight, but sympathy. Fenrin knew his story well—a babe discovered in the snow, kept and cared for by the late queen as her own. Another sigh, and a prayer for the many dead from the realm from which his daughter's murderers had come. Perhaps this was penance, not that Fenrin would have wished such atrocities upon the city and her people. They were not responsible for Alor's death; that had been a select few—and *they* had paid dearly. For a half second, Fenrin thirsted for blood, but the craving passed as quickly as it had come; he was not that man, that monster anymore.

But maybe I ought to be. Things were mad. Maybe monsters were necessary. Maybe only monsters could fight monsters. What was the old saying? From chaos, law. Dren had taught him that; Dren was dead, had gone mad ages ago. Fenrin had seen his memories prior to his death. Temporal alteration. Lieworlds. Fascinating. Horrific, even. Fascinating, nonetheless. He should like to see them. Maybe they held the key to... to what? Rectification? Reclamation? All of that, temporal alteration, the price... seemed far too high, far too risky. And yet... *From chaos, law.* Gods knew this was a lawless world, growing less by the day.

He was in the courtyard, now, of his home, a mountain manor. At the center stood those triptych effigies, winged and cloaked. They had been here since before Fenrin and his people had come to be, so said Dren. Creators. He took the walkway with measured steps, breathing the chill air. Shadowed foot-steps, though, drew his eyes, and from the trees to his left came a rather frazzled looking woman.

Fenrin cocked an eyebrow. "Never one for the straightforward path, my girl."

"I... Something—spell," said Erath hastily. "I did *something*. Saw, heard things." She doubled over, catching her breath, then rose to meet his eyes. "Has to do with Dren."

Fenrin narrowed his eyes. "What of him?"

Erath looked frantically about. "I... I think I'm *seeing* his memories and..." She looked at Fenrin unblinkingly, such fear in those stark white eyes. "It has to do with The Raven's Rage."

———

THEY SAT in Fenrin's study, Erath in a chair by the window, Fenrin at his desk. Silence reigned, had for some minutes as Fenrin went through everything that Erath had relayed about Dren, The Raven's Rage, the Burn, and this newfound ability of hers. Truthfully, it was a lot to take in, but Fenrin had time. Gods knew he had *so much time.*

"I'm not mad," he said. "If you were worried. Not at you, at least." He sighed. "I suppose I shouldn't be surprised about Dren, yet I am... and am not at the same time, if that makes any sense." Erath nodded. "First things first—*you* now wield the power, the energies that resided in The Raven's Rage."

Again, Erath nodded. "But I don't know what it is."

"Radich, I would venture," Fenrin said. "Possibility. The power wielded by the person Dren was *before* he was Dren. This Varésh Lúm-Talé, whomever he was. *Whatever he was.*"

"Do you think I'm seeing his memories?" Erath asked. "Hearing them?"

"With radich, anything is possible," said Fenrin. "Or so I understand. As I have never wielded the energy, I cannot say for certain." He frowned. "Did he mention anything more of this *She*?"

Erath shook her head. "He seemed afraid of whatever *She* was, *is*. Said he couldn't be trusted, so he bestowed"—she gestured wildly—"upon me, the lot of good that's going to do. I have no idea what I'm doing. I haven't for ages."

"If it makes you feel better," Fenrin said, "neither do I. I simply take things one day at a time." There was a twinkle in her eyes. Something on the tip of her tongue. "Ask your question."

"I'm afraid it might be rude," Erath said, averting his gaze.

Fenrin stood and approached. He knelt before her, hands on her shoulders, and looked her in the eyes. "Whatever the question, it's important. Please, Erath—ask me."

She heaved a ragged sigh. "You were untouched by the Burn, yet you dwell in the darkness of the Peaks as do the rest of the drenarians. Why? Why not be free?"

He caressed her cheek. "There is no freedom for me when the rest of my people are in chains. I am not free until we *all* are free, however long that may take. I'm not going anywhere, Erath."

She closed her eyes a moment, swallowing; he could tell she'd forced back tears. She opened her eyes. "What do I do? What do *we* do? Sinhounds and this thing, this *She* running amok. This power of mine, if you can even call it that. *What* is happening?"

"I'm not sure," Fenrin said. An honest answer. "We might start with the prince you rescued from the snow. Dead, now quite alive—not a feat attainable by many."

"He's lost so much," Erath said. "His mother."

"Ahnil Norrith was a noble woman," Fenrin said. "Her

passing pains me, as does Helveden's ruin. It disturbs me too. Sinhounds not bound to the will of Te Mirkvahíl—to what, then?"

"As you said, my king," Erath said. "We might start with the prince."

PARABLE

Day. Night. In the Peaks it was all the same; the persistent darkness made it impossible to tell, made it feel like time had all but slowed. So much on his mind. His mother. Virtuoso Khal. Norema. Helveden. Even strange Nameless Head, whom Avaria presumed dead. Never had gotten his name, never had gotten his story. Had he found what he was looking for in Rach Na'Schuul? Hard to say as Avaria had been dead the entire time.

His thoughts shifted to—could he even call it a dream? Whatever it was he'd experienced before waking in the snow. Alerion. Bringer. Find Bringer. Find a woman. Find himself. Seemed clear as day yet muddled all the same. He wished Geph was here, first so he could ring the bastard's neck, maybe gouge his eyes out based on what he'd seen, then to have him help Avaria make sense of all this shit. Geph had always been good at that, interpreting dreams.

"What happened, Geph?" Avaria murmured to the trees. Walking helped; he got antsy if he sat still for too long. "What I saw... was that really you?" Could have been; there was a lot Avaria didn't know about the longhound—sinhound?—and it made him wonder what secrets Geph might have been keeping. Had his kind been something more at one point? Gods, but his chest ached. *Everything* ached, outward, inward to the depths of his being. Felt like vines constricting his heart, vines with knives that liked to twist in wounds.

Mother's grin.

Norema's corpse.

He started, leaned against a tree, feeling winded, exhausted.

Any of you, he thought wearily. To his sinhounds or whatever thing now lurked within. *Please. Just...* He heaved a ragged sigh, on the cusp of sobbing for the second time in what, an hour or two? How the hell was any of this real? Was this what it had been like as a babe, alone in the snow and trees? Was this what utter helplessness felt like? Cold and hollow. Dark. Avaria closed his eyes—where had he come from? The thought had grazed his mind a few times over the years, but only now did it linger, festering like an open wound, *begging* for attention. Where. What. Why. Where had he come from? What was he? Why was he here? Surely the universe would see fit to answer these questions after subjecting him to such a torturous life, a hellish fuck-knew-how-many weeks since he'd departed Helveden looking for that sword. He clung to the tree as the tears came, as sobs racked his body.

"Mama..."

But that safety was gone. Dead, lingering only as a maddened grin stretched wide across his mind. Haunting every step he took and everything he dreamt.

"You know what you must do," said a voice. Commanding, soft. Avaria looked around, realized it was in his head. *"Stand*

up, Avaria Norrith. Stand up, Prince of Ariath. It would pain your mother to see you so."

He pushed himself to stand straight, tall; wiped his tears away with his arm. *You spoke to me the other day,* he said. *I saw you in my dream, whatever it was. You were beside me as I faced Alerion.* A hound of light. *What are you? By what name do I call you?*

"I am Jor, the allhound," it said, "and when last we truly spoke you were but a boy. Much has changed since then; dying has a way of, shall we say, resetting things. In dying, in rebirth, you freed me, made the seven whole."

Sins. Seven sins, you mean, Avaria said. *The worst of me.*

"No," said Jor. "It is not so black and white as that. Sin—true sin—is not indicative of evil, nor is it a representation of your worst self, just as true honor is not indicative of good intent. Sinhounds and honorhounds are merely two sides of the same coin."

What are allhounds?

"We are the balance," Jor said. "The middle ground."

I see, Avaria said, trying to comprehend it all. *What more of me do you know?*

"Nothing you don't already know yourself," Jor said. "What mysteries remain, we shall uncover together in due time—and I think you know where all roads lead."

Banerowos, Avaria uttered. *Dead city of a dead race. So many times, I saw it, walked it in my dreams. Never thought that it was real. Not until...* Images flashed across his mind. The tower. The descent. Alerésh. Schisms in continuity. A city vast and bright; a city dead, snow-draped ruin and a symphony of shrieks. *The answers are all there.* He could feel it in his bones, in the tingling of his heart. The howling of his mind, something buried yearning to break free.

"Her," he murmured. That girl of burnt paper flesh. He suddenly yearned for her presence, that connection. Everything had been predestined. "Luminíl." The name came to his lips, escaped his tongue of its own volition. Her name was Luminíl. To the darkness and the cold, he whispered, "Find me."

Then, he sat and waited.

———

LUMINÍL HAD SEEN NO FURTHER than this moment. Everything from here on out was fate's design. She found the Prince of Woe, as the drenarians had taken to calling him, in a copse, leaning back against a tree. He met her with an unblinking stare.

"You told me my words would be of little use to you," he said, standing to his full height. "But you, Luminíl—yes, I know your name—have words that would be of great use to me. I can feel it." He tapped his skull. "You claim to have seen what I experienced in The In Between—but did you see *everything*? My escape through the labyrinth of my mind? A girl in the forest 'neath a tree—"

"What girl?" Luminíl asked. "What tree?" Trees. So many trees.

"Beneath a tree of corpses strung to dance the dance of death," Avaria said. "Garbed in black. Eyes like the abyss. Like you—but *not* you." He paced. Muttered to himself. "...Dreams and memories braid together with those belonging to a monster." Looked at Luminíl. "Never saw that tree, never saw that forest around Banerowos in my life, in my dreams. I felt her fear as if it were my own. She—whatever *she* is—possessed my corpse in Rach Na'Schuul. I need answers."

"She calls herself Hush," said Luminíl. "And I loved her

once. She will not stop, and I cannot rest until she is stopped—but she is strong. Desperate. And desperate people do monstrous things." She averted Avaria's gaze. "So much horror..."

If you had not left her...

If you had helped her, not tormented her...

Gods. Was Luminíl to blame? Had she driven Hush mad all those millennia ago atop the ruins of Banerowos? *No,* she thought. *Hush was mad long before that.* But maybe Luminíl had been the straw that broke the camel's back. Maybe she had snapped Hush beyond rectification.

"What does she want?" Avaria asked.

"Me," Luminíl said. "Reclamation. We are all of us prey to the world maker parable. This"—she held her arms out wide—"was wrought by Hush, Alerion, and myself, and damn it all if we three are not monsters."

She expected shock of a sort from Avaria, yet he remained calm; something in him had changed. *He* had changed consistently over the months; Luminíl yearned to know why. He was more than he seemed.

"Power corrupts. A small taste is toxic, seductive. Especially destructive when wielded by liars," she said. "Hush betrayed me, tainted me; as long as she roams, as long as she is awake, so too am I."

"You seem exhausted," Avaria said. "And I'm not just saying that."

"You are different," Luminíl said. "Grieving yet composed. What changed?"

"I died," Avaria said, "and it released my allhound. Restored internal balance."

Allhounds were rare, especially now, though their numbers once had been great. That was millennia ago, however, during the time of the Reshapers. Luminíl had interacted with them scarcely, but their center, their equilibrium, was renowned.

"You will need that balance if you are to confront Hush," Luminíl said. "If *we* are to confront her. She is mad; whatever means to reclamation she seeks is sure to be desperate, destructive."

"Temporal alteration," Avaria said. "Only thing that would make sense."

Luminíl nodded. "Decidedly desperate and destructive, especially if the whispers are true." Avaria tilted his head. "Lieworlds. A multiverse as some would say. New realities wrought through changes to the past."

Avaria furrowed his brow, tense his jaw. "...Might explain things. Alerésh, Varésh, Alerion, and another—different, yet so similar." He looked at Luminíl. "If what you say is true then... might they all be one and the same?"

Luminíl sneered at the mention of Varésh. "In a manner of speaking. What you must understand is Varésh and Alerion are —were two very different people. As I said, power is seductive, corruptive; Varésh murdered Alerion and wore him as a guise. Alerésh is nothing more than a sorry abomination—and very much dead. I found his corpse in Rach Na'Schuul."

Silence. Calm snow. Avaria's chest rose and fell slowly as he contemplated what she had said. He was so very different, almost unnervingly so. "What happens now?" he asked.

"We seek Hush," said Luminíl, "and put a stop to her madness lest she break the world." Footsteps. She spun about— the drenarian king and a young drenarian woman. Familiar... Luminíl breathed deeply, narrowed her eyes. Familiar and wielding something great, wild. Dangerous.

They stopped short of Luminíl. The king regarded her with bright silver eyes; he kneeled, motioning for the young woman to do so as well. They bowed their heads. "Great Luminíl," he said. "We are humbled by your presence."

Gods but it had been *ages* since someone had referred to her as such. Honorifics were... Well. Used far too liberally in reference to far too many monstrous people. But him, this drenarian—king was befitting.

"Rise," Luminíl said. "Your respect is admirable, but you need not refer to me as such." She cocked her head. How had he known her—

Dren. Of course. She eyed this king. More than what he seemed.

"I am Fenrin," he said, he and his companion rising. "And this is Erath." He met Avaria's eyes. "I am glad to see you well, all things considered." Did not wait for a response; looked from Avaria to Luminíl and back. "There are matters I would discuss in the safety of Nil-Illúm."

There were ears everywhere. Wicked eyes. The trees watched silently. Hush was mistress of the night, of shadows, shade, and silhouette—she would learn of things eventually. As such, Luminíl cared little where they spoke. She gave a small nod.

"As you wish."

———

Judging by Avaria's yawn, it was late when they had caught each other up on everything. Allhounds. Radich. The potential for Erath to see Dren's memories, to bend time recollectively. Hush. The many lies of Varésh Lúm-talé. What a mess. What an absolute, chaotic mess. Not that he was surprised. Everything was out of sorts, had been for a while, so why not make it even fucking crazier?

"Breathe," Jor said in Avaria's mind.

Trying.

"I learned a saying," Jor said. *"Remembered, rather, and I think it pertinent to the situation, to the world at large—from chaos, law. Do you understand?"*

Familiar words, though Avaria swore he had never heard such an aphorism. *From madness comes order, or something along those lines,* he thought. *But how strong a hold must pandemonium have before it finally relents, before the balance shifts and peace prevails?*

"In this case? Quite strong," Jor said. *"This thing, this Hush..."* He trailed off. *"She is entropy. Desperation. She is* the source— the mother *of mirkúr."* Luminíl had been clear as day about that. Hush—the Vulture. The thought made him cold. Memories flashed; darkness in a dead wood. She had scraped his mind; in doing so, however, she had let him into hers. New bits and pieces had arisen in the last several hours.

"All roads, it seems, lead to Banerowos," said Fenrin after a time. So much silence. Pensive. "What remains of it at least." He acknowledged them all unblinkingly. "The way is long—I have been there once myself." Drew a look from Erath. "As the sunlight stings my kind, I propose an alternative route—Underlight."

What the fuck was Underlight?

"Through Gil'an Mor, City of Hounds," Luminíl murmured. She sounded less than thrilled. "Dead city of a dying race. Dangerous. Hush is the mother of sinhounds."

Geph. Sinhound? How? So many questions. Bastard hound. Was he alive? Hounds. Strange beasts. Existed internally and externally—how? So. Many. Questions. Maybe Gil'an Mor would lead to Geph; maybe he could save Geph or... something. Avaria rubbed the spot between his eyes and sighed.

"Chaos squeezes tighter yet," said Jor.

No shit. Know anything of Gil'an Mor?

"Dangerous. Old."

How informative.

"You said we seek Hush," Avaria said to Luminíl. "But the way it sounds? We're luring her—to the genesis and the end. The genesis *of* her end." Poetic, that. Sad. What a sad thing Hush was. What sad things they *all* were, immortals and mortals alike.

"I imprisoned her there once," Luminíl said. "I will do so again—permanently." Permanence was a scary thing, especially, as Avaria had come to learn, it meant jack shit when things saw fit to resurrect. Luminíl looked at Erath. "You are the key—your radich."

Erath swallowed. "That's reassuring." She yawned; Avaria yawned.

"For now, though, sleep," said Luminíl. "The journey ahead is long."

"You mean for us to leave tomorrow?" Avaria asked, and Luminíl gave a brief nod. "Right then. Sleep."

———

Blink.

Ouran was, and the world was. He stood in tall grass, gold beneath the sun; a crisp breeze swayed the feathers of his wings. In the distance he saw snowcapped mountains, and the shadow of a memory said that that was where he had to go.

He stretched his wings, sore with the ache of sleep; he could tell that they had not been used for some time. The breeze knocked his hood back; the cool air against his face was refreshing and it made his beak tingle—the sky called to him. He tried to flap his wings but could not, so he walked.

And walked.

The world was placid. Thick wispy threads of light flittered through the air and he watched them, cocked his head as they descended toward him. They had eyes and mouths, their bodies were translucent and encasing orbs of light.

Memory pulsed. They were Indrisori eels, carriers of light—the sheep to his people's shepherds.

Another pulse: where were his people—who were his people? Ouran waited for a third throb to present the answers, but none came. Perhaps they would later.

He saw trees on his journey toward the mountains. Their flowers bloomed like white stars and the eels followed him like hungry cats, expecting him to lead them to a bowl of warm milk. He ran a gentle talon through his feathers, subduing an itch above his eyes, only for it to retreat down to his wings.

Fly. He strained to flap.

Fly. His great wings twitched.

Fly. With one massive buffet he ascended.

And ascended further yet.

This place, this world... it looked so different from this height, like a painting or a pastel piece on paper. The landscape swayed and swirled beneath the breeze and Ouran shot forward with another beat of his wings, the Indrisori eels at his heels.

The plains below gave way to copses small and large; then to a lake, still as death; and finally, plains again, these littered sporadically with trees. Ouran thought of his people again; he thought of people in general, and of fauna. Where had they all gone off to—why was this beautiful place so still?

Ouran flew straight for hours. At dusk he descended into a valley that spoke of ages long passed. Buried underneath the grass and dried out weeds he saw the rusted remnants of train tracks. Trains, memory reminded him, had not been used for thousands of years, since the last of the humans had gone extinct.

He saw the carcasses of great locomotives, some electric, others undoubtedly steam. This place was a graveyard, a wasteland for the old and unnecessary things of the world. There were automobiles and airplanes too. Maybe, he thought, this place had once been a museum of sorts; he could make out the faint remnants of a structural base.

Much later he settled in for the night against the base of a tree. The eels revolved around him as if he were a planet. His wings were drawn about him like a cloak; his hood was pulled past his eyes. Stars blinked, and he watched a volley race across the sky.

Ouran closed his eyes to the night and dreamt of snow, of stars reflecting in the snow, of beams of light ascending from the earth and rocks.

And darkness.

———

Twilight.

A series of cerebral pulses shook Ouran from sleep, and for a while he stared at the distant peaks that he must reach. They were called Phantaxis: The Door to Heaven, the Indrisori lands. "Come and know," they whispered on the breeze. This far out he could smell the snow and rock. They were memories, but of what?

Another pulse informed him he had sought Phantaxis before. A second and third—these painful, like his skull was being squeezed—told him that his people, the Indrisori, the

Celestials, were there and awaiting his arrival. They had to be, for their time on Indris was coming to its end.

Thunder shook the cloudless sky; the tree trunk buzzed against his back. Instinctively Ouran started to his feet and took to the wind. He rode the current north amidst the booms and intermittent burst of stars, the eels mewing at the bedlam. They snaked around his arms, quivering, their light flickering. Ouran picked up speed, and the faster he went the less the eels' light became, until they were translucent, slumbering shells.

At dawn he touched down in the gray corpse of a once proud city.

Pulse.

His city.

He walked at a measured pace, wings half-cocked. The breeze of the world remained here too, slipping through old windows and doorways, through cracks and crevices—a dirge of days long past, a specter.

Clank.

He froze.

Clank. Clink.

He looked about, talons splayed.

The sounds came again, louder, closer, more.

Ouran ascended with a flap and took perch on the edge of a ruined tower. A couple hundred feet below the sounders manifested, dragging rusted limbs around street corners and over debris. They bore his image, rusted, wings mangled, twisting all directions. Their heads groaned as they scanned for Ouran, so he assumed, and shrieks like metal scraping metal slipped between their beaks.

"Let our earthen children cleanse the damned," said a voice in the center of his mind. Images flashed: forges and foundries, figures of great height; threads of light erupting from the tips of silver swords, ricocheting off tower shields of glass. A rebellion. The figures in the pictures screeched and Ouran tottered from his perch, dazed by their refrain. His wings went numb; it was a hand of trembling talons gripping the perch that kept him from plummeting to the street. He shook away the strange fatigue and hoisted himself up and in to sit on a ledge, back to the wall, cloaked by his wings.

His eyes fell shut, and once again Ouran dreamed of the mountains Phantaxis and his people awaiting his arrival. He was their king, and he must be the one to first set foot into Heaven, the Indrisori realm. He saw beams of blue, wreathed in a flurry of snow; beyond them a window into green pastures; in those pastures stood and beckoned figures wrought from wind— no! They were the creators of the wind.

Stars. Snow.

Ouran blinked the dreams away, greeted by the white dusk and the mountain breeze. His feathers were frosted, and icicles hung from the tip of his beak. He snapped them off and pushed himself to his feet, wings spread. The eels, still coiled around his arms, had regrown a morsel of their light, it like the wool of the sheep of old, infinite.

"Come and know." The wind's words were taunting now. "Come and see."

Ouran flapped and fled this place, this city of dead metal and ruin. Through the trees he went, to the mountain's base, and up its face. A cry escaped his beak, like a dragon woke from sleep. Gray and white was all he saw as he ascended, and soon just white, the cold chaos of the world engulfing him as memory surged and nearly shook him from the sky.

He landed on a small cliff, drawing on the eels' light, what they could offer at least, to steady his mind. More constructs, more technology; Indrisori brand he now knew. He saw his people struck down by their fabricated twins, turned to ash by light, carved for supper by swords.

Ouran pushed himself to complete the ascent, to reach the highest peak, which he found was not incredibly high so much as it was a gradual northward incline. He touched down on the snowcapped rock and hurried toward the cave mouth yards away. It yawned like a leviathan, wide enough to fit perhaps one hundred figures abreast.

Silence greeted him inside and he was reminded momentarily of the stillness he had found in the plains. It was done away by a violent tremor and a loud atmospheric crack. Behind him stars crashed against Phantaxis—the end was near.

Again, he hurried, coming to the center of this barren cave in minutes. An archway reared before him, seven hovering diamonds of varying size, and before it a console of sorts—a lightway marker. And his people were not here. Ouran clucked, perturbed.

"Again, the Eel Lord enters lightless," hissed the cave, hissed something in the cave. "Like so many times before, and forever shall it be."

Light javelined toward him from the shadows. Shock kept him from crying out as his wings fell clean away; the brilliance had cauterized the stumps. He leapt to one side as the burst came again, the hiss fluctuating, now a sonorous cackle.

The assailant leapt from hiding, a monstrous metal-flesh amalgamation—a cyborg, it would have been called centuries ago. It swung its great blade in arches, choreographing the light, making the destructive essence dance before it wound toward Ouran and caught him square in the chest.

Images came hazy as he writhed, grew fuller as the writhing turned to spasms.

"When you attempt to play god, Eel Lord, sometimes you create monsters."

The amalgam vaulted toward him. It froze halfway and sputtered, leaking something black and foul. And then it crumbled to the floor, one eye blinking erratically. "I-I—Indris-ori-ori—i-Ind—risori haaaiiiillll..."

It powered down, dead by the unknown.

No, Ouran realized, discerning a thin barrier between them, projected weakly by the eels around his arms. They mewed, their light pulsating—it was his key away from this beautiful, awful world he had called home.

He stood, groaning, feathers hissing with snuffed smoke. The lightway marker blinked, ready to accept the eels' light as payment for an egress. Ouran held his arms above the orb and the light streamed forth, and the archway shimmered with a picture of the Indrisori land beyond.

Ouran stepped toward it, into it, and through it—but he had not gone anywhere.

And he shrieked like a creature butchered in the night as the memories came in full, a tidal wave of chaos. Light snapped, his people screamed, his people turned to wispy motes of luminescence and ascended through the archway as the Indrisori chained him to this place so long ago.

"Those who are not gods, those who are not judges, should not attempt to be what they are not," the Indrisori snarled in his mind.

Ouran saw—he saw himself, sword in hand, blue light cutting down his people under proclamations of impurity. So many turned to ash.

To ash.

To ash.

Ash.

Ash.

Ash

Ash.

Ash.

He sputtered. From the center of his chest emerged a blade, and he heard that horrible metal-flesh whisper in his ear as darkness took him from Phantaxis.

———

Blink.

Ouran was, and the world was. He stood in tall grass, gold beneath the sun; a crisp breeze swayed the feathers of his wings. In the distance he saw snowcapped mountains, and the shadow of a memory said that that was where he had to go.

MONSTERS

Indris was but a distant memory in a dream. Likely dead and gone, as were so many of the things and people Varésh Lúm-talé had known. Destruction was a cruel legacy, unforgiving and relentless. He breathed deeply the air of this place, this underdark, this underlight—*the* Underlight as it was known, as the dead halls whispered. What a wretched place in which to have emerged. Alas, to swim the Temporal Sea was to invite chance. So be it.

Varésh winced, snarled at a snap in the center of his mind. He'd been afraid of that—the Varésh Lúm-talé of this reality yet remained; he would have to take a different name lest the consequence of paradox erode his cognizance and turn him into something rambling and mad. Such was the rule by which the lieworlds were governed.

Ouran, he thought at the pain, this sentient, phantom reaper of identities. For all his power there was still much Varésh—no, *Ouran*—did not understand about temporal alteration and the lieworlds, about the consequence of paradox—mainly the reason for its existence. Why should anyone care about myriad iterations of an individual running amok? Why should the universe give a shit?

"*Because,*" said the voice in his head, "*such a thing breeds chaos.*"

There is much that does, Ouran thought. *Why should it matter?*

"*Still ignorant after all of these years,*" the voice chided. It called itself Alerion; its very existence made Ouran sick for it reminded him of who he had been, was, and always would be. "*Have you learned nothing from the illum network, nothing of and from the lieworlds?*"

I have learned plenty, Ouran thought.

"*Then you would understand the consequence of paradox is only relevant should you encounter the Varésh Lúm-talé of this reality,*" Alerion said. He paused. "*Oh—I see. You* are *aware; you simply choose to wear your given name, your* true *name* as *opposed to running further.*"

The guilt will always call you back, Ouran thought. *Best embrace my sins and seek redemption. Penance, even.* Gods knew he'd done horrible things. Atrocities. Genocide. What a monster. *Maybe this undertaking* is *my penance...* He shook his head. Hell was certainly a place of one's own making.

Ouran walked the darkness at a measured pace, wings furled like a cloak. Dim light emanated from his feathers; strange pastel illumination bled from wispy strands of... something. Ouran reached for one, felt cold and fear as the gossamer thing brushed his hand; shattered memories shrieked across his mind.

"Memories," he murmured. His stomach dropped. "*Souls.*" Gods—what had happened here? He sniffed the old air but discerned nothing he was not already familiar with—illum and mirkúr. Even still, their presence here concerned him.

Do you think it was her? he asked Alerion. *Mirkvahíl?*

"Her or *Luminíl*," Alerion said. "*No telling which. The journal was not clear.*"

It all feels horribly repetitive, Ouran thought. *Seeking the Phoenix and the Vulture.* Hell was history rounding the corner to repeat itself. *A place of my own making.* He shuddered to think of what this reality was like, hoped it wasn't too far gone. Gods knew the lieworlds were a whirl of entropy and law, locked in a constant tug of war; many realities had fallen prey to desolation.

Did this place exist whence we came? Ouran asked.

"*In one way or another, yes,*" Alerion said. As with every-thing, there was much about Alerion that Ouran had yet to comprehend despite their millennia of coexistence. "*Everything is a reflection of itself.*"

Darkness, cold, and hush. Quietus. A labyrinth of a tomb—a tomb of memory. Ouran longed to be free of the despondency, to smell fresh air and taste the open sky—but instinct kept him here beneath the light, drove him deeper into silent madness. *A sign. Anything—point me in the right direction.*

Whatever that was.

———

Te Mirkvahíl has proven to be far more of a problem than Hush had anticipated. When she slew her by the stream, Hush did not foresee the three-month coma and confinement in a labyrinthine mind that would follow. As she ascends the Peaks of Dren she feels... strangely whole—but why? She ruminates a moment, but the answer keeps concealed. Nothing she saw, experienced in three months of sleep sticks out unless one counts the various mental blocks now guarding Te Mirkvahíl's most precious thoughts.

You will tell me all you know, she thinks of the stolen flesh she wears. *They always do.*

A child sprawled atop the rocks. Blanketed in snow. Breathing. Faint yet resolute. In the distance, Ouran'an—the corpse of it at least.

The memory fades. Hush feels pain in her chest, in the depths of her heart—this momentary recollection is hers. But what is the significance? Who is the child? What brought her so near Ouran'an—and when?

"Time and memory are such troubling things," an inner voice opines. This thing too is familiar; Hush is no stranger to voices in her head.

Which one are you? So many—too many to keep track of.

"The worst one." Such certainty. It fails to give a name—a silent challenge.

And where have you been all this time?

"Here. Caged in the abyss. Waiting..."

Waiting. For how long, Hush wonders, and for what?

"You were always a fan of puzzles—you have plenty of pieces to put into place."

Another challenge. So many questions.

"Keep it together, now." Or else.

Silence. Cold air on stolen flesh. An ache in the center of her mind. The difficulty of this undertaking has increased—and that is saying quite a lot as temporal alteration on the scale that Hush envisions is by no means guaranteed. The reiteration of this fact sends shivers up her spine; the notion of a life sans Luminíl brings tears to Hush's eyes, forms a lump in her throat.

Walk. Do not think. Just walk.

The shadows whisper of a temporal rift. Small, but significant, nonetheless.

A name rides the darkened mountain wind.

Hush smiles.

———

DREAMS ARE FILLED WITH BEAUTY. To Hush, that is what defines them—the absolute surrealness of a pale sky and the warmth of her beloved's hand. But Hush cannot recall when last she had a dream, for her thoughts and reveries are monstrous things. Labyrinthine phantasmagorias at the end of which her lovely Luminíl fades to ash. To smoke. To nothingness. Her nightmares are such that she cannot recall, exactly, how things fell apart.

The voice inside her head laughs. *"Mother Sin. What a name. The irony..."*

Hush knows of what it speaks, of the atrocity so profound she buried it within the darkest corner of her mind. Suppressed it. Feared it—*still* fears it. She shudders, not from the chill of the Peaks or the ever-present darkness nipping at her cheeks, but from the knowledge of a lesson she learned long ago: the guilt will always call you back. And oh, how guilty a thing Hush is. She does not need to know, to remember what she did to taste the lingering iniquity, to feel that harsh, violent tugging at the center of her chest that pulls her toward the past—to the corpse of Banerowos bordered by the Hang-Dead Forest and its myriad restless souls.

"I will fix this," she murmurs—to herself, to Luminíl, and to the world.

Hush does not want to be a monster.

But she is.

Her thoughts drift, drawn to the memory of the boy and the rocks and the snow and the distant ruin of the city Ouran'an. It tugs at her, whispers—but what is the significance? Who is the boy? Hush clenches her hand into a fist, hard enough that her fingernails pierce the flesh of her palm. No blood. Just...something. Whatever it is that sustains her. Smoke and fluid smelling of old rain and rot. A twist of mirkúr.

"Tell me," she whispers. "Please."

The memory fades—now is not the time.

Hush walks.

And walks.

And.

Walks.

Geph thought of his mother and wept as he crossed the old meadow. This horrible place seemed to exhume the sorriest of things, of memories and dreams. Seemed to amplify the guilt and longing and despair. What would she think could she see him now? Sinhound. Murderer. Betrayer. Weakling. To have been so easily swayed by Hush...

But she promised—so much had she promised. Where was she, then? Three months—three months and not a sound, memory, nor scent. Nothing to betray her whereabouts. Did she yet endure?

The question nagged at Geph, for he had headed south of his own volition. Compelled by curiosity, spellbound by the history of Hush; she had, for but a single moment, given him a glimpse inside her mind. Wondrous. Horrifying. Not of his own accord, then. Rather, of and of not. Perhaps it was his very nature—drawn to madness, monstrousness, and misery—

that pushed him onward toward a place called Hang-Dead Forest. A cursed barrier behind which sat the corpse of Banerowos. The first great city to arise; the first to fall. Hush's home.

"Always were a curious one, Gephorax," said the voice that'd come to him the night of Helveden's fall. Nameless even now. *"Do you think it wise, your destination, or does something deeper drive you on? Someone, perhaps?"*

Would that he could, said Geph, *any boy would bring his mother back.* Ah—there it was. He felt some weight evaporate, foolishness constrict. Of course, his mother was his motivation. No reason to evade the truth—right?

"You worry you shame her memory," said the voice. *"But you know she would do the same for you."*

The Hounds of Gil'an Mor had most certainly possessed the intellect and technology to rewrite to history once upon a time—but would his mother have done the things that Geph had? Committed such atrocities? What he recalled of her said otherwise. But, then again, he never could have imagined himself as he was now. Not in all his years had Geph foreseen such bleakness, such a swift and horrid transformation of himself.

But maybe this is who I always was.

So many threads of possibility streaming from that thought. Geph pushed them away. Bad to dwell on such a notion now.

Reclamation, despite so many moving parts, so many sinhounds, was a rather solitary undertaking. It had been days since Geph had caught scent of his dark brethren—this was typical; there was much to raze and many a soul upon which to feast. Geph shuddered. Disgust churned in his gut, and he swallowed the urge to retch at the thought of such slaughter. What was the point? What reason had they for such rampant destruction? If Hush was to remake the world, rewrite histories wronged, was such... *barbarism* necessary?

"Sinhounds, Gephorax—we sniff out and eradicate excessive sin wherever it may be. It is in our very nature," said the voice. The fur along Geph's spine stood on end. The voice chuckled. *"As I said the night Helveden fell, there is false sin—excessive-ness—and there is* true *sin. We are requisite. We are tempered sin, given leash enough to sate our hunger, but not so much we lose control."*

You and I, perhaps, thought Geph. *But what about the others?*

"Time will tell," the voice said. *"You will know—trust me."*

———

UNDERLIGHT. Vast nothingness. Rock and ruin kissed by shadows, sick from darkness and millennia of solitude. Occasional snaps of light. Sad. Dim. Whispers of the distant past swimming aimlessly and biting at his ears. Ouran felt cold in his heart and bones. Whatever it was that kept him here, dragged him on through silent, phantom horror, he prayed he found it soon lest madness keep him here forever as its pet.

How long had he been walking? How far had he gone? Straight. Straight. He furled his wings about him tighter; the feathers shone warmly before their brilliance was devoured, plunging Ouran into nothingness once more. Was this place trying to tell him something, or was it trying to slowly feed of him? What, exactly, was Underlight? Where?

"It is only as dark as you allow to be," said a voice. Firm, measured. Everywhere. "It can taste your shame—are you truly so devoid of hope?"

Ouran stopped. "Who are you?"

"Many things to many people," it said. "Many a lost soul has come to Underlight—I provide them solace whether living or deceased." Ouran felt—thought he felt—a gentle hand caress his cheek. "What, weary wanderer, do you long for?"

So much. There was so much he—

She came to him as if a memory from a dream, his Sonja Lúm-talé. He could feel the darkness of Underlight enfolding him, constricting him, yet his eyes saw only her, backdropped by the city Banerowos, spires rising, glinting like a thousand distant, monstrous teeth. She extended him her hand.

"Is this... real?" Ouran whispered. Lump in his throat. Hot tears welling in his eyes. When last he had seen her, she had been a monstrous, vengeful thing in Hang-Dead Forest. A rusalk born of violent death. "Please—what is this?"

She took his hand, led him to the center of the spire city.

Dissolved to nothingness and took the gilded memory of Banerowos.

Ouran gasped as the darkness lifted, as the weight vanished and he found himself within the center of a city, yes—but not Banerowos. Something else entirely—a cavern city built into the rock walls of Underlight, architecture rough yet gentle. Motes of light flittered through the air; whispers swam about, lingering like a favorite song. In the distance stood a grand flight of stairs, atop which sat a temple. Ouran walked, spellbound, desperate.

"What is this?" he inquired once more. "What are—" Souls, he realized of the motes of light, the whispers. "Gods..." So much weight. Felt his lungs would burst. Just breathe. Fucking breathe. Panic welling, breathing quick and short. Was she here, his Sonja? He ascended the stairway with hastened, clumsy steps. Almost tripped a few times.

Being draped in light. Wings. Eyes the blue of a clear sky reflected in the sea.

"Welcome," it said, "to the city Seleneth. I am Irgi, Warden of Souls." Its voice was softer in such proximity. So gentle... calming. "I have long been expecting you—but by what name shall I call you? You have worn many..."

You have worn many... Ouran shuddered. He could tell this entity knew. There was a nonchalance to its upright posture, to the softness with which it spoke that, despite mollifying him slightly, also set him on edge. Made him feel naked, bones exposed—*soul* exposed.

"I..."

"*Second thoughts?*" Alerion asked.

Endless. Gods, but who was he? Ouran? Varésh? Alerésh or Dren? His skull screamed; he dug fingers into his scalp, biting back the urge the shriek at the pain. What was happening?

"Nameless," he uttered. Gods, but he didn't want to be *any of them.*

Irgi cocked its head. "I see." It approached, towered over Nameless by a head. Gazed into his eyes, its blue stare mesmerizing. Hand upon his cheek, a soft caress provoking tears and stripping him of mental and emotional weight. Nameless shuddered; he felt weak in the knees and allowed himself to collapse into Irgi's firm embrace and weep. Just stand there as rivulets of sorrow streamed slowly down his cheeks. Never had he felt so uncertain, so confused. Bare. Lacking in identity.

"A bed for the night, I think," said Irgi. "Rest in Seleneth will do you well."

Eyelids heavy. Shuddering yawn. Darkness. Nameless felt the Warden scoop him up into its arms. Warmth. A voice in his head, a whisper distant and inviting; leaves rattling in the wind.

Dusk in a meadow of tall grass.

Rain and a girl of light.

He had seen this all before.

PRELUDE

What an odd collection they four were. Two drenarians, a resurrected prince with a voice in his head, and a goddess. Avaria breathed deeply as they departed Nil-Illúm. Dark. Always dark, save the glow of a single illum wisp orbiting Fenrin. Avaria felt comfortable here, knew the feeling would fleet the further from the city they grew, for things beyond the walls of Nil-Illúm were never as they seemed; nothing in this world was, as Avaria had come to learn.

His thoughts drifted once more to Helveden, to his mother, Virtuoso Khal, and Norema. Gone. All of them. Wretched grin. Headless corpse. Avaria winced at the images, hissed through his teeth. They'd never fade, he knew, felt. Horrible tattoos. Chest stung, felt like a knife had been twisted in an open wound, plunged further. Fuck—they were gone. Dead.

Khal and Norema fell to the wayside and his mother occupied his thoughts wholly. His last words to her had been harsh; she had struck him across the face. That had been their final interaction. No pleasantries, no affection, no parting words of encouragement—just pain. Such had been their relationship soon after he'd been sent to the Hall. Pain and loathing, sorrow and loneliness. Fuck. The numbness of the past day thinned, waned, and tension gripped him wholly, squeezing like a serpent. It was going to be a long journey.

What if? The question dogged him as they walked. Nipped at his heels for hours on end. What if their last interaction had been different? Might it have changed the outcome; would she still be alive? What if Avaria had never departed Helveden to find the sword? Might Helveden yet remain? Might he have been able to stop Geph? What if?

What if?

What if?

What. Fucking. If.

"Breathe," said Jor. The measured softness of his tone snapped Avaria from thought and the cold dimness of the world provided him something other than retrospection to focus on.

I'm trying, Avaria thought. *It's difficult.*

"I understand," said Jor. *"To recall such profound loss..."* There was something odd, reminiscent to the way he spoke. *"I too have lost much. I too have mourned. Before we two were one I dwelled in Gil'an Mor."* He paused again. *"I... don't know how I remember that."*

Something about death resetting things? Avaria asked. *You told me so the other day.*

"This feels different," Jor said. *"Like a memory from a dream. Distant, yet so very vivid. The halls of Gil'an Mor were grand once. The streets were ripe with crystal. And in the Angelarium she sat—Ybot: Mother of Hounds, Reader of Time, First of Her Kind. The most graceful of them—of us—all."*

The corner of Avaria's mouth twitched as an image of a winged hound manifested, lingered momentarily, then dispersed in specks of light in his mind. He blinked, briefly seeing stars. That had not been his memory, and he felt an ache in his chest, constricting. Mournful.

"She was always kind to me," Jor said, a recollective airiness to the way he spoke. *"Treated me as... more than what I was."* He sighed, and Avaria felt some of the tension flee, was able to breathe a little easier. *"The closest entryway to Underlight is through Gil'an Mor."*

More ruins. Great.

"Gil'an Mor," Avaria said.

"What of it?" Luminíl asked.

"Is that where we're headed?"

"Yes," she said. She offered nothing more.

"Gil'an Mor," mused Fenrin. "What a relic."

"You know of it?" Avaria asked.

"Been there on several occasions," Fenrin said. "Dreams are interesting."

He too offered nothing more, and Avaria exchanged a brief glance with Erath, who simply shrugged. Her eyes betrayed her exhaustion. Why was she so tired? Not that Avaria blamed her —he was spent too, driven by adrenaline. But what had changed? Was it the radich she wielded now? He knew little about the energy other than the fact it allowed its wielder the ability to bend time, but he suspected there was so much more to it than that. It meant possibility, after all. Avaria fell back to walk in step with her.

"All right?" Stupid question. Erath quirked an eyebrow. Weary-eyed, but a smile played on her lips. "Yeah, me neither."

"I don't expect anyone would be after..." She sighed. "Well, after all of this. Death. Destruction." Heavy eyelids. Distant sorrow swimming in her eyes. There was more than she was letting on.

Avaria squeezed her shoulder gently. "Won't press, but if you feel like talking..."

Erath nodded. "Thank you."

That was that. He understood. Had to gather yourself for the heavy things lest you crumble underneath the weight before you could get the words out.

Walk.

Silence.

Repeat.

———

How would this end? Erath couldn't help but linger on the question. So many variables. She swiped absentmindedly at the air, tore a momentary window to the past—to wherever. Too obscured to tell. Startling, nonetheless. It would be a while before this newfound gift—could she even call it that?—didn't make her jump every time she involuntarily used it. Gods... was this how the rest of her life would be, looking into memories and such with every gesture she made? She'd go mad if that were the case.

How long had they been at this? How far had they trekked? She knew the Peaks of Dren well enough, had explored their vastness over the years, yet she'd never been wherever it was they were now. Somehow, she'd managed to avoid it—or had *it* evaded her? Dead trees caked in rime. Spent glyphs and the ruin of myriad effigies—hounds had they been? Hard to tell given how far gone they were. Time and weather were gluttonous that way, feasting slowly on their meals, on whatever they saw fit.

"A prelude to the corpse of a once great city," Fenrin murmured. His fingers brushed along the effigies with gentle if not mournful reverence, and Erath wondered if perhaps these monuments were something more—*had been*, rather. "I dreamt of Gil'an Mor this walk. I see things even now." He held a hand to the air; faint threads of energy wreathed around his hand, snaked along his forearm.

Not energy, Erath realized, and Luminíl seemed to have taken notice too. A creature of a sort. Almost completely translucent save a pair of stark blue eyes.

"An Indrisori eel," Luminíl said. "This creature is foreign, of another world entirely." She frowned, looked at Erath with cold eyes. "Your radich is doing more than you are aware, girl. Pulling strings of its own accord."

"How do you know that?" Erath asked. Fenrin and Avaria looked to the Phoenix too. "What, actually, does that even mean?"

"You aren't entirely in control," Avaria said. "And radich *literally* means possibility, right? What if it's physically manifesting the past? Luminíl said the eel is alien to our world, and I suspect it's place of origin is..."

"Little more than a memory," Erath said. She felt a *tug* in the center of her chest; immense sorrow flooded through her, weighted her down, and she grabbed Fenrin's arm to steady herself. That had not been her emotion. Goose pimples rippled up her arms and neck at the possibility her body wasn't entirely her own.

"Gil'an Mor will test us all," Luminíl said as they started on their way. Snow and leafless trees. Weeping wind and muffled sobbing in the depths of Erath's mind.

The city wall appeared, gateless ingress warded over by a pair of towering hounds. Flee, they seemed to say, stay away from this awful place.

Or maybe it was the fear that had been festering in her for

the past few days, emboldened, nourished by the woe and melancholy of the land and her companions.

They crossed the threshold.

Erath's memories wept.

———

EVERY INCH of Avaria begged he flee this dead place as they descended into Gil'an Mor. A tomb of memories old and sad, all but lost to time save by those with long enough teeth or an allhound's presence in their mind.

A labyrinth of streets infected with the fissures and dead geodes. Old azure beneath their feet, wisps and threads of waning light adrift in the air, almost as if frozen in time. One brushed against Avaria's cheek and a shriek from the depths of his mind cleaved his skull in two. Felt like it had, at least. He doubled over, hissing through his teeth. Felt heavy.

"They are called Threads," Luminíl said, "and they are the memories of this place. Ghosts of longhounds past, bloated with the history of Gil'an Mor." Murmured, "And its violent end."

She held her hand to the Thread nearest Avaria and it came to her, snaked around her forearm, weak and slow. Mewed faintly at her presence and her touch.

"Sleep, now," the Phoenix whispered. She caressed the spirit's length... and it fell to mist and motes of light. Vanished in the gloom of Gil'an Mor.

"What did you do?" Erath asked.

"Relieved its suffering," Luminíl said. "Took it for my own—the pain, that is." Such sorrow in her words. A hint of something dark. "Sometimes pain is the appropriate price." She looked to where the Thread had been just moments ago. "Her name was

Alesana and she died when Hush attacked. The last to fall before they caged the Vulture in the depths of Underlight."

"A way to go before we reach Underlight," Fenrin said. "We had best move on." His upper lip curled slightly. "I do not like the air about this place, nor will I enjoy that about Underlight. The quicker we leave, the better."

They started on their way, Luminíl at the head and Fenrin taking up the rear. Something beautiful about ruins. Maybe it was the silence. Maybe it was the mystery of what had been.

"It is the connection," Jor said. *"The longing."*

How do you mean?

"Everyone connects to history in one way or another," Jor said. *"And whether or not they care to admit so, everyone desires adventure—longs for a taste of that which came before."*

Did you?

"Of course," said Jor. *"Just as you do now. Your quest, in its simplest form, was born of a need, a desire to be free of the confines of Helveden. Now? Now, you seek that which came before."*

Banerowos.

Avaria shivered at the city's name and knew that Jor was right. He had yearned for adventure for the longest time—but he hadn't thought that desperation would lead him here to the corpse of Gil'an Mor, or that his home would fall along the way, everyone and everything he'd known slaughtered. Little more than memories.

Mother...

They walked.

SAGES

The village was called Yll and Geph was surprised it stood. Surprised that anything at all endured here in the vast sickness of the meadow. The village was an odd, gray amalgamation of leaning not-quite-towers and uneven buildings which looked as though they were all cobbled together from the ruin of much uglier things. And the smell—gods, what an unforgiving thing. Apple pie atop the odor of rotting flesh. Geph's stomach churned as he padded on his way.

Scarcely populated was Yll. By the time he reached the village square Geph had only seen a dozen or so finite occupants. They had paid him no mind; he was practically a ghost. While he should have been content with this invisibility of sorts, he was not. How long had it been since he had spoken with someone or something beside the voice in his head?

"Nice doggy."

Geph turned to the voice. Gaze fell on a dark-haired child with amber eyes and a grin. His nose twitched as the child approached. Without hesitation, he scratched *that spot* behind Geph's ears.

"Whatcha doin' here, doggy?"

Was an actual answer expected? Was the child aware of what Geph was?

"Passing through."

The child continued scratching. "To where?"

"A bad place. An old place."

"Why?"

"You would not understand, little one."

The child cocked an eyebrow. Stopped scratching. Frowned, turned and started off. Geph sighed. *Children.* Ears perked up. Something more than just a child—its shadow was *wrong;* met the light instead of fled.

Geph trailed the child-thing at a distance. The stench of Yll grew more profound with every step he took, with every corner that they turned, until Geph was sure he would be sick.

An ugly, twisted patchwork remnant of a tower greeted him, and the child-thing halted at its door. "Why do you follow, doggy?" Agitation.

"To converse," said Geph. "We both are more than we appear. I apologize for my dismissiveness. It was ignorant, and I wish to make amends."

The child-thing said nothing. Twitched a finger—they were in the tower, now. In the depths and darkness of a place that made Geph's neck fur bristle. Light was all but dead here, save the intermittent flickering of dying wisps.

Geph sneezed. A familiar and haunting scent.

"You reek of her," the child-thing said, abandoning all pretense of ignorance and youth. "Of the Vulture, Mirkvahíl."

"I do," said Geph. "What is she to you?"

"Can I show you something?" The child-thing turned and

reached for Geph. Eyes like dying stars. Tapped his nose, and Geph was in the center of a ruin wreathed in wispy threads of smoke. Glass and stone hung in the air, ignorant of gravity; the entire ruin turned its nose to law.

A lanky shadow manifested several feet from Geph. "Misten Fahg was a place of power." Child-thing. "And then the Vulture came..."

———

THE DRENARIAN CITY IS CALM. For half a moment the stillness reminds Hush of home, and she longs for those evening walks by the lake. Just the two of them, she and Luminíl. But the feeling fades, slips away in the snowfall, and Hush is alone.

Loneliness tugs at her again, but this time Hush can feel it belongs to Te Mirkvahíl. Something about this place—some*one*, perhaps. Many, in fact. She walks, each step as aimless as it is meaningful. What is this city and its people to Te Mirkvahíl? What *was* it?

"Aveline." Hush turns to the voice, hardly of her own accord; Te Mirkvahíl remains. A woman stands a yard or two away.

"My Queen Silith," Hush says. So many questions.

The drenarian queen nears Hush, bores into her with hawkish yellow eyes. She is beautiful, but she is worn. Weary. Time is such a rotten thing, Hush thinks; she can feel the rot beneath her flesh, swimming in her heart and scraping through her mind.

Silith touches Hush's cheek. So tender. She can feel the queen's sorrow. She allows Silith to embrace her; reluctantly, Hush returns the gesture. It feels... nice, the firmness, the longing. It reminds her of Luminíl.

They pull apart. "I've not seen you since..." Silith sighs. "Since Alor." The name *stings* Hush physically, and it's all she can do not to wince. "I thought you dead all this time. Once news reached of Te Mirkvahíl's demise..."

Hush cocks an eyebrow. Play the part. "You knew?"

"We *all* knew."

Borrowed shame. Hush hangs her head. Sighs.

"What is done, is done," Silith says. Touches Hush's cheek. "I would show you something if you'll follow. Something of Alor's."

Hush nods of her own volition, pushes back against the will of Te Mirkvahíl. Humor the queen. Play the part, for all things have their use.

Silith takes her hand. They twist through the drenarian city and out into the trees, their mountain kingdom kissed by mist like darkness and a silence eager to infect what little sanity of Hush remains.

"*What a thing to admit,*" the voice inside her says. Hush says nothing; the voice does not relent. "*Pertinent, for no one sane could do what we have done. Too much fear. A lack of passion. Loveless, wretched things.*"

A totem in a glade. An effigy of something long and winged. Hush has seen these many times before; they are strewn about this dying world of hers. Its very presence stings her borrowed flesh.

She screams.

Has been screaming for so long.

Silith kneels beside her, eyes aglow like dying moons, lips drawn to a thin line upon which Hush smells blood and rage and woe.

Smoke. Her flesh is burning.

Burning.

BURNING
and she wails—
not this place again.

———

"You had the dreams again, didn't you?"

Rhona stood atop the tallest spire in all Banerowos. Below her were miles of ruin. Before her stood Djen, pale flesh cracked and webbed with mirkúr.

"This is the dream," said Rhona.

Djen frowned. "Have you truly learned nothing from all of this? How many more times will we repeat this song and dance? How much longer do you intend to run?"

"I'm not running," Rhona said.

"You *are*." Djen held her arms out wide. "In circles. How many times have you escaped this place only to have it draw you back? The guilt will always call you back if you allow it to." She approached Rhona. Cupped her cheeks. "Is this what you want to be?"

Tears. Hot.

"Stop."

"Answer the question."

Rhona screamed. Shrieked, and the force of her anguish sent Djen sailing through the air and off the edge of the spire. Fragments of the gray sky fell like sheets of ash. Rhona fell to her knees, sobbing. She could hear them as they manifested, neared at gentle glides—myriad shadows of self. A cacophony of chaos somewhere in between a whisper and a hiss.

"*Wake.*"

"*Rouse, before you kill them all.*"

"*Feed.*"

"You are more. You are better than the cracked and broken shell you wear."

"Feed."

"Rend. Feast. Sleep."

Wet hand. Warm. Rhona blinked.

———

So many dead. So much blood.

So many body parts strewn across the glade.

Her hand is warm and slicked with blood—Silith's blood. And her mouth... Hush retches, wills her tongue to kill the taste of iron. Begs her sense of smell and taste to die.

The drenarian queen is dead. Dead dead dead.

Dead.

Hush screams—almost. Swallows the shriek; her insides burn like the hell she has wrought. How many times must she dream and wake and dream and wake and—-

She pushes herself to stand. Stumbles forward. Who knows where? Just away. Get away get away get away. Such a cracked and broken thing.

I will make this right. I will fix it all.

How many times has she told herself that lie?

She bites back tears.

Help.

———

"What is this place?" Geph asked. "What are you?"

"A monster," said the child-thing. "I am a monster, and this is my home."

"Might you care to elaborate? You called this place Misten Fahg."

"The tower at the center of the village Sleep," said child-thing. "When they say, 'I am going to sleep,' this is where they come—Misten Fahg. The epicenter of The In Between."

"So, you are quite literally a thing of dreams," said Geph. He inched closer, intrigued. "But what is Mirkvahíl to you? And what is Misten Fahg to her?"

Child-thing sneered. The silhouette flared. "As without, so within. Mirkvahíl brought ruin to your world, but what she did to Misten Fahg was far more monstrous. She *created Hell.* Perdition. Down Below. Call it what you will—her cowardice infected *all.*" The silhouette recoiled. "I was beautiful once. The Dream Wolf, they called me. Time."

Geph frowned. Ears twitched. He felt sympathy for this strange, canine soul. "And now—what do they call you?"

A twist of shadow. A trembling of ruin. A black wolf, eyes like dying stars and a form that trailed to mist. "Than Sor'Al."

Wide-eyed. Bristling fur. Geph bowed deeply. He was in the presence of a god-thing. "Great One," he whispered. "You humble me. My mother told me tales of you when I was but a pup. I never thought... You are *real.*"

"The most monstrous things are often times hidden in the subtext of a child's tale," said Than Sor'Al. "Such little nightmares do I bring...."

"What do you wish of me?" Geph asked. "Why show me Misten Fahg?"

"As without, so within," repeated Than Sor'Al. "Mirkvahíl is such an old and splintered soul. A tower at its tipping point, so to speak. One need only give a little push—"

Geph howled himself awake. Found himself in tall grass beneath a sea of stars. Trembling like mad. That had all been...

real—hadn't it? His skull ached horribly, like it'd been split in two, and he couldn't quell the distant whisper—*"One need only give a little push."* Had this anything to do with what he'd seen of Hush's memories? That strange and twisted place called Hang-Dead Forest. Banerowos.

"*Get up, Gephorax,*" said the voice in his head. "*Get up and walk.*"

So, he did.

And the night endured.

———

NAMELESS WOKE to pale blue light and a feeling of absence in his head. No—not absence. Intrigue? That didn't sound right either. Nagging? Caged chaos?

"*Amnesia,*" said Alerion. "*Selective amnesia.*"

No use in asking what he'd voluntarily banished from his mind. Though how he'd done so... Nameless recalled nothing past the Warden Irgi placing him in bed. Emptiness, then pale blue light; now.

He slipped from bed, garbed as he had been prior to his sleep, and instinct drew him back to the staircase atop which he had first encountered Irgi in the city Seleneth. The Warden was there when Nameless arrived, its aura of nonchalance doing more to rattle Nameless than to ease his nerves. What was it about this entity that cause him such distress? Those eyes, bright as a blue sky echoed by the sea. Wise in a way that made him shiver, for why should anything know more about a person than a person knew about themself?

"You are a man of many lives," said Irgi. "Yet you acknowledge none—are you truly so controlled by fear and guilt? By fear *of* guilt?"

"I want to be a blank canvas," Nameless said.

"Many do," said Irgi. "But tell me—how can you be a blank canvas when you're haunted by the unknown? You let sleep take from you the source of your suffering, yet now you suffer, and you can't say why."

Weight. Tightening chest.

"Repression is intoxication without a drink," said Irgi. "It will destroy you from the inside out unless you face your fears. What is the saying? The guilt will always call you back. The longer you run, the worse it will be." The Warden bent over, leaned in close. "And you have been running for *such* a long time."

Hot tears. Burning, like a fire in his chest. Cracks in the tapestry of his mind; lost things aching to be remembered.

"How do I fix this?" Nameless whispered.

Portal of azure luminescence. Gossamer threads of light. A voice beyond it all. "Hell is a place of one's own making."

Seleneth dissolved, fell away in rivulets of muted color; with the cavern city went its host, and there was only Nameless and a brilliant doorway at the center of a vast and endless blackness. Nameless blinked. Was he dreaming? Had he died? The portal shimmered, shifted, and he saw a meadow of tall grass. Beyond it...

"Hang-Dead Forest."

Nameless stepped through the portal

and found himself lying on his back.

Starlight blinked.

A feeling in his chest.

Parable.

UNDERLIGHT

O uran'an was dead. Had been for a time. The city stood
in the distance like the jagged, snow-tipped maw of
some gargantuan beast. It was not the first of its kind to fall, and
Avaria knew it would not be the last.

How did he know that?

He blinked. Gulped the crisp air of this place now called
the Deep Rock as he gazed at Ouran'an. It beckoned, and he
longed to walk its streets, to stand atop its many spires and kiss
the morning sky.

But why?

Blink.

Such a ruin. Such a sorry thing the city was. Streets of
blackened bones encased in ice. Threads of mirkúr coiling
through the air like rivulets of angry fog. A breeze like knives
against his flesh. Swore it'd raised the dead for he could hear the
countless screams entwined with grief and joy like some abomination wrought in Hell.

Blink.

Ghosts. Aimless wanderers where in life they'd walked with purpose, for Reshapers and their magics were how so much of Harthe was wrought.

Hand to his head—how had known that?

"Bzzz." Sentience in a sea of silent resignation. "Bzzzz." Avaria searched for the master of the voice like gravel tossed by waves. Again—"Bzzz."

A swirl of mist, a snap of light; he was elsewhere now. Before him stood a man. What had been a man, at least, for mirkúr streaked his flesh, trailed beyond the realm of physicality, dancing in the wind. He was blond of hair, lithe, with arms and shoulders graced by intricate tattoos. His eyes were white and Avaria felt the stranger's gaze *inside his mind*.

"Stop." He retreated half a step.

"Bzzz." The man cocked his head. "Bzzz."

"No," Avaria said. "I've no idea why I'm here, let alone how I arrived. Don't know who you are either—*get out* of my head!"

Mirkúr flared inside Avaria; a short sword manifested in his hand. Jagged. Nasty. Hungry. He pointed the tip of the blade at the man.

The man held his hands up. "Bzzz." Half-turned, pointed to an archway and the many hills beyond, up from which an endless throng of tombstones rose.

"The burial grounds?" Avaria held his stance. "Why?"

"Bzzz," the man said softly. Turned and started on.

Blink.

Ouran'an had never had burial grounds.

Blink.

An oak tree cloaked in snow. Beneath it stood the man. Beyond it, thing of wings and shadow. They beckoned; Avaria obeyed.

———

"Where will you go?"

"East. I think."

"Are you not happy here?"

"It has nothing to do with happiness."

"What, then?"

"Dreams. I thought you of all people would understand." Silence. "You saved me, raised me as your own and I am grateful —but my purpose lies beyond this place of rock and snow and death."

"Death is inescapable."

"But slaughter can be quelled."

"Yes...."

———

Calm snow. Sky of trees.

So cold.

———

"Do you not love us, Erath?"

Erath sits against the trunk of a tree. It is spring and the air is sweet though momentarily poisoned by the inquiry. She looks at Alor. "Of course, I do. Why would I not?"

Alor says nothing.

"You let us die," Leru says. She sits at Erath's left. A shadow falls across the world and chokes away spring. All becomes cracked and withered, dry and dead like grass that's gone millennia without rain. "You let us die to sate your insecurities."

A twist of smoke and a snap of light. They are standing now in Nil-Illúm.

"Middle child, lost and full of woe," the specter of Alor taunts. She is naught but incorporeal burnt-paper flesh and ravenous eyes like dying stars. She trails to nothingness, to the planes beyond with every step she takes. Leru is her half-head shorter shadow twin.

"What will father think?" Leru inquires.

"What will mother think?" Alor hisses.

Erath trembles. "I..." She what? Did not mean to let her sisters die? To let the monsters of the world slaughter them? "I'm so sorry...."

Screaming snow.

"You are a cruel girl," Queen Silith whispers in her ear.

Erath starts, spins. "Mother..."

"Our girls," her father, Fenrin, murmurs and his eyes are red. "Your sisters... How could you, Erath?" Her heart stings: they four encircle her like the wolves to her trembling lamb. Fenrin weeps. "You are no daughter of mine."

Erath falls to her knees, hugs herself, bites back tears, swallows a sob.

Hand on her shoulder. Gentle voice in her ear. "The guilt will always call you back, dear girl." Dren, glorious and sad. "And such a monstrous thing it is, especially when we know there is nothing more we could have done."

Erath leans into Dren. Traitorous, mad Dren. The only thing here that feels safe. The tempest of emotion circling Erath slows, as if time itself desires sleep. Motes and threads of soft blue light flitter through the air, caress Erath as they pass.

"I can help you from this awful place," says Dren. He stands, pulling Erath upright. "I can help you gain control. You *must* gain control if you are to upset the sickness." He sighs.

"Underlight is such a twisted place..." He snaps his fingers and the two stand 'neath an archway warded over by a pair of effigies that Erath does not recognize. Winged, faceless things; four-armed, wielding blades. Beyond the archway, stones of light; a pathway leading elsewhere, from here, somewhere new.

"A word of advice," says Dren, taking Erath's hand. "Nothing in this place—nothing in this world—is as it seems. There is truth in madness and madness in truth. We must find the balance in between."

They walk and the stones shimmer.

They walk and the air chills

screams

weeps.

Gods, what is this place? So beautiful and twisted. Swirls of ruin in a sky of colors Erath cannot name. Blinks of places elsewhere, somehow, somewhen, beyond comprehension.

"Somewhere in the midst of all this," Dren says. "Balance."

Snap.

All dilates.

Contracts.

Snap.

Tower ruin. Glass and stone adrift, suspended in the air.

"How many masks will you wear? How many times will you stain this place with your presence, Varésh Lúm-talé?" something growls. "Speak, or I will consume you and the flesh you wear."

What did it—

"I come seeking balance," Erath says, but it is not her voice she hears. She feels wings protruding from her back, feels her bones reshape; she is on fire, burning from the inside out as Varésh Lúm-talé—whomever that is—takes her body for his own. So much guilt inside this flesh. Infection. Plague. Were she in control she would retch.

"You helped her destroy this place," the entity snarls. Manifests—black wolf. Eyes like dying stars and a shape that fades to mist. "Who are you to enter Sleep and make demands?"

Varésh Lúm-talé sighs. "I have made many mistakes." He locks eyes with the wolf. "Please, great Than Sor'al. If not for me then for the soul with whom I trek. She has suffered much to reach this place." Whispers, "*I have caused her so much pain...*"

Than Sor'al snorts. It clouds before the beast's nose. "Release her from your flesh that she might manifest before me."

Varésh nods.

Blink.

Erath starts. Than Sor'al's nose is cold, makes her shiver as it sniffs her up and down.

"Radich," says the wolf, with a hint of disdain. Bows its head. "What a cruel thing you are, Varésh Lúm-talé, to have tainted her with such a thing. You and your many names, your countless, rotten iterations. How many times until you learn? How many more worlds condemned to wither 'neath the consequences of your desperate guilt?" Starlight eyes burn red. "Leave us."

Blink.

Erath stands beside the massive wolf in the blasted remnant of a town on either side of which the tower and a forest loom. "Sleep is not what it once was," Than Sor'al laments, "but I shall do my best."

Blink.

———

CALM SNOW. Oak tree rearing in the night.

Sky of trees. Buzzing man. Thing of wings and shadow. Cricket serenade; the biting cold inside his flesh. He cries and it is small and desperate. Man and shadow watch but do not move. He is weak. So frighteningly weak. His tiny frame is fading, losing to the dark and snow. Won't somebody—

A forest cloaked in mist, the melody of distant death. He is older now yet haunted by the dreamlike memory of that night. Or a memory like a dream. Nothing in this world makes sense, not when he can summon beasts of Hell. Not when he's been banished to the Hall, the fucking lot of good that's done. Erudition and achievement are the falsities that ward the truth—the Hall is where they murder happiness, mold abandoned boys to function as the tools that drive their wars. Fuck Helveden. Fuck Ariath. Fuck—

He hugs her tightly. How many nightmares must a little boy endure before the gentleness of dreamless sleep takes hold? How many times must he relive that wicked night inside the woods? Cold and dark and snow.

"You are safe," she whispers. "Safe and warm and found and I will never let you go."

"What if the darkness tries to take me back?" he whispers.

She pulls him closer, kisses his forehead. "It will meet my blade."

He sniffles. "And if it takes you instead?"

"It won't."

———

THEY ARE all of them dead. He remembers little save the shadow from the forest of trees and spire rocks. It came, and Ouran'an fell. It came, and they went—his memories and the people whom the city housed.

Everything has led him here—but why? What is left in the shadow of a ruin, of a distant memory, for him to find?

You know, the sky says. *You have always known.*

Scenery of three lives stitched together over one another like a mangled corpse with mismatched parts. The triptych melds and the sky is black despite the blazing sun. They stand there, boy and hound and man, eyes fixed knowingly on one another.

"Why have you forsaken us?"

They turn, do boy and hound and man, come face to face with individuals who stoke in them a tempest of irrationality and rage and grief.

"Mother..." breathe the boy and hound, withering in the presence of a thing of starlight eyes and tattered wings and a woman red of hair and wielding mirkúr blades.

The man says nothing as he looks upon the queen.

A grin rips across her face; a cackle-shriek erupts.

Chaos.

———

SLEEP IS DEAD. Beyond dead. Erath trails Than Sor'al. How does any of this relate to balance? How will wandering through this corpse of stone contribute to her gaining dominance of her radich, weird and poisoned power that it is? What is Than Sor'al? Erath hugs herself for warmth; this place is cold. Beautiful. Haunting. Every step she takes pulls back the curtain just a little more. Screams and whispers, fleeting visions of... what?

"You reek of chaos," Than Sor'al says. "Chaos and fear."

"I'm scared," Erath says. "Afraid to fail. Of... all of this."

"Balance is not easily achieved," says Than Sor'al. They stop at the edge of a silver lake in which the cosmic brilliance of the sky reflects. "Were it so, perhaps then Sleep and Misten Fahg might rise anew. As without, so within—ruin."

"You speak simply," Erath says, "but there is a deeper meaning to your words. This place is a reflection of the waking world, isn't it? An analog of sorts."

"Clever girl."

Erath kneels before the lake, gazes in at her reflection.

The wind whispers in her ear; she shrugs it off. It will not relent.

They come from all around, manifest from nothing like a million waking stars. Motes and threads, a brilliant symphony. They encircle Erath, pull her to her feet. Whispers like a song she swears she's heard before.

Whispers like a dying voice.

A resurgent voice.

Her eyes are wide; she understands.

"Please," she asks of Than Sor'al, "deliver me from Sleep." The light-song caresses Erath's mind. Something in her snaps, surges, awakens. "I can save them yet."

"As you—"

———

A CITY SLEEPS. They safely sleep.

The Phoenix. The Father-king.

The Prince of Countless Names is gone.

"Peel back the fabric of the world," says a gentle voice. Winged figure wrought of light. "Every moment bends beneath your will."

"How will I know?" Erath asks.

"Follow the light. Close your eyes and follow the light."

———

THERE.

———

WAIT—WAIT!
So close.

———

TOO FAR. Too far.
Peel it back.
Follow the light. Follow the thread.
Oh gods...

———

HE WAKES in the amalgam of the cities he has known. They are a crush of ruined, crooked stone and twisted spires rising at impossible, if not unnatural angles. Gossamer threads of pitch swim through the air with the lethargy of basking snakes; the sky is red, the moon sits high and black, a dilated pupil-of-a-thing. His skin crawls; his mind screams, each shriek less intelligible than the last.

Toll the Hounds. Their cries descend, directionless, without origin. He makes no move to flee; he waits—sin is relentless. The amalgam shifts: the scenery bleeds and he is standing at the gates of Ouran'an. The city is a monument to failure, the roost of desecration. His heart aches to see it, dead and silent; he flees the necropolis he once called home—

Cold. Can scarcely breathe. Rocks and snow. So horribly alone. Best to lay here, die. Fade to memory like the rest.

A shadow thing of wings. Beautiful, a thing conceived of woe and dread, colder than the darkest night; in comparison, the snow and rocks are warm. Waning world, he sees their faces in his dreams, yearns to hold their hands; he is but a boy.

Gentle hands. A dark embrace: the longing floods him.

He will live.

———

WHAT A DEAD WORLD.

———

"HERE YOU ARE AGAIN."

Wings of midnight feathers, tapering into mist. Eyes like summer storms. The night is blood; the grass is dead. Save the gnarled and twisted tree, they are alone.

Avaria clasps his hands behind his back, walks past Alerion to the tree. Lost Tree. Memory, Sorrow, Thorn. Bringer. He caresses Bringer's bark and the dream world fluctuates, the great tree groans.

"It took me a while to understand," Avaria says. "I have been asleep a very long while, trapped in memories, manifesting dread, letting anger feast upon me as it's wont to do."

"You know then they are dead," Alerion says. "Those with whom you ventured into Underlight. The world is dead, and you are here."

"Luckily, *here* is not yet dead. Nor is the world." He kisses Bringer; white light threads the ancient bark. Rejuvenates. Leaves stretch from infancy; they shimmer. Bringer sighs.

"*How?*" the tree inquires.

Saplings rise. The sky congeals; the blood-night fades to ash, reveals the soothing colors of a setting sun. Virgin stars have roused.

"You," Avaria says. "Bringer—the very illum network itself." He breathes deeply of the fresh air. "I told myself that death has a funny way of piecing things together. It just takes time."

Alerion nods. "Well done, Jor."

A shiver up his spine. It's been so long since Avaria has been called by that name. The memories snap, flash on repeat—cities, death, and cold.

"Mother," he whispers, and he thinks of Aveline and Hush. Of Ahnil and her maddened grin. "How I failed you all..." Three dead, one beyond redemption. He sits.

"What now?" Alerion asks.

Avaria shuts his eyes. "We wait."

ACT III

O, CATASTROPHE

BLEAK

Lost. So incredibly lost. How could things have gone so wrong?

Erath kicked the dirt of the dead world in which she stood. A blanket of ugly night devoid of stars. A deafening silence and a wind that sliced at her with every dry gust. The stumps of myriad trees checkered the world, wherever and whenever she was.

And how was she going to get back to Underlight? To Luminíl and Fenrin—to the Phoenix and her *father*. Gods, what a mess. She swallowed the lump in her throat—do *not* lose composure.

Breathe. Balance. Find it, cage it. Otherwise, what was the point of any this? What had the point of this nightmare been if she gave up now?

But it would be so easy, a part of her thought. *Just sit here in the darkness. Let the world corrode—let them all wither, fade to ash.*

Timelessness.

Time meant nothing.

The eternal yawn.

She screamed

…

…

…

Again.

A shimmer in the gloom. A twist of light.

"Why do you despair?" a voice inquired. Erath blinked; before her stood a man. A ghost of a man. A ghost of a memory of a man. Something. "Erath?"

She started at her name.

At the caress of her cheek. His hand was warm.

"I'm so lost," she whispered. The emotional weight was banging at the chamber door. "Lost and… Is this just a nightmare? Am I dead? Is this where my soul is fated to remain?"

"What do you believe?" the man asked.

She didn't know.

He asked again.

Still, she didn't know.

He wilted; the darkness ate his light, and the barren earth consumed his corpse.

She was alone.

So

utterly

…

alone.

———

She had come so close so many times—yet Avaria had not been able to reach her. Waiting had not meant inaction; rather, it had meant patience until the moment presented itself, and so many moments there had been.

"She is stuck," he said to Bringer and Alerion.

"Perhaps it was too much to expect a novice wielder of radich to find us here," Alerion said. "Trapped in the Temporal Sea..."

"No," Avaria said. "She wields it for a reason. I think..." He frowned, winced at a sharpness in his chest; his corporeality fluctuated. "Her anchor wanes."

Fuck.

"If that happens..." Alerion sighed. "Then you die. We die. She remains adrift and the world whence you came fades to ruin."

"So, what do we do?" Avaria asked.

Alerion frowned. "We wait. We hope."

———

HUSH RETCHES BLOOD. Retches something. Spews rot and bile and woe until her stomach is a growling pit. The abyss from which her hunger manifests to ruin worlds.

Worlds. Obscured images snap across her mind. Her sense of smell is overcome with scents from days dead and those yet to arrive. She falls to her knees; she can scarcely catch her breath, collect herself. She feels the old dry grass between her fingers and its touch sparks dread—the rot of Banerowos has a long reach. The dead have memories longer yet. She trembles, struggles to steel herself in such proximity to the ruined city and the forest behind which it remains.

"*Are you going to give up?*" the voice inside her asks. It goes by Mirkvahíl now. Mirkvahíl, who betrayed her lovely Luminíl, who with the liar Varésh Lúm-talé condemned the city

Banerowos and its people to their ends. Who like so many others things in Hush's life was just a lie. A conglomerate of falsities.

So many lies.

"*So close,*" Mirkvahíl hisses.

When did Hush become this *thing*? How did she allow this monster to regain its foothold in her mind? *Weak*, she laments. *I am forever weak*

"*But you can be strong,*" Mirkvahíl urges. "*You can rectify it all—every broken world erased... You can save your love before it all goes wrong.*"

Snap.

So many trees.

Hush trembles. Tears well. Her jaw quivers.

Not here—not again.

———

THE MEADOW at the end of time—that was all this was. It would have sounded more poetic had it not frightened Erath. How far had she gone? How long had she been at this? Where was the light, her guide? Follow the light. Gods, she couldn't even do *that* properly.

She dropped to the dead earth and screamed, pounded the dirt with her fists. Pull back the curtain of world—ha! She had done that, all right, and look where it had gotten her. What a fool she had been to think she could wield radich. What a fool she had been to think she could save it all, *them* all. Her shoulders slumped. She sniffled.

"Oh Avaria... Where are you?"

A sign. Something. Anything. The utter silence of this place tore at her. An endless night, a silence in black and white. She heaved a ragged sigh, forced herself to stand. She was empty, emptier than she had ever felt. Doing this, this... world-hopping, reality-swimming, whatever it was, drained her like nothing else had, fed on more than just simple stamina. This was more than exhaustion.

"*...anchor wanes...*"

Erath blinked. She had heard that, hadn't she?

"*...wait... hope...*"

Words like a whisper amid turning pages.

A twinkle, a luminescent dot so far away it may as well have not existed—-yet in the darkness here the brilliance blazed. Her father had always said that in the darkest night, the faintest light was blinding. She was the moth to its innumerable snapping flames.

Snap.

"*...gone ...all gone...*" Weeping. "*...please...*"

Snap.

She dug deep, called—*begged* what little she had left. Feet ached. Heart stung. Blood and breath so cold she felt the kiss of fire. Her very *existence* fluctuating—yes, that was it. Could feel her tethers to the place whence she had come evaporating, splitting like dry strands of hair.

Had to reach that light.

Snap.

Snap.

Snap.

SNAP.

"Erath?"

YORE

Hang-Dead Forest smelled of her, and she reminded him of home—of the home that once had been. Nameless trembled at the memories, at her phantom touch within his mind, pulling, tugging, clawing. Atrocities.

He walked, a pitiful sack of fear and adrenaline, remorse and self-loathing. The corpses and the ropes from which they'd hung had faded long ago, but Nameless felt their presence nonetheless—nothing ever truly left Hang-Dead Forest, the accursed place it was. He was proof enough that guilt would always call you back.

He stopped in a grove illuminated by the muted glow of the moon. At its center stood the woman he had once called wife—what was left of her at least. Hung those countless centuries ago, returned to haunt the forest as a rusalk. She eyed him.

"Sonja," he rasped. Shivered at the myriad eyes blooming in the darkness behind her. "After all this time..."

"*Why have you come?*" Her voice was dry wind.

"To fix things," he said. "To fix myself, I think."

Sonja snarled. "*You are beyond repair.*"

She had attacked him when last he'd come. When he had been Varésh Lúm-talé. Was his abandoning of the name the reason why she held her ground, why the others like her made no move to rip him limb from limb? He clenched his teeth at the exhumed memory; threads of history were seeping through the cracks of his mind. Burning like cold fire.

"Maybe," he murmured. "What should I do?"

"*Have honor for once,*" Sonja said. "*Be brave.*" She turned to the trees. "*Atop her throne sits Mother Sin, the Ruin Queen. If whatever it is you are has any remorse, confront the demoness and free us from this hell.*"

Nameless nodded. "I will try."

Sonja eyed him; for a moment, her eyes were gentle. "*You will. You are not Varésh.*"

She withdrew from the glade and melded with the trees; one by one, the faceless eyes fell silent. Nameless was alone.

So, he walked.

———

A BREEZE. The air was warm and gentle on her cheeks; the sunset and the rousing stars adorned the sky, and the light and colors did not burn. The sensation was so jarringly wonderful Erath almost forgot someone had called her name. She blinked. A short distance away stood a grand tree and two figures, one regal and winged, the other placid and wreathed with intricate tattoos. She recognized them both to a degree.

"Dren? Avaria?"

"Almost," the winged man said. "I am Alerion."

She looked at the tattooed man. "And you?"

"Avaria," he said. Smiled. "You found me. Us."

Darkness snapped across her memory. She hugged herself. "I was afraid I wasn't going to." Felt that sharp tug at the center of her chest. Winced. "I can't stay much longer."

"Your tether is waning," Avaria said. "We should go."

So tired. Gods, she was exhausted. Sweat dripping down her face. Avaria caught her as she slumped forward, kept her on her feet. *Focus. Grab the light.* She urged her radich, reached inside herself to stoke the energy into action; its signature was faint. *Just one more time...*

Her flesh bloomed; rivulets of pale blue luminescence manifested in her veins. Threads of mist braided outward, wreathing her and Avaria, enfolding and depositing them elsewhere—elsewhen.

The odor of ancient rot snapped her to her senses.

"Banerowos," Avaria murmured. Then, to himself: "Farewell, Alerion. Bringer."

He had clearly not expected *this* to have transpired so quickly; Erath felt a minuscule pang of guilt, but it was banished by a throng of disembodied screams and a maddeningly quick succession of Dren's memories as her radich ripped the veil apart. So many dead. So much woe. Gods, the anguish burned her from the inside out.

Her breath was shaky, but she forced herself to gulp the sick air and steady her nerves. "The guilt will always call you back," she whispered; the words were addressed to what remained of Dren.

"Where are Luminíl and Fenrin?" Avaria asked.

She'd nearly forgotten about them. "Underlight last I was aware, but..." Erath shook her head. "Everything is chaos; I can hardly make sense of anything. They may still be in Underlight, or somewhere else entirely."

Avaria frowned. "We can't take her just the two of us." He

meant Hush. His eyes narrowed and his tattoos shone faintly in the gloom. "There's something else here. Some*one* else." He inhaled. Tensed his jaw. "More than one."

———

GEPH RETCHED. No idea how long he'd been lost in Hang-Dead Forest. No idea how long his mind and nerves had been subjected to the remnant woe and anguish of this awful place. He shook violently as the hot sick dripped from his tongue and smacked the dirt. Gods, what he would do for a whiskey and a lack of smell...

Nose twitched. Geph composed himself as best the forest-eyes and city-corpse allowed. Others here. Familiar and not. His ears twitched and his forehead drew taught with shame. Avaria was somewhere near—how could he look him in the eyes? How could he speak to him after... Geph may not have spilled her blood, but he had bayed the sinhounds into action. Helveden and Ahnil were on Geph's paws and conscience. Could he bring himself to fight back if Avaria came at him, tried to kill him?

"You did what was necessary, Gephorax." Still had no idea what that voice was. *"There is a reason for everything."*

And what, pray tell, is that? Why did Ahnil Norrith and the city Helveden have to die?

"Patience, Gephorax," the voice urged. *"All shall be revealed."*

Geph snarled. *Does that include you?* Would that he could, he'd have ripped the voice from his head so that it might manifest and perish by his bite.

The voice chuckled. *"Slow for such a cunning thing. You and I, Gephorax, are one and the same. I am the courage you concealed, freed and fed by Hush. You know this, but you fear it, as you have feared so many things in all your years."*

The air around Geph chilled. An inky blackness manifested through the folds of reality, and Geph found himself standing face to face with a wolf with eyes like dying stars.

"How long do you intend to run?" said Than Sor'al *"How long do you intend to sleep?"*

Distant voices. Trembling world.

They called his name.

"The guilt will always call you back," said Than Sor'al. *"Embrace it and be free."*

The world shattered.

Myriad fragments.

A thousand shards like broken memories and dreams.

"They call me Time," said a voice.

Said Geph, and the black-eyed woman smiled.

———

"You had better not be dead," Avaria snarled. Geph was motionless. The night about them screamed. "You're not allowed to die like this, damn it. Not until..."

Until, what? Until he had beaten the longhound senseless for his mother and Helveden? Until he had killed Geph, only to resurrect him for a second throttling? Avaria sighed, felt the hatred dissipate at the sight of Geph, still and silent as a drowned pup. He picked the longhound up, cradling him; he was surprisingly light.

"What did this to him?" Erath asked.

"This place," Avaria said. The sway and sentience of the corpse of Banerowos made no efforts to conceal itself. It *wanted* them to know the memory of its ruin, of its murder, pulled the strings. It, along with something else. The rot festering in the wound. "This place and Hush."

"Is that the name by which she now goes?"

They started, eyed the master of the voice as he approached. He looked every bit of Alerion, midnight-feathered wings and all, but Avaria knew he was not. He reeked of guilt, of anguish. Of pained intent.

"If by she, you mean Mirkvahíl, then yes," Avaria said.

The man eyed him unblinkingly. His stare was glossy, as if Avaria had roused a memory. The man approached; he towered over Avaria, cupped his face and stared into his eyes. "I knew it..." he whispered. "Eyes never lie. Jor Dov'an, as I live and breathe."

He embraced Avaria, clutched him to his chest as if he might fade from existence otherwise.

Avaria returned the gesture; for half a second, it was as if he were home. Varésh Lúm-talé—the name by which this man had gone—had been an uncle to Avaria—Jor—whilst growing up in Ouran'an. A storyteller and a conjurer of possibilities and dreams. He had instilled in Jor the certainty that one day he would see the world beyond the walls of Ouran'an.

Oh, how right he had been.

They pulled away from each other.

Erath looked somewhere in between confusion, exhaustion, and acceptance of the fact that nothing made sense anymore. Sense had all but died the day Avaria departed Helveden.

"Here we stand," murmured Varésh. "In the heart of guilt. So much weight..." He eyed Avaria and Erath. "A man who has cheated time and a woman harboring a power none have ever used for good." He touched his temple at Erath's frown. "The Nameless are afflicted with the memories of every retched life that we have lived. Such is the way of the illum network."

"I pulled this one"—Erath nodded at Avaria—"from the edge

of oblivion. That must be a start toward something good, right? To balance. I think."

Varésh touched her cheek. Nodded. "Balance is evasive. Sought by many, found by few. But you..." Erath's flesh bloomed with rivulets of gentle light. "Something in you wakes."

Gods. What was it with gods and oracular statements? Avaria arched an eyebrow. "Something being...?"

Varésh shrugged. Typical. "Left to hatch as time wills."

"What now?" Erath asked.

"We follow our guilt," said Varésh.

To the heart of Banerowos.

The genesis of mad worlds.

"Time," mused the black-eyed woman. "A beautiful name."

Her smile fell.

"What ails you?" Time asked.

"Many things," she whispered, and her torment spilled from trembling lips.

"I see," said Time. "You are dying in your world."

She was so young. Did he dare?

"What is your power for if not to keep the balance?" a voice inside him asked.

"Some things," said a second voice, *"ought not be meddled in."*

Time gazed at the young woman. Bore into her abyssal stare and dreamt her pain. She was fading. Her world waned. An important one. It whispered in his mind.

He withdrew his stare.

"Fool," the second voice hissed.

"There is a way," said Time. "Words have power."

THE TREE in the center of Sleep was the last to fall.

Time bowed his head to the pile of ash and wept.

Yowled. Fell to the dead grass graced with the corpses of a million stars, a million dreams, and writhed. Shrieked. Retched. This was what it felt like to be sundered from the inside out. So cold he felt aflame.

"You fool," that distant second voice hissed, wept. *"You utter fool."*

Time was still. What a fool, indeed.

Silence so profound he could hear the shrieks of all whom he had failed.

Darkness.

"Hell is a place of one's own making."

Had he said that?

Blink.

The gloom of the world bloomed like fire in grass.

Geph gasped. Sputtered.

Sobbed.

PANDEMONIUM

When had they arrived?

How long had they been here?

Fenrin groaned. Blinked, took in the ugly gray. So many holes in his memories. Not the first time that had happened, not that he was a fan of such obscurity.

He forced himself to stand, nearly stumbled forward thanks to legs weighted by disuse. Truly, how long they been here? They. Them. Kept thinking in pluralities. Looked about—no Luminíl. Just a gorgeous nightmare wrought from darkness, flame, and the light of countless dead and dying stars.

Fear compelled his tongue.

"Are you the one called Hush?"

"In a manner." A voice like dry leaves on an autumn wind.

Lieworlds and effigies snapped across his mind. Memories not his own.

"I see," said Fenrin. He feared this thing, yet his heart ached for her. "Mirkvahíl."

"I never left," she murmured. "Not entirely. This place is cruel... *I* am cruel."

Fenrin clenched his teeth, pushed fruitlessly against the unseen force that brought him to knees. Mirkvahíl was still, eyed him with that horrible starlit gaze. Tattered wings fluttered sadly in the breeze. "You should not have come, Wolf King. I will ruin you." A ragged sigh. "I do not want to—but I will."

Distant shrieks. Disembodied, trapped beyond a veil. Fenrin swallowed a howl.

Mirkvahíl turned, paced slowly, wings trailing like the train of a dress. "...I never wanted *any* of this. Fool... what a fool, I was." She cackled. The tower—Fenrin saw now they were at the pinnacle of a tower—trembled. The cackling fell to a deep sob. "What a fool..."

"You have agency over your actions," Fenrin said. Gasped at the release of weight and rose to his full height. "Why not end this?"

She shook her head. "You know nothing..." Drew a ragged breath, exhaled; the city wailed. "And you know not of what you ask." She tilted her head. "Can you hear it, Wolf King? Can you hear them cry? They are hungry—and they are here."

That ugly voice in his head.

"*Rend. Rip. Repeat.*"

Their anguish as he tore them limb from limb.

"*Blood. Blood for the gods of old.*"

Such fountains of exaltation.

Fenrin closed his eyes. The monster in the darkness met his stare.

"*Guilt is mighty,*" it said. "*I knew one day you would come.*"

Memories of a world beyond, of a tree and a town that once had been.

I will be the Dream Wolf once again, he whispered. *Such little nightmares will I eat.*

The corpse of Banerowos bloomed before his eyes. Fenrin howled, the ruin shook. He flexed his muscles, twitched his tail; this felt right.

He took a running start and leapt.

———

Hush whimpers in the cold and dark of Hang-Dead Forest. Retches at the memories stoked by whispers from the bodies that the trees once wore like festive bells.

"*The veil is weak here.*" Hush starts at the voice. Whirls around. An iteration of her lovely Luminíl. A phantom from a dream. Her name is Djen. "*Nightmares touch what once they could not.*"

"I did this," whispers Hush.

"*Hell is a place of one's own making,*" Djen says.

Hush shivers. She has lost count of how many times that phrase has scraped across her mind like a rusted blade.

"*Why have you come?*" Djen asks. "*What more could you possibly do? How many more ways must I suffer at your hands?*"

"No more suffering. I can fix this," Hush says. "I *will.*"

Djen snorts. "*You* won't, *because you never do. You only ever make things worse.*" She pointed beyond the trees. "*The culmination of your recklessness and arrogance stands atop the spire at the center of the city. You will destroy it—her—if you truly mean to make amends.*"

She sighs. Shakes her head. Her eyes are soft, sad. "*Look at you, my love. This monster you've become. So far gone you have to wear another's face.*" She reaches for Hush, brushes her cheek. "*My Rhona.*"

Rhona.

The forest wanes and waxes, slips in and out of dreams; corpses swing from trees in a pendulum dance and Rhona leads her quarry through the gloom by a tether 'round her neck.

"I do as the Raven wills," she murmurs, and she knows it's all a lie.

She is a lie.

The forest dilates into darkness.

A man screams.

"*We are all of us puppets*," Mirkvahíl uttered. She tugged on Hush's soul from atop the spire. Heard a man scream. "*I'm destroying me, my Luminíl. Colliding worlds will set you free.*"

She walked to the edge of the spire and jumped.

How *many times* was a man destined to see his mother's death?

As Avaria, Queen Ahnil.

As Jor Dov'an, Aveline and Hush.

So wicked was the world that he should lose his mother thrice. He cradled Aveline Dov'an, the monstress wearing her at least. Hush, who'd found him in the rocks and snow near Ouran'an, who had raised him as her own.

She touched his cheek with a cold hand. "...My Jor." Two voices. Avaria choked back a sob. All this time, Aveline had lived. "My boy..."

"You have to rest," Avaria said. "I..."

Fuck.

Fuck.

"So many sins," she whimpered; there was a wholeness to her voice, one that Hush had always lacked. She looked at Geph, at Erath. "I never wanted"—she coughed blood—"this. I did not want to murder them—but I did. Colliding worlds make monsters of us all."

Her flesh peeled like dry paper in the breeze. Threads of mirkúr twisted from the cracks. Braided, swam like serpents toward the center of Banerowos.

"Please... kill me."

And he was holding ash where once had been his mother.

———

THE REMNANTS of Hush's essence brushed Erath as they were drawn away. Kissed her flesh, her mind, and she understood what Hush had meant about having not meant to murder "them."

Aveline. And...

Her knees trembled; it was all she could do to keep from dropping to the earth.

Silith, Queen of the Drenarians, was dead.

Her *mother* was dead.

———

"WE HAVE TO END THIS," said Geph. He could smell the woe on Avaria and Erath. The remorse on Varésh Lúm-talé. This was enough. At its root, this broken world was his creation. He had given Mirkvahíl the keys to monstrousness. Had let her taint and twist a million times a million worlds with her toxic desperation. "Before it's too late."

Maybe it already was.

He yelped, whimpered as the temperature fell. So cold. Such anguish. Only the Vulture had ever touched him with such ice.

She approached at a measured pace, trailing tattered wings, eyes like flame and dying stars. "Welcome home," she said with a voice like dry leaves on the wind. "All of you—so pleased I am to see you here. So long it's been since last I felt your woe."

Gods but there was madness in those eyes.

"We can change things, you and I. Rewrite history to right our wrongs. Return to us the ones we left behind. So special, each of you..."

Avaria, who had leapt through time with every death.

Varésh Lúm-talé, who had swum the Temporal Sea.

Erath, wielder of radich.

And Geph, the previous personification of Time.

"You knew," he uttered, more to himself than Mirkvahíl. "You knew trauma would draw us here—you strung us up like puppets." He snarled at the Vulture. "I helped you once and you destroyed my world. I helped you, and you betrayed your Luminíl."

They encircled Mirkvahíl; Geph felt their rage, *fed* of it. So pure. So hot. *True sin, Gephorax. True sin.* Wrath to strike the monstress down. Wrath to save the world.

———

"Even now you hide. Even now you lie to yourself," said Luminíl. "And for what? Are you so afraid to face the weapons you have wrought? Are you coward enough you cannot look them in the eyes—the lives of whom you robbed of mothers?"

Mirkvahíl whirled to face her. What a sorry thing she had

become. Little less than a remnant of the woman Luminíl had loved those millennia ago when the world was new.

"Underlight is a peculiar place," continued Luminíl. "Labyrinthine, yes, but offering clarity for that is how places of its nature work. These... Pockets of Arcadia as they're known. Do you know what I saw?" She stepped toward Mirkvahíl. "Failure. Dead worlds. You cannot fix what you have wrought, dear Mirkvahíl, because that point in time is lost."

"You lie," said Mirkvahíl. The wind howled; battle sang. So much agony in those ruined streets below. "You are my guilt come to sway me from my prize. *I can fix this!*"

Tentacles of shadow fanned from Mirkvahíl; Luminíl deflected them with ease. The Vulture lacked focus and so unknowingly bled strength.

"*I can save you, Luminíl. I can save us!*"

Us. Them.

Luminíl sighed. "We ended long ago, my Mirkvahíl. And when this night is done, either one or both of us will be a memory."

She unfurled her great, feathered wings and launched herself at Mirkvahíl, but there was only mist. It descended, melded with the spire.

"Have it your way," Luminíl said, and she leapt, hurtling into chaos.

Avaria swung mirkúr blades at Mirkvahíl, but the Vulture moved too quickly to be hit. He stumbled, barely managing to evade retaliation as a spear of darkness screamed past his ear.

"*You are swinging far too wildly,*" chided Jor. "*Do you*

remember nothing? Balance is the key. You cannot bend beneath the madness of this thing."

That was easier said than done for Mirkvahíl exuded frenzied rage. Desperation. She was a parasite of woe infecting all within proximity of her rot.

Avaria rolled behind a slab of ruin. *What do you suggest?*

"Trick her."

How the fuck was he supposed to do that?

He peeked around the debris, watched tendrils of myriad hue and luminosity twist and javelin through the air. Watched Geph and Erath dance as best they could. Heard the shrieks and howls of nearing beasts.

Watched Varésh run the Vulture through with a mirkúr blade and—

Cold air and the kiss of darkness. A throng of distant whispers in his ears.

His eyes adjusted; he was in the bowels of the spire.

———

Varésh Lúm-talé's people called this place the Temporal Annex. He called it his last resort. Jor Dov'an was dead, and this time the old rites wouldn't be enough to bring him back. Something—some things—had to change.

"Are you sure about this?" Erath pulled her cloak tight to ward away the valley wind.

Varésh nodded. "That boy was the closest thing to a son I ever had."

"I understand," Erath said. "I miss him too but consider the consequences."

"I already have."

Varésh stepped toward the stone door embedded in the

mossy earth. He knelt and traced the symbols with his index finger, imbuing them with light until the door dilated to reveal a flight of stairs. The pair descended silently into the odorless abyss.

"Tell her," his conscience urged. She deserves to know before you bleed her dry.

And she will, Varésh promised. Just before.

His conscience sighed. *"When did you become so lost? The you of yesteryear would not have once considered something so extreme. The old you frowned upon such blatant use of temporal alteration. What changed?"*

My heart. He understood now, after all these years, the bond between creator and creation. Planets and people were so much more than playthings, momentary means to entertainment. *All of this, all of them... they were my children—*

"And you have not yet erred so monstrously to warrant going through with what you plan," his conscience argued. *"There is something to be said for that. No parent is perfect, Varésh Lúmtalé, but compared to your fellow Architects you have more heart, more compassion in your index finger than they do combined."*

Varésh offered the argument a melancholy smile. *If only that were so. I'm afraid you have confused my ignorance for moderately sound judgement.* He banished the voice to the abyss of his mind and continued his descent.

Erath cleared her throat. "Do these stairs ever end?"

"Eventually," Varésh said. "Though I can't remember when, exactly."

"Hmm." She rapped the hilt of her dagger. "This place is what...?"

"Far beyond your comprehension, cherished female." Varésh could practically feel her glare. "Beyond anyone's, really.

Imagine, if you can, the absence of time, or yourself existing independently of time."

Erath was silent as the stairway bottomed out into an anteroom of polished white stone. She offered nothing save a deadpan stare and Varésh could tell that she was flummoxed. Or, at the very least, highly annoyed. So, he grinned.

Erath glared. "Could you at least tell me where on Harthe we are?"

"I could," Varésh said, "but it would be irrelevant. We aren't anywhere. Or perhaps we're everywhere. It really is hard to keep it all straight." He wrinkled his nose and blew a strand of dark hair out of his eyes. "Call it... an island somewhere in the Temporal Sea."

Her glared persisted. "Sometimes I really want to stab you."

Varésh chuckled and kept on across the room. "You and many others, cherished female."

He had gone little more than halfway before an inky mottling bloomed along the walls. It spread like flames through grass, forsaking heat in favor of the ether's biting chill.

And then it was gone.

Varésh blinked and looked about the room.

"Varésh? Are you okay?" Erath jabbed his ribs.

He brushed her hand away, still scanning. "...Yes."

Erath arched an eyebrow. "Lead the way."

They crossed the threshold to the passageway beyond, its length pervaded by the scent of rain, its domed ceiling dusted endlessly by dots of light. "Each one, an instance," Varésh said. "A second or a year. A millisecond or one thousand years. Every measure of time the mind can comprehend is represented there."

"And those are every instance of time?" Erath asked.

Varésh chuckled. "Hardly a fraction."

The passageway serpentined; the instances multiplied. Varésh's heart thumped, and his palms were sweaty. *You've come this far*, he urged himself. *Commit, or else your journey here was all for naught. Or else Jor Dov'an remains a ghost, a memory lost to time.*

They kept on in silence.

"Has it occurred to you," his conscience said, *"that something here is wrong? See the frost and rot the walls and ceiling bear. See it suffocate the instances; see the memories die. You have brought a poison to this place."*

Varésh scanned the passageway, and all was well.

The only poison I have brought, he said, *is my intent to bleed this woman dry.*

His conscience growled. *"So, I'm the problem here?"*

The poison, yes, Varésh thought. *If I weren't so ridden with guilt—*

"Then you would sense the foulness creeping through this place like water permeates the earth," his conscience spat.

"Varésh." Erath's hand upon his shoulder startled him from thought. "You're spacing out again."

Varésh chewed his lip. "Just... overwhelmed." He sighed when his conscience made no attempt to refute his claim. "This place and the weight of its... its everything. It can be a bit much sometimes, which is why I endeavor to frequent the Annex as little as I can. I..."

Varésh trailed off. The weight. The rule: no mortal-born may set foot outside time. He eyed Erath; conjured his blade and placed its length between them. "What is this place?"

Erath held her hands up. "The Temporal Annex. Varésh...?"

He shook his head. "If that were so then the laws of time-lessness would have ripped you to bits." He advanced, the glow of his blade reflecting in Erath's eyes—her black eyes. "Who are you? Think carefully before you answer, lest I divorce your head and neck."

Erath sighed, and with her sigh came rime and rot and blackness. The Annex dissolved into a city ruin, Erath into a black-eyed silhouette of rage and woe. *"You have no name,"* she rasped. Grabbed his blade. *"You are a lie, and so you are mine."*

Darkness spread in webs beneath his flesh. His illum blade decayed to ash. He wheeled about and started toward a hound and a dagger-wielding woman, each footstep leaving threads of shadow its wake.

Each footstep conjuring the distant cackle-weep of Sonja's ghost.

THE INTERIOR of the spire was dark, save for the small threads of gray light seeping through the cracks. The floor was stone with varying spherical designs. On either side were columns, running all the way to the end of the room. The density of the walls all but kept the sounds of chaos out, and that meant his own screams would go unheard without.

The darkness here is stifling, Avaria thought. More powerful and ravenous than anything he'd ever felt. He could hear them in his head, whispers. They spoke gibberish at first, but it quickly turned to cackling, and that cackling became a ram, bludgeoning the barriers of his mind. Norema's headless corpse. His mother's face, clear as day, that mad grin stretching nearly ear to her, eyes white as snow.

It was only when Avaria momentarily pushed the images from his mind he realized he was trapped inside the darkness with no light to guide him out. The cackling returned, this time intermixed with childish giggling and the intermittent spoken word.

"*If I am dead upon your reading this...*" the words began. The laughter echoed and Avaria heaved, spewing bile. "*Then know that I thought constantly of you. Know that I am watching over you and am proud of who you have become.*"

"You monster," Avaria growled through his tears.

"*...are arrogant at times...*" There was volume to the cackling now, a physicality that had not been present. "*...I have come to find that people with such glaring faults are often the best...*"

Avaria could not banish her twisted visage from his mind. "STOP IT! STOP IT!" He sprinted blindly, boots smacking stone. He could feel his illum waning; could feel the sinhounds Envy, Pride, and Wrath, his mirkúr swelling like a coastal storm, and he did not care.

"*...I know who you are; I know who you can become. Never be anyone but you.*

All my love—"

Avaria shrieked, swinging wildly, blindly, with his blade.

"*—Mother,*" the voice finished, howling. The blackness swirled, swayed by a gust of wind. It retracted into itself and swarmed to its origin—the outstretched gauntlet of a thing of smoke and flame, the figure from his dream those months ago.

His shadow.

"You have to admit, that was a damn good trick. It makes this little meeting of ours that much sweeter, would you not agree? I told you she would set us free." It breathed a ragged sigh of ecstasy. "You've no idea how long I've been asleep here, waiting. Mother kept us fed"—it licked its cracked lips—"but nothing beats the real thing. Nothing tastes better than slow-cooked self-loathing."

Avaria roared, lunging forward, but his strike was turned

aside with the flick of a wrist. The counter floored Avaria, the force knocking the wind from his lungs. He pushed himself to his feet and leapt again, turned away once more, a mocking laughter bouncing off the walls.

"Fight me, you fuck!" Avaria snarled, wiping blood from his nose.

"So soon?" his shadow asked. "Not until you've heard how much Ahnil screamed inside her mind, how much she begged for mercy as Norema slid her blade into her flesh. Have you ever heard a woman die, Avaria Norrith?"

Avaria swung feebly, too blinded by his rage and tears, to land a hit. The shadow sidestepped easily; Avaria lurched and hit the stones, curled into a ball of misery. The shadow kicked him in the face, shattering several teeth and splitting his lip as its sabaton dragged across Avaria's mouth. Avaria spat blood and fragments, dazed, his vision threatening to fail. With the ounce of willpower that he hadn't yet been robbed of, Avaria forced himself to his feet and conjured his blade again.

The shadow grinned.

Avaria rushed.

———

AVARIA HIT THE STONES AGAIN, spitting blood. A couple of ribs were broken, something in his leg had fractured, but he forced himself to stand, to face this monster, the worst of himself. He brought his blade up, feebly deflecting the shadow's strike. It missed his chest by inches, instead screaming down his left arm. Hot pain bloomed almost immediately. There was no conversing with this creature any longer. Whatever joy it had taken in taunting him had vanished. He had to end this quickly.

Avaria dodged another blow. With every swing of that

sword, the shadow's attacks gained speed and momentum. It roared, slamming a gauntleted fist into Avaria's chest. Avaria tapped his mirkúr, stepping through the shadows. He emerged on the far side of the chamber, winded. Hadn't done *that* in ages.

Like smoke, the monster was before him. It gripped Avaria by the throat and tossed him like a rag doll, but Avaria rushed again. He vaulted through the shadows, barreling shoulder-first into his demon twin. His right hand found purchase on its armor. Instinctively, Avaria imbued the plate with illum until it shattered like glass.

"You are a Reshaper," Jor urged mentally *"You have all the power you require."*

Avaria grasped at the breastplate. The shadow, though, had caught on to his plan. Face contorted with rage, it lashed out with a series of furious strikes, drawing crimson grins on Avaria's arms and face.

"*Again,*" Jor said. "*Illum is the key. Balance.*"

Balance—that was it. The shadow was conflicted, off kilter. So much mirkúr, so little illum.

"Come here, you fuck," he growled. He had to end this thing.

He had an idea to weaken Mirkvahíl.

———

How sweet they tasted. How divine their deaths in a ruin long condemned to rot. He had eaten each and every one as they arrived. Every wrong and twisted soul, hound and Jémoonite alike. Devoured and delivered from millennia of hell. All save one. Pale-eyed, dead of flesh, hair trailing to mist.

"Sonja," he said. Such horror. "You seek vengeance."

"*No,*" she hissed. "*Catharsis.*"

Her fingers were talons, her memories were black, a master of the pendulum dance. A partnerless waltz in the dark of the wood.

"*He will falter,*" she said. "*As he is fated. He is nameless yet he is also a lie.*" Her eyes shone. "*They* both *are lies. He and the Vulture up high. But I know where she sleeps; I know where she hides.*"

Fenrin lowered himself; Sonja climbed onto his back.

"*In the heart of the tallest tower stands a tree.*"

———

AVARIA HAD DISAPPEARED. It was all Geph and Erath could do to push back against Mirkvahíl and her puppet. Varésh Lúm-talé had fallen prey to her rotten touch. Rather, he had fallen prey to himself, and the Vulture had done what carrion creatures do best.

He lunged at Geph with that dark blade, propelled with a flap of his wings. Geph leapt to the side. Where he'd stood, where the blade made contact, was ash. Whatever it was the Vulture had done to Varésh Lúm-talé had turned him into wither made manifest.

He vaulted toward Geph again, using his wings to add strength to his strike. Geph faltered—but the blade was turned back a sword of brilliant blue light. Erath pushed against Varésh, her flesh alight with radich. She swung with the prowess of a seasoned warrior, and each strike seemed to slow Varésh's moves.

Geph shifted focus to the Vulture. Bared his teeth and closed the distance between them with a single leap. He clamped his jaws around her shoulder and shook, tasting the sour sick of the fluid oozing from the wound. He dug in, bore his claws into her side; fed on the wrath of countless dead as he mangled her arm.

She flung him back with a shriek; Geph landed on his feet.

"I made you," he growled. "I will end you."

Something snapped, popped in the center of his mind and he could perceive time as sharp fluctuations of temperature. So frigid was the past, so seething was the present. He danced the temporal current; waltzed between the golden years and corpse of Banerowos as he zeroed in on the Vulture. She had been beautiful once—a thousand times over, in fact. But he had made her *this*. Abetted insanity.

He emerged from the current in a blur, barreling into her with the weight of a thousand years behind him—but she was smoke. Geph plunged into the temporal current, searching.

Something smelled wrong.

———

Erath parried, drove her blade into Varésh all the way to the hilt. The moment stilled; the world fluctuated; memories shifted. So many failures; so many desperate iterations doomed to fail. How could they not have seen? How could they wield such energy as radich yet be ignorant of the past? So much possibility, so little wisdom.

She yanked the blade from his chest with a squelch and he fell to his knees.

"Such... hell," he murmured, tears trailing down his cracked cheeks. "What a lie." He met her eyes. "We never deserved such power, did my temporal twins and I. Power... does terrible things." He titled his head back to look at the ugly night. "I thought I was a god... but I was only a fool."

Gradually, he wilted, and his body fell to ash.

"You *all* are fools," Erath whispered of his iterations. "And you will never learn."

Time was not a thing to be meddled with. She lamented their arrogance—theirs and Aveline's. Mirkvahíl's, even, curse the wretched beast.

Erath looked about; she was alone.

She started for the center of the city at a run.

HOUSE OF THE DYING SUN

Avaria lunged at his shadow, grasping desperately at the plate carapace it wore. If he could just shatter that armor and reach the flesh it concealed...

"Every move. Futile." The shadow caught him with an elbow to the throat.

Avaria spat blood. His muscles ached; his bones screamed. He could hardly find the strength to move. What small amount he still possessed served little more than to allow the shadow a shot at his face. The sabaton connected with a crunch.

"This?" It stomped again. "Fun. Simple sport."

"Reshape," Avaria gurgled. His vision was clouded, speech partially obstructed by a broken nose. He spat more blood, fragments of teeth. "Remake." He coughed. "Fix... the past."

"Mother has already begun," the shadow hissed, sword raised above its head.

Avaria could hardly move.

A burst of illumination rippled through the chamber and

speared the shadow in the chest. It hit the wall with a crack, sword knocked from its grasp.

Through the growing haze, Avaria saw two figures charge the room. Both female from the looks, though it was hard to make out much except the fact that one looked dead and the other gripped a blade of brilliance unlike anything Avaria had ever seen.

———

"Damn it all," Erath cursed. She knelt beside Avaria's mangled... Fuck, she hoped 'corpse' wasn't the right word. Not now. Not when mad-as-shit goddesses saw fit to send the world to its end.

"Avaria Norrith... Jor Dov'an—whoever the fuck you are— you had best open your eyes." She touched a glowing fingertip to his chest. "A little pain never hurt, hmm?"

Avaria gurgled. Then came a word. Or was it a name?

Erath frowned. "What was that? Ee? What the hell does that mean?" She leaned in closer; her eyes widened. "*Me—you.*" She looked up, wincing as Sonja—her new companion—took a forearm to the chin. Shadows of self had such violent tendencies.

Erath stood and danced her way into the fray, she and Sonja trading blows with Avaria's shadow, memories rushing to the forefront with every swing. Erath's sword screamed down the breastplate. She pushed, urging the radich to leave her blade, to saturate the plate. It was something that had simply come to her on her sprint through Banerowos. If she could imbue these monsters with enough counter energy to achieve balance, there was a chance she could restore their minds.

At least enough to avert disaster. She punched the shadow in the face, grasped its gorget and took an elbow to the eye.

"*Play nicely,*" Sonja hissed. "*Your* true mother *abhorred such violence.*"

That touched a nerve.

The shadow staggered, caught off guard by Sonja's jibe. Erath took the opening and gripped the breastplate and left pauldron, imbuing it with radich. A loud crack sounded as the tarnished plate shattered in several areas.

"How haunted you must be," Erath hissed. "I wonder if you know—"

The shadow snarled. It charged recklessly, blade striking stone as Erath and Sonja parried.

"—that your beloved Mother Mirkvahíl murdered your *true mother*, Aveline." What a shit thing to say. Erath ducked—she was surprised by her newfound agility—and swiped at the shadow's legs. Her sword crashed against the demon's greaves, tripping it. "How many times now has your mother died? And to think—this time you're to blame."

The shadow rolled over, exposed by the fractured plate—an invitation.

Sonja leapt at the opportunity; Erath cried out.

———

Luminíl entered the central spire. The moment she crossed the threshold she knew that something was wrong. Old energy waned. Old life, old memories. She had seen the girl Erath and the rusalk Sonja enter not minutes ago.

She crossed the antechamber, the density of this ancient spire once more silencing the madness without. Presently, she reached the central chamber. No Erath. No whatever it was they had been fighting.

Her breath caught—Avaria, still as death. Just beyond him, Sonja, writhing. Luminíl crossed the room, dropped to her knees beside the rusalk, lungs tight in her chest.

"Sonja," she whispered.

Sonja groaned, hardly able to sit up. Luminíl conjured an illum wisp and set about analyzing the severity of the rusalk's wounds. She could make out the deep gash in her chest. It hissed and smoked where she had been run through.

"Just a little longer." She pinched the flesh together with one hand, dragging an illuminated fingertip across it with the other as Sonja hissed. It was temporary; Luminíl knew it wouldn't hold. And maybe that was for the best. Maybe Sonja could finally rest.

The tower quaked. Sonja managed to sit herself up, though she looked ready to pass out at any moment. She pointed... Was it up, maybe toward the doorway—outside? Further in?

"*Illum*," she whispered raggedly, spitting blood. "*You have... to flood them.*"

She fell back and her eyes fell shut.

"How many times," Luminíl whispered, "must we suffer for their sins?" She kissed Sonja on the forehead. Her oldest friend, the two of them betrayed. "Rest now. You are free."

Behind her, Avaria groaned. She rushed to his side.

"D-Down," he stammered. He looked beaten to a pulp, yet still he persevered. She pulled him to his feet. "They went... down."

Luminíl's ears twitched. She turned, greeted by Geph and Fenrin. Such auras.

Fenrin eyed Sonja. He bowed his head. "May she finally rest."

"We need to end this," Geph said. "Banerowos is unstable. The more energy Mirkvahíl exerts, the more the city shifts between the veil of time. Whatever it is she's done, whatever monsters she's created, it's quite literally deteriorating the temporal barrier."

"Into the depths," Fenrin said, "for in the heart of the tower stands a tree."

Luminíl sneered. She knew that tree well.

"What a twisted puzzle," Avaria murmured. "It's not that she's deteriorating the temporal barrier. Her mind is labyrinthine, and we are simply pawns." He spat blood. Frowned. "No. Not pawns, I think. Predators—and she is our prey. She is afraid and she runs just as she's always done. Reality bleeds with her internal fictions."

He eyed Sonja's corpse; worry fell over him. "I saw another enter. Was it Erath? Where is she?"

———

"WHAT DO YOU FEAR?" the darkness asked. "Whom *do you fear?*"

Daylight and a blazing sun. *"For what do you long?"*

"For that which you desire most, what price will you pay?" Laughter. A meadow in fall. *"For whom you desire most, what price will you pay?"*

A fluttering of wings. Distant screams.

"Stay away," the darkness wept. *"Stay away from this awful place."*

Erath's footfalls echoed; she was in a hallway somewhere, seeking something wrong. Faded symbols lined the walls; the air smelled of a dying breath. The odor dragged her onward, deeper; spellbound, she descended into screams and snaps of falsities. Nightmares lived repeatedly of their master's own volition.

Radich bloomed at the center of her chest, emanating outward as an aegis. Chaos ricocheted off the gentle light as Erath walked, fruitless in its efforts to abscond with her lucidity.

Her descent yawned into a forest dark. Corpses hung from trees and held each other in a dance. Had it not been so macabre, there might have been a beauty to it all. A twisted elegance.

"Are you going to show yourself?" she inquired of the shadow she had chased. "Or are you going to hide? What a coward, hiding while I stalk your mother's tortured dreams." She had sensed upon entering this place that it defied reality, that somehow Mirkvahíl's insanity was so profound it had infected Banerowos like an incubus, subjecting all to the Vulture's guilt and dread.

Silence.

"You will," she pressed. "Because you don't exist, not entirely. Another lie." Her barrier bloomed. "How many, Mirkvahíl? How many lies do you hide behind? Will you not show yourself to me?"

"You have to know where to look." Luminíl emerged from a twist of light. "She'll not willingly reveal herself to anyone, not even me—but I know where she sleeps. After all this time."

———

A TREE STOOD NEAR A LAKE. Neither was an approximation of reality, but an amalgamation of what had been so long ago when the world was good. Rhona slept against its trunk and the wind kissed her cheeks. She could stay here forever. She *would* stay here forever. At least here she was safe; at least here *they* were safe from *her*.

How many horrors had she wrought? Mirkvahíl and Hush. So many more devoid of names and ripe with pain.

"How do you know you're even real?" the voice inside her asked. *"How do you know you're not the lie?"*

Truth be told she didn't. All she knew was she was mad, and the world was dead.

"It didn't have to be like this," the memory of Alerion said.

"But you chose power over people," said the whole of Banerowos.

"Power over love," said the memory of Djen.

"Lies," said a wolf.

Not a memory. She cowered against the tree at the sight of the incorporeal beast. Eyes like dead stars and a form that trailed to mist. "Than Sor'al, please leave me be."

How did she know that name? Why was this monster here?

"I cannot," said Than Sor'al. "Now that I have found you, Vulture, I cannot. You have taken from me—you have taken from us all." It neared her; dropped beside her like a pup. "You have taken from yourself, and that is the most profound sin of them all." It nuzzled her knee; its nose was cold. "It is time for things to end." It shifted shape; before her stood a man of silver hair and eyes. He held his hand to her. "Will you come with me? Will you let me deliver you from this nightmare?"

She stood, took his hand. Tears streamed from her eyes. "I wish I could." The sanctuary melted and a forest dark of dancing corpses bloomed. "But I cannot, and you were a fool to have come here."

"That's the thing," said Than Sor'al. "I am not here."

———

CHAINS OF ILLUMINATION bound the Vulture where she stood. Behind her reared a tree that Avaria had seen so many times in memories, dreams, and things of each. The Lost Tree. Memory. Sorrow. Thorn. Bringer, the very illum network itself. Encircling the Vulture were Erath, Luminíl, and Fenrin. It was by chance they had come across the former in this twisted place, and it was by greater chance that Fenrin had been far more than he seemed. Wolf King. The Dream Wolf.

Geph stood beside him, fur like needles, teeth bared. His eyes were restless.

"Hang-Dead Forest was beautiful once," Luminíl said softly. She approached the Vulture, stopped just shy of their noses touching. "You were beautiful once, but you lost yourself somewhere and when." She caressed her cheek. "My Mirkvahíl."

"Rhona," said the Vulture. "I am Rhona. Rhona!"

Luminíl shook her head sadly. "Lies. Even now, at the end."

"Rhona!" she sobbed. "I want... to be Rhona. To *be*—"

In a flash, Rhona fell to luminescent mist. Blades of darkness strafed the trees and Avaria's shadow erupted from the woods, a sick amalgamation of his inner darkness and what essence of the Vulture remained. He parried the blade, but only just, while Luminíl and Fenrin each were felled before they could retaliate.

Geph howled as corpses fell from the trees and rose like ugly puppets. Howled like Avaria had never heard before and all seemed to *slow*. Together they assailed the shambling dead, and from the corner of his eye Avaria saw a blue light wrap itself around his shadow's neck and *pull*.

He wheeled around and reality was all but still.

No, he thought. *I'm just too slow.*

Erath took his shadow into her, bloomed like an eclipse.

What is she—no! There was another way. "*Erath!*"

She shone like a beacon, pulsing with the brilliance of radich.

Time caught Avaria like the raging sea. His ears rang. He stumbled toward her—

but the blade was already buried in her chest.

And she was on her knees and her eyes were wide.

And the world was silent.

———

Dying hurt far less than Erath had ever anticipated.

Blood leaked from the wound, from her lips. She was cradled in her father's arms. "I had to," she whispered. She looked at Avaria. "There was no other way. Only..." She gestured vaguely at the dagger, at the glow of radich. "Possibility."

"Then you can save yourself," Avaria whispered. Dropped beside her, held her hand. Tears trickled down his cheeks. "Possibility. You—"

She shook her head. She was cold and the world was growing dark. "Doesn't... work like that." Spat blood. "Only one impossible thing... made possible." Lest the cycle never end; lest the Vulture's madness only spread. She touched his hand, smiled. Looked at her father, Fenrin. "Papa..."

It was good to finally call him that again.

EPILOGUE
TO THOSE LEFT BEHIND

One Year Later

Avaria had never been fond of heights, but even he had to admit the world looked brilliant from so high a perch. Geph sat beside him, tongue hanging lazily from his mouth.

"What a long, strange year it's been..."

Avaria thumbed the bundle in his arms; a lump formed in his throat. It was time.

To express what'd taken him a year to figure out.

To finally say goodbye. Tonight, she'd leave him on a breeze.

Tonight, he'd give his mother's remnants to the world.

A wet, ragged sigh escaped Avaria's lips; he cleared his throat.

"Your mother would be proud," said Geph, "and I'm proud for her."

Avaria twitched a melancholy smile. Not just a strange year, but a busy one at that. He'd swum the Temporal Sea for educational import. With Geph and Fenrin at his side he'd walked the Fountainhead and seen the madness of it all—the beginning and the end.

"How many worlds, Geph—how many worlds beside our own?"

"A fathomless amount," said Geph. "Where do you think we'll end up next?"

"Somewhere with a gentle breeze, I hope—to remind us both of home."

Footsteps.

"I was wondering when you'd show," Avaria said. He'd detected Fenrin in the illum network several minutes prior. "How are you feeling?"

Fenrin spoke no reply as he joined them. He too held a bundle in his hands.

Avaria gave his arm a pat. "They would be proud of you."

Geph nodded.

Fenrin allowed himself a hint of a smile. There was sadness in his silver eyes; there had been for as long as Avaria had known the man. These days it was simply *more*—and Avaria understood.

"We had little of Alor, and nothing of Leru," said Fenrin softly. "That I should have my Erath's ashes brings me warmth in the worst of ways. If only—Silith..." He fell to his knees, tears streaming from his eyes. "I miss my family."

Avaria bowed his head. A memory bloomed.

Moonlight. Virgin snow. The looming Hall and his mother's gentle hand. She'd always said being drafted to the Hall was the best thing that happened to people. Avaria had never understood why until now. The realization made him weep.

She'd wanted him to have a choice. She'd never wanted him

to be a slave to familial convention like Avaness and Maryn, never wanted him shackled to this place, to a city and a country glorifying war. She had loved him in the ways she knew how, the ways by which she'd been shown love for all her life—and she had freed him.

Wind.

A breeze. Cold and comforting all at once—the goddess Luminíl.

"Your sorrow drew me here."

Avaria looked at her, bore into her dead-moon eyes. They held something she had never shown—hesitation. He beckoned Luminíl to join them in the glade. They were not the only ones to have lost their loved ones in a war, and Luminíl had lost hers twice.

"You are welcome here," said Fenrin to the Phoenix as he rose.

"You're a friend whether you like it or not," said Geph.

Luminíl quirked a smile, the first from her Avaria had ever seen.

"One year," she said. "One year to the day." She heaved a sigh and the shadows wept. "Is it possible for joy and misery to be so heavily entwined? We are all of us free from Mirkvahíl, from her pestilence and sway, and yet her spirit seeks to harrow me with thoughts of better days..."

Avaria gave her hand a gentle squeeze.

"I want to sleep," said Luminíl. "Would you begrudge my absence?"

"Not at all," Avaria said. Sleep in the context of a goddess was a very different thing. "You've earned your rest."

Luminíl smiled and pulled Avaria into a tight embrace. This, he realized, was the true Luminíl; the Phoenix that'd been buried in the shadows for a thousand years and more, bound by misery and guilt. Her tension bled away as he held her close; a spark of warmth bloomed above Avaria's heart.

She was gone.

"I hope we see her again," said Geph.

"As do I," said Fenrin. He walked to the edge of the glade, overlooking the world. From his bundle he procured a glowing illum orb. It hovered in his palm as Fenrin drew its light. When he was done, there lingered several smaller beads as bright as, if not brighter than the source from which they'd come.

"They're beautiful," Geph whispered. "*She's* beautiful."

Avaria swallowed the lump in his throat. He'd thought of Erath with increasing frequency these last few months. She'd saved his life—saved *everyone* by letting Mirkvahíl enthrall her form. Would that he could, he'd find a way to bring her back, but the dead were better left to lie.

He and Geph joined Fenrin at the cliff. From his bundle he procured a similar orb, drew its energy until a dozen motes remained. They hovered there above his palm; for a moment he was scared to let them go, for if he did it meant that she was well and truly gone—and how could he accept the finality of such a thing?

"*Letting go is always hard,*" said Jor.

I know, Avaria thought. *I just...*

"*Regret what never was,*" the allhound said. "*Grief has no chronology; there are many stages, many paths walked many times. In grief we* meet *shame, but there is never shame* in *grief, Avaria.*"

Avaria nodded. He felt better for the words. Better, yet still afraid of letting go. *But I must.* He sighed deeply and broke his mental tether to the wisps. Beside him, Fenrin did the same.

They stood there and they stared. And when Fenrin finally withdrew, Avaria lingered longer yet with Geph, watching the remnants of his mother and Erath enfold themselves within the winter night and stars. He trembled.

Geph licked his hand. "Do you remember when we met?"

Avaria smiled—and he sat there in that memory of happiness and snow.

Just a boy

and a dog.

THE WORLD REAPER
ODYSSEY

BEING A DREAM WITHIN THE NIGHTMARE

"There is no greater sorrow than to recall our times of joy in wretchedness."
— Dante Alighieri, *The Inferno*

WALKER

I *am not ready for this.*

Rhona stared down the forest pathway leading from her village. It was black as pitch. Her knees knocked together and she wished she had never been able to understand the words now ringing through her head. It would have brought her father shame, but it would have kept her from the task ahead. Alf elo nor meant one for all; they marked her as a Walker. Rhona knew she would never live up to those words and its mantle.

This is not right, she thought, but the hunting knife strapped to her belt suggested it was.

Rhona glanced at the tether in her hand. At its end was a silver doe with azure eyes. The self-repugnance rose like a river in spring. How could they expect her to gut and bleed such an innocent thing?

"You have until the Vulture's Moon to reach the shrine," her father said.

Both were half a month away. Rhona choked down bile rising at the thought of failure. A belated offering to Yll, the

Raven of Jémoon, would be disastrous; it had happened several times before. Rivers would dry up. Game would grow sparse. Plagues would spread and people would starve. As the Raven went so too did the people of Jémoon.

"Alf elo nor," said Rhona. She kissed her father on the cheek then started on her way.

The doe was silent as they walked and Rhona could not decide whether or not it was because she simply had nothing to say—*As if a doe could speak!*—or if she was scrutinizing Rhona's unease and plotting her escape.

"I wish you *could* speak," Rhona said. "I wish you could understand I have no desire to spill your blood."

The doe tilted her head and Rhona sighed. She kept to the path as best she could; the way was dim. She drew her knife, pricked her index finger, and held her hand out to the forest. "Alf elo nor." Something brushed across her finger, drinking from the tiny wound, and the pathway bloomed with light.

"Alf elo nor is more than just words," her father had said. "It is the way of things in the forest. An offering of blood for aid."

The small birds—gleamers—now flittering through the air were proof of this—a drop of life for all the light they could give. Rhona's blood would keep them healthy for the year and their radiance would guide her for the night.

How long I have been walking?

Rhona had departed shortly after midnight, armed with just her knife as per Walker custom. The journey to the shrine was so much more than just an offering to Yll. It was a time to test one's mettle and resourcefulness.

"I have the blood, they will come," she whispered. A part of her worried about keeping track of time, but Rhona heaved a sigh, deciding, for the moment, it was pointless to fret. *Dusk is dusk and dawn is dawn. Just focus on the path and keep yourself awake. Your longest yawn will tell you when to sleep.*

IT WAS BARELY daybreak when that yawn came. Rhona stretched her arms, eyes open just enough to see the hints of sunlight creeping through the dense canopy of the Korjin Forest. It refracted off the moonstones scattered here and there and zigzagged through the trees, like needles drawing thread.

Rhona tied the tether to a branch, watching momentarily as the doe nibbled at the grass. She sat against the trunk of a tree and massaged her legs; her calves burned. Her mouth was dry. She drew her knife and made a shallow cut along her arm, then dug a half foot into the dirt and let the blood drip. It bled into the earth, absorbed into the tree's roots. In return the tree presented Rhona with the means to quench her thirst.

Rhona cupped her hands and drank feverishly until there was nothing left. She leaned back against the tree and closed her eyes. It would be a miracle if she made it to the shrine alive. Two cuts, two offerings, in a span of several hours. At this rate she would bleed out quicker than the Vulture's Moon arrived. The other Walkers would be shamed by such dependency.

Focus on the journey, Rhona told herself in an attempt to ward away fear. The Korjin Forest ran roughly twelve miles before it spilled into a meadow. Beyond the meadow was the Nohl Waypoint. She had gone four or five miles alread.

Rhona opened her eyes and looked at the doe. "You lucked out," she said. "I will probably die of blood loss before we reach the shrine and then you will be free."

The doe looked up a moment, tilted her head, then returned to chomping the grass.

. . .

Alf elo nor was the way of things in the forest; it was the food chain, the circle of life. Despite knowing this, Rhona found herself angry and fearful as a pack of dusk wolves descended on her from the darkness of the trees. Dusk wolves only prowled the forest at night; Rhona cursed herself for having slept through the day.

The doe flailed wildly on her tether. Rhona stumbled to her feet and placed herself between the doe and the wolves, knife drawn, extended toward the growls. She trembled, biting back tears. *I will not be their one.* So long as scarlet coinage flowed in her veins, Rhona knew she had a chance. The dusk wolves neared, their hoary eyes ablaze, and an idea reared its head.

Rhona had always been a strong and willing reader. Her mind was as absorbent as her reluctance for this task was strong. Had she not been a Walker, she would have been unable to request assistance from the gleamers and the trees. But—

She steeled her nerves and dragged the knife across her palm. "Alf elo nor!" The dusk wolf nearest her lunged and lapped the blood feverishly as Rhona shook. She retreated once the entranced beast had finished gorging itself, untied the doe, and took off down the mote-lit path. In her wake the dusk wolves snarled and the sounds of fight and tearing flesh screamed through the night.

Some hours later, Rhona reached the edge of the forest, the pathway shifting from dirt to a mottling of stones and tall grass turned reddish-orange by the moon. A breeze tousled the reeds as Rhona tied the doe to a branch. Once more she took a seat against a tree. Adrenaline had kept her going; she had rested maybe once or twice since fleeing the wolves, though she was not really sure. The entire trek still seemed a thankfully bloodless blur.

Rhona gazed out at the meadow, fingering the makeshift

bandage wrapped around her hand. She took a deep and contented breath, mind relaxing as a mixture of vanilla and honey permeated the air. She realized now why a Walker's path went straight through here, why they always dropped bundles of this grass in the village fires, why everyone went about their days in peace.

A yawn escaped.

She closed her eyes.

MEADOW

R hona doubled over to catch her breath. She was little more than halfway across the plains now, sweat dripping from her brow, wishing she had traded for hydration earlier when she had roused. Her throat was dry and itched horribly. She rubbed her legs, the muscles tight and knotted beneath her fingers.

A gentle melody swam through the air. *Singing?* Rhona straightened up and squinted east; eventually the figure a woman came to light. She was tan, her long red hair swam on the air, and she wore a simple white gown and nothing else. Her eyes were silver; Rhona decided she was radiant.

And most likely an illusion. Surely fashioned by thirst.

The singing ceased. Rhona blinked and the woman was just feet away.

"Greetings, weary wanderer."

Rhona shifted slightly, looking past the woman. "Where...?"

"...Did I come from?" The woman smiled. "A village just a

couple miles east. Yanegé. I walk the plains each day to gather flowers from the lake."

Rhona cocked her head.

"Just west of here." The woman narrowed her eyes. "You look a bit ill."

"Water," Rhona said weakly.

"Come with me to the lake. It isn't far. A conversation would be nice. It will quell my boredom and distract you from your thirst." The woman eyed the doe, reaching toward her with a steady hand, but the creature stepped away and munched the grass.

"Does she have a name?"

Sacrifice. Rhona lowered her eyes. "No."

"I understand. I am called Jeynar."

"Rhona."

"Well then, Rhona. What say we seek the lake?"

"Lead the way."

They walked in silence for a time.

"Why come all this way for flowers?" Rhona asked. The world around her spun a little more with every step; she hoped the lake was near. "And how does a lake—I see no hint of a river in sight."

Jeynar chuckled softly. "You trust your eyes too much."

"Is the river underground?" Rhona stumbled. She could not help laughing. "Ravens, I could really...use...a drink."

"We are nearly there."

They crested a small hill and there the lake sat—placid as the evening sky in spring. Rhona bounded toward it. Behind her Jeynar sung.

Rhona's reflection stared back as she cupped her hands and brought the water to her lips. It was cold and refreshing. Before she knew it she had dropped the tether and was wading through the shallows toward the center of the lake. Jeynar's song infected her with urges and she twirled along.

The water was up to her nose now.

She was underwater.

Her knife was in her hand.

Her blood was in the lake.

She was in the plains. It was sundown and the lake was screaming. No—some*thing* was screaming, silhouetted by the westward setting sun. A gangly shadow, fingers spindly, hungry.

Then it was night.

Rhona bolted upright and the world spun.

"Easy, now." The displaced voice was stout but gentle. The speaker rested a hand on Rhona's shoulder. Gradually the plains and evening came to rest. Rhona took several deep breaths. The doe slept beside her, nose against her leg. Before them was a figure of daylight, like a mannequin with a cloak, faceless but alive.

"What...happened? There was...Jeynar. The lake—"

"She is bound once more to the lake," said the voice. "I sealed her there myself and pulled you from her grasp, though I was nearly too late. The song of the Jétjune Queen is mesmerizingly deadly."

Rhona groaned and cursed her stupidity. *I should have known.* She had read about the Jétjune Queen as a child, and her father had told her stories to scare her to sleep. For the longest time that was all they had been—stories. She could hear her father's chiding in her head: "Everything has a purpose." That meant stories too.

Rhona looked at her savior. "Thank you. Who are you?"

"I am a spirit called Orjem."

Rhona perked up. "Like the waypoint?"

"Indeed. It was built by my family..." The spirit trailed off. "But their blood is no more; I am all that remains and that is not much. It does not pay to be careless. To bargain with the Jétjune Queen means death...

"Moons ago I loved a woman named Oroe and she loved me. We lived east in the village Yanegé. We were happy. But she passed and I went mad. They told me not to seek the dead. They said souls were not to be reborn, but I was deaf to their advice and so I journeyed to the very lake I pulled you from.

"I tried to barter with Jeynar. I offered everything," said Orjem, "and got nothing in return. She took my flesh and blood, took my Oroe's body as her own, and walked the Sorjen Plains, seeking Walker blood to keep her frame. But she is trapped again now and the sward is safe."

"I am sorry," said Rhona. She gazed at Orjem's fiery, flickering shape. "Your appearance..."

"In the darkness I am sunlight," Orjem said. "I can touch the world as though I still had flesh and bone. But by the light of day I am naught but wind."

"Are there more like you?" Rhona asked.

"Trickster stricken? Undoubtedly. For every spirit in this world there live a dozen imbeciles a finger snap away. If there are others like myself—shadeseen—our paths have yet to cross."

Rhona looked beyond the shadeseen.

"You are anxious," Orjem said.

"I had hoped to be at the waypoint hours ago."

Orjem rose. "I will guide you on your way. At the waypoint you will sleep, and on the morrow we will depart for Misten Fahg, the northernmost waypoint of Jémoon."

"You are familiar with the path?" Rhona asked.

"Yes," said Orjem. "You are far from the first Walker I have guided."

Rhona smiled wearily. "I am grateful for your help."

She gave the doe a gentle, rousing pat and stood, the graceful creature rising up beside her, eyes alert. Rhona took the tether and followed Orjem, brightened by the spirit's warming glow in more way than one.

BERRIES

Rhona yawned and flexed her muscles. It was early; the sun had yet to rise and the moon had yet to fully wane. She led the doe along, the pair approaching Orjem at the waypoint's northern edge. The spirit waited like a beacon, and the closer Rhona got the warmer she became.

Soon I shall be halfway toward the shrine. What did it look like? How would she know when she arrived? What would await her?

Rhona started slightly, aggravated by the remnants of a dream. *Perhaps the plains' perfume does more than just relax the mind.* That made no sense, though. Or did it? She eyed Orjem. Was there a chance the spirit's presence was to blame?

It was just nerves, Rhona decided, as she led the doe after Orjem. It had not even been a week since she had departed from the village and already she felt the weight of her task. Wolves, thirst, and murderous spirits. What next?

Rhona took a small sip from her newly acquired waterskin. How refreshing it was! So cold and crisp, no blood required

She was thankful for that, for the fact the waypoint had a well. Her stomach roared.

Rhona was *not* thankful for her hunger.

"The land beyond this waypoint is filled with game and roots. You'll find nutrition there," Orjem said. He paused, "Another drink would do you well, my friend. You look tired."

Rhona did as was suggested. She rolled her shoulders back and set her jaw, the waypoint fading as they ventured forth.

Every step she took was the farthest Rhona had ever been from home. It was as frightening a notion as it was exciting. Her stomach rumbled for the umpteenth time that day, and it was all she could do to keep from groaning in complaint. She hoped every step she took was also one more toward a meal.

Rhona took one last backward glance at the plains before they crossed into the woods. Immediately she felt cold. There was something ill about this place, something old. Something watchful. The hair on Rhona's neck stood tall. Everywhere she looked she felt but saw no eyes. She trembled, looking to Orjem for an answer, for relief.

"Keep your focus on the path," the shadeseen said. "Those who mind the forest's rules are safe. Wander where you ought not, though, and pay a heavy price."

Rhona attempted to subdue her trembling but doing so was folly. She frowned, looking at the motes of light—they were veering west and off their path.

"Do not stray," warned Orjem, as if sensing her curiosity.

"But the trail of light—"

"*Do not stray.*"

They continued on, Rhona's arms folded against her chest, the doe walking vigilantly at her side. A creature fated for a sacrificial ending, she felt like a friend to Rhona, and she hated herself. Did the doe know Rhona meant to spill her blood in offering to her god?

"Sunrise must be soon," said Rhona. "Yet the forest only seems to darken. Why?"

"The Dusk Ones," Orjem said. "They rule the Korjin Wood for miles in all directions."

"The Dusk Ones?"

"Mages," Orjem said. "Exiled by the Korjin Empire; afflicted by the wild Dusk."

"Is that why it is so relentlessly dark?" Rhona asked.

"I am not completely sure," said Orjem. "The wild Dusk is...well, wild, perhaps even sentient. It is a power source the mages are unable to fully control. As the stories go, it warped their minds, made them violent and aggressive toward the careless wanderers who occasionally invade their shadowed world."

"How did this happen to the Dusk?" Rhona asked.

"Some believe it went rogue when Jévim, the previous Raven of Jémoon, was cast out by her brethren, but who can really say? Come. Our egress lies just ahead."

Rhona nodded, wondering if the shadeseen's glow would ward the Dusk Ones off or rile them into action. She hoped it was the former. Even if Orjem's words were true, the wayward mages would not harm them if they stayed their course, even with the spirit's glow a possible antagonist.

At length they reached a clearing and the Dusk dispersed. Rhona sighed, eyes closed, face tilted toward the sky. The sunlight warmed her and she felt her fear begin to fade, superseded by a renewed sense of hope.

"Our journey through the wood is not yet done," said Orjem, "but this clearing runs about a mile. Long enough to let the touch of Dusk evaporate completely, though you will no doubt feel it more than once this journey."

They continued on their way, the sunlight pleasant, Orjem's phantom presence calming. Eventually the threshold to the Korjin Wood took shape and the shadeseen manifested in the shadow of the trees, gesturing they rest.

Rhona sprawled out across the grass while the doe reached down to chomp the sward. She ate quickly, her dark nose twitching every now and then. Rhona's stomach roared and she glanced at her hands and arms, mouth watering pensively. She shifted focus to the trees just yards away. Would they offer sustenance like they had the other night?

"Keep your knife," said Orjem.

It was only now Rhona noticed her hand was wrapped around the hilt. She chuckled sheepishly, if not a little wearily, and set about watching the clouds.

"It is tempting," Orjem said, "especially when you are privy to the fruit your blood bears. But trials greater than a rumbling stomach lay ahead. Let that knowledge help to temper your urges."

Rhona stood and ventured toward the trees, stopping just before their shade. She gazed hard into the murk. The leaves rattled and she swore something whispered from within. A chill pushed through her flesh, like weeds erupting from the earth. It was likely, she decided, she would invoke alf elo nor before the day was done, and not to sate her hunger.

"WE HAVE NOT ONCE GONE ROUND a bend nor cut and crossed through the trees," Rhona said. "We have walked straight all day. Why?"

"Ley lines," Orjem said. "They connect the three Jémoon

waypoints and the ancient places of the world. We spirits see them clearly."

"Are they dots of light?" asked Rhona hopefully.

"No. A constant stream of energy."

Rhona frowned. What, then, were the motes of light? They not yet led her astray, but were they actually leading her at all? Perhaps they were a test as well. She decided she would watch them closely. If she saw them at the second waypoint she would know they had led her true.

At length they entered a grove. "Here there is food to be had," Orjem said. "Plenty of berries, and game if you know where to look." His tangibility fluctuated, like a candle in the wind. "Relax, fill your rumbling gut. I will only be a moment."

Sunlight trickled through the grove in ribbons, bouncing off the moonstones scattered here and there. The trees bore leaves of spring and fire; purple flowers blossomed near their roots. Amidst it all, though, Rhona spied the motes of light, winding in between the trees and bushes, just a couple yards away. Where did they lead?

She tied the tether to a branch and followed the lights. She raised her nose, attention garnered by a sweet aroma. Her stomach roared and Rhona scanned the bushes, sniffing all the while, hoping the odor led her to a meal. She kept to the motes, halting just before the grove dissolved. The scent was strongest here; the dots of light had grown brighter. Rhona looked around and there they were—a treasure trove of berries, waiting to be picked.

Stomach screaming now, she dropped to her knees and picked the black and orange berries, shoving handfuls into her mouth, the juices running down her chin. The more she ate, the more she wanted. The more she wanted, the less there were.

Then the bush was bare, though her hunger yet remained.

Rhona stood and looked about in desperation—there were no berry bushes to be seen. She wanted to cry, to scream. If she did not eat more she would surely die of hunger!

"Breathe," she rasped, feeling hot. There *had* to be something here!

"Are you all right?"

Rhona looked up. Several feet inside the trees, basket in a hand, was a young girl, perhaps not more than thirteen years. She wore a black dress and orange cloak and mantle; her dark hair was tied back, and her hands were stained with...was it berry juice?

"Miss?" she asked.

Rhona stumbled, reaching toward the girl, toward the basket. Her vision shifted in and out; the forest fluctuated and another figure manifested in the trees, just behind the girl. It too wore a cloak and hood. Beyond that, though, Rhona saw nothing else. The world was spinning and she was spinning the opposite direction.

Then it stopped. All was still, and in the corner of her memory was a distant scream and puff of smoke. She swallowed, gazing up at the sunlight streaming through the leaves, tickling her face.

"Fool," a voice beside her said. "You are lucky I was here."

Rhona sat up, lightheaded but otherwise unscathed. The rumbling in her stomach had been silenced. She looked to the voice, the *multivoice*—the cloaked and hooded figure.

"You nearly lost your mind." The figure tossed a berry at Rhona. "The jétjune's fruit. Fox berries."

Rhona closed her eyes, groaning. "A trickster spirit?"

"Yes." Her savior snorted. "A particularly nasty breed at that." The figure drew a knife, pricked its finger, and wiped the blood along the roots of a tree. "Alf elo nor." Cool clear liquid burbled in between the roots. "Drink."

Rhona did so without question, sighing as her strength returned. She withdrew from the small pool and took a swig from her waterskin, just to slake her thirst and wash the earthy taste away.

"Thank you." She watched the figure stow away the knife. "Are you a Walker?"

"I used to be."

"What are you now? Who are you?" Rhona asked.

"Djen," came the reply, head turning slightly.

Rhona followed the presumed gaze. There was Orjem, with the doe.

"Orjem," said Djen. Rhona was not sure if that was a name or title.

"I am thankful you were near," the shadeseen said. He cast his gaze on Rhona. "It does not pay to wander, friend."

"Blame her youth, for they are wont to roam," said Djen, who Rhona now discerned was a woman. "Blame inferior education. Even novice Walkers know to stray from motes."

Rhona frowned. "Why?"

"Motes show us where we ought not walk," said Djen.

Révin cursed her stupidity. Dusk wolves. Jeynar. Dusk Ones. Jétjune fruit. "I am such a fool..."

"But alive," said Orjem. "We shall rest a while then continue on. The Nor'Forjét—the forest mages—have agreed to give us aid."

Rhona stood and took the doe by her tether. Serenaded by the rustling of the leaves, she followed after Orjem, wondering who and what Djen was and where exactly they were headed.

GUARDIAN

Ⅰt felt good to eat. It felt good to eat food that was not a hallucinogen.

Rhona sat on a stone bench, on a covered veranda overlooking the trees. The meat was juicy, freshly prepared, and tasted of wild herbs. It was accompanied by a cup of wine. The Nor'Forjét had offered berries, but Rhona had politely declined.

She sat, watching as the sun fell back behind the distant peaks. It was the most peaceful part of her short journey. It felt nice to be protected, to have the assistance of at least one individual to whom she could relate to as a Walker.

She glanced at Djen, cloaked in white, countenance veiled within a hood, character further obscured by the multivoice.

"You stare too much," Djen said. "You stare when words suffice. You speak when observation would be best. To reach the shrine you must rectify this. You must be more aware. You must exercise more caution."

Rhona turned her eyes back to the peaks and swallowed.

"Sorry. I...suppose I shall be better at that now. Since I know about the motes."

"Do not be sorry," Djen said. "Be vigilant. Vigilance prevents the need to apologize."

Rhona nodded. "You said you used to be a Walker. What was your first Walk like?"

"Awful," Djen said. "People died. I was not vigilant. I was not wary. I failed to watch the moon; I let the Vulture rise. Alf elo nor is the way of things. I did not understand. Not about the consequences. You might not see them right away, but eventually they will come."

Djen sighed. "Alf elo nor works in and out of favor. To ignore its call is sacrilegious. It would do you well to remember that. We Walk not for ourselves, but for the whole of Jémoon."

Sacrilege. Rhona was not sure whether the weight on her shoulders had lessened or increased, but she nodded appreciatively at Djen nonetheless. "Thank you, truly. This was not something I wanted. I am not brave. I am clumsy and panicked easier than the sun rises. I cannot hunt to save my life. I just..."

She trailed off. "I suppose 'thank you' sufficed." She stood from the bench, feeling flustered, but Djen motioned for her to sit. So she did, exhaling into the night. "What are the Nor'Forjét?"

"Guardians," offered Djen, and nothing more.

THEY LEFT the Nor'Forjét the following night and headed east for Éjor's Rest, the second waypoint of the Walk. Rhona ruminated on the way. She had not paid attention to her dreams until the previous night but they were strange as of late, painful. Like crawling over needles, but instead of flesh wounds, they tore at her very soul. Flashes of light and muffled screams—they made little sense, but she reasoned they were simply the manifestation of her fears and doubts.

She glanced at the doe, walking beside her, and groaned inwardly. To ignore the call was sacrilegious, Djen had said. There *had* to be another way.

Rhona brooded silently, listening as the mage and shadeseen shared a conversation several feet ahead. Something about "the old ring."

"Focus," Rhona whispered to herself. "Push away the anger."

She took a deep breath and exhaled slowly, feeling a bit of the stress disperse. She felt lighter, more aware, and realized the mage and shadeseen were speaking to her.

"Cast the wax from your ears, girl," Orjem said. "Are you listening?"

"Yes. Sorry," Rhona apologized.

"Vigilance," reminded Djen.

"Sorry."

"We are near the second waypoint," said Orjem, pointing.

Rhona gazed at a hill and gathering of stones, silhouetted by the pale glow of the moon. She trained her ears and inhaled through her nose—they were near the sea. The air was salty; it grew saltier the more she paid it mind. She could hear the distant waves rolling over each other.

Rhona took a swig from her waterskin and started past Djen and Orjem, doe in tow, a youthful energy aroused. She had never seen the sea, only heard and read of it. Was it truly as marvelous as her lessons told?

Rhona slowed himself—and just in time. Her footsteps kicked up pebbles and they turned to ash against a barrier. She leapt back, startled, looking at Djen and Orjem.

"What was *that*?"

"Protection," Djen said. "Éjor's Rest is sacred. Here the fallen Nor'Forjét are laid to rest. At the top and very center of this hill, deep below the earth, our founder sleeps a dreamless sleep."

Rhona furrowed her brow at the cryptic words. "So...is he dead?"

"*She,*" corrected Djen. "And no. She is in hibernation, granting peaceful passage to our dead. She is *alf elo nor.*"

Djen peeled back her hood, revealing ghost-white eyes and even paler flesh; platinum hair pulled back behind her ears. She drew her knife and dragged it clean across her throat without so much as a twitch.

"Ravens!" Rhona yelped.

The wound was bloodless. Instead a wispy, silver essence leaked between the grin and slithered in between Djen's outstretched fingers. The essence touched the barrier and dissolved it. Rhona looked at Djen as they stepped across the threshold, as her wound sealed shut and she replaced her hood, once more veiled in secrets. What was she? What, exactly, were the Nor'Forjét? What kind of power did they wield?

They crested the hill. At the center was a circle, a giant glyph. The shadeseen flickered as he took his place on the easternmost section of the circle. Djen stood south and pointed Rhona west. She took her spot and looked at them.

"Kneel as we do," Djen said. "Feel the grass, feel the dirt, and take a breath. Keep your wits and do not fear. The Nor'-Forjét will light the way."

The hill exploded out of sight, devoured by a warm and blinding brilliance. Rhona wrapped her arm around the doe and pulled her near, her free hand on the grass. The wind roared and something wormed up her arms, around her neck, her face, her body. Her stomach lurched and she cried out.

Then all was still and she was glancing up into the night.

Rhona groaned, sitting up. The doe was at her side, a little dizzy, but unscathed besides. A couple yards away were Djen and Orjem, the pair unfazed.

Rhona stood, nearly toppling over, but managed to steady herself. Before them was an archway, choked by vines, engraved with symbols. Beyond it stood a town, and around the town ran a wall of stone. In some of the distant buildings there were lights. From the very center of the town rose a stream of smoke.

Behind them was another cliff, and beyond the cliff, the sea. Rhona felt disoriented. "What just happened?"

"We Leapt the sea," Orjem said.

"Leapt?" Révin asked.

"Alf elo nor provides as necessary," Djen said. "Some tricks, however, call for more than one mind. This time we all invoked it." Rhona searched herself for cuts or nicks, but there were none. Djen chuckled. "The Nor'Forjét employ it in ways Walkers cannot. We deal in soul and offer fragments of our spirit. But do not fret. Like your blood, your spirit will renew."

"Right," said Rhona, feeling suddenly exhausted, more than she had ever been.

"Keep your legs beneath you just a while longer," Orjem said. "We have reached the final waypoint. Welcome to Misten Fahg."

SPELLSCARRED

R hona tossed back her cup of wine. Misten Fahg. She was halfway to the shrine. She felt at ease. She knew what lay ahead, but being here had lessened the weight on her shoulders significantly, enough for her to enjoy the town.

It was like nothing Rhona had ever seen, which was not saying a lot because she had not seen too much beyond the forest back home. But it was still something. A small harbor sat a couple miles northwest, which explained the abundance of fish and shellfish that the inn and tavern offered, as well as the constant smell of sea salt.

"Misten Fahg is a place of magic, young and old, from far and wide," Orjem said. His figure burned like sunlight, giving warmth and drawing looks. Those who stared did so for a second or two before scurrying off.

"A beacon," Djen added. "One of many. A place of refuge and acceptance for the mages and the spellscarred of the world."

"Spellscarred?"

"They are among the most powerful beings on Harthe," said Djen. "Their magic is dangerous, unpredictable. They are rare, and most are dead."

"Have you ever met one?" Rhona asked.

"Yes," said Djen. She offered nothing else.

They sat in silence, watching people weave between the firelight and shadows, then decided to retire to the inn for the night.

"WE ARE fortunate the moon has held her color for the past two nights," Djen said the following morning. Her hood was down; the early sunrise swirled in her eyes, the silver irises ablaze. She could not have been more than seven or eight years Rhona's senior, but her pale visage lent itself to her general mystique.

She led Rhona northward, out of Misten Fahg, to an egress from the grove in which the hill town sat. "Our destination's start," she said, pointing toward distant peaks. "The shrine sits within the mountain's crown."

Rhona squinted. The jagged range was little less than a grayish blur concealed by fog; the mountaintop was not even visible. Trials greater than a rumbling stomach lay ahead. She swallowed, steeling himself. When the time came, she would be ready.

Rhona still needed a solution, though, an alternative to sacrificing the doe. She considered asking Djen for advice, but she knew what the mage would say: "To ignore the call is sacrilegious." She sighed, following silently as Djen led them back to town.

Her mind itched. There was something strange about these woods, about the town. There was an aura of familiarity around it. Had it been here all this time?

The leaves rattled in a breeze and pine needles fell from their branches. As the wind dispersed, it seemed to whisper Rhona's name. At least, she thought it had.

She shook her head, trying to clear her mind. Maybe it was the magic of this place. Maybe she was simply overwhelmed. Maybe it was another trickster, though wouldn't Djen have sensed it too? It was something else, she decided.

The air about Misten Fahg was different as they made their way to the inn. Rhona could smell the salt but it was fainter than it had been when they had arrived, had been smothered by a sour, ashy stench. Rhona wrinkled her nose. Djen glanced casually about the street, inconspicuous to passersby, but vigilant enough for Rhona to detect. Whatever abnormality was near, Djen was privy to it too.

"Trickster?" Rhona whispered.

The mage said nothing and proceeded toward the front door of inn. They stepped inside, crossed the lobby, and ascended to the second floor, to Rhona's room. She pulled the key from her pocket and unlocked the door. On the other side were Orjem and the doe. With the curtains shut, the Shadeseen was corporeal, allowing him to gently pat the doe curled beside him on the floor.

"She has yet to rise," said Orjem. "She trembles in her sleep." His figure flashed erratically. "Something is amiss here."

"We noticed," Djen said.

"Trickster?" Rhona asked again

"Maybe." Djen narrowed her eyes. "Maybe not. Either way..."

Her words hung on the air. Rhona frowned.

"It is best we leave this place today," Djen said.

"But we just got here," argued Rhona. "We can rest, strategize, restock supplies, and—"

"We have been here long enough," said Djen, pulling up her hood. "Do not be foolish like I was." She cast a glance at Orjem. "Wait 'til sundown. Then head north as long as she can go." Djen drew her dagger from its sheath and dragged the blade across her hand. She knelt and held it before the doe. "Nor elo alf."

The doe lifted her head, eyes half open, as the wispy essence leaked from Djen's hand. The doe absorbed it and within seconds looked livelier than she had a few minutes ago.

Rhona looked at Djen. "Nor elo alf?"

"If our intent is pure and just, the Nor'Forjét can occasionally rewrite the alf elo nor," said Djen. "Nor elo alf: all for one."

In theory it seemed simple enough. In practice, though, Rhona was completely clueless as to how the Nor'Forjét worked their magic. Blood was offered easily enough, but how did one deal in soul and spirit? She was about to ask but Djen grabbed her bag and yanked her from the room.

"North. Stop before the woods."

"Hold on!" Rhona demanded, digging her heels into the floor. "I cannot just leave; I cannot leave the doe here. She is my..."—she paused—"responsibility. If I get to the shrine without—"

"Go," hissed Djen.

So Rhona did, withdrawing from the inn as nonchalantly as she could, pack slung across her shoulder as she headed north. She passed beneath the archway, leaving Misten Fahg behind. Her steps led her toward and through the clearing, with the path sloping downward toward the copse below.

Rhona kept pace despite the shift in terrain. She stumbled a couple of times and nearly lost her footing on loose rocks, but managed to make it down the hill. Even here the sour stench was as strong as it had been in Misten Fahg, if not stronger.

The motes of light had also returned. Rhona eyed them, leading back to Misten Fahg. Why had they not appeared before? Maybe they were not indicative of inherent danger, but rather mal intent. He hoped Orjem and the doe were safe.

Rhona turned away from Misten Fahg. As she did, she noticed the motes stretched in all directions. The sight was disconcerting and she could not help trembling. She took a deep breath then set one foot forward, then the other, and soon found herself moving toward the forest at a reluctant jog.

Vigilance. Composure. The motes' volume multiplied as she neared the entrance to the woods, but Rhona did not stop. Djen said north so she was heading north. She halted where the trees began, listening to the leaves rattling in the wind.

"Vigilance," said a voice.

"Djen!" Rhona started as she entered from the left. "What now?"

Djen drew her knife and motioned for Rhona to do the same. "An offering. Alf elo nor." She dragged her blade across her throat, her stomach, and her wrists, the wispy essence seeping out, devoured by the trees. She looked at Rhona. "Wrists. Then wait."

Rhona eyes widened. "I could die."

"Could," said Djen, her wounds already sewing shut. "If you do not, you will. The Old Things linger here and taxes must be paid. Do it. Now."

Reluctantly, Rhona did as she was told. The blood rushed from her veins, staining her flesh, splashing the earth. Time itself seemed to stop. At last, when she started wobbling, Djen grabbed her wrists and steadied her.

She sat Rhona down, cut her wrists, and murmured, "Nor elo alf." The essence lingered in the air. "Take it."

Vision shifting in and out, Rhona nodded and the essence

drifted toward her, into her. Gradually her strength returned and her wounds sealed shut. Djen helped her up and they started into the woods.

"The Old Things will not protect us but they will not attack us either," Djen said. "Our followers will have to pay a tax as well. If we are lucky, they will be slowed a bit."

"What are we running from?" asked Rhona, shivering as they ventured on.

"The spellscarred," answered Djen.

What could the spellscarred want with them, Rhona wondered. Why were answers so hard to come by?

All around, the woods were bright and open. Sunbeams pierced the canopies and lit their way. Birds chirped, toads croaked. Red and orange leaves fell from the trees. It was a stark contrast to the smoke and shadow of the Korjin Wood, but somehow, all the color, all the light—Rhona knew in her heart, her mind, and her flesh, this place was inherently wicked.

Light could be deceiving. She thought of the motes, how she had followed them like a guide, only to learn they warned where not to go. She suppressed a shudder and kept hes focus on Djen, on the path they walked.

OBSCURITY

Dusk was upon them. Rhona could hardly feel her feet. Her legs were cramping, her stomach was roaring, and her throat was dry. She took a quick swig from her waterskin, unsure of when or where she might be able to fill it again. Djen had made it clear they were not to invoke alf elo nor in search of hydration; the Old Things had tainted the water in the woods.

Rhona sat on a log, leaning back against a tree. Djen sat beside her, breathing laboring just a bit. "I lost track of the spellscarred an hour back," she said, frowning.

"Not good," said Rhona, pausing. "What were they like? The spellscarred you mentioned."

Djen rested her chin in her hands. "Her name was Djorev. She was brave and kind. The Nor'Forjét accepted her as one of their own after she was exiled from her home." Djen bowed her head. "The Korjin Empire's been at war with mages for a century; people fear what they fail to comprehend. I found Djorev by the river. They had taken her tongue and eyes. 'If a mage cannot speak or see, they cannot curse you,' goes the saying."

"I'm sorry," Rhona said.

"We need to start moving again soon," Djen said abruptly.

"Will Orjem be able to find us?"

"Hopefully."

Hopefully. Rhona chuckled inwardly. Old Things, tricksters, and spellscarred. It was a bit hard to feel hopeful considering all of that. And she still had not figured out a way to avoid sacrificing the doe. Sacrificing herself would not solve anything. The cycle would continue as it always had and would.

Djen rose to her feet. "We have a ways to go before we stop for the night."

Rhona rose and followed after the mage, trembling. It was impossible to be calm inside these woods, especially with the Old Things touching her thoughts. What were they, what did they look like? Everything had a purpose; alf elo nor decreed as such. What was theirs? She considered asking Djen but held her tongue, deciding silence was better, safer.

Dusk melted into night and the stars blinked. Like thousands of eyes, reddened by the moon, Rhona observed, teeth chattering. Not from the cold, but out of fear, from watching shadows dance beneath the moonlight streaming through the trees. Or maybe fatigue. Everything ached, her eyelids were heavy, and her mind yearned...for sleep...

Rhona's eyes snapped open. The strange sense of familiarity she had felt in Misten Fahg had reemerged. She squinted through the darkness. In the distance stark white fabric flowed gracefully in a breeze—except there was no breeze. Rhona rubbed her eyes; the fabric had vanished and the leaves were rattling madly, as if they were trying to speak.

Stay vigilant. She kept her eyes glued to Djen, only to

realize the figure in front of her was not Djen but a girl in white, with hair like night. Rhona went cold as the girl turned to face him. She was gold-skinned with eyes the color of a late summer night.

She reached toward Rhona.

"Rhona."

She started.

"Rhona."

"Djen..."

"We shall rest here for the night," Djen said, gesturing toward a maw beneath the trees.

Rhona nodded airily and trailed the mage into the earthy darkness, the girl in white tattooed to her thoughts. The sound of rattling leaves grew fainter, silent, though not before it etched a name and question in her mind.

Who was Ahnojem?

How LONG HAD they been here? Provisions were scarce, the spellscarred had yet to reemerge, and with no sign of Orjem and the doe, Rhona found her worry mounting. She had grown skittish, prone to jumping at the smallest of sounds. The longer they remained inside the woods, the more alive the shadows felt; the more invaded her thoughts became.

And who was Ahnojem? Djen had offered nothing but an "I do not know," an answer Rhona took with half a grain of salt.

What are you really, Djen? What is your play, your endgame? A Walker with a town's worth of blood on your hands... Rhona's heart beat faster. What if Orjem and Djen were conspiring against her? What if Djen sought to sacrifice her at the shrine?

No. That was insane. Djen was here to help.

Or is she? Rhona's hand drifted to the hilt of her dagger. If she was quick, quiet...

"You whisper far too loudly, Rhona," Djen said, turning to face her. Her ghost-white eyes bore into Rhona's own; her lips were drawn to a straight line. She made no move for her blade. "You let the Old Things in and now they do not want out."

"How many times have you lied to me?" Rhona asked.

"Your words are swayed," Djen said.

"Tell me."

"The Old Things work your tongue."

Rhona brandished her knife and lunged. Djen sidestepped and landed a blow to the side of her head, shocking Rhona from her paranoia. Djen gripped her by the arm and spun Rhona to face her. "We run and do not look back."

The woods were a blur of dusk and color as the sunlight slowly waned. The Old Things whispered all the while. They prodded Rhona's thoughts, slithered where they ought not be and begged she ask them why. Their rattling-leaf requests were like a flame inside her mind, far too constant and profound for her to really focus on. There was undoubtedly some deeper meaning. There was even something familiar, but by the time she and Djen reached the forest's edge, Rhona was far too drained to care.

They took refuge there in a cluster of boulders. Rhona leaned against the smooth surface, breathing hard, relaxing slightly as the whispers died away.

"Such a wretched place," she said to Djen.

"Think if we had been in there more than a day," replied the mage, offering a slight tremble. She shrugged at Rhona's gape. "The Old Things like to play; the forest shifts. Be thankful we stayed the path, for it is not unheard of for people to be lost in there a week, sometimes longer. Forever, even."

Rhona shivered. She pulled her waterskin from her pack. To her dismay, there was only air. She looked at the ground, at the trees several yards away, and swallowed. Best to ignore the thirst for now, at least until they were a ways beyond the forest's taint.

"Do you think they are okay?" Rhona asked.

"I can only hope," Djen said. She was frowning intently. "Sleep a while. I shall keep watch."

"Djen—"

"*Sleep.*"

AHNOJEM

It was late as they walked, or early depending on perspective. Rhona yawned, trailing Djen along a dirt path riddled with rocks and patchy brush. The dirt was of a finer consistency than usual and a couple of times she spied little objects—shells, she realized, recalling sketches from books.

At length they reached the top of a small hill, upon which stood a henge comprised of six gnarled and twisted pillars. The one nearest them began to glow.

Djen pointed beyond the henge to distant peaks. "Only Walkers may pass beyond this point."

"We Leapt the sea," said Rhona, following her gaze.

"We cannot Leap land," said Djen. "Only water."

A tingling sensation trickled through Rhona's body as they passed beyond the henge. It settled, superseded by a thought.

"Is it wise for us to head to the shrine without, well... my offering?"

"Keep moving."

Rhona opened her mouth to protest but there seemed to be no point in doing so. Djen had led her this far and she was still alive. That had to count for something, right?

Hours later, when the sun was rising, something in the distance caught her eye. It flickered erratically before it finally vanished. In its place remained a silhouette, its shape familiar and welcome.

Rhona and Djen broke into a run. The doe was munching the patchy grass when they arrived, looking no worse than the last time Rhona had seen her. The flickering had undoubtedly been Orjem, but where had they come from? Rhona scratched her head, puzzled.

"Orjem? Are you there?" She felt a faint breeze and watched the sand scatter. Rhona took a seat on the ground and sighed. "Thank Ravens."

She reached up and stroked the doe's ears as the creature came near. She nuzzled Rhona's hand took a seat beside her, resting her head in her lap, eyelids heavy.

"It looks like she missed you," Djen said, offering the tiniest of smiles.

Rhona smiled wearily as she caressed the doe. Truthfully, she missed it too. Her spirits dropped as she remembered that, unless she found some other way, she would have to spill the doe's blood once they reached the shrine.

I will find it. *I will* make things right.

"Alf elo nor," chanted Djen. She cut her palm and let the blood drip into the earth. A minute later, thick muddy liquid burbled out. She cupped her hands as the volume increased then raised them to her lips. "Drink."

Rhona did the same. It was earthy but refreshing nonetheless. She let the doe drink from her palms as well.

"There are not any trees around. Where did this come from?"

"The earth has her own reserves," Djen said. "Alf elo nor provides for those who use it properly."

Rhona drank and did not press further.

THEY CAMPED beneath a patch of trees that night. Orjem flickered into sight, warm and bright as fire. It had been a couple of days since Rhona had seen the spirit and she was happy for his return.

"I am glad to see you well," the shadeseen said. "Our journey was laborious to say the least. I have little doubt you faced oppression of your own." He flickered briefly, almost as if trembling. "That forest was not meant for spirit, man, or beast, let alone the living or the dead."

"I never want to go back there," Rhona said, trembling. "I saw..." She paused, lowering her eyes. "It was a hallucination. Obviously. Ahnojem. Do you know the name, Orjem?"

"Ahnojem was my eldest sister," the shadeseen said slowly. "She passed when I was just a boy. Struck by lightning in retaliation for seducing the Raven Jévim, or so the rumor goes. For distracting Jévim from her obligations."

"I am sorry," said Rhona. "Did she—I mean...I think I saw her in the forest." She sighed and rubbed the spot between her eyes. "None of it makes sense."

"There is a rumor among the Nor'Forjét," saud Djen, "that the Old Things in the forest dredge the minds of their visitors, reawakening memories lost to time. Perhaps there is something in your past that links you to this girl."

Rhona tensed her jaw and let a soft hiss escape between her

teeth. "But what? I have never heard that name before. I had never even seen Ahnojem until I hallucinated her, if that is even who I saw."

She leaned against a tree and closed her eyes.

ASCENT

Rhona dreamt of lighting, of spirits screaming in the woods. Of Ahnojem erupting into flames, her golden skin reduced to ash. She dreamt of blackness, endless and devouring, as double voices bellowed in their foreign tongues.

She awoke to sunlight, warm and gentle. The doe was curled beside her. Djen was up and gazing at the northward mountains looming in the distance. Orjem was nowhere to be seen.

"We will reach the base of the mountain by nightfall," Djen said. "Our journey there will be a time for thought and reflection. It would do you well to clear your mind of any obstacles or reservations you may have. Once we begin our ascent there will be hardly any time to rest."

"Are there spirits on the mountain?" Rhona asked.

"Yes and no. It is a matter of perspective," said Djen. "Are the fears and horrors we encounter simply tricksters longing for our Walker blood, or are they manifestations of our inner selves we must confront in order to better ourselves?"

Rhona lingered on her words, curious and afraid of what she might come face-to-face with during their ascent. She had plenty of fears, plenty of reservation about this Walk in general. Would they come to haunt her, or would something else?

She cast her gaze from the mountain, instead focusing on the doe. She had roused and was chewing at what bits of grass she could find. Rhona stroked her ears, feeling a sensation of warmth pass through her body, doing away with the trepidation.

Vigilance. Keep your wits about you. Focus on the task. Right now that was getting to the top, to the shrine. She decided she would figure out the rest when they reached it.

The terrain was flat and boring the entire day. Hills disappeared, packed sand fell loose, and grass all but disappeared beneath the golden, grainy earth. Halfway through it had begun to rain and by the time they stopped beneath the rocks at the base of the mountain they were soaked to the bone. Their journey had been so uncomfortable Rhona found herself looking to her problems as a source of solace.

Her thoughts wandered home to the people who were depending on her. A failed Walk would lead to disappointment and worse—much worse.

Orjem flickered into being and the tiny henge they had taken shelter beneath was drowned in heat as pure and warming as the summer sun. The shadeseen's glow was so profound the rain evaporated as it neared, as though the henge were inside a barrier.

Djen had risen and was standing at the entrance to the mountain path, the rain beating down on her all the while. She stood there for a moment then returned, white eyes more intense than Rhona had ever seen them. Her stare lingered long enough for Rhona to discern she was hiding something.

"We will need to be careful. But first"—Djen yawned—"we must sleep." Then, looking at Rhona: "This will be the worst climb of your life."

RHONA DRIFTED OUT OF SLEEP, greeted by the pink sky above. The storm had passed and Orjem's glow held strong. The doe was still, Djen was bundled in her cloak, and Orjem sat in the center of their rocky encampment. Whether sleeping or awake, Rhona was not sure.

She stood and stretched, muscles aching from a poor night's sleep. She withdrew a few yards from their camp, stopping at the start of the mountain path. The peaks loomed above and Rhona could not help but shiver.

"It will only get worse."

Rhona started. "Djen. I thought you were asleep."

"I have been watching the color bleed from the moon. We will need to ascend quickly," said the mage, at Rhona's side. "Time is no longer on our side. The obstacle presented by the mountain may very well lead to failure." She touched her shoulder. "You will learn things, remember things—memories you have suppressed. If you wish to reach the shrine and make your sacrifice before the Vulture's Moon rises then you must accept the truths you will learn."

"What did you learn of yourself?" Rhona asked.

"I learned," the mage said softly, "the past is inescapable." Djen pulled her cloak away. Her eyes shone brightly as they shifted white to black. Dark veins webbed outward from her eyes.

Rhona took a few steps back. "What—what *are* you?"

"Spellscarred," she said sadly. "Twisted by the wild Dusk

when the Raven Jévim fell. I thought I could forget, that I could be something, some*one* different. But I was wrong. This mountain made sure my past transgressions would not stay buried."

"What happened?" Rhona asked softly.

"She died because of me. I killed her, accidentally, in a fit of rage and self-loathing. My older sister, Djen."

"Wait—your *sister Djen?* But I thought..." Rhona paled. *"You* are Djorev, aren't you?"

"Yes," she said, replacing her cloak and hood. "But everything I have told you *is* true. Djen failed her Walk; she found new purpose with the Nor'Forjét. They took me in when I was exiled from my home. For a while everything was fine. And then...

"We had been arguing. I exploded. When the rage subsided Djen was dead and the land around us scorched. I knew the Nor'Forjét would cast me out. I knew the mage hunters would track me down, so I did what I thought best. I stole my sister's name and face. I pulled the lifeless spirit from her corpse and took the body as my own. And to make sure no one ever found out, to make sure I could never hurt anyone again, I wiped my memory clean. Doing so entombed my power deep inside me, where for decades it lay dormant, 'til the mountain called me back."

Knowing Djorev was spellscarred made Rhona wary but she could not bring himself to fully fear her. She was stern, hardened by a harrowing past, but she was also kind in her own way, perhaps eager to repent for what she had done. And she had never led Rhona astray.

Rhona touched her arm. "I am sorry, Djorev, about your sister, everything. No one deserves that."

"Thank you," whispered the mage. She glanced behind

them as the doe and shadeseen roused. "You must steel yourself. You must be ready. You must be vigilant."

Rhona nodded. "The spellscarred we were fleeing from...?"

"My own instability, an occasional mirror image I must flee," said Djorev darkly. "Collect your doe. It is time to move."

JÉVIM

The mountain was not very high. They wound around sharp bends and hefted themselves up over even sharper lips. Rhona picked at the cuts on her hands and arms, grumbling inwardly.

She looked at Djorev and the mage gazed back, her eyes ablaze within the depths of her hood. Not once did she blink; Rhona wondered if she were in some sort of trance. Maybe she had remembered something.

She frowned. Why hadn't *she*? She strained her mind for something, anything. Ahnojem flashed briefly but did not linger long enough for Rhona to extrapolate the reason for her frequent manifestation in her thoughts. She gave a low growl and chewed her lip. What was it about this girl? What was the connection?

Rhona started, roused from thought by the doe's nose against her hand. She stroked her ears, watching as the doe closed her eyes and fell asleep. What could she do? Spill her own blood until she was an inch from death? Plead—to who, to what?

"You look conflicted," Orjem said, his warming glow pervading their rocky encampment.

Rhona chuckled wryly. "I have followed alf elo nor as best I can, but...I do not know if I can do it." She fingered the hilt of her knife. "Killing, hunting..."

"Sometimes," Orjem said, "we do things we know to be outwardly wrong, but right for the heart."

Something pulsed in the center of Rhona's mind. Ahnojem lingered momentarily before she disappeared. Rhona took a deep breath, her heart pounding, adrenaline coursing through her.

"Rest a while," Djorev suggested. "You look absolutely spent."

Rhona nodded, half paying attention to the mage, half invested in the strange sensation, the image of the girl in white. She leaned back against the rock, gazing up at the moon, now nearly white. It would have to be tomorrow.

It could have been the lack of food. It could have been dehydration. It could have very well been the mountain playing tricks. All three, even, causing the landscape around them to change, to shift upon their cresting of a jagged slope.

Maybe it is the blood loss. How many times had they invoked alf elo nor in the last day? Four? Five? Maybe they should have forsaken hydration for a time, Rhona thought as she dropped to the ground, rolling over onto her back. Her hands stung, the cuts riddled with rocks and dirt.

She gazed up at the sky, threads of sunlight peeking through the clouds. She rolled her head back, looking at the upside-down world beyond, the forest several hundred feet away. She listened to the rattling of leaves. It was soothing in a way, inviting. Rhona sat up and rose to her feet.

"Best continue on before exhaustion takes its toll," said Djorev, moving toward the wood.

The first things Rhona noticed were the trees that lined their path. They were gnarled and twisted, with roots that grew above ground. Their leaves were black, their bark was white.

Next was the absolute stillness, the utter silence. The further they ascended through the mountain wood, the denser the trees became. Orjem's glow was little more than a dot of light despite his close proximity to Rhona, Djorev, and the doe.

Rhona shivered as the shadeseen waxed and waned. The density, the darkness of the wood—it was sentient. Something haunted their steps.

Or maybe my mind is playing tricks. Rhona's focus drifted to Ahnojem. Was this her doing? Was this her way of saying they were connected?

She jumped at the doe's nose against her hand. The creature nudged her again and licked Rhona's fingers. She gave her head a pat and sighed, looking to Orjem's minor glow. Beside the shadeseen wandered Djorev, silent.

Rhona lingered on the mage. What business did she have at the shrine? She was genuine in her attempt to help her Walk succeed buts he still felt as though Djorev had some other reason for being here. Perhaps it was related to her sister, or to the awesome, wretched power she commanded as a spellscarred.

And Orjem? He remained as well, but why? Rhona felt Orjem too was genuine in his efforts, and yet she could not help but feel as though the shadeseen's motives had been swayed. Was it because of *his* sister as well?

Orjem's glow dispersed and Rhona found himself alone in blackness. She could not feel the doe beside her anymore either, could not feel anything save the ground beneath her feet. She exhaled utter nothingness. No heat. No cold. No breath. Just the illusion of decompressing lungs.

The emptiness endured and a single, dominating thought took form: *Ahnojem.* Rhona mouthed her name, savoring the syllables her tongue could not release.

Rhona.

Her own name resounded in her head despite the fact she had not heard a sound. The forest spoke through the transference of thought, she realized.

Rhona.

"I am coming."

She stepped blindly as the voice grew louder in her head. She heard others too, words as familiar to her as they were foreign.

Our kind is not to mingle with the humans of Jémoon.

The darkness swirled, intermixed with streaks of blue and blasts of white. Rhona stumbled through the chaos as the throng of voices tore into her thoughts.

Rhona!

Welcome to the Forest of Retention, where memories are lost and found.

"Ahnojem!" she cried, shattering the silence.

JÉVIM!

The droplets smacked Rhona's flesh and ricocheted like pebbles off a stream. She looked about. She was standing in a henge. Misty luminescence swirled and twisted through the air, funneled toward the obelisks and the archway at the far end of the henge. To her left were Djorev and Orjem, their respective white and orange frames stark contrasts to the darkness of the storm that raged. To Rhona's right were several dozen figures wreathed in shadow, gazing out with ghost-white eyes that mirrored Djorev's.

And before her, only feet away, was the doe. They locked eyes, and Rhona knew. "Ahnojem," she uttered. "My Ahnojem."

"Rhona," Orjem spoke.

No. *Not* Rhona. Had they ever actually called her that or was that simply what she had wanted to hear?

"Jévim," said the shadeseen once again. "We searched for years. We scoured Jémoon, hoping for a sign, an inkling of your presence. Imagine my surprise at finding you helplessly wandering the Sorjen Plains. I felt hope the bedlam drowning Jémoon would be quelled, that my sister's curse might be reversed."

"How long have you known who I was?" Jévim asked.

"Since that day," said Orjem.

Jévim looked to Djorev.

"Since the day we met," the spellscarred said.

Jévim touched her fingers to her forehead. Memories she had known for years were whisked away or swayed like grains of sand beneath a breeze. Ever-shifting.

"Why did you not tell me?" she asked slowly.

"We could not," Djorev said. "The wild Dusk around you made your ears impermeable to the truth. We could guide you, yes, but only you could rouse your dormant past and make your memories whole."

Jévim tensed her jaw and closed her eyes. "They knew. My father and the villagers who tasked me with this Walk..."

"They are *your* Walkers," said Djorev. "Of course they knew. They are privy to your aura. We *all* are."

Jévim's temples throbbed, her chest heavy. She opened her

eyes and looked at Djorev; then she shifted focus to the figures cloaked in black, memories twisting, mending. The Nor'Forjét, the spellscarred, the Dusk Ones...they were all one and the same. Exiled mages cursed with the wild Dusk.

Jévim looked at Djorev. "Djen, was she...?"

Djorev frowned, her brow folding. "Because the Dusk repelled the truth," she said, "you think I simply made my sister up? Djen was *real*. Her death was the consequence of the chaos your negligence unleashed and cursed me with."

Jévim bowed her head.

"We mages are what the world needs us to be." Djorev continued, expression darkening. "Sometimes what the wild Dusk *necessitates*. Surely you can relate, Jévim. For so long you were the Raven of Jémoon: the Keeper of the Dusk. But when the other Ravens saw fit, you became an example, and that poor creature there"—she pointed at the doe, Ahnojem—"became the consequence." She held her arms out wide. "We *all* became the consequence of your infatuation, of your decision to forsake Raven mandate."

Jévim's memories surged. She saw herself with Ahnojem beside a lake, the very lake Jeynar had nearly drowned her in. Then they were lying in the plains, gazing at the stars. Dancing through the trees near Misten Fahg.

"Alf elo nor. Your mantra, your credo," said Djorev, advancing. "You were supposed to be the one for us all, but instead you were the one who *failed* us all. You strayed in favor of your own desires. Because you failed to claim the sacrifice you so readily depend on in a timely manner, Jémoon floundered underneath the unbounded Dusk."

Jévim was trembling. This was why Ravens were not to mingle with the humans, lowers as they were often times called. She was crying now. She had not meant for this. She had wanted only to be with *her*, Ahnojem. She gazed into the doe's eyes, Djorev's words cutting into her like a knife.

"I am sorry," she whispered. She knelt before Ahnojem and kissed her nose. "Please forgive me." Jévim rose to acknowledge Djorev and Orjem. "I will make things right."

She marched toward the archway and the obelisks, humming with power. It was familiar, like rousing from a dream. She drew her knife. *O brethren, O Ravens of Harthe, please accept my blood and soul as penance for my sins. Return to Ahnojem the life my ignorance deprived her of. Allow the people of Jémoon to live good lives.*

"*Alf elo nor!*" She held the knife high, called upon the Dusk, and plunged it through her chest. The enchanted blade punched through bone and muscle, piercing Jévim's heart. A stream of lightning javelined from the clouds and set her soul and flesh ablaze, the fire paying little notice to the rain cascading from the sky.

Jévim's sight held long enough to see the last drop of color from the moon. The darkness welcomed her as radiant motes encased the doe.

She found herself in a forest dark.

She ran.

ACKNOWLEDGMENTS

If I really think about it, the seeds for *Adjacent Monsters* were sown back in 2016. I had just received a rejection from Fantasy & Science Fiction for a novelette entitled *The Walker and the Doe*. While the world building was solid, the story had pacing and structural issues. I took those comments to heart, set about revising the story, and, after several more failed submissions to other markets, trunked it.

But the story kept nagging at me. There were bits and pieces I still dreamt of. Eventually in December 2019 and January 2020, I revisited the story and took notes. Before long, I had a draft of a novella called *The Hang-Dead Parable*, which was eventually published as *The World Maker Parable* and has gone on to receive humbling praise.

"But what about the rest?' I kept asking myself.

Well, in this omnibus, the answer to that questions is made manifest in the form of *The World Reaper Odyssey*, a companion story to the horrors faced by Rhona in *The World Maker Parable*. Dreams have always fascinated me, which you'll undoubtedly have learned having read this book, and I wanted the chance to explore one of Rhona's delusions in-depth. I'm fond of the final result and I hope you were as well.

That said, I have many people to thank, starting first with my wife Jenny. We've had our ups and downs, we had children at the onset of a pandemic, we dealt with mid-career employment changes, we even moved house. Still, here we are. You've always been supportive of my writing and I cannot thank you enough. You've always pushed me to be better and you stood by me while I spiraled into a blackhole of depression. I love you.

In no specific order, the many friends I've made in the science fiction and fantasy community: Nick, Clayton, Thomas, Krystle, Angela, Rowena, Sarah, Ashley, Mark, David, Sara, Krina, Ryan, Zack, Jeremy, Dom, Dyrk, Tom, Shawn, Tom, Jonathan, Dan, Justine, Jodie, Justin, Tori, Nathan, Aaron, Adrian. My god, the list goes on. There are so many of you. So many fellow authors, so many dedicated book bloggers and reviewers, so many readers who lift up self-published fantasy and genre fiction. Where the fuck would we be without your continued support?

Lastly, a special shoutout to the following people who have been such ardent supporters of the *Adjacent Monsters* stories: Victoria Gross, editor supreme; Ashley Brennan; Justin Gross; Nick Borrelli; Rowena Andrews; Mark a.k.a. The Fantasy Book Nerd; and Sarah Chorn.

Thank you, everyone. This series was written in the midst of guilt, depression, grief, and delusion, and it's completion and reception has been so incredibly humbling and weight-lifting.

Thank you eternally.

ABOUT THE AUTHOR

Luke Tarzian was born in Bucharest, Romania. His parents made the extremely poor choice of adopting him less than six months into his life. As such, he's resided primarily in the United States and currently lives in California with his wife and their twin daughters. Somehow, they tolerate him.

Unfortunately, he can also be found online, and to the dismay of his clients, also functions as a cover artist for independent authors.